Evermore

Also by Brenda Pandos

The Emerald Talisman
The Sapphire Talisman
The Onyx Talisman
Blood Wars

Evergreen, Book #2
Everlost, Book #3
Evermore, Book #4

Glitch
Switch

Evermore

Mer Tales ~ Book Four

By
Brenda Pandos

OBSIDIAN MOUNTAIN PUBLISHING

Text Copyright © 2015 by Brenda Pandos
All rights reserved.
Everlost: A novel/by Brenda Pandos

This novel is a work of fiction. Names, characters, place and incidents either are a product of the author's imagination, or used fictitiously. Any resemblance to actual events, locals, organizations, or persons, living or dead, is entirely coincidental and beyond intent of the author. No part of the book may be used, reproduced or stored in retrieval systems, or transmitted in any form or by any means, electronic, mechanical, photocopying, recording, or otherwise, without written permission of the author.

Photograph by Kelsey Keeton of K Keeton Designs
Cover Design © Brenda Pandos

Published by Obsidian Mountain Publishing
www.obsidianmtpublishing.com
P.O. Box 601901
Sacramento, CA 95860

ISBN: 978-1519339881

Printed in the United States of America

Dedicated to my amazing fans

Mindy Minz Janicke

Nicole Hanson

Barbara Stoker

Emily Krouk

Katie Doan

Stacey Nixon

Amanda Hughes

Jennifer Lessard

Valerie Martinez

Debbie Poole

*"I have wept for joy to think
that you are mine,
and often wonder whether
I deserve you...
What would I not do
for love of you!""*

Robert Schumann (1810-1856)

German composer

1

ASH

May 15 – 12:59 p.m.

"So, can we finally talk wedding? I'm dying to get started."

I startled out of my thoughts and swung my gaze to Tatiana, my best friend since we were ten.

She gave me a guilty smile as she pinned up my hair. "I mean, together."

"Started?" After everything had happened, I wasn't sure if both sets of family, mer and human, were ready to have an actual wedding on land.

"Starfish! You're killing me here." She grabbed another bobby pin from between her teeth. "At least tell me the colors."

I let out a gentle sigh. Visions of promising my life to Fin on the beach in Tahoe with my friends and family surrounding me made me smile. Yes, I wanted to plan it and finally be his wife more than anything, but there was a lot to do before we could start our happily ever after.

My stomach spasmed in fear and excitement. Fin and I were planning to return to Tahoe in an hour and check in with my parents because we'd mind-jacked them about a supposed mission trip to Africa when leaving for Natatoria. Fin's dad was coming along to check out the damage left after his brother, Alaster, burned down their house. I wanted Tatchi to come, too, like it wouldn't have officially made things right unless she returned home with me.

"If you come with us today, I'll tell you the colors," I said as a bribe.

She let out a long sigh. "You know I can't. Not with the merling."

"What about Pearl?" I asked. "Can't she watch Nicole?"

Tatiana rolled her eyes. "Last time I left her with Pearl, she cried the whole time. Nicole is super attached and wants me right now; like she's worried I'll disappear, too."

Nicole, Prince Azor and his servant Xirene's orphaned merling, had been adopted by Jacob and Tatiana, making them parents overnight. I looked away to hide my disappointment. Though I'd grown to love my adoptive niece, I knew that until Nicole was older, college and land life with Tatchi—like we'd dreamed—would be on hold.

The shell-encrusted ceiling of their room shimmered green, purple, and silver light onto the mirror, illuminating my red tresses as Tatchi continued to pin them up. Fin and I had a similar apartment of our own in the palace, but I still couldn't get over how surreal Natatoria was, almost like a dream. Normal had been plunged underwater without a chance to dry—new rules, new ways of living, new beauty. And even though we'd been living here only a few short weeks, returning home would be a culture shock to say the least.

"Being a mom won't stop me from planning the wedding if that's what you're worried about."

"I'm not worried." I rotated and smiled at her. "Nicole would make an adorable flower girl."

"Wouldn't she?" Tatiana giggled.

"In something green or pink…"

Tatiana's mouth gapped. "Are those the colors?"

I shrugged sheepishly. "Maybe."

"You're such a tease." She slid open the drawer next to me. Inside was a notebook stuffed with what looked like magazine pictures.

Sitting next to me on the bench, she laid the notebook on the desk.

"Okay, don't kill me, but I've been putting together a visual masterpiece for your approval."

She flipped past page after page of gowns, flowers, decorations, and cakes.

"Where'd you get this?" I said, salivating at the gorgeousness.

"Girra's magazine stash. Where else?"

Of course my curious little sister Girraween, with her love of all things human, would have had someone smuggle in wedding magazines for her. At the visual masterpiece, my heart flipped. Could this finally be happening? My dream wedding finally coming true?

"And Desirée said we could have whatever you wanted. Spare no expense."

At the mention of my birth mother's name, something pinched inside me, like she was overstepping my human parents' bounds, which was ridiculous considering she was my mother.

I ran my hands over a picture of a beaded gown. "She doesn't have to do that. My parents have some money."

"You can't say no to Desirée. Trust me."

Trust. That was a hard thing to do when your mother switched you at birth because you weren't a boy. Even still, I wanted to mend that relationship, considering my strained one with my human mother.

"And technically, I'm still the Queen," she finished. "So, I decree it!"

"What?" I nudged her arm. "No, you're not."

"Tell that to the mer. They keep bowing, and calling me Queen, even though they know Azor wasn't born royal. They see the mark and bow as if on instinct."

She pushed out her hip to flaunt her fleur-de-lis tattoo. I had a matching mark, one I'd always thought was a birthmark, but was actually a tattoo given to me at birth. But Tatchi's point was made. Half the time, though, the mer confused me for Princess Galadriel, my rude older sister, and snubbed me.

"Old habits die hard." I licked my finger and flipped the page.

"And Queen Desirée isn't about to give up her title."

"Regent, you mean," I corrected with a snotty tone.

King Merric, who'd come to the rescue when Azor was about to kill all the rebels for trumped up charges, thought it would be less of a blow to the mer people than to take away all the customs overnight.

"Regent, shmegant. Luckily, it's just a title and she'll never rule again. It was horrendous being on the court with her." Tatiana rolled her eyes. "If I had to listen to one more complaint, especially when her son was the one causing all the problems, I would have screamed—no, sirened."

From what I could see upon arriving at Natatoria compared to now with the Council ruling, I couldn't agree more.

There was a knock on the door interrupting us, and then someone pushed it all the way open. We both jumped.

"Tatiana?" Regent Desirée said with a large smile.

"Mom," I said, getting to my feet.

Tatiana did the same.

Her eyes brightened. "I didn't know you were here. Sorry to interrupt." She gazed toward the merling's room. "Is Nicole sleeping?"

I gave Tatiana a sideways look. Had she overheard us?

"She's still napping, Regent." Tatiana bowed.

"Oh," she waved her hand, "you don't have to do that. Call me mom… or, um…" Her gaze met mine. "Desirée is fine."

"Okay."

At the sound of Nicole's cry, Tatiana scurried toward the baby's room.

"Allow me," Desirée said, intercepting.

"Oh, okay." Tatiana stopped, then spun to me, biting her lip, when her ex-mother-in-law entered the child's room.

"Why is she here?" I mouthed.

"She feels a connection since it's Azor's child," she whispered back.

Tatiana kept a close eye on the opened door, body taut, ready to spring into action if Nicole needed it.

"I don't want the wedding to be too ostentatious, considering the audience," I said quickly to distract her.

Tatiana touched my arm. "Well, actually... I was hoping to ask a favor."

My gaze swung to hers. "Okay?"

She paused. "Could my students come?"

I felt the blood drain from my face. "Your students?"

She bit her lip. "I've been wanting to test them. I think they'll be ready for some human interaction by then."

My mouth dropped. "At my wedding?"

"Well..." She cocked her head. "They are Fin's friends and family. It would give them a chance to use their aliases, and they could help with the planning. And with a good handful of mermen ready to sing away any flub ups, it'll be perfect. I mean, I'm guessing it'll take three or four months to plan everything—like late August? Don't let me set your date for you, but I do need some time, and that'll be right before we start college." She winked.

I pinched my eyes shut, massaging my neck. I could just imagine the nightmare, especially with Girra, the most curious of my sisters, interacting with the likes of my high school friends, like Georgia.

Nicole started to wail, almost at the point of a siren. I plugged my ears while Tatiana darted to the door.

At the last second, she pivoted toward me. "Just think about it, okay?"

"Okay." I most definitely didn't want them there, but how could I say no to my best friend?

"I've got it." Desirée came out of the room with Nicole wriggling and shrieking while she reached for Tatiana, blasting everyone's eardrums.

"She's hungry," Tatchi said anxiously. "Let me feed her, then you can hold her."

Reluctantly, Desirée gave Tatchi the merling. The babe calmed instantly.

"Did you have a good nap, sweetie?" Tatchi asked Nicole as she settled on the settee.

I marveled at how she'd taken to motherhood so easily. Nicole settled in her arms, her little hand shooting up, tugging on Tatiana's blonde hair as she nursed.

"I'm still in awe that she bonded with you," Desirée said.

"Bonded?" I asked.

"A merling knows their mother's voice. It starts from the womb. They respond to it like a magnet, swim to it, calm to it, crave it. It's instinct, which makes adoption so… difficult."

I sat back and thought of my human mother. Was that why things were never peaceful between us? That I couldn't bond to her because I didn't recognize her voice?

"Really?" Tatiana asked.

"Yes. Many times the merling is inconsolable, especially the boys." Desirée's eyes lingered on me. Was she thinking about my adoption? About what she'd done to me?

At the awkward pause, I returned to the wedding notebook, flipping past the pages, trying not to think about what we'd been through as of late… it started after Fin and Tatiana didn't return after a family emergency, and I'd stupidly fallen into the icy waters of Lake Tahoe, nearly drowning. That fateful day, April 3rd, Fin happened to be visiting the bay and was forced to give me mouth to mouth while I was unconscious, to save my life, thus entwining our souls together with the mer promise in order to save my life. I didn't remember a thing, but that little kiss changed everything. No more dreams of college, or going to the Olympics. Finding him became my obsession, but I had no idea where they'd gone.

Tatiana and Fin were just trying to break free from Natatoria and find their dad, Jack, but they were captured on my beach by Prince Azor and his goons, and that's when I finally saw what they really were—merfolk. Before Jack could stop him, Azor stole Tatiana's promise—at his ruse of a promising ceremony—and she'd become bonded to him and wouldn't leave. Accused of treason, Fin and his parents narrowly escaped, destroying the gate bridging Natatoria and Lake Tahoe. But they weren't safe for long. Azor and his minions swam up the rivers from the Pacific in a tactical attempt to capture the family, which forced them to abandon their house and go to the safe house in Florida. I was to finish out high school in Tahoe, then join up with Fin's family once I attended college.

But Fin's treacherous Uncle Alaster and his son Colin had other plans. After moving into Fin's house and interacting with me, they quickly discovered my birthmark and assumed I was the lost princess Galadriel. With aspirations of becoming royalty, Alaster had Colin kidnap and force promise me. Since I was already promised to Fin, the plan failed. But Alaster still fed me the essence anyway, converting me into a mermaid.

In the meantime, Fin and Galadriel (the real lost princess) crossed the country to Fin's house, in a mad rush to rescue me. Then, in a last ditch effort to hide his treachery, Alaster burned down the house, trapping me, along with Colin, Galadriel, Jax, Ferd, and Fin inside the basement. We narrowly escaped with our lives.

At the same time, Azor used the disruption of his promising ceremony to cleanse Natatoria of Jack's rebel alliance. Tatiana, after discovering he'd committed promising polygamy with his servant,

Xirene, who was pregnant with his child, did something very few mer were capable of doing: break the promise connection between them. After the babe was born, Azor murdered his father, King Phaleon, because his desire to be king outweighed everything else. In the meantime, Tatiana had fallen in love with her bodyguard, Jacob, who secretly was one of Jack's rebels. Azor blackmailed Tatiana with Jacob's life, so she'd pretend the babe was hers so he'd fulfill the requirements to take the throne. She succumbed to his bidding, and Azor was crowned King, as he'd wanted. When he was about to execute the rebels, starting with Badger, the Lost Ones—those condemned to die on Bone Island, led by former King Merric, returned and demanded justice. When the babe was discovered to be a girl and not the required boy, Azor's control unraveled, and the people demanded his life as punishment. When he tried to escape through the Pacific gate, the sharks devoured him along with his Dradux guard.

And the mystery was explained about my pesky birthmark that looked like a fleur-de-lis that wasn't a birthmark at all, but a tattoo given at birth to show that I was of royal blood. I'd been switched at birth with Azor, a human child turned mer, so Phaleon could be king. Of course, none of that mattered now with the royal family dethroned and the Council leading the colony.

So much. Too much.

"What are you looking at?" Desirée asked, standing over my shoulder.

I looked up from the notebook, pulled back into reality. "It's a wedding idea book."

"Oh?" Her face brightened. "May I?"

I handed her the book and watched her eyes as she flipped through it, skipping the pages with anything to do with the outdoors or land.

"Oh, my. So many lovely ideas." Her gaze met mine. "So I'm taking it you're moving ahead with things. Are you planning to have it here? In the remodeled audience hall?"

I bit my lip. With everything we'd been through to mend our past, I didn't want to anger her. Could I tell her the truth? "I…"

"She wants to have it on land," Tatiana interrupted. "On her parents' beach."

Her eyebrows puckered, and I wanted to take back the mention of my human parents the moment it was said.

"It'll be a perfect opportunity, actually, to introduce mers to land, to human culture," Tatchi added.

Desirée kept staring at me, fear and pain radiated somewhere deep within her irises. "But what about the humans? Aren't you worried about being discovered?"

I shrugged. "Tatchi and Fin were my closest friends growing up, and I never suspected a thing. And considering my background, I'm an expert on humanity."

"She should be teaching my class with me," Tatchi added.

Desirée nodded slowly. "I'm sure you're right, but we should discuss it with the Council."

Though Desirée had expressed reservations, I already knew the Council had discussed this, and recently decreed that mers could go on land if they wanted. The only restrictions were they needed to graduate from Tatchi's classes, and then be accompanied by an experienced merman during the first visits until they'd fully acclimated.

"So, are you excited about going home?" Tatchi asked as if to break the tension.

At her use of the word "home," Desirée frowned. I cringed, not wanting my mother offended any more than she already was.

"I don't know if we'll go on land," I said quickly. "Probably just look at the house from the water… a quick trip."

Please stop, Tatchi!

Though I knew seeing the burnt house would be horrific for Jack, he'd most likely want to hunt down his slimy brother and give him hell right then and there. I merely wanted to get home and tell my family all about my supposed Africa trip and make sure they were okay.

"That reminds me." Desirée returned her attention to the babe momentarily. "Fin is looking for you."

Nicole let out a coo and sprang into her fin, shredding her diaper.

"Now, now, sweetie. We only phase underwater," Tatiana said.

Nicole arched her back and screamed, and her tail morphed back into legs. Once Tatiana was able to put on another diaper, she set the merling on the floor. Nicole took off crawling, her bouncing, dark curls flowing down her back.

"Aren't you going to burp her?" Desirée scooped up the child and attempted to hold her over her shoulder. "She'll get a tummy ache."

Nicole arched her back again and screamed in Desirée's ear.

"No, no." Desirée smacked Nicole's behind.

A blood-curdling shriek came from the merling. Tatiana stood aghast, putting her hand to her mouth before she snatched the babe from Desirée's arms.

"Look who's starting those terrible twos." Tatchi chuckled nervously.

Desirée watched on with a disheartened look as Tatiana returned Nicole to the floor. The merling crawled over to the closet.

"She needs to be disciplined."

Tatiana trailed after her daughter, her lips into a taut line. The tension mounted.

I popped to my feet. "That's just crazy how quickly mer kids grow. I wouldn't have thought her to be the same girl, considering she's crawling already."

"I know." Tatiana took a flip-flop from Nicole before she could stick it in her mouth. Nicole let out a wail, shifting back into a mermaid. "Do you have time to come with me to the park? I want to take Nicole for a swim before she... Holy crawfish!"

A puddle gathered under Nicole's tail, and she started to splash in it.

I ran and grabbed a towel from the bathroom and handed it to Tatchi. "I'd love to, but I think the guys want to leave once Badger finishes with his sparring lessons." Glancing out the window, my eye caught Badger and Jack swimming in the courtyard. "Oh, shoot. I think I'm late."

"I'd love to go with my grandmerling," Desirée said with a smile.

"Okay. Let me clean up this mess first." Tatchi swaddled the wiggling girl in the towel, then put her on the changing table.

"You two have fun." Feeling left out, I faked a smile and headed for the door before disappointment settled in. "I'll see you soon."

Desirée turned with a concerned expression. "Please be careful, my sweet. Promise me."

"Sure, Mother," I said, still not comfortable with calling her that. "Always."

She gave me a dejected smile, then returned to the babe, cooing over her. For a brief moment, I got the feeling she was disappointed in me, that I would never be important to her until I produced a merling of my own.

2

FIN

May 15 – 2:15 p.m.

Walking down the hall toward my sister's apartment, I watched as the door swung open and my favorite redhead walked into the hall. My eyes swept over her pink beaded dress that hugged her curves just right, and my insides squeezed.

"There you are, my Ginger Girl," I said before she saw me. She looked over her shoulder at me and smiled. Her beauty left me speechless. Poseidon. Breathtaking.

"Why are you looking at me like that?" she asked.

I took a few long strides to close the gap between us, just to touch her. "It's too easy losing you here. We need cell service."

"So you can call me on my shell phone?" She laughed, sending a thrill through me, and I kissed her to capture it inside me. My love. My girl.

She pulled away, breathless, but I couldn't let her go. She looked up at me with those long eyelashes, a coy smile on her lips. "If you keep kissing me like that, we'll never make it to Tahoe today."

"Oh?" My arms squeeze her tight as my lips meet hers again. "Is that what we're supposed to be doing today?"

"Maybe."

Someone cleared his throat behind me. Ash let go and jumped away from me.

Dad stood off to the side. "Didn't mean to interrupt. Badger is ready when you are."

Ash's cheeks flushed red as she giggled, moving nervously next to me, her hand molded into mine. "Hey, Mr. Helton."

"Call me Dad," he said.

"Dad." She looked down.

"You ready?" I asked her, unable to think straight momentarily.

She nodded, but there was something behind her eyes. Fear?

Jack headed down the hall. "Knowing Badger, he probably already left without us."

As Ash and I followed, Dad shared his plans to remodel, but as we got closer to the porthole entrance, Ash seemed to stiffen next to me.

"You okay?" I whispered.

"Me?" She kept her eyes forward. "I'm fine."

We exited through the porthole and shifted into our fins. Badger swam across the courtyard.

"Aye, lad. You look a little flushed," Badger joked. "Whatcha been doin' making us wait like this?"

I cocked my head to the side. He'd been teasing me every chance he got after he found out I'd run off and ended up promised to a human. "Nothing. I couldn't find Ash."

"Ah, sure, lad." He winked at me.

"You ready?" Jack asked.

"Yes. Let's git before the barnacles have a time to fasten on me tail."

Dad and Badger swam ahead, and I stuck back with Ash to get out of earshot, confused about what happened to her normal spunk.

"Okay. Something is wrong."

"It's nothing."

"It's not nothing. Are you nervous? Do you not want to go?"

Thinking back to the disaster that had happened the last time with Ash's family, I could see her apprehension. Ash had hated that I'd sung in order to persuade them to believe we were going to Africa on a mission trip, that it was more important than finishing school and becoming an Olympic hopeful.

She shook her head. "No. I need to go."

I waited, but she didn't say anything further. "Did something happen with my sister?"

Her expression became puzzled. "No. Of course not."

"Then what is it? You were fine this morning."

"Well…" She bit her lip, and I imagined the worst—that the conversation of being converted into a human would come up again. "She wants her students to come to our wedding."

I stared at her, stunned for a moment, then my shoulders sagged in relief. "And you don't want them to?"

"No. I do." She lowered her head again. "It's stupid."

"What?" I put my arm around her waist and pulled her close to me, stopping us in the current. "Is this about me asking your dad?"

She sucked in the water and flashed a coy smile that made me want to kiss her lips.

"I'd like you to do that, yes. I just… I'm not good with all this mer mojo stuff."

Instantly, I felt bad. Though she'd just recently found out she'd been switched at birth, and then forced to become a mermaid at the hands of my uncle, she'd lost everything—her family, her home, her security.

I lifted her red hair so I could see her eyes. "We don't have to rush anything."

She sighed. "What are we going to tell them?"

"Whatever you want. It's up to you."

She paused for a second. "I feel like a totally bad daughter leaving like I did."

"You're not a bad daughter. We had no choice." I squeezed her tighter.

"I want them to be happy about it, about us getting married."

I highly doubted they would, considering our age, but then again, with the song, I could make them.

"When they see how much we love each other, they'll be happy for us," I said as a cover, knowing she hated it when I manipulated humans, especially her parents.

Her gaze rose, gauging the looming rock wall up ahead. "My dad will question you about a job and where we'll live."

"Already got it covered. I'll be taking over the charter business, and Dad's building a cottage for us."

She leaned into me, eyes filled with worry. "Really?"

"Yeah." I tugged her close and kissed her nose. "I've got this. Don't worry."

"But then what? I can't stay at the house at night, and what about school?"

"Well..." I paused for effect. "That'll be something I'll have to mojo..."

Her body tightened.

"It won't be bad. Maybe I'll tell them they can't open your door when it's shut, or bug you after you say goodnight to them." I snuggled up closer and waggled my eyebrows. "Then you'll have to sneak out of your window each night so we can... you know."

I grinned mischievously.

"Fin... focus." She dipped her head. "My room is on the second story."

"Don't tell me you've never snuck out before."

"Well..." She rolled her eyes. "Maybe once, but what about school?"

"What about it?"

"I'm going to have to go... I don't want you singing away that, too." She let out a sigh. "I only have 4 more weeks left... I mean, for my parents' peace of mind I should go."

"Sounds fun. I'll go with you."

She nudged my arm. "Stop it. No, you won't."

"I will."

"You need to rebuild the house."

"Look," I cocked my head, "there might be questions when you get back so you might need my services."

She pinched her eyes shut. "You just want to mind-jack everyone."

"No, I don't." I lifted my hands. "We'll just take it one step at a time."

The fissure to the Tahoe Gate came into view. Once a beautiful arch my father carved by hand was now nothing but a crevice in the mountain with a big pile of boulders stacked haphazardly off to the side. The damage made me sad, destroyed because of Azor's greed. And then the memory of what my uncle did to the house made my anger boil over once more. It was almost like everything my father created secretly crushed their egos. After we rebuild the house, I vowed that I'd bring the gate back to its original splendor if it killed me.

As Jack and Badger entered the crevice, Ash slowed. A slight shiver convulsed through her and she held tighter to me. Alaster had attacked her in this cave and severed her ring finger and pinkie to pass her off as Princess Galadriel. Luckily she was able to reattach them.

"You ready?" I asked again like an idiot.

"I'm fine."

The need to say something more to comfort her burned on my tongue, to tell her not to let being here bother her, but I didn't want to patronize her either.

We eventually made it through the tunnel and out of the gate to the other side. We both pulled in deep sips of the snowy, crisp water of Lake Tahoe.

"Home," she said quickly, spinning in a circle. "The water is unlike anything I've ever tasted. Clean."

"I know."

Dad regrouped with us outside the gate. "Okay, so I don't know what to expect up there, so stick together—"

"We're going to check on Ash's parents," I interrupted.

"Okay." Dad gave me a look of warning. "But it's just like always. Since it's daylight, we need to check the surroundings before we surface, and once we're on land, don't overdo the song, okay? We may just need to assess things from the water and see if there's anything salvageable."

"But we're rebuilding," I said firmly. I'd just promised Ash we'd have a place to live—that was part of the deal.

Dad's lips formed a hard line. "I want to see the damage first."

I sighed. From what I remembered, there'd be nothing left from the inferno the night Alaster burned it down.

Cautiously, we neared the top and carefully crested the surface. I scanned the horizon, and my heart plummeted. All that was left was the lone chimney surrounded by burnt timber and yellow caution tape.

The deathly silence was cut by Dad cursing. "When I get my hands on Alaster—"

"Aye." Badger put his hand on my father's shoulder. "You and me both, mate."

"We'll make it good as new, Dad," I promised.

But Ash wasn't looking at the ruins. She was drifting toward her childhood home. I moved to catch up with her, tugging on her hand to pull her under.

"We have to stay hidden," I reminded her.

She ducked down but kept moving forward, trance-like. "Do you think they remember?"

"They'll remember only what we told them, which was not to worry, remember? It'll be fine."

She surfaced just by her dock and stared at the house.

"Everything looks okay," I said to reassure her.

"Yeah, unless they tried to contact me." She worried her lip.

A police car drove up and over the hill, parking next to her house. Two officers got out and walked to the door.

"Holy crawfish. Why are they here?"

The door opened, and I tried to listen with my bionic hearing but was unable to catch much. After a brief conversation, the two were invited inside.

Before I could stop her, Ash leaped onto the dock and phased into legs.

"Ash!" I whisper-yelled, looking around to make sure no one from the nearby beach saw her.

She ran up the dock toward the house, dripping wet. I swam to the shore and shifted, trying to catch up.

"Wait!" My hands couldn't fasten the Velcro on my board shorts fast enough.

I looked up, and to my horror, she'd already charged inside.

3

ASH

May 15 – 3:39 p.m.

My heart pounded with thoughts of why they'd come. Did something happen to Dad? Gran? My mother? Once I entered the house, the taller of the two cops stopped talking.

"Ash?" My mother blinked at me, eyes red and swollen. Then she jumped up and attacked me with a hug.

My arms circled around her, squeezing tight. I didn't understand why the happy reunion since I'd only been gone for a few weeks. Tears wet my cheeks anyway. I'd wanted this, for her to miss me. Gran hugged me next, followed amazingly by my sister, Lucy. Then they all stared at me like my head might pop.

"What's going on? Why are they here?" I gestured to the cops.

Mom eyed me up and down "What are you wearing, and why are you all wet?"

I looked down at the puddle under my feet from my pink beaded gown, realizing my mistake. Luckily, Fin walked in behind me. He quickly sang, using his mer mojo to get them to ignore my attire.

"I'm sorry to interrupt the reunion," the shorter cop turned to me, "but you're under arrest, Ashlyn, for arson."

"Arrest?" I leaped backward.

Mom stood between us. "I told you. She didn't do this. I don't care what evidence you have!"

"Ma'am, please…"

Fin started to sing, "Ash is innocent, and it's time for you both to leave."

The cops' eyes glazed over.

"Sorry for the confusion." The taller of the two looked at the shorter one, then nodded and they left. "We'll be going."

I swallowed hard, my heart thundering.

Then my mother's gaze turned cold. "Where have you been?"

I flicked a glance at Fin. She'd been mojoed. How could she have forgotten? "I was on a mission trip in Africa."

She chuckled. "Really? And where are your plane tickets? Your visa? Your passport?"

Fin opened his mouth to sing, but I grabbed onto his hand to stop him.

"No. Let me handle this." They deserved answers, not some fishy mind-jacking makeover. I turned to my mother. "You're right. I wasn't in Africa."

Mom's jaw tightened. "Then where were you?"

"I was with Fin and his family."

"Doing what?"

I gritted my teeth. What could I say that didn't sound totally lame? "Just traveling."

"Traveling?" Mom barked out a laugh. "Are you kidding me? Oooh! Jack and Maggie are going to get an earful!"

"Karen," Gran said. "I'm sure there's a logical explanation."

"Let me handle this, Mother!" Mom snapped.

"Please," Fin whispered to me.

I held up my hand for him to wait, but I had no excuse to give her that wasn't a lie. How was that any better than just singing them a story? "Mom, just trust me—"

"Trust you? You disappear without a word, and I'm just supposed to look the other way?" She stretched the small space between us and slapped me. "This is unforgivable, and your life will be over as you know it, Ashlyn Francis Lanski. You can leave now, Fin."

"Karen!" Gran scolded. "That's uncalled for."

I turned away, gasping while I held onto the stinging flesh. My mother and I may have had a strained relationship, but she'd never hit me before.

Gran begged for Mom to calm down, while Lucy let out a rude cackle. Fin sang for everyone to sit and be quiet. Tears trickled down over my hot face, and my stomach turned over, making me want to vomit. I knew coming home wouldn't be blissful, but this? The wedding most definitely wasn't happening now.

Fin walked over to me. "Let's just smooth this over and find out what's happened."

I wanted to, but with the cops ready to arrest me, I knew whatever had happened was irreparable.

I barked out a laugh. "Smooth it over? Isn't that what we were doing the last time?"

"Trust me." Fin gave my hand a squeeze before he moved to the couch and sat down next to my mother. "So… what's been going on since we left?"

Lucy cocked a brow. "Justice."

I glared at her. "Having Mom and Dad all to yourself isn't good enough for you?"

"Ash! This is serious," Mom interrupted. "Haven't you seen the news?"

I gritted my teeth. "No?"

"No?" She shook her head. "Where have you been? A hole?"

Something like that.

"You were missing, dear," Gran interjected.

"What?" I mouthed, but nothing came out.

Mom clenched her jaw. "When I told the authorities you were in Africa on a mission trip, they just kept asking questions, threatening that I was covering for you when they couldn't find anything to support you'd left the country." Her head swung around to Fin. "You told me not to worry. You told me everything was fine."

I cringed, ready to let Fin just sing and get it over with.

"There's a warrant out for your arrest, too," Mom hissed.

"For what?" he asked calmly.

"You've been charged with arson. The both of you."

I swallowed, my head swaying. Didn't she remember what happened? That Fin was presumed dead when they couldn't find him in the basement. It didn't matter. This was too big to fix. Unless we mojoed the whole police force, someone else would show up to arrest me.

"We didn't start the fire. Fin's Uncle Alaster did," I defended.

Mom's eyes lost focus and she wrung her hands. "Well, there were witnesses who saw you, and when you disappeared, it looked suspicious, and I didn't have any answers to their questions. I just…" She glanced over at the door, confusion crossing her face. "Why did the cops leave?"

I pressed my hand to my forehead. "Because I didn't do it, Mom."

"It wasn't arson," Fin said quickly. "It was an accident. And now that my family is back, there's no need to panic, and no one is pressing charges. In fact, my dad will start rebuilding this week."

Mom let out a pent up breath. "Well, I'd like to talk to them."

"You always get out of everything," Lucy huffed and left the room.

My shoulders slid downward, and I slumped onto the couch. I didn't want to get away with anything. I wanted to stop the deception. The truth needed to set me free. But how do you tell your human parents you're… inhuman?

"We ran away because we want to get married," I muttered.

Mom spit out the tea she'd just sipped. "What?"

The front door flew open behind us, and Dad appeared, eyes wide and face flushed. I took in the site of him, terrified. But he wasn't angry. Tears were streaming down his cheeks. He stumbled forward, arms outstretched. I jumped up and ran toward him.

His giant arms slid around me and squeezed. "Oh, my baby girl. I knew you'd be alright."

For a brief moment, I believed I was his baby girl, that he was my only father; that I was human again and not stuck between two worlds. My stomach, though, knew differently and tightened all the same. How could I have lied to the one person who loved me unconditionally?

"I'm so sorry, Dad," I said through my tears.

He pulled away and studied me, pressing his hands against the sides of my head. "There's no way you started the fire. I didn't believe it. Is that what kept you away?"

"No."

"Then why?"

"I—I," I stuttered.

"Was someone threatening you? There was this witness who saw you, but I knew there had to be a good reason why they couldn't find your documents."

"It's 'cause I didn't go, Daddy," I said through sniffles.

He stopped for a second. His disappointed look zinged into me, making my heart squeeze.

"Where'd you go?"

"I…" I couldn't tell him.

"They were getting ready to elope," Mom interrupted.

"Cantaloupe? What does that have to do with anything?" Gran asked from across the room.

Mom growled. "No, Mom… ugh. Don't you have your hearing aid in?" She turned to Dad. "When I see Jack and Maggie, they are going to get an earful…" Mom's glare swung to me. "You're pregnant, aren't you?"

"What? No." I pinched my eyes shut to think. "It's just… with the fire… Fin had to leave again, and I couldn't be without him. He was the one that saved my life when I fell into the lake. We have a special bond, one that I can't explain. He understands me. And I love him. Lying was just… easier."

"You lied?" Dad gave me a despondent look, confusion covering his face. Then he looked down at my beaded dress. "What are you wearing?"

Fin quickly sang for him to ignore my attire. Dad's eyes glazed over, driving a dagger into my subconscious. I couldn't keep doing this, especially to him.

"Forget it." I jumped up and stormed out of the room, running upstairs.

I went to my room and slammed the door. A row of cards blew off my desk and hit the floor. My gaze panned to the dresser. Cards and flowers, some new and the others wilted and drooping in their vases, covered the top.

I sucked in a strangled gasp, then caught a glimpse of something shiny outside. Mylar balloons were tethered to a sign nailed to our tree in the yard and flapped in the wind. Stuffed animals and candles crowded the trunk underneath. I leaned against the window, legs weak. Reality sunk in.

I was missing.

4

FIN

May 15 –4:20 p.m.

"Stay here," I sang to her parents, then followed Ash upstairs. Only one door was shut, so I approached slowly.

"Ash?" I knocked, then turned the knob.

She sat curled up on the bench seat under the window, fingers pressed to the glass. "They think I'm missing."

"Who does?"

"Everyone."

I walked closer and placed my hands on her shoulders.

She yanked away, popping to her feet. "No."

"Ash?" I stepped backward.

"Your Uncle Alaster did this. He needs to pay." Her voice was shaking.

"I know. And he will—" I started.

"No, I'm serious. You find him and make him pay." Her voice deepened. "Not only for this, but for what he almost did to me." She lifted her hand to show the scars on her ring and pinkie fingers. "He's a monster and he forced me into a life I wasn't prepared for. This is his fault."

"I promise you, if it takes my entire life to find him, he'll pay."

She blinked at me, then swallowed. "We need to fix this because I'm not disappearing from my parents' lives again. I mean... I know I'm not their biological daughter, but to them I am. So... I want to make them happy."

"Okay," I agreed. "Let's go downstairs and I'll ask for your hand in marriage right now. Weddings make everyone happy."

Her mouth opened, then shut, her eyes wide.

"Or not," I added, unsure how to fix this.

"I just…" she sniffled. "This isn't how I'd imagined it to go."

I nodded, not quite understanding, wishing she'd give me a little more go to on. "How did you imagine it?"

"I know it's corny, but I just want my dad to agree… on his own."

"Oh?"

"And we can't tell anyone about this."

My brow furrowed. "Tell anyone about what?"

"About the arrest warrants!" She shook her open hands at me. "Where have you been?"

I sucked in a breath. "Well, sure… yeah. Of course."

She gawked at me, determination wrinkling her forehead. "You can tell your parents, but…" she stood and took my hands in hers, "if we truly want the mers to have the freedom to live on land, then no one can know about this. We're supposed to be the masters at it."

"Oh," I said, thankful I finally understood. "Yeah. Right."

"So, you and your dad have to figure out a way to fix this before anyone visits. Find Alaster, pin it on him, or come up with a convincing story about how the fire was started, and where I went. Not something that the press would go after and not let go, but something decent."

Decent. Right. I had no clue what that could be, but I'd figure out something. Anything to make her smile.

"Until then," she lifted her chin, "I'm finishing out my senior year."

I nodded, suddenly regretting that I'd agreed to join her.

"That's a good idea," I said.

The space between her eyes puckered in that cute way I liked.

"You're coming with me, right?"

"Of course I am."

"To high school."

"Yep."

"For four weeks."

"If that's how long it is, then yes."

"You're not going to argue with me?"

I dipped my head. "With my wife? No way. We're a team, remember? And if this is what you need, so be it."

Her eyes teared up again, her lip quivering. My insides seized. What did I say wrong now?

"What did I do to deserve you?" She grabbed onto me, laying her lips on mine.

I almost collapsed in relief and deepened the kiss. "No. I'm the lucky one."

Her body softened in my arms. "Thank you, Fin."

I squeezed tighter. What was four weeks anyway? Piece of crab cake.

After Ash had found me one of her dad's shirts to wear, she changed out of her dress into yoga pants while I searched for an alibi on the internet. Luckily, there was a city located close to the border in Arizona that would be an ideal place for a mission tour and sounded similar enough to be confused with Africa.

We walked downstairs, finding her parents where we'd left them, and smoothed things out the best we could before I headed over to the singed pile that used to be my house. Ash decided to stay behind to clean up the shrine in her yard. Glancing over to my parents' driveway, I was momentarily jolted that my Jeep was missing until I remembered I'd left it in Florida.

"Where's Ash?" Dad crossed over to me, his hands blackened with soot.

"She's cleaning up the shrine in her front yard, and breaking the news to her best friend."

"Shrine?" Dad asked.

I shrugged. "We didn't think through the whole mission trip thing, so when they couldn't reach her, they thought she was missing."

"Oh."

"Yeah. There's also a warrant out for my arrest," I said.

"For?"

"Arson." I gave him a fake smile. "Got any pull in the police department?"

Dad grabbed onto my shoulder and squeezed while he laughed. "Oh, don't worry about it. I have to go sweet-talk the county for the building permits later anyway, so I'll take care of it while I'm there."

Hope filled me. I knew if anyone could fix this, he could.

"This is quite some mess."

Dad gave me a disheartened look. "Yes, it is. I can't believe my brother would do such a thing."

"Have you seen him at all?"

Dad let out a low whistle. "No, but knowing him, he's lurking somewhere embarrassed. He knows he's not welcome." Dad lifted another charred board. Underneath was a burnt picture of our family. He cursed. "He'll more than pay. He'll suffer."

Oh, yes he will.

Forcing himself on Ash to be his mate, and then trying to pass her off as Galadriel by chopping off her ring and pinkie fingers, set my teeth on edge. I'd made a promise, and I intended on keeping it.

"In the meantime," Dad continued, "we've got our work cut out for us. And I could use a break from the politics in Natatoria, I bet you could, too."

I nodded. How people could be happy one minute with a decision, to turn around and be upset was beyond me.

Dad's bushy beard lifted with a smile. "Great. I could use all the help I can get."

"Of course," I said with a smile. "I'll be here... uhhh, I mean, in the afternoons, I can."

Dad's eyes narrowed. "Ash already have you on wedding errands?"

"No. It's even better than that." I laughed and shook my head. "I'm going to attend high school."

Dad deadpanned. "What?"

"It's only for four weeks until she graduates. She just wants things to transition smoother than they have with her parents, and a high school diploma won't hurt when asking her dad for her hand."

"I see." Dad's head bobbed up and down. "You're a good mate, you know that?"

"I know."

"And humble."

"The humblest."

Dad chuckled and then lifted his chin to Badger, who paced around the back side of the property. He raised his hand to acknowledge me but kept shaking his head at the mess. How we'd clean this up and rebuild seemed daunting.

Dad let out a long exhale. "Well, I need to get over to the office. Hopefully, my basswipe of a brother didn't wreck the work truck. I know of a houseboat for sale at the pier, and we'll park it at the dock for appearances sake, and then order the lumber."

Come to think of it, I'd need clothes for school, and if I had my Jeep, I'd pick up Ash and we'd go shopping.

But most importantly, I'd prove to Ash I could fix this without always resorting to the song. I'd show her I could fix everything.

5

ASH

May 15 –4:35 p.m.

Pushing another stuffed animal into the garbage bag from the shrine outside my parents' house, I deleted yet another voice message from Georgia. I couldn't believe she'd actually filled my voicemail; I wanted to scream.

"Ugh," I cried out as I spilled hot wax from a recently lit candle on my arm. Why did people light candles for me?

A guy next to a work truck labeled Sierra Cable eyed me suspiciously, giving me the creeps. I cinched up the bag and walked over to the alcove next to the garage to toss everything away in the garbage, then stayed hidden while I dialed Georgia's number.

"This better be you," Georgia said, voice quivering.

"It is me."

"Holy mother of Jehoshaphat!" The phone jostled as if she'd dropped it.

"Georgia?" I asked.

"Where have you been?"

I held the phone out from my ear, prepared for her piercing outcry, my left eye squinting. "On a mission trip."

"To Africa? Try again."

"No… Arivca."

Silence.

"Georgia?"

"You've been in a town called Arivca? I could have sworn—even your parents said Africa!"

"I know," I said softly.

"You disappeared!"

"Not really… there just wasn't any cell service, or Internet, or TV. That's the point of a mission… total O.T.G."

"O.T.G. What the heck does that mean?"

"Off the grid."

"You've got to be freaking kidding me! Ashlyn!" she seethed. "You were totally the talk of the town. Talk of the nation."

I let out a long sigh, questioning why I was doing all of this. *Talk of the nation* was quite an exaggeration. Maybe I should have let Fin sing to her like he'd wanted.

"Off the grid. It's all part of the experience."

"What's it called?"

I crinkled my brow and walked out from the garbage can alcove, watching for the weird guy. He wasn't by his truck any longer. "What's what called?"

"The place off the grid?"

I swallowed, then pinched my eyes shut. "Why do you care?"

"'Cause I don't believe you anymore, that's why."

"Come on, George."

"Come on nothing. What's it called?"

I licked my lips. "I forget."

"You forget? You were there for three weeks."

"Okay… you caught me. I ran away with Fin and got married."

Georgia began to choke. "Seriously?"

"I'm kidding."

"You better stop doing that, because you worried the CRAP out of me and everyone! I thought for sure you were kidnapped and sold into slavery by that guy… Fin. I scoured the Internet for hours looking for you."

My stomach twisted. "I'm sorry. It's… really just a misunderstanding. I'm home now."

I contemplated telling her that I was secretly engaged, but then I didn't want her to step on Tatchi's fins as wedding planner.

"Did you run off and get married?"

"No." I let out a sigh.

"But you lost your scholarship."

"I… put it on hold, remember?"

"Hold?"

"I'm sure that can be fixed after I talk to the coach, considering I was volunteering for a charity."

Again. Silence.

"Georgia?"

There was a sniffle. "Just don't do that again. I… I didn't know how to survive without you."

My eyes lost focus. I'd almost done to her what Tatchi and Fin had done to me when they'd left. "Yeah. I'm sorry."

"Well, I'm glad you're sorry." She sounded half-hurt half-sarcastic. "I'm just glad you're home and you're okay."

"Me, too." My stomach was still in knots, though for the most part, things were fixed between us. But tomorrow would be a totally different scenario, most likely needing Fin's mojo. Good thing he was coming with me. I sucked air between my teeth, not looking forward to it.

The crunch of gravel grabbed my attention. I turned, expecting the weirdo, only to see Fin stroll up, wearing his favorite black baseball hat.

"Georgia, I need to go."

"What?"

"I need to go. Can we talk later?"

"But… I want to come see you. You're still not *forgiven*."

I laughed. "I'll see you tomorrow."

"Tomorrow?"

"At school," I said.

"Oh. School. Right." She let out a huff. "I'm still coming over."

"Bye, Georgia."

I hung up just as Fin approached. His blue eyes zinged into me, making my stomach do flips.

"You found your hat."

"The only thing that survived the inferno." He waggled his eyebrows. "Hey, sexy. Wanna give me a ride?"

I stepped forward, trying not to grin. "You trying to mer-mojo me?"

"Always."

I looked upward, my lips pressed out like a duck's bill. "I don't know."

He grabbed me, then leaned me over, hungrily kissing my lips. "Stop! People are watching?"

Fin looked left then right, all spy-like. "Who's watching?"

I busted up laughing and he covered my lips again. My toes curled in my flip-flops, and I knew we'd done the right thing being together, until my phone rang in my pocket.

"I think I like being shellphoneless," Fin joked as he set me upright.

"Oh, geez," I moaned, looking at the screen. "It's Georgia."

"Let me mojo her."

I sighed, then shook my head. "Can you do it over the phone?"

He shrugged. "Never tried."

I handed him the phone. "Hello?"

"Who's this?" I heard her say.

"Stop calling," he sang over the phone.

"Stop calling? Who is this?"

I flapped my hands. "Hang up. Hang up!" I whisper-yelled.

He pressed the button and handed it back to me. "I guess it doesn't work."

The phone started to ring again.

"Don't answer it," he said.

"I have to. If I don't, she's going to poke more holes through my story. I need a name of a mission or a charity… something in Arivca. Where I was."

He pressed out a sigh. "Fine. Let's go inside."

But the more I thought of it, the more I didn't trust that Georgia would actually call to corroborate my story. And after learning Fin couldn't mind-mojo someone over the phone to say I'd actually been there, I was screwed.

"We have to tell Georgia the truth."

"What?"

"It's just better… then when I spring the wedding on her, she'll cooperate. It'll work," *I hope.*

Fin looked at me apprehensively. "Are all your friends this difficult?"

I laughed. "No, just Georgia."

After the second time she called, I picked up. "Georgia?"

She started to yell, so I pulled back the phone, then I told her I'd run away to be with my boyfriend to once again leave her speechless.

6

FIN

May 16 – 7:50 a.m.

I parked Ash's car, if you could call it a car, and eyed the building before us. "This is your school?"

"Yup. You nervous?" she asked as she slipped out of the passenger seat.

I wiggled my toes in my shoes, wanting to take them off already, and slammed the car door a little too forcefully. "No. You?"

"Hey, be nice." She gave me the stink eye.

I lifted my hands in mock surrender.

Her lip turned up in a smile. "It's only four weeks."

Four weeks of boredom. Kill me now.

She came around the car and wove her tiny fingers into mine, peering up at me, her long lashes causing me to think of other things I'd rather be doing right now.

"Just be good," she warned.

Oh, I'll be good.

My winning smile returned, and I put my arm around her shoulder. "I've got this, Ginger Girl."

Her apprising look was met with a quick kiss, but I knew where this stemmed. The evening prior, after she'd snuck out of her window so we could stay in the lake, she'd begged me not to mer-mojo everyone today. I'd promised I wouldn't. Dinner with her parents was proof. Little did Ash know it took all my strength not to mind-slap Lucy about a million times, the little brat.

"Ash!" A girl with dark hair ran toward us and tackle-hugged her before I could stop it. The girl then pulled away and eyed me curiously. "Who's this?"

"Oh." Ash smiled. "This is Fin."

Her dark eyes turned cold. "Fin, huh?"

"Come on, Georgia. He's not the enemy."

Oh, the infamous Georgia. I held out my hand. "Nice to meet you."

Her expression still suspicious, she waited for a second before shaking. "So you're the sweet talker—"

My jaw tightened.

You can do it, Fin. Self-control, man…

"Ash?" another girl said behind them.

Another hug led to more people swarming in, girls and guys pelting her with questions. I stood at the ready, my vocal cords taut to sing away anything, my patience tried to the point of exhaustion. But once Ash explained, the group handled the mix up pretty well, much better than I would have expected.

The bell rang and Ash looked up at the clock. "Oh, crap. We need to see the principal first."

"After you." I gestured she lead the way.

After I had dazzled Principal Wright with a little song and dance, I was officially a Lake Tahoe High student, headed to English Literature in room 203.

"Lanski?" a woman said behind us.

Ash turned around. "Oh, hey, Coach Madsen."

The coach's eyes narrowed. "You're back?"

"Yeah," she said with a chuckle. "Big misunderstanding about *where* I was, actually, if you haven't heard."

"Oh?" She appraised Ash with a suspicious expression, then eyed me quizzically. "Well, that's good to hear. We were all very concerned."

Ash gestured to me. "Have you met Fin yet?"

I stuck out my hand.

Coach Madsen's eyes flashed with recognition for a moment like everyone else's had, and she paused before she took my hand. "No, not yet. New student?"

"Yeah," I said.

"Where from?"

"Florida. He just moved," Ash said quickly. "Big adjustment."

"At the end of the year?"

I let out a sigh, then sang. "Don't worry about that."

The coach's eyes glazed over momentarily, and I hated myself for deceiving her, but it had to be done.

"You didn't have to do that," Ash said tersely. "I was handling it."

Yes. I did.

"Whoa, sorry about that." She pressed her palm to her temple. "Must have been something I ate. What was I saying?"

"Uh…" Ash started.

"Oh, yeah." Coach dropped her hand. "So I have good news and bad…"

Ash stiffened. "You do?"

"Yeah, your blood samples got lost on their way to the lab somehow."

"Blood samples?" A faint memory of Ash telling me that the school had requested her blood for some reason came back to me.

Ash nudged me in the side, a signal to be quiet.

"That's okay. If the Hamusek's are still upset, I don't need to keep the record," Ash said quickly. "I disqualify myself."

"You get to keep the record. And—"

"What blood samples?" I sang, impatient.

Coach's eyes glazed over again. "I took blood, suspecting Ash did performance enhancing drugs before the swim meet because she broke the NCAA record."

Ash glared at me. "Stop doing that."

Coach blinked, then shook her head. "What was I saying?"

"You were talking about the lab results," Ash said while giving me a sideways glare.

"Oh, right. So the good news is the hair test came back clean. There was a weird protein they noticed, but for the most part, it looked good. You're cleared."

"Oh." Ash blew out a breath. "That's great news."

But I couldn't believe my ears. She let them take her blood and hair sample to check for performance enhancing drugs. When?

Coach's eyes narrowed. "So, what are your plans for the Olympic trials? I'm sure once people realize the… mix up, I'll be getting calls again."

"I—I don't know."

I opened my mouth to sing, but Ash zinged me with a hard look.

"It's a big decision, but I know a few coaches who would love to train you… and anything you need, just ask. I'm here for you. You'll be swimming the last meet on the 28th, right?"

"Yeah." Ash shifted her weight, leaning away from me.

I couldn't believe what she was saying. School was one thing, sure, but I didn't think she'd still be swimming, too, especially now that she had one fluke up on everyone.

"Great." Coach's face lit up. "We've got a lot to plan. College wise and everything. It's all very exciting."

"Yeah." Ash fake laughed. "Well, we're late for class."

"Oh, right. Nice to meet you Fin."

"Likewise," I said.

Coach went on her way but kept her eye on me. Once we were alone, Ash turned.

"What are you doing?" she said through her teeth.

"What am *I* doing?" I asked sarcastically. "I think I should ask what the heck you're doing. Swimming? You can't swim."

"I'm living my life like a normal person, that's what I'm doing."

"You gave blood and hair? When?"

"I don't remember… after you left. But you shouldn't have sang to her."

"What if they had found something?"

She pushed out a breath. "You said there'd be nothing in my blood. Remember?"

"When?"

"When you were driving to Florida!"

I scrubbed my hand over my face, trying to remember beyond the insanity of our road trip. "Even still, you can't take chances like that."

"Well, after you left, I had to make do," she said between clenched teeth. "And you don't have to mind-mojo everyone who's questioning me."

"I'm not… she just kept *looking* at me like that."

"Like how?"

"Like she knows our secret."

Ash blew out a breath. "That's crazy. I'm sure she recognized you from the news reports."

"Maybe." I looked down the hall to see if Coach was listening. "Wait! There are news reports about me?"

"You're missing the point," she said, storming off.

I followed after her. "But I can't believe you're going to swim in the meet."

"I have to. It's part of the deal."

"Ash," I grabbed onto her arm to stop her, "you think you swam fast before? Wait until you swim as a mer."

"I'll purposefully lose… then these coaches will leave me alone." She pulled away from me. "Look, if we're going to assimilate, you need to use your song as a last-ditch resort, okay?"

The need to defend myself rolled through me, but I clamped my mouth shut. Demanding she listen wasn't going to change her mind. I was here to make her happy and keep the secret safe. "You're right."

She yanked her head backward. "I'm right?"

"I don't want to argue."

Her expression radiated confusion. "So every time we get in a disagreement, you're not going to argue with me so we won't fight?"

"No." My jaw tensed. Clearly, no matter what I did, I couldn't please her. "I'm going to stop singing. I don't like it anyway."

She looked at me, a mixture of anger and bewilderment.

"Aren't we going to be late?" I gestured to the door.

"Yeah." Ash opened the door and stepped inside. I followed. Thirty pairs of eyes landed on us, and I questioned everything.

What the heck was I doing here?

"Why, hello," the teacher, whom I assumed to be Mrs. Keifer, said.

"This is Fin." Ash handed her the paperwork and marched to a seat in the middle of the room.

The only other empty chair was in the front row.

"Nice of you to join us, Finley. Have a seat." Mrs. Keifer gestured to the empty seat in front.

I opened my mouth to mojo myself a spot next to Ash, when I caught the warning in her eye, and stopped.

Taking the seat in front, I stared straight ahead at the board. High school was nothing like TV shows depicted.

"Okay class, let's open our books to page 215."

The girl next to me nudged my elbow and held out a small paperback, *To Kill a Mockingbird*.

"Here. I already read it." She smiled at me, eyes twinkling.

I took it from her. "Thanks."

"I'm Brooke, by the way."

"Oh." I straightened, and held out my hand. "Fin."

She took it, then giggled.

The teacher cleared her throat, eyeing us. "Now, who wants to tell us about the symbolism of…?"

I glanced over my shoulder at Ash. She pinned me with a heated glare.

Slinking down in my seat, I flipped through the book. We hadn't even gotten through first period and I'd already managed to piss her off—twice.

At least I liked the story we were reading.

7

ASH

May 20 – 3:00 p.m.

Fin turned onto our street, and the cool lake air flowed throughout my car, refreshing my flushed skin.

I opened my calendar and marked a big X over Friday, before slamming it shut and shoving it into my bag. Shaking my head, I couldn't believe what we were doing for pretenses with my parents.

"We survived the week," I said.

"Yeah," Fin said tersely.

"Oh, it wasn't that bad."

"You could have clued me in about a few things ahead of time. Like… Brooke, for starters."

"Oh…" I punched him playfully in the side. "I was only mad for like a minute."

Fin reached over and tweaked my knee. I shrieked and moved away from him, giggling. "Stop!"

Fin laughed while he drove over the hill and parked on the street. A crane assisted in raising the wooden forms of the walls while the workers scurried back and forth to secure them. "Your dad isn't wasting any time."

"He's not good at being idle."

I slid out of the passenger seat and slung my backpack over my shoulder. Fin tossed me the keys, and I shoved them into my pocket.

Maggie waved from the houseboat. "Hey, kids. You hungry?"

Once we got closer, the smell of freshly baked cookies wafted over and my tummy rumbled.

I dropped by backpack and jogged down the dock as fast as I could, and took a few before she could hand me the plate.

"I have milk, too."

"Awesome, thank you," I said around a mouthful as I took a seat at the table. Lately, I'd been hungrier than normal, which I attributed to all the extra swimming.

Fin joined me at the table, and we watched the action while we devoured the entire batch. Afterward, I undid the top button on my jeans. "I'm stuffed."

"Does Dad need any help today?" Fin called over his shoulder to his mom.

"Yes, I imagine," she answered while rinsing dishes in the sink.

"Are you going to sing away your homework for tomorrow? Or actually do it," I asked.

He eyed me, a naughty grin on his lips. "Maybe, or see if you can do it for me."

"No way."

"Or I can ask Brooke for help."

"What?" I threw my balled up napkin at him. "Not if you know what's good for you, you won't."

He moved closer, rubbing my thigh. "What's good for me?"

My breath hitched, but I worked to keep a straight face.

"Doing your homework *yourself*."

"And what's my reward for doing my homework *myself*?" His hand moved higher.

"A good grade, for starters—"

His lips covered mine and I gave in to him, my stomach tingling. His kisses grew deeper, and I giggled, then pushed him away. "What if your mother sees?"

"What's the big deal? We're promised."

Something caught my eye just off shore, and I moved to see what it was. Correction, who it was.

"What the shell?" I pointed.

Fin's head whipped around just as Desirée and Pearl walked right out of the lake onto the beach like two goddesses unawares.

He hopped onto the dock and ran toward them before I could get out of the chair. I followed the best I could, my stomach full of milk and cookies.

By the time I'd caught up, Jack had joined as well.

Desirée's regal, white, beaded dress that rose up high in the front, showed off her long legs and gained the attention of the workers. She'd also yet to stop wearing her crown. Pearl, no longer wearing the servant's attire of a white skirt piped in blue, wore a yellow tulle and chiffon skirt, a bit less ostentatious.

"Regent, what brings you to Tahoe?" Jack asked. "Everything okay in Natatoria?"

Pearl stood nervously next to her prior mistress, her eyes round as she took everything in.

"Oh, yes, Jack. Thank you. The Council is in working order under Merric." Desirée smiled. "I'm here to speak with my daughter, actually."

"Mother." I walked up and gave her a hug.

The coolness of her wet skin helped ease the heat coming off of mine.

Desirée swept my hair off my cheek and stuck it behind my ear. "I think you're becoming more beautiful every day, my sweet."

My heart warmed. "Thank you."

"It's a shame you could never be queen. You would have been stunning."

I chewed my fingernail. Queen? Not likely. I couldn't even manage things with my family, let alone a kingdom.

A catcall came from the construction site.

Jack spun, annoyed, and motioned to the gawking crowd. But the song exploded from Badger's mouth.

"Come on, yea blokes, and get yerselves back to work!"

In unison, they all turned and started hammering again.

"That's better." Jack dipped his head. "Your Regency, I hate to be rude, but I have people to babysit."

"Of course. Don't mind me." She chuckled.

He then trudged off.

Pearl eyed me up and down. "You're wearing pants?"

"Jeans, yes. It's the style. We do have to look the part."

"Oh?" Pearl smoothed her hands down her tulle skirt, then eyed the workers. "We're out of place, aren't we?"

"No… just a little dressed up and… wet."

"Oh, we can fix that." Desirée's skin grew red and her hair began to steam. Within seconds, they were both dried.

"There." She fluffed her blonde hair. "Is that better?"

"I'll say." I'd yet to master that trick as quickly as the others had.

"What a gorgeous little place this is here, with all the people and the buildings." She turned to gawk at the surroundings. "I… it's so good to see you grew up in such a luscious place." She looked wistfully off. "Is that the house you grew up in?"

"Yes."

"You know…" she started, then stopped. "I'd love to meet your parents… when it's time, of course."

"Yeah. We should have dinner—er." I folded my hands together to keep from fidgeting. "A meal."

"How's the promising… I mean wedding planning going?" Pearl asked quickly.

I sighed, wanting to tell them both the truth that we hadn't started planning, but didn't for the future of Natatoria. "They're slow in coming with the house building and everything. Cranes don't make a pretty backdrop for a wedding."

"Oh, so you still plan to have it here."

"Yes, under the evergreens."

"It'll be lovely." She held out her hand to me. In her palm was a small beaded sack. "I thought you could use this. It's not much."

I took the bag and opened it. Inside, a mountain of gems sparkled. "Oh, you shouldn't have."

"Oh?" Desirée's smile fell and she side glared at Pearl. Pearl looked away, clearly embarrassed. "Is it not customary for the bride's family to pay for the wedding?"

"Oh," I said quickly. "Yes, yes… it is. I'm sorry. It's just… with so much going on, I've not thought about things." I tied the bag shut and slid it into my pocket. "Thank you," I added. "It's very generous."

Desirée's smile returned. "Do you have a date set?"

"September—" Fin started just as I said, "August."

"I—I see," she said.

Fin cleared his throat a little too aggressively. "I still need to ask Ash's father."

I clamped my mouth shut.

Desirée chuckled. "What's stopping you? Catfish got your tongue?"

Fin's panicked glance found mine. "That's another custom that requires some finessing."

"And you can't sing?"

"I'd prefer he didn't manipulate my father," I said.

Desirée sighed. "All these rules. So confusing."

My rules were confusing? I wanted to argue that Natatorian law was far more confusing but didn't say anything.

"So…" Fin gestured to his parents' houseboat, obviously wanting to get them out of sight. "Why don't we go inside? I'm sure my mom would love to say hi."

"Oh, yes." Desirée eyed the houseboat. "Is that your *home*?"

"It's called a houseboat." Fin proffered his arm.

Desirée took it, and the two walked toward the dock.

I glanced around, thankful the unseasonable chilly weather kept visitors away from our beach. Pearl came up alongside me.

She pulled something out from her waterproof bag. "Princess Tatiana wanted me to give this to you."

She handed me the wedding notebook. Tears pinpricked my eyes looking at it. The fact she didn't bring it herself once again solidified my worries that I'd be planning this alone.

"Thank you."

I quickly stuffed down my emotion. Why was I crying over something so silly?

Pearl reached out and squeezed my hand. She gave me a coy smile. "You are looking radiant."

"Me?" I coughed to cover my surprise. "No. Just… concerned. Though it's a semi-private beach, we don't… um… encourage mers to walk out of the water onto the beach in the open like that."

Pearl put her fingertips to her mouth. "Oh… right."

"Aren't you taking Tatchi's classes?"

She tsked her tongue and leaned in. "I am, but you know Desirée. When she gets something in her head, she doesn't take no for an answer."

I nodded. "Why is she here?"

"Oh, she wanted to visit and… she'll tell you…" She stopped and stared at me. "When are you due?"

"Due?"

"Never mind." Pearl clamped her lips together.

"What do you mean due?" I swallowed, my head swaying.

"Ash, dear," she said softly. "I'm pretty sure you're pregnant."

And at that moment, I almost fainted.

8

FIN

May 20 – 3:45 p.m.

When Ash didn't follow, I looked over my shoulder for her. Whatever Pearl had told her, the smile on her face had vanished.

"Maggie," Desirée said. "It's so good to see you. How quaint this little place is."

"Yes, Regent. It makes a nice front until Jack can finish the main house. How lovely of you to visit."

As Desirée passed, my mother shot me a glare. I shrugged. How was I to know the Regent would visit?

I paced on the dock until Ash and Pearl finally joined me. Then I helped Pearl step onto the deck of the houseboat first.

"What's going on?" I asked Ash softly.

"Nothing." She smiled, but I could tell it was forced.

"So, Ash, my sweet," Desirée drawled. "I have to confess. We came for another reason." She patted the seat next to her.

Ash took a seat, eyes wide. "Yeah?"

Oh, great. I braced myself for what Desirée would say next.

"Do you want to tell her, Pearl?"

Ash's shoulders stiffened and she deadpanned her.

Pearl smiled. "Well, we came to check things out first before Regent Desirée allowed Girra to come help you with the wedding planning."

"Girra?" Ash clarified. "What about Tatchi?"

"Well, with Nicole being so young, I didn't think it a good time to be visiting land, especially now that she's walking. She'll just toddle to any body of water, and shift without knowing any better, and she's been so clingy." Desirée paused, sounding almost jealous. "Well, unless you want to wait a year."

"No," Ash said abruptly. "We need to get things going. Girra is fine."

My brow furrowed. What was she agreeing to? Ash would never allow Girra to take Tatchi's spot in her right mind. Was she just trying to please her mother?

"Great," Desirée said. "She has been taking Tatiana's classes, and of all my daughters, she's the keenest on human lifestyle. I see you have the planning book."

Galadriel was pretty keen, too, but I didn't necessarily want her here interfering. In Ash's lap was a notebook that had pictures sticking out of it.

Desirée leaned forward. "But she'll need to be chaperoned."

My head jerked backward, and I knew exactly where this conversation was going, and I wouldn't be her chaperone. No way. Especially not after my disaster with Galadriel.

"Desirée—" Mom's voice was low.

"I think you mean Regent," Desirée clarified.

"Regent," Mom said with a pert grin. "I think Jack should sit in on this meeting."

"Did I hear someone say meeting?" Jack stepped onto the boat and dusted off his hands. "Ooh, cookies."

Mom quickly filled Jack in on Desirée's concerns as he wolfed down a few.

Desirée pursed her lips, eyeing Dad with disdain. "I know you and I don't see eye to eye on this, Jack, but the rules have been passed down through our generations for a reason. The fact I'm even letting her come here is a stretch for me."

"I understand," Jack said around a mouthful. "But we've decided as a Council that we want to allow properly-trained mer to come on land."

"Yes, but I know my daughter," Desirée interjected.

"Well, if it will make you feel any better, I was going to suggest Fin."

My hands formed into fists, and I tried not to show my frustration. With everything going on, the last thing I wanted to do was babysit another princess. "I'm a little busy—"

Desirée's watchful eye landed on me and I stopped talking.

"He's promised. He's responsible, and of anyone, he's very qualified on human matters," Dad added.

Desirée lifted her chin, appraising me. "Then it's settled."

"Wait," I said quickly.

Dad glared at me.

"I think Ash should decide, I am her promised mate, which will mean she won't have my full attention, right dear?"

I hated that I put her on the spot, but she had to save me.

"What?" Ash's eyes flicked upward from the floor. "Sure whatever you guys want."

My mouth gapped open, then shut. Did she not hear the question? Then she bolted out of her seat.

"Ash?" I asked.

"I just remembered something. I need to go." She leaned over and hugged Desirée. "Good to see you, Mother."

"Likewise, my sweet." Desirée kissed her cheek. "Don't be a stranger."

"Ash?" I asked again.

She passed me, kissing me on the cheek. "Just stay here. I'll be back."

I watched her cross the deck and head toward home. Then, she turned and headed toward her car. Where was she going?

"So if Girraween comes tomorrow, what should she wear?"

"We'll give her something appropriate," Mom said.

But I couldn't listen. Something was wrong, and once again Ash didn't trust me enough to tell me what.

9

ASH

May 20 – 4:45 p.m.

After a visit to the drug store, I ran upstairs and locked myself in the bathroom. Hands shaking, I took the kit out of the bag and ripped open the package.

According to the directions, I just needed to pee on the stick. My stomach turned over. Did the test work the same for mer as it did humans?

I did as instructed, then waited, watching the stick like it would talk to me. What if I was pregnant? Then what? And how did Pearl know by just looking at me?

What did this mean for our plans? How would we have a wedding with my big, bulging stomach? I mean, we could sing away some things, but I didn't want to be a pregnant bride.

How could I have a child? I mean, I enjoyed Nicole, but for the most part, I didn't even like to babysit. My sister was proof I couldn't raise anyone.

I glared at the stick, willing it to do something. Was it a dud? Did I need to do another test?

When I didn't think I could wait another minute, a duplicate pink line began to appear on the stick.

My head felt like it would burst. How could I be pregnant? Yes, I knew how, but Fin and I had used protection. It was as if my mother had guessed and spoken this into existence. A baby. A merling.

The air rushed out of my mouth, making me lightheaded. I mean, it wasn't that I didn't want a child with Fin. I did. Just not right now. Not at eighteen. Not before we had time to get everything settled between our two cultures. Time together as a couple, at least.

My dreams of a wedding, of normal human life were quickly vanishing before my eyes. What was I going to do now?

Someone banged on the door.

"Ash?" Lucy whined. "What's taking you so long?"

Wiping away a tear, I glared at the door. "Use the other bathroom."

"I can't. Gran's using it."

A sigh slipped from my lips. "Use Mom and Dad's."

"A-a-ash-ly-y-yn. Mom's taking a nap. Hurry up."

I couldn't move. I couldn't breathe.

"Ash!"

"Okay!" I yelled and stood.

Shoving the stick and the box into the bag, I wiped my eyes and opened the door.

"All yours," I said as I brushed past her.

"Finally." She darted inside without so much as a thank you and slammed the door.

"You're welcome." I pressed my eyes shut and leaned against the wall.

Lucy would be my merling's aunt. Oh, Poseidon. This was affecting so much more now than just me.

Why was I pretending to be human? Why did it matter? Other humans turned mer had faked their deaths when they couldn't let their human families know, like Maggie. But I didn't want to do that to my family. I loved them. And as silly as it sounded, a wedding on the beach had been my dream as long as I had a crush on Fin.

Fin's parents would be elated to find out they were expecting another grandmerling, especially with how they doted over Nicole any chance they got. And my mother, Poseidon help us all, she'd be over every day, wanting to raise him or her.

I just wasn't sure my parents would be happy without some mer mojo. But then what? They'd want to show him or her off, take pictures, go on outings. And after witnessing the unpredictability of Nicole, there was no way I could allow that.

I trudged down the stairs like a zombie.

"Is that you, Ash?" Mom peeked her head around the corner from the kitchen. I jolted and stuffed the bag behind my back.

"I thought you were taking a nap."

"Me? No." Her smile lit her face. "I didn't know you were home. Fin's looking for you." She stopped, smile melting away. "What's wrong?"

I choked down a swallow, my mind too overloaded to be mad at Lucy for lying. Even if Fin had asked for my hand in marriage, we'd need to get married now before I showed. I had wanted more time before we sprung the wedding on them, on everyone.

"Oh, nothing." I tried to smile, appreciative that Mom had been a lot nicer lately. A baby, as horrible as it sounded, would ruin everything.

"Are you sure?"

I opened my mouth to tell her, then closed it. All I'd ever wanted was a close relationship where I could tell my mother anything. But with this, I didn't even think I could tell Fin.

Then my heart stopped. Pearl. I had to stop her from saying anything before it was too late.

"I just remembered something."

Darting out of the house, I ran down the path to the beach toward Fin's dock. Heart pounding, I scanned the houseboat, not seeing them. I let out a groan, then slumped to the sand.

Nothing was working out as expected, and though it would disappoint everyone, I knew we shouldn't hold the wedding. What we should be doing is figuring out how to erase me from history.

"Ash?" Fin called from the houseboat.

I twisted toward him, barely keeping my tears inside. A frown disfigured his lovely face. He'd been working so hard to make everything as normal as possible for me, even to the point of convincing his dad to build us a cottage.

He crossed the yard and walked over to me. "What's going on? Where did you drive off to?"

"I…" I swallowed down the lump growing in my throat.

He moved closer, then gently took my shoulders between his hands. My muscles stiffened under his palms.

"What's wrong? You're scaring me."

"Nothing."

His blue eyes were intent on mine. "What did Pearl say to you? Is this about the wedding?"

I ground my teeth together. If I told him I was pregnant, he'd want to sing my problems away and elope. "Where did Desirée go?"

"They went back home."

I let out a soft sigh. Knowing the closeness of their relationship, Pearl would tell Desirée everything and then my secret would be out.

"You don't want Girra here, do you?"

I tried to think, but couldn't. "It's not that."

"It's Tatchi, isn't it?"

I shook my head, my heart racing.

"It is. Just tell me, Ash. I'll do whatever to fix it."

"It's not something you can fix," I blurted out.

His jaw grew taut. "What do you mean?"

My eyes prickled with tears. "I don't think we should have the wedding."

"What?"

"Let's just elope and be done with it."

His expression hardened. "Wait, what?"

"I don't need all of this fuss."

"Okay," he said slowly, eyes tight. "I don't know what's going on, but eloping won't solve anything. We're technically already married in mer culture though we didn't have a ceremony. But that's the reason we're having a wedding. To satisfy your human culture along with the mer."

"Our human culture," I corrected.

Fin took my hands. "Ash, I'm not human, and technically, neither are you. I only live here. Everything else is… pretending for us."

"I see." Though he was right, his words cut me like he'd rejected a part of me. I dropped his hands and swiveled away from him.

"Ash, please," he begged.

My mom appeared on the trail, waving at me.

I pushed the tears off my cheek, then grated. "Don't you dare sing to her. You hear me?"

I popped to my feet and left him there to greet my mom.

"Hey," she said as she approached. "I've been calling…"

She stopped and frowned.

"I don't have my phone on me."

"Ash, what is wrong?" she asked. "You haven't been the same since you've been home. Is everything okay at school? With Fin?"

She put her arm around my shoulders, and something inside my stomach fluttered. Was it the baby? I withheld my gasp and held my tummy. "I'm nervous about everything, Mom."

"There's nothing to be worried about. You're growing up. This is part of life. Moving out, going to college. Responsibility."

I sniffled. "What if I don't want to go away to school? What if I just wanted to stay home?"

"That's fine, honey. We're not forcing you to leave. There are good schools here."

"What if I wanted to go to school here and marry Fin?"

Mom pulled her head backward. "I…"

"We've got it all planned. Fin will work for his dad at Captain Jack's, and I could help you run Tahoe Tessie's Treasures."

Mom's eyes crinkled at the corners. "The world is your oyster, Ash. Don't sacrifice your freedom because you're worried about me. We'll be here when you're done with school, and then you can decide where you'll settle down."

I took her hands. "I want to marry Fin. He's got a good future ahead of him, and…" *I'll make it work, somehow.*

"You're set on this?" Mom asked, face concerned.

I nodded. "I love him with all my heart. He's the one. You knew with Dad, too. Right? High school sweethearts. I mean what did you tell Gran and Papa Frank?"

Mom sighed and pressed her lips together. "I told them the same thing you're telling me."

"So you made it work."

"We had help, yes."

"And we have help, too. Right?"

"You do," she said, apprehensively. "It's just… it's not easy."

"So you'll talk to Dad. Butter him up?"

Mom gave me a forced smile, and I braced myself for her true self to emerge and be angry. "You know your dad loves Fin, as I do, too… it's just you're so young—"

"I know we're young, but it's like he has an old soul. And he knows me. He's killing himself to make me happy as we speak, and… he has my heart. Please."

Mom folded me into a hug, squeezing tight while she let go of a long breath. I waited to hear the condemnation, the plea to wait. "And that's all I could wish for my little girl."

I startled at her words, and then my heart bloomed with warmth. I'd blamed our disconnection on the fact I wasn't her biological daughter, never having felt bonded to her, that was until this moment. I trembled with a sob.

"Okay," she said, petting her hands down my arms. "None of that. Don't worry. I'll talk to your father."

I collapsed with relief, sobbing more. "Thank you, Mom."

She touched my hair, then my chin. "I don't know where you got this red hair, but… you're just so radiant. You'll make such a lovely bride."

A tear trickled down her cheek.

We hugged one more time, then she smoothed her hands down her apron. "Invite Fin for dinner. I'll set up some time afterward for Fin and your father to talk. Okay?"

I blew out a breath. "Perfect."

When I turned to tell Fin the good news, he was gone.

10

FIN

May 20—5:10 p.m.

Snapping my tail, the cold water felt cool on my scales after the heated argument on the beach. Once Ash had stormed away from me, taking a piece of my heart with her, I couldn't stand there, waiting around like an idiot.

Why did I say that about being human?

I'd caught enough of Ash' conversation with her mom, college and me proposing, but I didn't think that was what this was all about. She's become impossible to please, and I was getting sick of the constant change. At least I'd thought to mind-mojo her mom to be nice to her, but I couldn't hack it anymore. I needed the one person who'd know what to do.

Once I cleared the Tahoe Gate and swam into Natatoria, my heart picked up speed. Where would my sister be? Just then, a mermaid crossed the ridge, mad as a hornet fish.

Tatchi! I called out in my mind.

She looked up and frowned. *Oooh. You give them a fathom, they take a freaking nautical mile.*

Nicole squirmed in her arms, squealing to be freed from her tight grip. Tatch swam closer, and from her irritated look, I knew I needed to get out of her way.

"Having a day?" I asked.

"A day?" She shook her head. "Girra's been parading it in my face all afternoon at the palace. That Desirée and Pearl visited to get permission for Girra to plan the wedding. Girra! My fin, she gets to plan my best friend's wedding! I want to hear it from the seahorse's mouth that that's the truth!"

"No, it's—"

Nicole opened her mouth and sirened.

I clutched my ears and fell over, paralyzed by the sound.

"Nicole, honey, Mommy needs to talk to Uncle Fin. You be nice."

The girl looked mischievously over at me and started to giggle. I struggled to right myself, my head spinning. This wasn't good that she was already sirening at such a young age.

"Something's wrong with Ash," I bit out.

"What?" She let out a groan. "Why didn't you tell me?"

"I'm telling you now." Needles of pain stabbed into my temples. "And another thing, when Desirée came and asked, Ash agreed, I mean, it is her mother, but just now she told me she wants to call the whole thing off."

"What?" Tatiana shrieked. "You're together without me for one week! One week! And you've let it come to this?" Tatiana ran her hand through her hair. "Oh, the poor thing. She must have wedding jitters."

"You've been busy."

"Yes, being a mom!" She gestured to Nicole. "But that doesn't mean you can't come find me!"

I backpedaled, hands up. "I know, and that's why I haven't bothered you. It's been a little crazy for me, too."

Nicole gave me an evil smile and for a moment I saw Azor. Chills ran up my spine.

"Crazy? This was worth bothering me for!" Tatchi hit me with her tail, spinning me sideways before she darted off to the Tahoe Gate.

Wait.

Nicole looked over my sister's shoulder, and sirened again,

freezing me in the current.

Stop her from doing that will you?

Can't you see she's just a merling?

Merling? She's a terror. My eyes rolled backward in my head. Thankfully, Ash and I had thought to use protection when we made love. I couldn't deal with this.

By the time I'd recovered, Tatiana had already disappeared through the gate. I followed behind slowly, taking my time. We needed my sister, yes, but bringing a merling into the public was asking for trouble.

I cleared the gate, but Tatchi was chasing after Nicole.

"You get back here," she said.

The giggling merling zipped past me, dark hair flying behind her.

Fin! Tatch whined in my head. *Help me.*

Why did you bring her with you? I mind-talked but still kept my distance.

Because, she cries when I leave her.

Nicole zipped by again, waggling her tongue out of her mouth like a dog.

And you think you'll be able to plan a wedding?

Shut-up and help, she yelled in my head.

Nicole turned, then swam right for me, arms wide, and as soon as I reached for her, she sirened.

I doubled over, grabbing my ears, groaning.

"Caught ya!" Tatch said.

Nicole yelped, then giggled some more. The two turned in a circular hug of bubbles.

Good thing she's not a boy, I said, meaning to say it to myself.

Tatch frowned. *After everything, I can't believe you'd say that!*

"No, I... ugh." Clearly, I wasn't winning any contests today. "Just the tail barb issue. He'd cut you to ribbons. I'm not trying to start a fight. I just need you to talk to Ash."

She landed a glare on me, and Nicole opened her mouth like she was going to siren again.

"Please." I moved backward in the current, wanting to distance myself from the merling's vocal chords. "I can bring Ash to you."

"No." Tatchi sculled forward with her free hand. "Get Mom. And… where are you "staying" while Dad fixes the house, by the way?"

"Dad got a houseboat."

Tatch's eyes brightened. "Oh, that's perfect."

She swam ahead and I hung back, terrified of Nicole's vicious lungs.

When I surfaced by the houseboat, I could see Mom holding Nicole. Tatiana was already running down the beach, wearing jeans and a T-shirt. Not soon after, the child's shrieking started, but at least it wasn't a siren. I leaped onto the edge of the dock and quickly put on my jeans, breathing a relieved sigh. At least I'd made someone happy today.

11

ASH

May 20 – 6:00 p.m.

On my phone, I stared at the empty text box addressed to Fin. My stomach, both hungry and nauseous, balled up once more. I'd been hard on him when this wasn't his fault, and I needed to let him know if he wanted to ask for my hand, tonight was the night.

"Dinner's ready, Ash," Mom called up the stairs "Your dad should be home any minute."

"Okay." Though I'd been starving because of my pregnancy, I'd lost my appetite.

A knock at the front door made my stomach lurch, and I froze mid-step. He was here. Mom wiped off her hands and answered the door.

"Oh… Tatiana?" Mom said. "My. What a pleasant surprise. I haven't seen you in… a long time. Come in."

My lungs seized, then my legs took off, hitting the stairs in rapid succession. I tackle-hugged her neck before Mom could let her fully inside.

"You're here!" I said, gasping.

Tatchi smiled, but not as brightly as I'd expected. "Of course I am, silly. I promised I'd come."

"So… should I set another plate?" Mom asked.

Tatchi shrugged. "Sure, why not, Mrs. Lanski."

"Good. And let Fin know, too. I don't want the food to get cold." Mom left to go to the kitchen.

Tatchi twisted her head. "She's taking this well."

"She doesn't know anything yet," I said between my teeth. The wedding was one thing, but a baby? That could set off world war three.

"Oh." Tatchi's eyes tightened. "So what's this I hear about Girra being your wedding planner?"

My breaths grew shallow. I was certain she'd come because Pearl would blab.

"She's not," I blurted out.

"Well, she thinks she is." She cocked her head. "That's if your wedding is still on."

I ushered her outside on the porch. "Shhh."

"What is wrong with you? Fin came in a rush telling me the whole thing is off."

I paused for a moment, guilt settling in. "If you want to plan this wedding, it has to be in three weeks."

"What?" Tatchi let out a huff. "I can't plan a wedding in three weeks. Why?" Her face fell, and then her mouth gapped open. Eyes wide, she said, "You're not…"

I bit my lip and nodded.

Tatchi screamed, startling me, then scooped my hands into hers and danced around. "Oh, my STARFISH!"

I let her pull me with her in a circle, trying not to burst into conflicting tears of sadness and joy.

"This is the best news! No wonder you're all over the board." She froze. "Fin doesn't know, does he?"

My eyes became transfixed on the worn paint on the deck. "Not yet."

"Why not?"

I held my breath. "I just found out." The lump rising in my throat wasn't helping things. "Tatchi, I don't know what I'm doing anymore."

She grabbed onto me and had us sit on the swinging bench. "What do you mean? This is good news."

"Is it?" I collapsed backward into the cushions.

She touched my knee. "Do you not want a baby?"

"I…" the tears slithered down my cheeks. "I… just… how am I going to explain all this to my parents?"

"Oh, honey," she said, patting my knee. "With mojo."

"I don't want to. I want them to be happy for me for real."

"I know…" She took a deep breath. "Look, it's hard, mixing two worlds. I get it—"

"Hard? We came home to two arrest warrants. How's that for an early wedding gift?"

Tatchi pressed her lips together as if to hide her smile.

"What?"

"It could have been worse," she said. "Your sister could have been mer-jacked by Alaster."

My body convulsed in full shivers, remembering his slimy lips on mine. She was a complete brat, yes, but I didn't wish that on her, or anyone. "Oh, don't say that."

"Look. The mojo is there to smooth it all over and protect the secret. If humans found out about us, it would just be bad. So… you have parents who love you, my parents who love you, your birth mom who loves you, a mate who loves you, and I love you… we all want you to be happy. This is about your dream. Don't let the timing of a child get in the way."

I shook my head. "It's just a wedding. I don't need it."

"No. It's not." Tatchi said sternly. "It's a commitment. It's a promise inside of the promise. And it symbolizes your parents' trust. They're giving you to Fin, for him to protect and take care of you for life. It's part of your transition to becoming a mer citizen, too.

Believe me. You're the talk of Natatoria right now. This wedding symbolizes freedom."

The pressure felt like too much, and I pinched my eyes shut. "Why does it feel like a lie? Like I'm cheating?"

"Because in your culture, people don't rush this. It's to prevent making a mistake. But you and I both know you're not making a mistake. You and Fin love each other, and this is a good thing. And having a baby is a totally awesome thing."

"Shhh…" I looked around to make sure no one was listening. "I don't know if I'm ready to be a mom, though."

She put her arm around me. "I didn't either, but you have no idea how much love you have inside of you. It's powerful, and Nicole isn't even my flesh and blood."

"Yeah, but it's just a party."

"Just a party? Were you not listening just now? It's not!"

I sniffed. "I don't even know how far along I am."

"Well, you're not showing yet, so… we have three weeks."

"Three weeks," I repeated.

"So we're doing it?"

I closed my eyes and sucked in a cleansing breath. I wanted to say yes but worried about what my human friends and family would think. I couldn't agree. It was just too much.

"You may not think so, but you need this and it is not selfish," she whispered.

"I don't know."

"It'll be the wedding of the century."

My stomach flipped. "I don't want all that."

"Fine, then a small one—a small, magnificent one." She paused. "What are you afraid of?"

I smirked. "Why do I feel like you're proposing to me?"

Tatchi snorted. "'Cause I am."

In the distance, I could hear a baby cry. "You brought Nicole?"

Tatchi sighed. "Yes. She's with my mom. But don't worry about that. I have it handled."

I blew out another breath, still unsure, as the merling wailed louder. If I ever wanted to fulfill my dreams of having a wedding with my human family involved, this would have to be it.

"Three weeks?"

Tatchi's face brightened as she clutched my hand. "Three weeks."

I squeezed back. "Okay. Three weeks. Let's do it."

Tatchi jumped up and whooped, doing a little dance.

I rolled my eyes, and though she always had a way of sweet talking me into doing what she wanted, I wasn't sure if this was the best timing. But then I was somewhat relieved.

I was getting married.

12

FIN

May 20 – 6:00 p.m.

I waited on the dock, nervous as hell. What were they talking about? Would Tatiana help Ash see reason?

Badger walked up to me, changed from his work attire back into his kilt. He stopped and clapped me on the back.

"Aye, Son, what's troublin' ya?"

I scrubbed my hand down my face. "What do you think? Women."

He laughed a big belly laugh. "They be trouble, but the best kind in my opinion. Anythin' I can be helpin' ya with?"

"Can you read minds?"

"Oh, Son. I don't think you be wantin' that. If she ain't talkin' to ya, it might just be she's scared. Weddins and funerals bring out the worst in people, I'm tellin' ya."

I swallowed. "She wants to call it off."

He jerked his chin down. "Whatcha mean, off?"

"I don't know. She just freaked out, like…" I groaned. "She hates it when I sing."

"She don't like your voice?"

"No." I let out a loud sigh. "When I persuade people."

"Aye." He nodded. "You been doin' a lot of that? Singin', eh?"

"Well, I kinda have to," I huffed. "I mean, we showed up and they wanted to arrest us because the house burned to the ground and we took off without a trace." I froze, remembering I wasn't supposed to mention that. "Between you and me."

"You be workin' yer magic with her parents, too?"

"Well, yeah, when I have to. Like tonight when I ask her dad if I can marry her… that's if she still wants me." I glanced toward the house, watching the girls on the porch, an emptiness filled the pit of my stomach. "I can't seem to do anything right."

"Does she be wantin' her family's blessin' without the song?"

"Well, sure, but…" I started. "He's not going to say yes."

"How do ya know?" Badger scrubbed his bushy beard. "Yer not some chump. You got a good noggin on yer shoulders and ye love her. That's all a dad wants for his daughter."

"He has a gun."

Badger busted up laughing. "Aye. Give him a chance, lad. You might be surprised."

Hearing him confirm what I knew I should do didn't help my nerves. Off in the distance, I heard my sister scream. Badger and I looked toward Ash's house.

Badger smiled. "Aye, Tatiana's here."

"Yeah," I rubbed my sweaty hands down my pants, "I called in for backup."

"Smart man." He raised a bushy brow and nodded appreciatively. "Looks like those girls be up to no good, though. I have ta admit, ye got yer hands full." He smacked me on the back once more, making me stumble forward. "But yer house ain't goin' to be built on its own." He guided me across the lawn, around my parents' house, and stabbed a finger toward the newly poured foundation slab by the lake. "Actions always speak louder than words."

"That's the cottage?" Eyeing the slab infused my confidence with a renewed vigor. This was really happening.

"Aye. Yer Da did that yesterday while you be out schoolin'." He gave me a hard look. "Listen to me, Son. A woman needs two things." He raised a forefinger pointedly. "To know she's the most important thing in the world to ya and ya'd die for her." He raised another finger. "And second, a home. It's easier being a mer to provide that, but right now, yer caught in the middle, tryin' to make everyone happy—mer and human. Focus on Ash, and let the rest fall where it may."

Goosebumps stippled my skin as courage swelled inside me. I wanted to ask her dad. I wanted to ask him now.

Out of the corner of my eye, I caught Ash's dad's truck pull into the driveway. This was my chance.

"Thanks, Badger!" I said, then took off running.

"Aye, where you goin'?"

"To show Ash how much I love her!"

Badger laughed behind me as I ran down the road to her house.

I reached the driveway, out of breath. "Mr. Lanski?"

"Hey there, Fin." His expression turned bewildered as he pulled his gear from the truck. "Am I late for dinner?"

"No. I... uh, need to ask you something," I said while following him into the garage.

He set his boots and fireman turnouts on the floor. "Can it wait till after we eat? I'm starved."

I waffled for a minute as he walked past and retrieved a grocery bag from the cab.

"No, it can't," I said firmly.

Bill stopped and spun toward me. "Okay."

My chin jerked upward, my heart pounding. "I love your daughter, and I'd like to have your permission to marry her."

His brows lifted, and I clenched my mouth shut, my courage evaporating and leaving me in a desert of doubt. The urge to sing burned in my throat. Why would it matter if I did? It wasn't like Ash was here to listen anyway.

"You think you're ready for that?" he asked.

"Ready?" I stammered. My heart continued to pound as his glare deepened. This was impossible. How could I convince him without the song that Ash was my soul mate? I ground my teeth, determined to make him see me as a legitimate suitor. "I don't think anyone is ready for marriage…"

"So, then why are you asking to marry my daughter?"

"Because I love her, sir, and I want to spend the rest of my life making her happy."

His eyes tightened. "And how do you plan to do that?"

"My dad and I are building a cottage next to my parents' house—where we'll live, and I'm taking over Jack's Charters, so I'll be able to provide whatever Ash needs."

Bill's chin lifted. He looked over my shoulder as if to verify my claim of a cottage. "I see."

"And I know you have a gun, but I'm still here asking you."

His jaw clenched as if to hold in a laugh. "I do, but… lucky for you, I like you, and there's no more room on my wall for your head."

I choked in a breath.

He put his hand on my shoulder. "I'm kidding. You're young, yes." He let out a long sigh, and I fought interrupting him to defend myself. "But you've matured into a fine, responsible man. And even though there was confusion with the mission trip, you took care of my girl like you promised you would. I can see she loves you too, and if I said no, I wouldn't hear the end of it, from her or my wife." He smiled. "So, yes. You have our blessing."

My legs almost gave way as my throat parched. "Really?"

"Of course. Now, come inside, Son, before my stomach turns inside out."

I wanted to whoop and holler, but I calmly followed him inside.

13

ASH

May 20 –6:20 p.m.

At the baby's wail that lasted long and loud, Tatiana darted off the porch and headed to the houseboat.

"Tell your mom I'm sorry I can't stay. We'll start tomorrow when you get home from school, okay? Get your mother's credit card."

"Okay?" Like that was going to happen. My mother needed to know there was a wedding happening first, then I remembered the bag of gems I'd hidden in my room. Maybe I could exchange that into currency.

As I watched Tatchi go, a tear gently slid down my cheek. One problem down, a million more to go, and I couldn't stop crying—dang it!

Out of the corner of my eye, I caught Fin running up to the house. He disappeared around the corner by the garage. I leaned over the banister to call out and clue him in on the plan, but he disappeared inside. Then I heard my dad's voice.

My heart jumped into my throat and I yanked my head back. Was he doing what I thought he was doing? Now? I held my breath and waited for the song, for him to force my dad to agree. But he didn't. Even after my dad heckled him about having a gun.

My heart gushed with happiness as I listened to him defend his love for me, that I was his everything.

Mom opened the front door, startling me.

"Ash? Dinner's been ready for fifteen minutes, and… what's going on now?" She walked over, and I couldn't stop myself, a hormonal hot mess, from crying more. Then Dad's blessing of my wedding could be heard clear as day.

Her mouth opened, then shut as we looked at one another.

She dipped her head. "I don't think you're supposed to be hearing this."

I pushed the tears off my cheeks. "I didn't mean to. I was just talking to Tatchi and…."

I stopped talking.

She gave me a sweet smile, then pulled me into a hug. "It'll be our secret."

"Thanks, Mom." I relished the warmth of her arms, in awe my decisions weren't making her mad. Was the missing persons scare what she needed to finally support me like a mom should?

"We should go inside before they do, though."

"Oh, right."

As we darted inside, I put on my game face and wondered how I'd keep my excitement contained throughout dinner. I was getting married, and all without the song.

Throughout dinner, I fought to keep from fidgeting and pay attention to the conversation, wondering how long we'd need to hang out before Fin and I could escape and be alone.

"I'll take care of that," Fin said while standing, collecting my plate and my mother's.

"Oh, no, Fin." Mom lifted her hand, shooing us out. "You two should go relax outside. Watch the sunset. I'll do the dishes."

"Are you sure?" he asked.

"Quite positive. Now go."

I caught my father's wink as Fin took my hand and led me outside. He said nothing as he led me to our bench, but I couldn't restrain myself. I tackle-hugged him.

"What was that for?" he asked while he held me, eyes bright.

"I just love you." I peered up into his face, wanting so badly to confess I'd listened in. "And I'm sorry about earlier."

He tilted his head to the side. "I should have convinced my sister to come a lot sooner."

I nudged him in the side. "It's not just that."

His eyes narrowed. "Then what else is it?"

"Just… that I don't want anything to stand in the way of me professing my love to you for all to see."

He gave me a funny look. "You were listening, weren't you?"

"Listening?" I gave him a coy smile.

"To my conversation with your dad," he said.

"You talked to my dad?" I could barely keep myself from blurting out the truth, and how proud I was of him.

"Yeah. Threatened to mount my head on his wall if I wasn't careful."

"What?" I rasped. That part I hadn't heard, but it totally sounded like Dad.

"And," he said slowly. "He gave us his blessing."

I grinned so wide, I thought my teeth might fall out, then threw my arms around his neck. "This is wonderful."

"You listened, didn't you?"

"What? No." I twisted my lips.

"You're such a terrible liar."

I laughed and hugged him tighter. "And you're terrible at being covert. I saw you run up to the house."

He glanced away. "I had to ask him when I had the chance."

I could barely contain my smile.

"So no more wedding jitters?" he asked.

I held my breath. With my parents' blessing out of the way, the next step was timing. We had to set the date, and Fin had to know why the rush. And if there was ever a time to tell him the truth, this had to be it. "Just maybe some… morning sickness."

Fin laughed, then his body stiffened. "Wait, what?"

I looked up at him, dragging my teeth over my bottom lip. "I'm pregnant."

Eyes rounded, he stopped breathing. "How is that possible?"

"It's called sex," I said sarcastically.

"No, I mean…" He paused and stared at me. "We used protection."

"I know, but…" My smile fell. How could he look at me like this was my fault? "It's not fool proof."

"How far along are you?"

"I don't know. A week? I haven't had a period since the conversion."

He scrubbed his hand through his blond hair, his eyes darting to my stomach. "How long have you known?"

"I took a test earlier today. That's why I left. Pearl guessed by just looking at me."

"Pearl knows?" He stumbled backward.

All the amazingness he'd just done to ask for my hand evaporated from my heart and left me there feeling naked. This wasn't how I'd expected him to react. Not one bit.

"You know, you could be happy for me. This is your baby, too."

"I know that… I… I'm…" He just stopped and stared.

"Well, it wasn't like I wanted this either." I balled my fists and turned, marching toward the front door.

He caught me by the wrist, spinning me toward him. "I'm sorry. It's just a surprise."

"Tell me about it," I barked. "And because of your stupid mer genes, we'll be parents in 6 weeks. So it's now or never, and I need a house. So you've got some work to do."

"You mean your mer genes. Have you forgotten you were born mer?"

I gasped, then tried to side step around him, but he wouldn't let go. I yanked against his grip. "Let go."

"Ash," he said calmly. "Wait."

"What?" Tears streamed down my cheeks.

He tugged me into a hug and squeezed. "I love you, and I love our baby. We'll get through this."

"Get through it?" My body stiffened. "You act like it's a death sentence."

"No." He pulled away and then grunted. "What I mean is, it's going to be a lot. But our love is stronger than just a promising kiss. Tatch is here to help you plan. I'll build the house with Dad. And all that's left is that we let your parents know."

"That I'm pregnant?"

"No." He blew out a breath. "That the wedding is in three weeks."

My glance darted to the ground. My original instinct was correct in not holding this wedding. How could I be happy about this now? "What will my friends think?"

Fin hooked his fingers under my chin and lifted so he could look me in the eyes. "It doesn't matter what they think."

My breath hitched, my pride wounded. Doing things in the right, respectable order had always been my intention. "It matters to me."

"Ash," he said more firmly. "What needs to matter is what I think."

"I know that, it's just you have to sing to manipulate everybody." My voice was hard.

"And I hate every minute of it," he said resolutely. "But this is why I have the song. To protect our secret. And unfortunately, your human friends can't be your friends forever. They're going to age and wonder why you look the same as you do now unless I sing to them. We're going to have merlings they're not going to be able to meet unless I sing to them. There's a compromise so you don't have to say goodbye to your family forever. You have to remember that."

I gnawed on my lip. "I know. It just hurts to manipulate them."

He let out a slow sigh. "Well, I didn't manipulate marrying you."

"I know."

He cracked a smile. "So you were listening."

I pressed my lips together, caught. "Just promise me you won't resort to singing first thing. That you'll try to rationalize a reason first."

"I promise." He took me into his arms. "We're a team, you and I. We have to be strong. We can overcome anything, but you have to talk to me. You can't try to solve it on your own, or keep things from me to protect me. I'm a grown man. I can handle it."

I closed my eyes, feeling guilty. Time and time again, I'd done just that to protect him and it always backfired. "And you need to do the same for me."

"All right." He kissed the top of my head, then he knelt down.

I startled. "What are you doing?"

He pulled something from his pocket. "Making it official."

"But you've already made it official." I flashed my hand where the ruby ring he'd given me covered my promising tattoo.

"That was a promise ring. This is the real deal." My eyes watered at the sight of the diamond ring sparkling in his hand. "Ashlyn Francis Lanski, will you marry me?"

I swallowed down the happy sob lodged in my throat. "Of course, I will. Today. Tomorrow. In three weeks."

I changed the ruby ring to my other hand, as he stood. He took my fingers gently, and slipped the ring onto my finger, then he grabbed me and twirled me around. "You've made me the happiest merman ever."

I laughed, baffled at the crazy life we lived.

In the corner of my eye, I caught two silhouettes watching us.

"I think we have an audience." I nudged my chin to the left.

"Ready to go tell them?"

"Okay?" I said, not meaning it to sound like a question.

"And I have your blessing to sing to them the date?"

I rolled my eyes. "Of course you do. Just… just not the baby yet."

"Okay." He put his arm around my shoulder and walked with me toward the house. My stomach bunched in nerves.

With the wedding happening in three short weeks, we had more than enough to do.

14

FIN

May 20 –7:23 p.m.

Walking alone across the beach toward the houseboat, my feet barely felt like they'd touched the ground. I'd gone from getting married to becoming a dad.

I stepped onto the boat and met the four pairs of anxious eyes of my parents, Tatiana, and even the merling, Nicole.

"So?" Tatiana asked hesitantly.

I gave them a baleful look, then raised my hands, unable to keep them in suspense any longer. "I'm getting married."

Everyone let out a whoop and jumped up to hug me. I backed up, stopping them. "But that's not all."

Their eyes widened.

I cracked a grin. "I'm going to be a dad, too."

My sister let out another loud whoop, clearly not surprised, while my parents' mouths dropped open. Nicole crawled across the floor to touch my feet, then phased into a mermaid, shredding her diaper.

"Another grandmerling?" Mom gasped, holding the sides of her face. "Oh, my starfish. This is wonderful!"

"Congratulations, Son. When?"

Tatiana scooped up Nicole, just as she started peeing everywhere. "Oh, sorry, Mom and Dad. I'll clean it up."

She leaped onto the dock and jumped into the lake. The merling wiggled in her hands, crying to be let loose.

I tore my gaze away from her and focused on my parents. "Uh…

five, six weeks? I don't know about incubation… pregnancy… stuff."

Mom snagged a towel and cleaned up the mess. "Pearl can confirm how far along she is, but where does that leave the wedding? Do we need to postpone it a year?"

"We're having the wedding in three weeks," Tatiana called from the water. "Here. On the beach. It's already decided."

Mom's forehead creased. "Are you sure?"

"Yes. Very sure." I turned to Dad. "But here's the hard part. I promised Ash's dad I'd have a house for her. So…"

"Three weeks?" Dad's eyebrows lifted. He turned to Mom. "I guess we don't have a choice."

I leaned forward, not trusting my ears. "You can build a house in three weeks?"

Dad laughed. "Well not alone, no. The biggest hold up is usually permits and inspections, but we've got that covered."

I blew out a nervous breath. "Okay. That's handled. What about the wedding?"

Tatiana yelled from the water. "Well, Girra has permission to come on land, along with the rest of my students so they can help, too. That includes several of the guard. I think between Jax, Jacob, Badger, and Dad, we'll be able to sing away any mistakes. Oh, and Fin too, when you're here. I think it'll work."

I inhaled quickly. It just sounded like so much, too much.

"It doesn't need to be elaborate, Tatchi. Just some chairs and dresses, and stuff."

Tatiana laughed. "Uh, sure. We'll have a few chairs. Won't we, Mom?"

Mom stepped from the houseboat deck onto the dock, a wide smile on her face. "You've done your job, Son, in both proposing and giving me another grandmerling. Let me and your sister add the frosting on the cake, with Ash's blessing of course."

"Uhhh, are you sure?" I stuttered. "'Cause I know Ash isn't going to want a huge thing."

"Huge?" Tatiana made duck lips. "Spectacular, yes."

Mom dove off the dock and disappeared under the water. She reappeared a few feet off shore, then leaped into the air.

"Mom!" I yelled, looking around to make sure no one saw. The last time I'd seen her this happy... Actually, I couldn't remember the last time.

Dad clapped me on the back. "Give her a moment. No one is watching."

Dad dove off and joined her.

I let out a long sigh and turned toward Ash's house. She'd agreed to a wedding, not a mer convention.

"Trust me," Tatiana called across the water.

I sighed and shook my head. I'd done half my responsibilities per Badger, the other half had yet to be finished.

With the wedding happening in three short weeks, we had more than enough to do. Why did I agree to attend high school?

15

ASH

May 23 –4:30 p.m.

I lugged my gym bag filled with my swim gear when a wave of nostalgia crashed over me. This was the last swim meet before the end of the year—my swimming career was finished.

"So, when do you want to start shopping for FAU?" Georgia asked as we walked to the parking lot. "You did reinstate your scholarship, right?"

My eyes lost focus. With everything, I'd forgotten about our plans for college.

"Uhhh," I stuttered. "Soon, I guess."

She started to ramble about her list of things she wanted, but all I could think about was the wedding. Maybe telling her we'd set a date would help distract her until I lowered the real boom. With the baby coming, I wasn't going anywhere.

Across the parking lot, a white van was parked on the sidewalk. The decal on the side, Tim's Landscaping, wasn't level, driving my OCD crazy. Then I saw him. The same dark-haired guy as last week leaned against the side, wearing black pants and a leather jacket. He smoked a cigarette and watched us. What struck me as odd was his attire—way too nice for that type of work.

"Earth to Ash," I heard her say as she snapped.

"Oh, sorry."

"Did you hear anything I said?" She unlocked her car door, then slid inside.

I climbed into the passenger seat and craned my neck to see the creep, but the car next to us was in the way. "Yeah... shopping."

I felt my naked ring finger with the Band-Aid over the top of my white promising tattoo, wishing my engagement ring was on my finger and not hiding in my jewelry box. Wearing it didn't seem like a good idea, considering the rumor mill.

"No. I was talking about the meet on Saturday. What's wrong with you? You've been in a daze ever since you returned." She pulled out of her parking spot, and I noticed the van was gone.

I turned to her, then swallowed. "I have news."

Her eyebrows peaked. "News?"

I closed my eyes and braced myself for a squeal. "I'm getting married."

She laid on the break, stopping way before the exit. I grabbed onto the door. "What are you doing?"

The car behind us honked, loud and long, but Georgia didn't move. "Don't mess with me."

"I'm not messing with you." I turned to look behind us. It was none other than Brooke. "Drive, please."

Georgia pressed the gas, throwing us back into our seats. "Married, like as in to Fin? Where's the ring?"

"I left it at home."

"Left it at home? Are you kidding me? When did this happen?"

"Yesterday... last night, actually."

She white-knuckled the steering wheel, lips pursed. I tried to imagine what she was thinking, then wished I had the song like Fin. It seemed so unfair mermaids had only the siren and claws as their defense.

"Georgia—" I began.

"No." She pulled over to the side of the road and parked, then she turned her whole body so she could glare at me. "Ever since Fin showed up, you've been distant and moody. I mean, I'm not so jealous that I can't deal with my best friend having a boyfriend, but this? Marriage?

You've got to be freaking kidding me! Next you're going to tell me that you're not going to FAU at all."

I bit down on my lip. Maybe telling her was a bad idea. Deep down, I knew this was all crazy—that having this wedding was stupid. Though it hurt me to think of it, maybe having Fin sing me out of her life was the answer.

"I—I," I mumbled.

Then I thought of Tatchi. What if Fin had done that to our friendship? My gut twisted. I didn't want the same for Georgia.

"I'm sorry I didn't call and tell you."

Georgia pulled away from the curb, then wiped her hand over her cheek. "Yeah, well… whatever."

"I need help with the planning. Do you want to help?"

"I'm going to be really busy with finals and the meet Saturday, then packing for FAU. When's your date, anyway?"

I looked out the window as the lake came into view—blue, so blue. Telling her in three weeks seemed cruel.

"We're going to look at wedding dresses today."

"We?"

"My mom, and my neighbor Tatchi. I've mentioned her before, right?"

"*Pfft*," she said. "Oh, your neighbor gets to know before me. Sounds lovely."

"She's technically my future sister-in-law… so…"

As we pulled over the ridge before turning down my street, the water came into view. Fin's yard was a bustle of activity. Mermen and human alike came in and out of the house, and just beyond was a little replica of the main house with walls and a roof. I gasped.

It was our cottage. Visions of moving in, having our baby there, of growing old made my heart sing.

"What?" Georgia's head snapped to scan the road for oncoming traffic. "Don't do that!"

"That's..." I started, then stopped. Telling her Fin was building us a house would seal her worst fears; that I wasn't going to college. "Incredible. Look at how much work they've done today."

Georgia grabbed her chest at heart level. "You scared me."

My eyes panned to Fin's parents' dock just before Georgia turned right. A crowd of mermaids busied themselves around several tables covered with what looked like tulle and ribbon. Desirée stood in the mix.

My mouth parched. "I, uh..."

What were they all doing out in the open like that? I'd agreed to Girra helping, not all of Tatiana's students and the entire mermaid finishing school.

Georgia pulled up to the house and parked. I looked for Tatiana when a girl ran down to the car from my parents' house. Girra.

I froze, unable to open the door.

"Who's that?" Georgia asked.

I almost blurted out that she was my sister. "My cousin."

"Oh, thank Poseidon. You're here." Girra fiddled with the handle, trying to open the door for me. "I'm just so excited. So much has happened once we all heard."

I pulled the lever to open the door, tried to step out of the car as she tackle-hugged me.

"Hey," I said with a grunt.

Georgia bent down low to get a better look out of the passenger window. "Heard what?"

"Oh, hi!" Girra stretched her arm into the car. "I'm Girra."

Georgia met her hand. "Hey."

"Oh, fun. More friends. Are you here to help with the wedding?"

I stiffened as I watched her jaw jut forward.

"You're going wedding dress shopping, too?" Georgia asked sarcastically.

"Shopping? Oh, no." She laughed. "The royal dressmaker, Mistress Wynie is making all the mermaid's dresses and the decorations."

I coughed, choking on my spit.

"Mermaids?" Georgia asked.

"She means bridesmaids," I clarified. "You know me and water. The theme is the ocean because I'm practically a fish."

Girra's eyes widened, realizing her error. "Oh, right. Yeah." She cackled long and loud. "Mermaids. Silly me. Why would I say something like that?"

One of Tatiana's students ran past carrying a green bolt of silky fabric and disappeared into my house.

"So soon?" Georgia asked while getting out of the car.

Girra's forehead wrinkled. "Soon? We have three weeks."

The color in Georgia's face drained and her head whipped to me. "Three weeks?"

I held up my hands. "There's a reason," I started.

"Yeah, she's pregnant," Girra said with a cheerful smile. "I can't wait!"

My heart stopped.

Georgia's mouth became unhinged. She steadied herself, leaning on the hood of her car.

"Girra, can you go find Tatchi for me?"

"Oh sure…" She frowned, then whispered. "Did I say something wrong?"

"No." I forced a smile. Out of the corner of my eye, I watched Georgia stand there zoning out into space. "I… I need Fin maybe, too."

"He's working on the cottage."

"I know. Just… mention that Georgia is here."

She nodded, then took off running. I walked up to Georgia.

"Pregnant," she mouthed.

My heart hammered. "Yeah."

"How—?" She looked at me, eyes hurt. "When—?" Then she just hugged me for a long quiet moment. "I'm sorry I've been such a poo. No wonder you've been so distant."

I blinked in shock. "I'm sorry, too. I should have said something."

Glancing over her shoulder, I saw Fin run toward us. Then he slowed, watching anxiously. I held up my index finger for him to wait.

She sniffed. "I've been the worst friend. All I've been talking about is me, me, me." She pulled away and stared into my eyes. "I'm here for you, whatever you need."

"I'm not going to be able to go to college with you," I said slowly.

Her shoulders dropped as the tears welled in her eyes. "Okay."

I swallowed hard. "But I'd really love it if you could be in my wedding."

"Of course I will." She hugged me firmly. "Anything, Ash. Just… anything."

"Thank you," I said through broken sniffles.

She tore away, and her face grew serious. "But you shouldn't be swimming. And the meet. The stress. Are you crazy?"

"I'm fine. The team needs me." I rested my hand on her arm. "Let's not tell people at school just yet, okay? It's embarrassing enough as it is with my family. And it's not a big wedding," *just a hundred mermaid family and friends.*

She nodded, her face childlike. "Okay."

"Thank you." I stared at her, sniffling, and then we hugged again.

When I looked over to where Fin stood, he'd returned to the construction site. Victory surged through me. I'd taken care of things without needing to sing, by telling the truth. Imagine that.

"Ash!" Girra called from the deck. "Come on. You need to get measured."

Georgia's eyes brightened. "You're getting married."

I shook my head. "Yeah, I know."

"Oh, my gosh!" She squealed, morphing into the Georgia I knew and loved. "You're. Getting. Married!"

She engulfed me in another hug, this time bouncing on the balls of her feet.

16

FIN

May 26 –5:30 p.m.

I looked down the table we'd made out of big, plywood boards stacked on sawhorses, and at the group of mers—female and male alike—, eating dinner together on my parents' lawn. Once Natatoria had heard about the merling, along with the need to finish the house in time, we weren't without assistance. Mer and human ate together, including Ash's parents, who sat next to mine.

Hot steaming plates of smoked salmon and tuna were being passed down, along with bowls of fruit and vegetables. Jax and Jacob sat across from me, piling up their plates yet again, then stuffing their faces.

"This is good," Jax said around a mouthful. "No wonder you love land so much."

I flashed a glare at him. We were supposed to not only act human but talk like humans, too.

His pupils dilated. "Oh, I mean… eating outside."

I rolled my eyes but then wondered what happened to his mate, Galadriel or my sister. From my vantage point, I didn't see either of them on the dock or inside the houseboat.

"Where's Tatchi?" Ash asked Jacob as if reading my mind.

He straightened, like any good soldier would do, and nodded respectfully to his former Princess, then lifted his finger to let her know he was chewing. He swallowed, then cleared his throat. "She's feeding the child inside, Prin—probably."

Old habits die hard.

Ash pressed her lips together to hide her smile, probably appreciative of him still wanting to use her royal title, but I noticed she'd rested her hand on her stomach. "I thought Nicole was eating solid food."

"She is... well, when she's not spitting it everywhere, ma'am." He shrugged. "As you'll see soon enough, this parenting thing takes some getting used to."

I tried not to smirk. Mom often gave me a firm slap on my cheek as a kid for such an offense. When our merling came, he or she would never be allowed to spit food. It appeared that he and Tatchi hadn't put their fins down and stopped letting Nicole swim all over them.

Badger grabbed his mug of ale and shoved it upward, rising to his feet.

"To the bride and groom," he bellowed.

Everyone lifted their glasses and let out a cheer.

I clinked my glass with Ash's, then took a swig while I gently squeezed her thigh under the table. She took a sip of her water, then leaned over, kissing me with cold lips. "Isn't this perfect?"

I beamed, feeling proud. "It's all coming together like I knew it would."

White sheets billowed in the distance, shrouding the front of the cottage: my house. With Dad singing to get all the inspections passed early, we'd managed to finish the plumbing and the electrical. Tomorrow, they'd install the HVAC, and then start the drywall.

"We should be feastin' outside every night, I say," Badger shouted. "To our maids and this fine feast!"

The group let out a cheer again, and I had a feeling this toasting session would last until sunset.

After Badger had put down his mug, he leaned over and kissed his wife, Sandy, long and passionate.

I cleared my throat, to which Badger gave me a kindhearted sneer. "It's all about the kissin'. That's why we're here, lad. Eyelashes and luscious lips that we can't seem to keep our hands off of."

"Barlemede," Sandy spat, saying his true name almost as if a curse.

"How's the food planning going?" I asked to rescue her.

"Good so far." She nodded. "We've arranged a caterer, considering the large group."

Ash sucked in a deep breath. "Did we secure the tables and chairs?"

"Yes, and the linens." Sandy looked upward as if she checked off an invisible list. "Decorations are almost done, and the flowers, oh, I can't wait to get started on that. Mistress Wynie has sewn her fingers to the bone, along with Gran and Maggie."

"That's good…." *I guess.*

Ash took my hand under the table and squeezed, leaning into me. "They've hand-stitch what looks like a million gems on my dress. I'll never be able to walk down the aisle, it'll be so heavy."

"Or you don't have to wear a dress at all," I whispered in her ear while caressing her thigh.

"Fin," she scolded, then looked up at me with a coy smile.

"Actually," I added, "that's what got us into trouble in the first place."

Thinking about our time earlier this afternoon, when we snuck off to her bedroom, sent a thrill through me. And I hadn't been able to think about anything else, other than scooping her up and christening every room in our new house—quite a distraction while working.

"Stop," she chastised with a slight blush. "Focus. There's an issue with the growing guest list."

Galadriel marched over and plopped down in her chair next to Jax. "Oh my gods," she said, exasperated as she dished a heaping plate of salad and fish.

Ash straightened. "What now?"

Since Galadriel had stuck her fin into the planning, drama followed.

"Mother has invited fifty more..." her eyes flicked to my parents, "guests. Where are we going to put them? The parking lot? I don't know how we're going to fit everyone in as it is."

"Fifty?" I reiterated.

Tatiana and I were going to have words after dinner was over.

"You need to put your fi—" she stuttered. "I mean foot down. She's... going overboard."

"I'll do it," Sandy said in a calm voice. "Don't add more to the bride's plate."

Jacob's head popped up when he heard Nicole's wail, then he excused himself and darted off. Watching him, I knew our life would mirror his soon.

"Who are the new guests?" Ash asked.

Galadriel leaned in, whispering. "Some of her friends that live on the outskirts by the Scotland gate. They hadn't even heard about the wedding, which serves them right for being such hermit crabs. I don't know why the water reception isn't good enough for them. The rule was you had to attend Tatchi's class first, and Garnet is coming with a date." Galadriel made a face.

"She is? Who?" Ash asked.

I cringed when I heard Ash's sister's name. She of all her sisters couldn't have been born with a heart.

She paused, looking left then right. "Colin."

Ash's mouth dropped open just as my blood froze.

"Yeah, tell me about it." Galadriel returned to stabbing her salad. "I guess they hit it off after all the rules changed."

"And Alaster?" I asked, unable to hide the vitriol in my voice.

"Dead." She speared a tomato on her fork.

Ash's muscles tensed under my palm. I gently squeezed her tight to reassure her.

"How do we know he's telling the truth?" I asked.

"We don't, but no one's seen Alaster, the son of a bass, excuse my language." She glanced at Jax's plate. "You going to eat that?" She stole a strawberry and popped it in her mouth before he could object.

"If he shows his mangy arse around these parts—" Badger started.

"He'll have more than his clock cleaned," Jax finished. "There's a line of guys who want at him, including me."

Not before I get a shot.

"But who would ever think Garnet would go for Colin, of all the mermen in the sea?" Galadriel asked. "He's just… gamey."

Ash stiffened at her mer reference and leaned forward. "Galadriel."

"Oh… oopsie," she said with a chuckle.

I glanced down the table to see if any of the humans noticed.

"You promised," I bit.

"Sorry. Sorry," she said quickly. "You know you can just sing."

I deadpanned, reminded of all the times in Florida where she'd tested me. "No. We are trying to avoid doing that."

Jax put his arm around his mate. "Awe, Gladdy. I'll sing away anything you want me to."

My internal heat began to rise.

"Do you think Colin is lying?" Ash's expression turned fearful.

I put my arm around her shoulder and drew her into me. "I don't know, but I won't let anything happen to you."

Her body trembled as she nestled against my chest. I hugged her, trying to reassure her. But the truth of the matter was, I couldn't be with her 24/7 and still get everything done. He'd be crazy to show his fin here. This was enemy territory.

After we'd sat around talking and drinking way too late, the mers filed off to my parents' nearly finished house to the hatch in the basement—a more discrete exit than the shore.

"I have to go with them," Ash nudged her head toward her parents as they walked home with Gran. "I'll meet you in a few."

Her eyes twinkled, something I hadn't seen in a long time. I grabbed her and planted a kiss on her lips.

"Don't make me wait long, my Ginger Girl," I purred.

Clearly, I'd had too much to drink.

She giggled nonetheless, then ran off, sliding in under her father's arm and taking her mother's hand. Seeing her with her human family pleased me.

I trudged past all the construction into the house. Since I'd been working on mine, I hadn't seen the latest progress. The wonderful smell of fresh paint on the newly finished walls filled my lungs. The hardwood floor had almost been completely installed. The charred rocks on the fireplace, evidence of the fire, rubbed me wrong, and made me wonder if in fact Alaster was really dead.

"Looks good, doesn't it?" Dad asked while putting his arm around my shoulders.

"Yeah." I nodded. "Colin's back. Did you hear?"

"I did. That means my brother is around, too."

I stiffened and stepped away from my dad. "Rumor is he's dead."

Dad guffawed, shaking his head. "Unlikely. Even still, he's not welcome here or in Natatoria. Desirée has made that abundantly clear."

"You act like she's still in charge."

"She's not." He shrugged. "But the mers like her and seem to need a Regent, and since the Council is keeping the peace, it works for now. After the wedding, we'll make greater strides at helping the people acclimate, and Chancellor Merric has also requested to retire."

"And you want me to consider the vacancy?" I asked.

"Actually, you would make a fine leader, Fin."

"Me?" I blew out a breath, not believing for a second they'd let a youngin' like me on the Council. Besides, I wanted to be on land as much as possible. "Why don't you do it?"

"I'm too old for politics." He leaned in. "The mers have no idea what to do with their new freedom, and you could lead them by example. Actually, your wedding will be the catalyst."

I huffed and shook my head. "All of them?"

"Sounds like it."

"Do you think that's wise?"

"And why not?"

"It'll be culture shock, and don't you remember the Hill Billy boys who shot me in Oklahoma? I almost died."

A twinge of pain radiated from my side, and I inadvertently rubbed the spot. The loss of blood almost killed me.

Dad laughed. "That was a different situation. With the lake nearby and mermen to sing away mistakes? It's foolproof."

"*As long as they're human and unpromised,*" I wanted to say, but it felt weird being the cautious one. This was what my parents had preached my whole life. Mistakes happened, as with anything, but we'd managed to keep the secret all the same.

Dad locked up the house, then headed with me down the basement stairs. A new bridge suspended over the empty pool. Piles of human clothing were strewn about in various places on the deck, ready for their owners come morning.

"We should put shelving over there, Jack, or maybe a bar for hangers." Mom motioned to the other side of the room. "And I was just thinking, that if all the mers are coming to the wedding, we are going to have to provide appropriate clothing—preferably store-bought."

I ran my hand through my hair. More stuff to plan. "Let them dress themselves," I said.

"The men can't wear skirts, Fin. And the ladies, their beaded dresses compete with the bride."

Dad pulled Mom into a hug and started kissing her. "It'll work out. Stop worrying."

She giggled, but I could feel the scales forming on my legs. Time was up.

I headed for the hatch first, disappearing into Lake Tahoe, but I couldn't help but think that by having this many mers who'd never experienced life on land in one place would be like herding cats and not a good idea.

Not a good idea at all.

17

ASH

May 26—7:20 p.m.

I darted inside my house, happy as ever. Nothing could change my good mood or our fortune. Everything was working out as planned. We could do this dual life.

"Ash?" Mom asked as I darted up the stairs. "I want to show you something."

The dimness of the oncoming twilight reminded me the sun had already ducked behind the mountain range. As if in response, my legs began to itch to reveal their scales.

"I need to study for finals."

"It'll just take a second."

She walked past me to her room, and I followed. On her bed lay the beautiful, long veil my sister and I had drooled over as kids, one I'd seen only a handful of times and was forbidden to touch, let alone try on. She lifted it up.

"I thought... for your something old."

"Your veil?"

"Yes." She led me to the full-length mirror, then slipped the veil's clip into my hair. I sucked in a startled breath at my reflection, the contrast of red under the white.

"It's so beautiful on you," she said breathlessly.

I turned to her, the emotion welling in my throat. "You think so?"

Her lip quivered and she nodded, her eyes watering with tears. "You're a vision."

"Oh, Mom. It's so beautiful. Thank you."

She swiped away her tears. "I know we've had our issues, but I feel like this wedding has healed us. That by bringing Fin into our family, I finally understand you."

I pulled in a gasp. After everything, I'd felt the same way—whole—even though, with the way mer bonded with their mother it really couldn't be. Maybe it was just, delayed.

I threw my arms around her neck and hugged tight, so thankful I had her, the real her, and not some mer-mojoed woman.

"I love you, Mom," I said. "So much."

"I love you, too."

She held me for a long moment and I didn't want to let go, but I knew if I didn't, there would be consequences to pay.

"I'm sorry, Mom, but I have to study," I finally said.

She let go, then wiped away another tear. "Okay. Yes."

As I darted into the hall, the veil trailed behind me, lifting in the air, all princess-like and romantic.

Lucy eyed me with disdain. "What are you doing?"

"Mom lent me her veil, and when it's your turn, you can wear it, too."

She snorted and shook her head. "That old thing? No thanks."

I pulled my head back, glancing to Mom's room. "That's rude."

"Laura Jane thinks you're only getting married because you're pregnant."

My mouth dropped open. "Well, you can tell Laura Jane she's not invited to the wedding."

"What?" Lucy put her hands on her hips. "Mom!"

Scales burst on my skin, and visions of me falling off the trellis as a mermaid rocked me. I had to get into the safety of my room and outside now.

"What's wrong?" Mom walked into the hall.

"Ash says Laura Jane can't come to the wedding," Lucy whined.

Mom tilted her head. "Ash. Is that true?"

"Mom," I started to argue, but my legs were starting to fuse at my crotch, slowly ripping my jeans. "Fine, she can come."

I ran to my room and slammed the door shut. Throwing open the window, I tried to lift my leg to step outside when the horrible sound of my jeans ripping down the seams filled the air. I lost my balance and fell over, yelping out in pain.

"Owwwwwww!" I wailed.

Mom knocked on the door. "You okay in there?"

"Fine," I squeaked out, grabbing the comforter off my bed to cover up. Tears leaked from my eyes as I rocked back and forth, rubbing my scales to try and stop the burning sensation. "I'll see you in the morning."

Though the song had kept them from opening my door after I'd gone into my room at night, I still felt the need to cover up all the same.

I stared at the ceiling until her footfalls fell away. What the heck was I going to do now? The guys would already be in mer form, and unable to slither up to the house to sing this away for me. Could I just stay in here in my room all night?

After a few minutes, my scales pulled tight from the lack of moisture, and the overwhelming need for water was all I could think about. Fin and I had never discussed that this might happen. What was I going to do?

Scooting to sit on the boxed seat under my window, I raised myself up and I scanned the lake, but saw no one. Fin should have his phone with him if he kept it in his sling pack like he was supposed to. Then I heard mine ringing downstairs.

"Crabfish on a cracker."

"Ash, honey," Mom called. "It's your phone. Do you want me to answer it?"

"No!" I fell to the floor and pulled myself to the door, opening it a crack. "Can you bring it to me?"

"Get it yourself," Lucy sneered as she walked by. "*Princess.*"

I cringed. More than one mermaid had called me that within earshot of my sister during the last week. "Please, Lucy. Can you get it?"

She laughed, then slammed the bathroom door. At the sound of water rushing in the sink, every cell in my body screamed for the moisture. The phone started to ring again.

"Ash?" Mom called, sounding more annoyed this time. I braced myself for her to change into the evil mother I knew well.

"I have a cramp. Can you bring it to me?"

After one ring, it stopped.

"Hello?" Mom said. "Fin?"

I held my breath. Blood rushed in my ears, making it hard to hear.

"Yes, she's studying in her room. What do you need?"

The toilet flushed, making me crazy to the point of not being able to think straight. I needed to get into the water, any source would do, and I needed it now.

The lock of the door clicked. Lucy walked out and sneered. "What are you doing on the floor?"

"I have a cramp. I need my phone," I grated at her as my talons began to form under my nails. "Go get it."

Lucy merely stuck her tongue out before she disappeared in her room. She was just like Azor, her real brother—a complete bassfish.

"I've put your phone on the stairs," Mom said. "I know you're trying to study, so call Fin when you're finished. He needs to talk to you."

Her footfalls faded to her office downstairs. Silence. Dad had left to go to work already, and Gran would be in her room watching her TV shows. This was as good a time as any to make a break for the stairs. Maybe I could slither outside.

I pivoted my fin out of the way of the door and rocked my hips to help me drag myself forward. Though I only had to go a few feet, it looked like a mile with how fast I inched myself. My heart hammered as I panted for air. If someone caught me, I had no idea what they'd do.

Something deep inside my belly pinched, at the spot where my merling grew, and a strong sense of survival took over. I had to get out of the house.

I army-crawled into the hallway while wiggling my hips, all the while cursing the carpet. If it were hardwood, I could have slid across easily. My throat burned with thirst as I tried not to grunt or hit the wall with my tail. Slowly I made headway. Inch by inch.

Memories of when Fin was chained to the wall in the basement by his evil uncle, finned up and out of the water, came to me. As a newly changed mer, I'd never experienced much time out of the water, but then I'd never asked how long we could survive without it. Was that the reason for Bone Island? The terror if it practically suffocated me, of shriveling up and dehydrating to death.

Once I got halfway to the stairs, I took a second to rest. Sweat dripped down my head, taunting me with its delectable wetness. I wiped it off and touched my scales. They sucked in the precious liquid, then pulled taut in agony, just wanting more.

Rolling onto my side, I sat on my butt. My fin snagged on the carpet. When I pulled to free it, I smacked myself into the wall.

Lucy's door opened, but I couldn't see her, thank Poseidon. "What are you doing?"

"Nothing." I quickly slid into the bathroom to hide. My fin smacked the door, then the tub, making a loud thump.

"Stop making so much racket!" She blew out an annoyed breath, then slammed her door.

My phone started to ring again. I could see it light up on the stair. So close, yet so far. Ring. Ring. Ring. The sound taunting.

Mom turned the corner, angered to see the phone unattended to. "Ash?" She called, then looked upward from the bottom of the stairs. "What are you doing?"

I froze. "Nothing."

"Are you on the floor?"

"Uh, yeah." I pulled my head into the bathroom, and once again yanked on the door to close it, but my tail filled the entire space. The creak on the third step of the stairs sounded loudly. She was coming.

In a panic, I tried to pivot, and put my tail behind me, making more thumping noises in the process, but then my body was in the way now.

"Ash?" Mom's voice was so close, too close.

"I'm fine, Mom." Heart racing, I curled into myself and had just enough room, when her hand made purchase with the door, stopping me from closing it.

"What's wrong, honey?"

She pressed harder as I knelt with my tail bent underneath me, the fin smashed up and inside the tub. Quaking in the dark, I pulled a towel off the wall and held it to my body, praying she couldn't see anything.

Then the urge to vomit overtook me from the strain. I dry heaved. If Mom had Kryptonite, that was it. Her hand released from the door.

"I'm going to be sick," I said quickly.

"Oh, honey," she said. "Was it something you ate?"

"Don't talk about food." Another wave rolled through me, making me gag. I broke out in a fresh glossing of sweat. I needed water, now.

She moved somewhere further down the hall. "Do you need anything?"

"No." I turned to the toilet, and let loose my dinner, unable to help it.

"Oh, gross," I could hear Lucy say.

"Don't come in." I closed the door and locked it.

"I'll leave your phone out here," Mom said through the door.

The ringing started up again, but I had to get into the tub. Turning on the water, I pulled myself onto the toilet, then dunked my tail in. A sigh of relief escaped from my lips as I slipped the rest of the way in.

Heaven.

Even underwater, I could hear the phone ringing, but I didn't have the energy or the willpower to get out and retrieve it quite yet. Fin would have to wait a few more minutes.

Then I remembered I was still wearing my mother's veil.

18

FIN

May 26—8:20 p.m.

The phone kept ringing, then rolled over to voicemail. I cursed. What the heck happened? Where was she?

Dad hovered in the current close by. "Where's Ash?"

"I don't know. Her mom said she was upstairs studying and that she'd call back, but now no one is answering, and she's not here."

My mind went to the worst, that she was too late and finned out in her room. Without water, she'd die.

"I have to get a closer look." I broke the surface.

My eyes zeroed in on the light illuminating out of her bedroom window, but there was no silhouette. Helpless, I called once again. This time, the phone just rolled straight to voicemail. If it weren't for the fact I needed it, I would have chucked the phone onto the beach. Instead, I stuck it in my sling pack.

I kicked my tail and swam to shore.

Dad intercepted me. "No, Son. You can't go up there."

"But I have to do something!"

"Let's just wait for a bit. I'm sure she's okay."

"Okay?" I was shaking with adrenaline. "How can you even say that? What if she fished out in front of her mom? They'd panic. I'm sure authorities are on their way." Then I had an idea hit. "Convert me."

"What?"

I sucked in a breath. "Convert me, then persuade me to go get her.

I'll bring her to the water, then you can bring me back. Mom has some essence on her, right?"

"No. That's ridiculous." Dad shook his head.

"I'm going to lose her!" I said, breathless. "She's carrying my child!"

Dad put his fist to his lips. "There're risks. What if she made it to the bathtub?"

"What if she didn't?"

"Do you have a friend you could call?"

"A friend?" I slapped the water. "Are you nuts?"

The longer we watched the house, the more my scales ached. We'd cut things too close, talked at dinner too long, gotten comfortable. This is what we'd been warned of ever since we were merlings.

"Please," I begged.

Dad closed his eyes, then balled his fists. "Fine, but we can't do it here. We need to do it in a place where we can collect your blood to revive you."

My heart raced. "Then where?"

He blew out a hard breath. "The houseboat has a tub."

"Okay." I kicked my tail, propelling me to the houseboat.

Dad followed. "It would be easier to persuade someone."

"Who's going to walk along this beach now? It's dark."

"If we made a scene," Dad suggested. "Someone would come."

Though his idea sounded better, her family would flip out if anyone but me walked into the house uninvited. "No. We can't chance it. She's running out of time."

"It'll break your promise to her," Dad said.

"I can easily kiss her once this is over. I can't lose her."

Dad's brow furrowed. "But we could lose you."

"How?"

"You could not be revived in time."

"So, you're saying it's between either her or me?" When he didn't answer, I moved closer. "What if it were Mom in there, huh? Would you sacrifice yourself or just stay out here and wait?"

Headlights illuminated the trees by the shore. A van came into view and parked in the lot. The engine died, and a man stepped out, eyeing Ash's house.

"Hey!" Dad called out before he did a backflip, creating a huge wave. "Over here!"

The guy turned toward the beach, and froze, just staring at us.

"Come here," Dad sang.

The guy leaped back into his van, but he didn't drive away.

Dad growled. "What is he doing?"

"Come here," I sang, hoping he'd hear me.

The guy flicked on his headlights, illuminating the beach and the water.

Dad kicked his tail and landed on the shore in the beam of light. His song burst from his lungs. "Turn off your lights and come here!"

The lights didn't go off. Instead, the engine started.

"Doesn't he hear us?" I asked.

"Probably not." Dad swiveled around and rolled into the surf, cursing the entire way. "Or he's deaf."

Deaf. Just like the one Hill Billy boy with the gun in Oklahoma. Each minute we wasted took chances with Ash's life.

Visions of when Alaster had chained me to the wall to dry out coursed through me. I wouldn't wish that torture on anyone, well, maybe him.

"Change me!" I yelled. "We're running out of time."

Mom's head popped out of the water. "What's going on out here?"

"Ash is stuck inside," I said, frantic. "I need Dad to convert me."

She pulled in a gasp. "What?"

"We need to get out of the light." Dad pulled the both of us underwater. "If he takes pictures—"

"Jack," Mom said as a warning.

"I don't care about pictures. Ash's life is at stake." I glared at the both of them. "If she dies, I'll never forgive myself."

Dad stopped and looked at me. "Come on, Maggie. We need to do this."

The three of us swam to the houseboat. One by one, we kicked our tails and leaped onto the deck. I slid across the floor, smashing into the table, taking out a few wedding decorations with me.

"Fin, be careful," Mom said as she unwove fabric from my tail.

After I was free, I slithered into the bathroom, and tried to stuff myself in the tiny tub. How would we do this without making a huge mess?

"Are you sure about this?" Mom asked Dad, her expression pensive.

"I—I don't think we have a choice."

My heart lumbered on, anxiety snaking through and choking me. Dad approached slowly, pulling himself across the floor with one hand while holding a knife in the other. Mom brought several bowls.

"I can do it fast or slow," Dad started.

"Just do it quick," I interrupted.

"Okay, I'm going to have to cut you on your neck, your upper fin, and your armpit—"

"Fine."

"Are you sure you want to do this?" His eyes flashed in warning.

"I don't have a choice. Do it already!"

He brought the knife to my neck and held it there. The cold metal felt like ice against my throbbing jugular. At the pinch, I held my breath. Hot blood poured down my neck and chest. Mom blanched and turned away while Dad grabbed a bowl to collect the liquid.

I leaned back, thinking only of Ash. Thinking of when I'd rescued her from drowning, of our first kiss.

"Lift your arm."

He sliced into my armpit, and I sucked air through my teeth to keep from groaning. My head spun, and I clutched the side of the tub for support.

"You're doing good," Dad said in a low tone.

He switched out the bowls with Mom's help. I imagined Ash's soul holding onto mine, not wanting to leave. Then my ears began to ring. I knew whatever happened, it would be soon.

"You should get that," Dad said anxiously.

"No. Keep going," I said, my throat raspy.

"What if it's Ash?"

Then I realized the ringing was coming from my sling pack. Dad put pressure on the wound while I shakily pulled the phone out. Ash's name illuminated on the screen, dancing around in small circles. I hit the talk button and barely had the strength to hold the phone to my ear.

"Fin?" Ash's voice cracked.

I almost dropped the phone in relief, and Dad quickly propped up my elbow. "Ash. What is going on?"

"Maggie, a towel," Dad mouthed.

"I'm sorry," she whispered, her voice echoing in the background. "I finned out… and… I'm in the tub… No one saw me."

"Poseidon. You freaking scared me."

"I know. I'm sorry. I'm so sorry," she mumbled over and over between her sobs.

I wanted to reach through the phone and hold her.

"No. Don't be." Delirious, I pressed my cheek against the cold wall as dad pressed the towel to my armpit. "I'm glad you're okay."

"It happened so fast, but luckily, I was able to make it to the bathtub."

"No, more," I said softly. "This can't happen again."

"I know." She sounded as weak as I felt. "I threw up, so I think they won't bother me in here. Dad isn't home tonight, either."

"I almost had to—" I stopped, realizing I was talking out loud.

"Almost what?"

I blew out a breath. She didn't need to know how close I'd come to risking my life by stripping my fins for her. "I would have slid up to your front door if I had to…" I lied. "Are you going to be okay?"

"I can't keep all of me underwater, so… I'm miserable, but… I'll see you in the morning. I have to go. I'm worried I'll drop the phone."

"I love you, Ash," I murmured.

"I love you, too," her voice faded. "Bye."

When she hung up, I let out a groan. The phone tumbled from my fingers and hit the floor.

"You're okay." Dad patted my head and turned on the shower. "Take your time."

The water cooled my aching scales. Opening my mouth, I swallowed away my dry throat. Then I tried pushing myself up, collapsing in the tub. Exhausted or not, I still wanted to go get her, but I knew Dad wouldn't convert me now.

"Let me help you out," he said.

Together, they heaved me out, and I flopped onto the floor. Blood and water smeared across the floor. "Sorry, Mom."

"Don't worry about that." Mom gave a kind smile. "I'll clean it up in the morning."

I turned off the shower and slowly slid past the dining area to the outer deck. Mom and Dad had already returned to the water, watching anxiously from the water. Glancing across the yard, I noticed the van wasn't in the lot anymore.

Tomorrow we'd have some mojoing to do, but for right now, all I wanted to do was sleep.

19

ASH

May 27—9:20 a.m.

My head snapped forward, and I woke up with a start, sucking in a loud breath. Georgia looked over the table at me with a concerned frown.

"That's the third time you've almost fallen asleep during lunch. What's going on?"

I wanted a bed. I wanted coffee. I wanted to be done with high school. Maybe I could just lower my stupid standards and have Fin mer mojo me A's on my finals so I could quit. I'd let him quit so he could finish our house.

"Is that a pregnancy thing?"

"Georgia," I scolded and looked around to see if anyone had heard. "I just didn't sleep well, okay?"

"Sorry." She clamped her lips shut. "They're going to find out sooner or later."

"I prefer later." I took my aggressions out on my apple by taking a huge bite.

She sucked her straw extra loud. "So, wedding planning after school?"

I took another bite and looked beyond her, at all the seniors milling about, thinking about how different things were for me. College and swimming used to be my concerns, now I had a husband, a child on the way, and responsibilities. The weight of the wedding made me even more tired.

"Yeah," I said with a yawn.

"How about you give me a list of what you need done and take a nap later."

"Okay." I leaned into my hand, too tired to chew, too tired to argue.

"Girra is just so funny, you know? Being homeschooled, she like knows stuff, but then doesn't."

I could imagine the conversation. "Yeah? Like what?"

"Oh, simple stuff, like driving for instance. She said something about pressing buttons to make the car go, I mean for really expensive cars, sure." She laughed. "She probably was messing with me, but it's good to hear that I'll get to see Colin again."

I swallowed hard. A piece of apple lodged in my throat. I swallowed again, but it wouldn't go down. I tried to cough, but couldn't get any air out. My feet hit the floor as my hands splayed on the table. I couldn't breathe.

"Ash?" Georgia asked.

Panic settled in. I tried to suck in a breath, or press one out, unable to do either. The sides of my neck tingled. I reached up, feeling my gills just under the surface. They were going to pop out any second, wanting air. Then the seam of my jeans between my legs started to strain. The delicate skin ached from what had happened last night. I was going to fish out.

No, no, no.

"Are you choking?" she asked. "She's choking!"

I backed away, lightheaded, tripping into my chair, trying to ready myself to run for the bathroom. No one could see this, especially if I sprouted my fin.

Arms slid around my middle, and whoever held me, made a fist. At the jerk of their hands upward, I coughed and the apple went flying across the room.

I pulled in a long breath, then turned to look up into Callahan's chocolaty warm eyes. My body reset to human form.

"You okay?" he asked.

Tears formed in my eyes. Without thinking, I reached up and hugged his neck. Students around us were deathly quiet, then one lone person started clapping. More joined in, and the room burst into cheers.

"Thank you," I said softly.

"I'm here for you, Ash," he said. "Anytime."

My heart warmed at his words. I let go and slunk down in my seat, embarrassed and relieved. The little baby merling leaped in my stomach as if to celebrate with everyone else.

All of these close calls last night, and then today, were going to put me in the grave. Why did we think the other mers with less experience could handle this better?

Georgia's eyes were wide. "You okay?"

"Yeah." I took a swig of my bottled water.

"That was like, wow."

Heat crept along my cheeks up to my ears. People kept staring, and I wanted to leave.

"Can we talk about something else," I suggested.

"Yeah, okay, so…"

My phone dinged with a text message. I looked down, scared Fin was checking up on me after he somehow felt my near death experience. It wasn't from Fin.

UNKNOWN: Your secret isn't safe much longer.

I blinked at the text, then looked around. Who had sent this? Then another text came. An image of Fin's dad lying on our beach, finned up and looking at the camera, flashed on the screen.

My hand started shaking. I quickly clicked the phone off.

"What is it?" Georgia asked.

"Nothing." I didn't want to be there anymore, pretend anymore. Things were getting out of control. "I, uh… don't feel good. I think I'm going to let the office know I'm going home."

Her phone dinged, too.

"What the—?" She held the phone toward me. "It's that Fin's dad?"

My heart nearly stopped. The picture was the same. Whoever had texted me, had texted her, too.

I chuckled. "What? That's so photoshopped."

She studied it, tilting her head sideways. "Looks pretty real. Is Fin messing with us? I'm going to text him back."

"No, don't…" I started to say.

"Where is Fin, by the way?" At the sound of Brooke's voice behind me, I nearly jumped out of my skin.

Lacking the mental energy to battle with her today, I plastered on a sneer. "Why do you care?"

She returned my look. "I care because he's supposed to be my partner in Biology, and I'm not doing all the work by myself."

Partner? Since when?

I continued to glare at her. "Well, you'll have to find a new partner I guess, 'cause he's not coming back."

"What?"

I gave her a fake smile. "Sorry."

"Figures." She gave me a snide look, then walked off.

Her entourage followed behind, all giving me smirks. I smiled sweetly at them.

"I so can't wait until high school is over."

Georgia watched on, clearly entertained by everything. "Me, too, though I'm totally going to miss you."

The bell rang, startling me. Though I'd missed Georgia, too, all I wanted was for this wretched day to end.

20

FIN

May 27—1:24 p.m.

At someone's whistle, I stopped painting the wall in the cottage and strained to listen. My armpit pulsed in pain, reminding me of my blood loss from last night.

"Fin! Get yer mangy arse over here. Your lady needs ya!" Badge yelled somewhere in the distance.

My lady? She was supposed to be at school.

My heart started pounding as I wrapped up the brush in plastic and tried to dart outside, my legs feeling too leaden down to get me anywhere fast. Slipping between the sheets we'd hung to keep the house a surprise for Ash, my eyes caught sight of her car. Ash smiled from the front seat when she saw me, her eyes tired but bright.

I walked up, still concerned, and kissed her through the open window.

"Everything okay? What are you doing home so early?"

Her eyes drifted to the scar on my neck. "What happened?"

I reached up and covered it with my hand. "Accident with... the... ladder."

"Mean ladder." A yawn escaped from her mouth. "I change my mind. You can sing me a diploma. I'm done."

I laughed and shook my head, relieved whatever had happened wasn't worse. "Oh, no. You made me promise not to."

"And you also promised you'd go with me."

I dipped my head. "I can't go to school and finish our house in time. You know that."

She let out a fake cry. "I hate it there."

I sighed, hating to hear her so upset. "One more week, then you're done. It gives you something to do."

"I want to plan the wedding."

My chin lifted toward the hubbub of mermaids huddled at tables on the dock. "I think that's being handled."

She leaned against her head rest, her lips pulled tight. I wanted to curl up with her in her room and kiss away her worries.

Taking out her phone, she touched the screen. "I think you need to see this."

She held the phone toward me. What little blood I had in my system drained from my face.

I took the phone from her to get a closer look—Dad on the beach, fin and all. "Where'd you get this?"

She shrugged. "It was an anonymous text."

The words underneath haunted me, then staggering backward, I ran my hand through my hair. "I need to show my dad."

She reached her hand out of the window for the phone. "Let me forward it to you."

Another yawn escaped from her lips.

"And you need a nap." My lips touched the tip of her nose as I set the phone in her fingers.

"Should I be worried about this?" Her eyes lingered on the picture long after she sent me a copy.

I inhaled a long breath, warring with what to tell her.

"No," I lied.

"When was it taken?"

We'd never had so much trouble staying hidden before.

"Last night. There was this guy and… we thought we'd get his attention." I stopped when her eyes bugged, then I shook my head.

"It doesn't matter."

"Why did you want his attention?"

"We were running out of options, and in our fins, it wasn't possible to get to you." I couldn't tell her about the near convertion.

Her eyes registered with understanding. "To persuade him?"

"Yeah... maybe." I looked off toward the parking lot, then at her family's house beyond, the terror still fresh in my tired muscles.

"That'll never happen again. I promise you."

Though I wanted to keep that promise, like it or not, one mistake could reveal our secret so easily. And without the song, we'd be fish out of water. The old laws insistence of male chaperones suddenly seemed logical and warranted.

Her eyes slid shut momentarily.

Badger walked up. "Aye, sorry to be interrupting ya, but the Queen... I mean, Regent Desirée is requestin' audience."

"With me?" I asked.

"No. With her daughter." He leaned down to talk to Ash through the window. "Can ya see her? She shan't stay long."

She didn't open her eyes right away. Had she fallen asleep?

"Now?" I asked weakly. "Can't you see she's exhausted?"

Badger shrugged. "Then, I'll be telling her ye can't."

"No. I'll go. She's never able to come here, so..." Ash opened her car door, her face strained.

I helped lug it the rest of the way open. "Are you sure?"

She took a deep breath and shot me a coy look with her green eyes. Poseidon, she was getting more breathtaking every day, even when she was tired. She cracked a small smile.

She gnawed on her thumbnail. "Just... uh... if I go to sleep in the lake afterwards, can you persuade my family?"

I returned the smile, unable to help it. I loved how cute she was when she was eating crow.

"Please don't give me any grief." Her eyes flashed with a warning.

"I'd never dream of it." My hands lifted in feigned defeat.

She slid her slender arms around me, squeezing. I wanted to promise once more I'd keep her safe forever, that this would be the worst we'd ever go through, but pictures were something we risked daily by living on land.

She let out a soft breath, relaxing in my arms. "I love you."

The sweet scent of honeysuckle infused in her hair filled my lungs. "I love you, too, Ginger Girl. Don't worry about this, just don't say anything."

"I won't."

Reluctantly, I let her go and disappeared behind the curtains as Badger escorted her to the dock. I needed to find Dad.

With Desirée popping in unannounced like she was, we needed to clean this up before any of the loose-lipped mer found out, exposing our mistake.

21

ASH

May 27—1:24 p.m.

I gave Fin one last kiss before he returned to our cottage, craning my neck to try and peek between the curtains when he walked through them.

"Aye, you shan't be lookin' yet, Princess." Badger proffered his arm. "Would ya like it if I be walkin' ya?"

My shoulders softened in relief, glad to have his help getting to the dock. "Thank you."

"I'm so happy for you and Fin. I wish me Sandy and I could have had a shoal of merlings."

"Oh, I didn't know. I'm so sorry," I said as he led me around work tables covered in saws and tools. Several of the mermen stopped and tipped their heads.

"M'lady."

"It 'tis what it 'tis." Badger lifted his chin. "Besides, it gives me a chance to look after the wee ones who need a little extra attention on the field, like yer Fin. He was a wiry one when I met him."

"And now he's less wiry?"

"Ah… takin' responsibility like a man. He came to me, green behind the ears. I'm right proud of how he shaped up."

"Me, too." My cheeks warmed.

Desirée caught my eye and lifted her hand in a greeting.

"Ash, my sweet."

I turned to Badger and leaned in. "Thanks for taking care of him."

Badger bowed his head. "Anytime, Princess."

She hurried toward me, barefoot, but wearing a gorgeous red velvet, sleeveless dress that set off her white-blonde hair. I admired the lovely headpiece that circled her head, very mermaidish. She folded me into a hug.

"Mother, you're here."

"I hear that congratulations are in order," she said while hugging me, her voice quivering momentarily. "I just… was overjoyed when I heard. Another grandmerling."

My stomach sank as we pulled away. With everything, we'd forgotten to visit her in Natatoria and tell her the good news in person. "I'm sorry you found out before…"

There was happiness in her eyes, but also sadness.

"Oh… no, don't think a thing of it. I understand with the distance and the planning. It's not like you're spending much time in Natatoria these days." She tsked. "I had a feeling anyway."

Behind her, Pearl walked up, and I knew exactly where the source of her elusive feelings came from.

"Oh, Princess. You are radiant." She gave me a hug. "Congratulations."

Desirée put her hands on her hips, inspecting the operation. "Girra has been coming home with daily reports of the progress. I didn't think you could pull off a wedding in three weeks, but it appears you may just do that."

"Not because of me," I chuckled. "It helps when you have many eager hands."

Several mermaids walked past holding long trains of blue and green ribbon. Mom followed with a handful of tulle, then caught my eye and stopped. Since when was she helping?

"Ash? How come you're home early?"

Busted.

I cringed, waiting for her to yell at me. "I'm not feeling well, still."

She stepped forward and balanced the tulle in one hand while she pressed her other hand to my forehead, completely opposite of what I'd expected her to do. "Oh. You are warm. You shouldn't be out here."

The mer in me always made me feel warmer than normal, but what was wrong with me today was my exhaustion, especially from the pregnancy. Not to mention I was starving—again.

"Is this—?" Desirée gestured to my mom.

"Oh, yes." My stomach balled in nerves, dreading how this would all play out. "Desirée, this is Karen, my… mom."

Mom stuck out her hand, her eyes scanning Desirée from head to her bare feet. "Nice to meet you."

"Likewise." Desirée shook her hand while eyeing Mom with what I suspected was jealousy.

I knew this awkward day would come, just not when I felt like crap. Desirée and I hadn't had time to discuss an alias for her or anything for that matter.

"This is Fin's Aunt," I said quickly, as a cover.

Desirée's head whipped to mine.

Mom nodded. "Are you Maggie's sister?"

"Jack's, actually," Desirée said, her voice toneless.

My stomach seized.

"Oh… I should have seen the family resemblance." Mom stepped closer to me. "Ash, let's get you home."

"Who's minding the store today?" I asked.

Mom smiled. "Gran's there. She'll be fine until I check in later. It's been slow since we're between seasons, and there's so much to do before the big day."

Desirée's lips pulled into a line. She leaned into Pearl. "Go get me Colin, please."

"Colin?" Mom's face lit up while my stomach soured. "Is that your son?"

Desirée's eyes narrowed. "You know him?"

"Yes… nice boy. He and Ash had—"

"A friendship," I interrupted while I gave Mom a sideways glance.

"Yes," Mom agreed. "Friends."

"He's Jack's other brother, Alaster's son."

Mom cocked her head. "You mean your brother."

Desirée's shoulders tightened. "Yes."

Pearl eyed everyone nervously, then bowed before she walked off. I hoped it wasn't to find Colin, the leech. He'd be bold to show his face here after he'd defected and gone back to his dad.

"I know you're not feeling well, but I wanted to show you something before I left town." Desirée leaned toward me. "Are you up for it?"

I opened my mouth, then I looked to Mom, unsure what to say.

Mom's glance went to Desirée, then to me. "Make it quick."

"Wonderful, my sweets." Desirée held out her hand to me. "I have an early gift."

"A gift?" Mom said, interest piqued.

Out of my peripheral vision, I could see Desirée's jaw tighten. Clearly she wanted time alone with me. "Give me a minute, Mom."

Mom's expression grew saddened for a brief moment. "That's fine, I need to, um, get the rest of this tulle to the house anyway. Don't be long."

I followed Desirée into the houseboat as Mom headed home.

"I'm sorry—" I started.

She smiled softly. "No, it was my fault. We should have discussed this." She waved her hand as if to suggest my life on land.

"Is it okay that I told her you're my aunt?"

"It's…" she closed her eyes, then hardened her exterior, "fine. I'm glad she was a good mother to you. If I could go back in time…"

I stepped forward and hugged her. She stiffened, then her arms slid around me.

"I've forgiven you, Mother. There's no need to explain. You… you did what you needed to survive."

She held me for a long time, then let go of me and wiped away a tear.

"Thank you." She sucked in a cleansing breath. "Now to the fun part. I wanted to show you this."

She opened her bag and pulled out a crown that had delicate interlocking chains holding gems, tiny pearls, and something sparkling—diamonds perhaps.

"This was my mother's and her mother's." She handed it down to me. "I'd love for you to wear it. For your *something old* tradition that Girra keeps telling me about."

"It's lovely," I rasped, for more than the fact it was an exquisite piece.

"Turn. Let me put it on you."

I did as she instructed and felt the crown encircle my head and the gems find homes in my hair, heavier than I imagined. Looking at my reflection in the mirror, I sucked in a gasp. *So lovely. So regal.*

What was I going to do? I couldn't tell Desirée that my mom had offered hers first, not after the fiasco with the introduction. Nor could I tell my mom I didn't want to wear hers, especially after it had strengthened our connection.

"Thank you," I said as the tears fell. "It's so beautiful."

"I knew you'd love it."

"You asked for me?" A male voice said.

My heart jumped into my throat at Colin's husky voice. I hadn't seen him since we'd encountered the Dradux guards when returning to Natatoria through the Tahoe Gate, and he decided to stay back with his dad.

"Ash," he said while bowing. "So good to see you again."

I quickly glanced at his left hand. No promising mark, not yet.

Desirée walked over to him and put her hand on his shoulder. "We should turn this into a double ceremony."

My heart jolted. "Double ceremony?"

"Colin has asked Garnet for her hand. He's going to be your brother-in-law. Did you not hear?"

"Uh," I started to say. There was no way in Hades I'd let Colin and Garnet steal my day, of all the mer. But promised? To Garnet? I never expected the two of them would ever hit it off.

"Thank you for the offer, Desirée, but Garnet wishes to get promised in Natatoria," Colin said. "She's not a fan of land."

I breathed out a sigh of relief, then wondered why Desirée had saved her veil for me and not Garnet. Maybe this was a sign that I needed to stop thinking of Karen as my mother, first and foremost, and let Desirée have that place.

Whatever I decided, it needed to happen after a nap. Otherwise, I'd be dead on my feet.

"You'll have to excuse me. I'm needed at home." I kissed my mother's cheek before I left the houseboat, half tempted to just dive into Tahoe and try to overhear their conversation instead.

I would have if I weren't so exhausted.

22

FIN

May 27 1:46 p.m.

"Hmmm," Dad said as he studied the photo. "Good thing it's blurry."

"Blurry? We need to find the invertebrate and mind-wipe his sorry excuse for a brain," I said emphatically. "He knows our secret and he's got Ash's cell number."

"It appears so." He handed back the phone and took out his hammer. "Have you seen him since?"

"Well, no."

"I'll look into it." He knelt down and began hammering the baseboard in place.

"When?"

One of the mermen yelled from down the hall. "Jack. Where are the rest of the two by fours?"

"They're over here. Oh, and Grommet. We need more paint."

"Sure thing," Grommet said.

Another guy walked by with a sink in his hands. "Can you give me a hand?" he grunted.

"Yeah." Dad put his hammer in his belt and started to follow the guy. "Grommet. I'm ready for more molding when you are."

"But what about the picture?" I asked.

"Let me get some of this stuff handled, then I'll help take care of it," he said, disappearing around the corner.

I blew out an exasperated breath and headed outside. Apparently, this wasn't that much of a concern for him.

"Excuse me, Fin," another merman said as he walked past, holding a corner countertop.

"Do you need help?" I asked.

"Nope. Got it."

I moved out of the way, then scanned the dock below. There were mermaids everywhere, but no Ash.

"Hello, cousin." Colin passed with a big smile.

I startled, and then grimaced. "What are you doing here?"

"Escorting my *almost* mother-in-law."

"Desirée?"

"Regent, you mean."

"Just because you're marrying Garnet doesn't mean anything, royalty wise. Just so you know that."

He leaned in. "And just because Jack is on the Council, doesn't mean we'll always have a democracy."

I pulled my head back. "Is that what this is about? Position?"

"No." Colin laughed. "I love Garnet, and I think palace life will suit me."

I stepped forward, jaw clenched. "Just know that I'm not against seeing you be prosecuted."

"For what?" He shook his head. "I never did anything wrong."

"Alaster did."

His eyes grew cold. "He's dead, and thanks for your concern."

Suddenly, I felt bad. "Sorry."

"It is what it is." He gestured to the driveway. "Hey, where's that old, red jalopy of yours?"

"My Jeep?"

"Yeah."

At the mention of my Jeep, I longed for it again. Would it be too much to ask Hans and Sissy to drive it out here from Florida when they came to the wedding? I didn't entertain his stupid question.

"It's gone," I said.

"Too bad." He raised a brow.

"I'm keeping my eye on you," I said.

"Oooh, sounds so ominous." His eyes slotted. "Hard to watch when you're so far away."

He walked past me and headed toward the dock. I unclenched my fists. Even though Alaster had turned on his son and tried to kill him, I still didn't trust Colin. And I certainly wouldn't believe Alaster had died until I saw his bones first hand.

"Fin? Oh, Fin!"

I turned at the sound of a girl's voice, one that wasn't Ash's.

"Brooke?"

She sauntered over like a deer in high heels that looked like they'd trip her, eyes wide. "What's going on here?"

"What does it look like? We're rebuilding."

She looked upward at the merman hanging off the side of my parents' house painting the trim. "Oh, that's right. You were accused of starting the fire that burned this place down. Pity." She flashed a smile.

I lifted my chin. "What's up?"

"Rumor is, you're too ill to be at school." She eyed me up and down. "But you look perfectly fine to me."

I clenched my jaw. Why did I promise Ash I wouldn't sing? "You shouldn't believe everything you hear."

"When are you coming back?"

"I'm not," I said as I headed toward the cottage.

"And why not?" she asked, following me.

"I quit."

"Quit?" She propped her hand on her hip.

"Too much to do here." I gestured to my parents' house and mine.

"But… if you don't take your finals, you won't graduate."

I smiled and leaned toward her. "The teachers love me. I don't think I have anything to worry about."

She stood taller and gave me a fake smile. "Well, it would help if you told that to Mr. Wellington because he won't reassign me to someone new. We're supposed to do the project together."

"Oh, right." I palmed my hair. "Well, I don't know what to tell you."

"Oh, Fin." Galadriel sauntered up to me with a determined look on her face, clipboard in hand, that was until she saw Brooke. "Well, aren't you cute as a fish fry. Who's this?"

"This is no one you should worry about," I sang to Brooke.

"Fin. That's rude." She stepped around me. "Are you on the guest list?"

Brooke rubbed her forehead. "Guestlist?"

"For the wedding," Galadriel pressed.

"Who's wedding?" Brooke's brows pushed together.

Galadriel waited for a second. "Ash and Fin's."

"You're getting married?" Brooke asked me.

I closed my eyes for a moment, feeling a headache set in.

"Oh, my mistake." Galadriel turned to me. "Fin. Do you like gold or silver?"

"For what?"

"For the men's vests."

I let out a gust of air. "I don't care. Whatever Ash wants."

"She's napping, you know, tired with the baby making and all."

If steam could blow out of my ears, it would be happening to me.

"You didn't hear that," I sang to Brooke. "And you don't know about the wedding either, and probably should be on your way."

Brooke staggered backward, then toddled off in her too high heels, confused as ever.

"My," Galadriel opened her eyes large, "your tune has definitely changed."

I glared. "Don't judge me."

She saddled up next to me, threading her arm in mine. "I like the new you, well... the one that sings at the drop of a hat, until Ash comes around. But we all know who wears the pants in your relationship." She playfully nudged her hip into mine.

I pulled my head back. "What?"

"It's okay. Happy mermaid... happy life."

"I think it's happy wife, happy life, but we're a team. There are no pants."

She laughed and busied herself with her clipboard. "Whatever you say. I'm choosing gold."

"Silver," I said.

"There. Now doesn't that feel good? Putting your fin down? 'Cause I think Ash wanted gold, too."

I blew out a gust. "Then why did you ask me?"

She let go of my arm and waved before walking back to the dock. "Toodle-loo. It was nice chatting with you."

I balled my hands into fists, wishing the guy who'd threatened Ash would show his ugly mug right now so I could throttle him.

23

ASH

May 27—5:31 p.m.

Something loud banged repetitively against the door. I startled awake to Mom's panicked voice. "Ash! Open up!"

Quickly glancing at the clock, I rolled to my feet. My head swam for a minute. How long had I been asleep?

"Ash!"

"I'm awake." My mouth felt like it was full of sand. "Hold on."

The doorknob rattled, but she didn't press the door open.

"Let me in."

I groggily walked to the door and opened it, finding it wasn't locked. Then the memory she was persuaded not to open the door when it was closed came into focus.

Rubbing my eyes, I refocused on her. "What's wrong?"

"I…" She gave me that concerned mom look. "You didn't answer, and I couldn't go inside."

"I was sleeping," *pretty hard, in fact.*

"Coach called. She was concerned 'cause you'd skipped practice today. She wants to know about tomorrow."

I pressed my hand to my forehead. The meet. "Um."

"I don't think you should swim."

"I feel a lot better," I said.

"You shouldn't push yourself after being sick like that."

I braced myself, waiting for her lecture to kick in. "It's my last meet, and I don't want to let anyone down."

She dipped her head down, eyes narrowed. "Are you sure?"

"Very sure."

The smell of garlic made my stomach rumble. "And I'm starving. Is that—?"

"Dad is making pasta, meatballs, and garlic bread. Carb loading, right?"

I smiled, my shoulders relaxing as I imagined that first bite. In fact, I'd probably eat the entire dish if they set it in front of me.

Out of nowhere, Mom pulled me into a hug and squeezed tight. I worried she'd see Desirée's crown on the bed, so I inched us further into the hall.

"Mom?" I asked when she didn't let go.

"Not too many more days like this," she said with a sniffle. "I'm going to miss you not living here."

Regret hit. I closed my eyes and relaxed into her. "I'll be next door."

"I know."

Part of me wished she knew about the baby, giving her something else to look forward to. But then again, we'd have to persuade them from the get-go: the fast pregnancy, fast maturation and of course, the shifting mishaps of a merling. More secrets.

Once the hug became awkward, Mom ushered me downstairs. "Let's go eat."

Lucy sat in the front room watching TV, surrounded by an explosion of bows, tulle, and decorations hanging from the curtain rods on hangers. Mom disappeared into the kitchen, asking Dad if he needed help.

A happy, loving family.

"It's not good enough that your wedding has taken over the house. Now you're taking over the beach?" Lucy gestured to the windows with a smirk. "Where does it stop?"

Scratch that.

I pulled in a cleansing breath, determined not to argue with her. Glancing out the windows, I noted several more tables had been added since last night's feast. "Sorry about that. Luckily things will get back to normal in a few weeks."

"You act like you own it," she drawled, not looking at me.

"Where else is everyone going to eat?"

"At their homes, maybe?" Lucy lifted a brow.

"You didn't seem to have a problem eating with everyone last night."

She glared. "I didn't have a choice."

"There's my girl," Dad said from the kitchen. "You're looking a whole lot better."

"Feeling better," I said with a smile. "When's dinner ready?"

"Just give me 10 more minutes."

I pulled out my phone and texted Fin.

ME: Eating here. Family dinner. I PROMISE I won't [fish emoji] again.

His reply came quickly.

FIN: You better not.

I chuckled to myself. I'd never *ever* do that again.

Lucy sulked all through dinner, ruining the mood. Was she upset because the attention was on me or was it because I was Mom's favorite for once? I tried not to let it bother me. Once I moved out, she'd have them to herself, and one day, she'd understand.

Slipping out of my bedroom window and sneaking across the lawn, I stopped for a moment. That same white van I kept seeing was parked up on the ridge between our houses. A big black spider was painted on the side this time. The red glow from a cigarette lit up in the darkness.

What was this creep doing?

I boldly decided to walk toward the van and ask him what was up. The red glow vanished. Then the engine rumbled to life, and the van drove away.

I put my hands on my hips, satisfied. Neighborhood watch to the rescue.

24

FIN

May 27—7:12 p.m.

I hovered in the water and waited anxiously for Ash to show up, eyeing the sunset. Was she being serious right now? Especially after last night?

The water around me bubbled from the heat rising off my skin, one out of anger and two out of fear. This was getting ridiculous. A promise that I'd personally escort her to her room for a good night kiss just to make sure she got out okay, crossed my mind. But that evaporated once her window opened and she crawled down the lattice to the ground, her gown blowing in the wind.

I swam over to the dock.

"Ash," I whispered, motioning her over. "Over here."

She hesitated, turned to face something I couldn't see. Then she ran toward me, her red hair catching the setting sun's rays, her short nightgown bouncing around her thighs. In all honesty, she shouldn't be shifting here. We both should be using the hatch like everyone else, but my parents had stayed in the pool doing Poseidon knows what.

She turned and looked over her shoulder one last time, concerned about something.

"What's wrong?" I asked.

"I thought I saw someone."

"Who?"

"Oh, it's no one."

She lowered her long sexy legs into the water, her nightgown hitching up, and I forgot my anger. Her feet morphed into a fin and unfurled—delicate and green, and all I wanted was her.

Without a splash, she slipped into the lake. My arms encircled her waist, and I smothered her neck with kisses, my desire for her building. "Stop cutting things so close or I'm going to have to punish you."

She giggled. "I'm not trying to. I'm actually early."

"Early?" I blew bubbles on her neck because I knew they drove her crazy.

She wriggled next to me, then moaned softly, and snuggled into me, entwining her fin around mine. "Well maybe if this is the punishment, I might be late every night."

My voice grew husky. "Not funny."

I continued to kiss her deeply, pulling her farther into the lake for some private time, but her body tensed under my hands.

Her gills flapped faster than normal. "Are you sure we're alone?"

"What do you mean?"

"Don't you smell that?"

I stopped kissing her and scanned the water. "Smell what?"

"All the other mers. It's like they're here, somewhere... watching."

I sniffed but knew I wouldn't be able to smell anything, being smell blind and all.

"Everyone's gone and my parents are in the basement pool," I said to reassure her. "It's just you and me."

My lips traveled down her neck to her cleavage while my hands ran up her sides in an attempt to remove the impinging nightgown.

Ash yanked away from me, pulling the fabric down. "I'd like to go somewhere more... private."

At the giggle to my right, I turned. Jax and Galadriel were spinning in the current, oblivious.

"Holy crawfish," Ash shielded her eyes and turned away from them.

My face burned with anger. "What are you two doing here?"

"Oh, hey," Jax said. "We… uh…"

"Oopsie." Galadriel pushed her tail in the current, and the two darted out of sight, but they weren't headed toward the gate.

"I guess we're not alone," I said apologetically.

"You think?"

"Did I ever mention that I'm smell blind?"

She quickly adjusted her nightgown and crossed her arms. "No. But seriously? Here? In our lake? Do they have no tact?"

"It's a big lake." I took her hand, knowing a better solution. Only problem was I'd wanted to wait and surprise her on our wedding day. Apparently, that wasn't going to happen if I wanted to have some alone time. "Come on. I have a surprise for you."

"Surprise?" Her frown softened.

I started to swim toward the house when Ash redirected me.

"Wait!" Ash tugged on my hand. "Jax and Galadriel just swam this way."

"Oh. Right." After we had taken a huge loop out of the way of where Jax and Galadriel might be, I took her toward the porthole leading to our house.

She flared her tail to stop us. "I thought you said your parents were in the basement."

"No. Here." I pointed to another tunnel—our tunnel.

Her eyes widened. "Is that…?"

"I'd wanted to wait until our wedding night, but considering…" Her nightgown gave me an idea. Tugging on the hem, I silently asked permission to rip off a piece. "May I?"

"May you what?"

"I need a blindfold."

She cracked a sexy smile, heating my parts that craved her. "Seriously?"

"I'll buy you another nightgown."

"Why can't I see inside?"

"It's not finished yet."

She pursed her lips, then finally nodded. I knew she was enjoying every minute of this, so I tore off part of the hem and blindfolded her while purring in her ear.

"You like teasing me, don't you?"

"Maybe." I pulled her close to me, extra hard, and swam into the hatch.

"Oh," she rasped.

Once we reached the porthole, I opened it and slid out. Her head surfaced above the water. She inhaled. "I smell paint and fresh wood."

"No peeking."

Sliding my arms under her armpits, I lifted her out onto the deck. She slithered over and lay to rest on her side. Her tail flipped over and splashed into another body of water.

"We have a pool in our basement, too?" She slid her hands forward until she reached the edge, her fingertips dangling in the water.

"Not exactly." I slipped into the pool, then grabbed onto her hands, helping her in. We dove under, spiraling down together.

"The water is salty," she said.

I curled around her, anxious to know what she thought of our private oasis. "So…?"

Her fingers grazed over the blindfold, then reached forward, touching my face, then caressing my lips. "Can't I take this off?"

My stamina waned. If she asked for the moon, I'd give it to her.

"Please?" she begged.

My fin shivered.

"For a minute," I said before I changed my mind. "But don't tell anyone."

"Our secret," she whispered against my lips.

She ripped off the blindfold and blinked. Though I'd wondered if she'd be disappointed because our pool wasn't very big in size. I'd compensated by making it deep. The walls had inlaid designs of abalone and gems I designed myself, like that of Natatoria. On the bottom were elevated platforms with weighted blankets for beds. She studied everything, her fingers trailing the designs on the walls.

"This is incredible."

She then glanced upward and gasped. Large windows that covered the pool's ceiling revealed the night's sky beyond. She kicked her tail to get a closer look, but I held onto her waist.

"Whoa there… that's for another time."

She pouted. "You're mean."

The side of my lip curled up and I returned the blindfold to her eyes.

"I have to save something for a wedding gift."

Bubbles trickled from her mouth, and I covered her lips to trap the air.

"You're not disappointed, are you?"

"No. It's amazing, Fin. So much better than I imagined."

My happiness soared, and I swirled with her in my arms.

"Now where were we?" she asked, wiggling against me.

I slid my hands once again up her sides, and the nightgown floated off on the current with ease. She giggled, but this time, she didn't resist me.

"I should blindfold you more often," I said in between kisses.

"Only if I can blindfold you," she promised.

I growled in pleasure and pulled her down deeper.

25

ASH

May 28—10:10 a.m.

I stood on the block, water dripping down my legs. The thought that I'd never get to do this again rolled through me. My last meet. The last time swimming with my peers.

My little merling zoomed around in my tummy, bouncing off the walls like a pinball machine. I touched my growing pooch afraid people might see. Did he sense my nerves?

Meredith Hamusek stood on my left, shaking out her arms and legs, already in her zone. After the incident with Meredith's family accusing me of doping, I wanted to beat her once again to prove myself. But if I did that, the attention wouldn't be off me.

I looked into the stands. Fin, my parents, Gran, Georgia, Girra and a few other mermaids were on their feet, cheering me on. Tatiana would be so proud of her little fledglings. The starter held up his gun.

"Swimmers, take your mark."

I bent down, watching the glistening water shimmer below inviting me to play, speaking a language I understood too well.

At the sound of the blast, we were all airborne, then underwater. My heart took off as I began to kick my legs, feeling the water flow up and over me, exhilarating me, making me feel alive.

The past two weeks had been torture to refrain from swimming the speed that felt comfortable. Being here, though, was like crack. My limbs twitched painfully with my effort to slow down.

I looked over at Meredith, her face determined and focused. The last meet, I'd still been human and beat her fair and square. But she couldn't accept I was better and demanded the test. My arms and legs pounded the water, aching to be let loose. No matter how hard I fought it, I wanted it. I wanted to beat her so badly.

No, Ash.

Another lap and Meredith pulled ahead, and I pinched my eyes shut to block out the overwhelming urge to just swim. I took another breath, though my gills had wanted to make an appearance, and kept going as slow as ever.

When I opened my eyes, there was no one next to me. Had she successfully passed me by? My legs kicked hard as if on their own. My body lifted to cruise across the water from the momentum.

I hit the wall and looked up. The remains of a wave of water left everyone standing on the deck drenched. Mouths everywhere flew wide open. Did something bad happen? I turned around to see the progress of the other swimmers just making the turn. Meredith was only half way across the pool.

Fish poo on a cracker.

A beautiful song erupted through the loudspeakers telling everyone to ignore me. The crowd's eyes glazed over. I craned my neck to find the source. Fin was standing by the announcer, holding the mic.

"Get in the middle of the pool and act like you're finishing your lap," he instructed me. "Now."

I did as he said, swimming to the center. Meredith made a weird sound underwater when she passed by. She apparently hadn't heard the song. Once she hit the wall, I finished the race behind her. Meredith pulled her head out of the water and gawked at me.

I leaned over to shake her hand. "Good race."

She recoiled. "What was that?"

"What?"

"Come on, ladies. Time to get out." Coach had her hand outstretched for me to grab. I latched on and let her lift me out of the pool. "Great race, Hamusek."

"You… you passed me," Meredith said from the water.

"Nope. You won. Fair and square." I spun on my heels, pulled my drenched towel off the chair, and put it over my shoulders before turning on my internal heater to dry myself off.

Even though the timers insisted she'd won, Meredith kept arguing from the poolside. Fin needed to come and smooth things over with her. Where was he?

"Ash," Fin called out.

I turned to find him glaring at me.

"What?" I shrugged.

He palmed his hair. "Poseidon, if I wasn't here."

"What do you mean if you weren't here?" I furrowed my forehead.

He continued glaring at me. "Do you know how much I have to do at home?"

"Yes, but I thought you'd at least want to come to one swim meet in my lifetime and cheer me on. Sorry to interrupt your schedule."

"You were supposed to lose the race."

"I thought I did." I gritted my teeth. How could he be mad about this? He sang. Problem over. "I lost track of my place. Geez."

"Carried away? Your fin showed."

"What? No, it didn't." I laughed incredulously and brushed past him to head to the team area.

Fin grabbed onto my arm, stopping me. "Yes. Your feet finned out and you made a wave. This was more than a close call. You broke the law and revealed yourself out there."

"Broke the law?" I rolled my eyes. "That's quite an exaggeration considering my suit is still intact."

"You don't need to ruin your clothes to shift your feet."

I pulled away from him, confused, then grabbed my swim bag. "I didn't shift."

"You know what? You're not going anywhere by yourself. And that's final."

My head whipped around. "What?"

"It's not safe, not in your condition."

I clamped my mouth shut as my body tensed, knowing I'd explode on him and say something I'd regret later. Instead, I pushed past him and walked to the girl's locker room.

He followed me. "I'm trying to protect you."

"By lying to me? I didn't fin out. I would have felt it."

Fin's lips pulled into a line. "You made a wave and drenched everyone. Half a foot of water was splashed out of the pool."

I dropped my bag and crossed my arms. "Is this how it's going to be being married to you? Controlling everything I do? Everywhere I go?"

Fin's expression hardened. "No."

I walked further into the alcove of the girl's locker room. "I'm fine. Stop hovering."

He tried to follow.

"You can't come in here." I pointed to the WOMEN sign.

He planted his feet, clearly showing me that he wasn't leaving after I went inside.

I snatched up my bag and leaned forward, unable to stop myself. "You're just as bad as the rest of the Natatorians! As Azor!"

He yanked his head backward.

"No. I take that back. You're worse!" I seethed before I marched inside.

I threw my bag against the bench, holding my tears at bay. Meredith came around the corner. She stopped, and just stared at me. I tried to ignore her, but she wouldn't stop glowering.

"What?" I finally said.

"What happened to you?"

I frowned. "What do you mean?"

"The cops thought I'd done something to you when you disappeared." She walked forward, eyes fixed on me. "They came to my house and arrested me. I was taken downtown for questioning."

The blood drained from my face, along with the feeble excuse that I was on a mission tour.

"And then today, I don't know what that was." Her eyes narrowed. "You have to be doping."

I shook my head. "No, I'm not."

"You passed me. I know you did because the time pad recorded you'd beat me by a minute. That's not humanly possible."

I looked away. Fin didn't know he needed to fix the time, too. "I don't know what you think you saw, but I didn't pass you."

"You swam back as if to taunt me. I watched it all happen!"

Her voice echoed in the bathroom, and I cringed. "You won. Can't you be happy with that?"

She leaned forward, finger pointed in my face. "You're a cheater, Lanski. Always have been. Always will be."

I curled my hand into a fist. If she touched me, I'd punch her.

"I'm not a cheater," I said between clenched teeth. "I beat you fair and square. I have the record to prove it."

She laughed, a grating, cackling sound that hurt my ears. I charged her, ready to do anything to stop the incessant racket when my talons burst from my nail beds. I skidded to a stop.

Her eyes went wide. "What the heck?"

I put my hands behind my back, but it was too late. I'd done it again. I'd revealed our secret.

"What are you?"

Snagging my stuff, I hightailed it outside, expecting to run into Fin.

He'd left already. Knowing I should find him to mind-mojo Meredith, I just stood there, heart racing. I needed air. I needed time alone to calm down. Swiveling in the opposite direction, I headed out of the front gates and plowed right into a man.

"Oh, I'm sorry." I looked upward at him.

He held onto my arm to steady me, a broad-shouldered guy with dark eyes and shiny, black hair. I might have thought him handsome if he didn't smell of cheap cologne and cigarettes.

"Thank you." I wondered why he looked so familiar.

He clamped onto my arm tighter and didn't let go. "No, thank you."

Then I was yanked forward and swiveled around at the last second. I opened my mouth to scream, just as he put a cloth to my mouth. Instantly, my gills began to form so I could breathe, but they wouldn't work if I weren't underwater.

I kicked and writhed as he dragged me behind a row of bushes. Did no one see?

"Don't make this harder than it needs to be," he said in my ear.

I eventually took a breath. The pungent smell made my head woozy and my limbs sluggish.

"That's better." There was a sick smile in his voice.

When I stopped fighting, he threw me onto his shoulder and carried me to the parking lot. I fought to keep my eyes open. There was a grinding sound of a door opening, and then I was tossed on my back looking up at a dingy white ceiling.

My heart stalled. It was him. The guy. The one that had been stalking me in the white van since I returned.

I tried to fight, to stop him from shoving my legs inside. My limbs remained lifeless as my eyes slid shut. Was he kidnapping me?

"Oh, no you don't, sea serpent!" a girl yelled, sounding an awful lot like Girra.

There was a grunt, then I was sliding down, out of the van toward the ground. My body flopped over at the last second, and my head hit something hard. Sparkles of light flashed behind my closed eyelids.

"Get back here!" Girra screeched.

An engine rumbled to life, and my body jerked away from squealing tires.

"Coward," Girra mumbled under her breath. "Come back and fight like a man!"

"Is she okay?" another girl asked. Georgia?

"I don't know. I need Fin," Girra said, but I couldn't open my eyes. Then I was moving.

"She's bleeding," Georgia squealed.

"Tubeworms, I should have scratched his face off!"

"Help!" Georgia yelled.

"No, don't," Girra warned. "Just… go get Fin."

"Are you sure?"

"Yes."

Footfalls slapped the pavement, leaving me.

"It's okay now, Ash." Girra petted my cheek. "That's it. Your cut is already healing. Just hang in there. Help is coming."

I tried my best to stay awake, but couldn't, cradled in the arms of darkness.

26

FIN

May 28 – 12:44 p.m.

"I'll crush the buggar," Badger promised as Mom and Dad sat with Ash and me in the living area of the houseboat. Tatiana stood off to the side, bouncing Nicole in her arms.

"I'm so sorry," Ash repeated while huddled under a blanket.

My hand squeezed tighter, trying to help her stop shaking as the drugs her captor used wore off.

"This isn't your fault." The horror that I'd almost lost her gripped me once again. I wanted to rip things apart.

"I should have not argued, and just listened to you," she mumbled.

My insides shuddered with guilt. "No. I overreacted." Why didn't I keep my mouth shut, not aggravating things, especially in her condition? "It's my fault."

Mom leaned forward. "What did he look like?"

Ash's eyes slipped shut slowly, her neck taut. "Dark hair. Dark eyes. Stunk of cigarette smoke and booze…. I don't know." Her body jolted as if she'd relived the near abduction.

Dad, too anxious to sit, shifted his weight. "Do you know him?"

"No," she said, breathlessly. "But he's been following me…"

Following her? My jaw hardened. Why hadn't she told me this before? I withheld my need to pelt her with questions, but my muscles coiled tight. I'd find this basswipe if it was the last thing I'd do.

"I didn't think anything of it until today. Each time the van had a different logo. A cable company, an exterminator… I don't remember them all…" she trailed off.

I rubbed her arm, wishing my family would lay off the questions already. "We should probably let Ash rest."

"No." She unraveled herself from the blanket and sat straighter. "His van is white and old."

Dad's knowing look in my direction hit my gut. He sounded a lot like the same guy who took our picture the night Ash finned out at home after dark.

"Is he mer?" Badger asked.

"I don't know," Ash said. "Maybe. He's very strong."

"Well, if he's who I think he is," Dad said firmly, "he's human, and was here that night."

"And he has Ash's cell number," I seethed through my teeth.

"I think we should persuade someone to give us this guy's address."

"How?" I asked.

"Cellphone records, for one," Dad suggested.

"It's a blocked number," Ash said.

Dad leaned in. "Somebody knows something somewhere. It's not all anonymous."

"I'll handle it," Badger said. "No one can say no to me Irish charms."

"Just call off the wedding," she whispered to me. "We'll go back to Natatoria, problem solved."

"No." I took her hand in mine. "We won't run because someone found out. He's just looking to make a quick buck. We just have to be smarter."

"Fin's right," Dad agreed. "This happens sometimes, Ash, and it's not your fault. But it doesn't mean we stop living. For now Ash needs to be under twenty-four-hour guard. She doesn't go anywhere alone. Not until we mind-wipe whoever this son of a bass is…" Dad stopped, clearly holding back what he really wanted to do to this guy, and rubbed his beard. "Is school over yet?"

"One week left," she said.

"Alright." Dad nodded "Fin? What's left to do on the cottage?"

"The electrical is almost finished, then the drywall and the interior," I said. "The outside is done."

"Good. Badge, take whoever you need off the main house so they can finish up Fin and Ash's cottage. I'll finish painting the outside of the main house and make sure it's presentable for the wedding, then get the records. Fin, you'll go back to school and help Ash finish up her finals." He turned to Tatch. "And where are we with the wedding plans?"

"We're just about there. We decided to cater the food, 'cause the kitchen isn't done. Extra chairs and tables are on order. We're having sod put over the parking area for the overflow since parking won't be an issue." Baby Nicole reached up and yanked on her hair. "Be nice to Mommy."

"How many extra mers?" Dad asked.

"Oh," she blew out a breath and unwove her hair from the merling's grip, "about five hundred."

"Five hundred?" Dad shuffled back a few paces.

"Everyone wants to come," she said with a shrug. "And you know the Regent. She gets what she wants."

"Maybe not after she hears about this," Dad muttered under his breath.

Ash leaned into me with her fists pressed to her face, her eyes closed tight.

"Desireé can't know or she'll call the whole thing off," I said forcefully.

"Right. I'll talk to Girra," Tatchi said. "She'll keep her mouth shut, considering she wants to have land visitation rights. She's the only one who saw what happened, right?"

Georgia had been there, too, but I'd already taken care of her memories.

"Saved my life, you mean?" Ash suggested.

"Yes," Tatchi agreed. "That she did."

"We need guards manning the property from now until the big day," Dad suggested. "I think that we should have Jax and Jacob—"

"Are in the wedding party," Tatchi interrupted. "You'll need to find someone else on the wedding day."

"I'll be doing it," Badger suggested. "No one will come on this here property without me knowin' it."

"Maybe we should cut the wedding party," Dad suggested.

Tatchi gave him a heated stare. "Do you want to tell that to the Mistress Wynie? 'Cause she's been working her fingers to the bone to make their outfits."

"We don't have to do this," Ash pleaded, her hands tugging on the collar of my shirt. "It's not that important."

"Now, now, honey." Mom scooted closer on Ash's other side and patted her knee. "This isn't something you could have avoided. He must have known about the mer before he saw Jack on the beach. It happens."

Her frightened eyes met my mother's. "You've been taken?"

"No… just…" She brushed Ash's hair from her eyes. "We've had a few close calls."

"This is a wake-up call that we've been too comfortable," Dad warned. "All strangers need to be persuaded off our beach."

Badger puffed out his chest. "My boys are ready and able. I've been workin' with 'em and they're right fine."

"Okay, Badge. That sounds great," Dad agreed. "Thank you for doing that."

"Aye, Captain."

Dad's lip quirked up in a knowing smile at the moniker from when he'd been in charge of the guard in Natatoria.

Ash pulled harder on my shirt. "This isn't necessary. We can postpone it."

"Ash," Tatiana said decisively. "Not with the merling coming, we can't. I am not postponing anything for the likes of some spineless little jellyfish who can't show his face. We're family and we've got this covered."

"That's right, Ash," Dad said. "You're my daughter now, and we stand together and protect our own."

"And if he dare shows his arse anywhere near me, Posideon, he's goin' to wish he never messed with the likes of me," Badger seethed.

"We'll find him. He's not going to ruin our wedding," I promised.

Nicole let out a squeal, wanting to be put down. Tatiana let her free and she crawled over to Ash, pulling herself up on her knee. She blew bubbles and smiled at her. Ash let go of my shirt to stroke the merling's hair. She then let out a shaky sigh.

Tatch bent down behind her daughter. "And Nicole will be crushed."

Ash sniffled, her questioning gaze landing on each person in the room. "Are you sure?"

"Are we sure?" Mom folded Ash in a hug. "We've all been awaiting this day eagerly, since the moment you two were promised. It's one you both deserve after what you've been through. Don't let this animal stop you."

I felt my resolve swell. She was right. We couldn't let this basswipe stop our day.

"And if I planned all of this for nothing—" Tatiana started, her glare fierce.

"Okay." She lifted her hands in surrender. "You're right. We need to stand up to him. Don't cancel the wedding."

The group collectively sighed in relief, but my mind was already spinning on how we'd find the guy. He was going to regret the day he messed with the mer.

27

ASH

May 30— 7:56 a.m.

Monday finally rolled around, but I couldn't stop myself from jumping in fright every time someone came up from behind. Walking through the halls, knowing this would be my last school week posing as a human felt surreal.

Posters announcing graduation Thursday night caught my attention. Even if I'd wanted to, I couldn't attend with it being in the evening. The swim meet fiasco, still too fresh in my mind anyway, was warning enough, and I could only imagine my reaction if I spotted Mr. White Van in the audience. Fin, my fearless bodyguard, had already decided I should dress up in my gown and take pictures with the family anyway, then he'd sing them a story of what happened that night instead—give them a good memory. Each time he had to do this, I felt like a part of my soul chipped away.

My focus had to be on surviving seven finals: two each day until Thursday when I only had one. Then I'd leave this place. Finally done. All with Fin by my side, of course.

Georgia ran up to me, a huge smile on her face. "Hey you two, can you believe it? Our last week?"

I shook my head and gripped Fin's hand tight. "No."

"It's like the whole year zoomed by just like that." She snapped her fingers. "I studied until my eyeballs fell out this weekend. How about you?"

I glanced up at Fin. I'd spent the weekend trying to calm down. Of course, her story might have been more exciting if she'd remembered Girra's heroic rescue when she conked Mr. White Van over the head with a rock.

"Yeah. Let's just get this over with." I moved to follow her through the door to English when Fin dropped my hand.

"What are you doing?" I asked.

"I don't think I should go in there."

I scrunched up my nose. "Why?"

He peered inside, then ducked out of the way. "I'd rather wait out here for you."

"Technically you're still a student," I whispered.

"Yeah, well... I'd rather patrol the parking lot for you-know- who."

I smirked. For some dumb reason, I wanted him in class with me. The bell rang, and Mrs. Keifer told everyone to take their seats. What was he afraid of? It couldn't be failing.

"Seriously?" I asked.

"No one is going to snatch you from your classroom," he insisted. "Especially if I'm outside of it."

"Ms. Lanski. Please come inside and shut the... Finley?"

"You didn't see me," he sang, then kissed me on the lips and darted down the hall.

"Fin!" I called, but he was gone.

When I turned around, Brooke was glaring at me with hateful eyes. I took my seat, ignoring her, but after everything that had happened, my nerves were once again rattled.

I finished my exam early, surprised at my recall. Actually, all my homework had been a cinch now that I had a near photographic memory—mer perks, I guess.

Waiting impatiently until someone else turned in their test first, my leg twitched. Enduring this week just seemed like a waste of time, but the plan was to continue on as normal, hoping to flush out Mr.

White Van.

Mrs. Kiefer gave me a kind smile when I brought her my test, and something about it made me sad. Originally, I thought living out my human high school experience would prove something to the mer and free me in the process. Instead, it just felt fake. A tear welled in my eye as I walked out of the doors into the hall.

Fin wasn't there like he'd said he'd be, upsetting me. I pulled out my phone and typed a text.

ME: Done. Where are you?
FIN: Already? Be there in a few.
My stomach growled fiercely.
ME: What are you doing?
FIN: Running an errand.
ME: You left?
FIN: I'll be there soon.

I growled, glaring at my phone. After what happened, I couldn't believe he'd left. I contemplated texting and telling him that I was starving. Of course, that would make him later. I paced the hallway, then leaned against my locker in the hall. What was taking him so long?

Someone stormed out of English, and I looked up, hoping it would be Georgia. Brooke's scowl landed on me.

"You're such a liar," she said.

I crinkled up my brow. "What?"

She crossed the hall. "You said Fin wasn't coming back to school, but he was here. I saw him."

"I..." Did she not hear him sing earlier? My heart jolted, and I looked at her hand to double check if she had a promising tattoo. "He was just dropping me off."

The sweet cinnamon smell of chai tickled my nose, and I turned to the double doors just as they swung wide. Fin sauntered in with a smile.

"Ginger Girl." He held up a bag in one hand and a cup of chai in the other. "Look what I brought—"

A peace offering.

He slowed, seeing Brooke's angered expression.

"Hey…" He chuckled nervously.

Brooke marched over, hands balled into fists. "Do you think this is funny? Lying to me, and showing up for finals anyway? I hope you flunk Biology, too."

She raised her fists as if she'd hit him.

"Whoa!" I ran and put myself between them, my talons just about to break the surface.

Her fierce glare darted between the two of us, then she chickened out and ran for the restrooms.

I swiveled toward Fin. "What was that about?"

The cinnamon goodness wafted from the bag, diffusing my anger over Brooke's rage.

"She came over last week wondering where I'd been."

Fin offered the bag, and I tore inside, ravaging the huge hunk of coffee cake. My eyes rolled backward when the sugar and butter hit my taste buds. Heaven.

I stopped chewing when his comment hit my newly fed brain cells. "She what?"

"Yeah." He held out the drink to me. "Don't choke."

My cheeks burned with the memory of almost finning out in the cafeteria, which I hadn't told him either. I would have hoped he'd mention Brooke, though, considering she came to his house. "And what happened?"

"Nothing. I told her to leave… mer-mojo style."

"Fin," I whined.

"So… I guess she flunked."

I continued to devour the muffin and eyed the bathroom door. Even though she'd made my life a living hell for the past four years, I suddenly took pity on her. "If she flunks, she might not graduate."

"And how's that my problem?" Fin pulled me under his arm and headed to the double doors.

I lifted my gaze to his. "Can't you do something?"

"For your nemesis? I think not."

I let out a soft sigh as he pulled me outside in the crisp morning air. "Yes, but… you were supposed to be her partner."

"And?"

I stopped him. "And maybe… you should sweet talk Mr. Wellington on her behalf."

"You said I shouldn't sing."

"Yeah, well. You sang when she came over, besides it'll give you something to do during my history final."

"I have plenty to do." He gestured I sit on a bench outside.

I refused, putting my hands on my hips. "Like?"

He gritted his teeth. "Like figure out who sent you that text. Okay?"

I stopped for a second, then realized where he'd gone during my final. "That's why you left."

"I just stopped in the cellphone store on the corner after I picked you up a snack, but they don't have access to the main files. I need to go to the corporate offices. They're in Reno, of course."

The bell rang and he walked me back inside. Students began filling into the hallway, some anxious, some excited. Brooke darted out of the bathroom, head down, eyes rimmed in red.

"Just smooth things over with Mr. Wellington, for me, okay? And, if you want to go to Reno, I'll catch a ride home with Georgia if you're not back in time. I think finding that creep should be a higher priority than babysitting me. He's not going to dare show his face with all these students around. I'll be okay."

He eyed me suspiciously. "Are you sure?"

I pulled out the pepper spray hiding in my pocket. "I'm armed."

"Where'd you get that?"

His mother had given it to me, but I wasn't going to give up my source. "I have my ways. Now go!"

Fin gave me a quick kiss before heading toward the double doors.

I snagged his hand and redirected him in the opposite direction. "No, handsome. This way."

I pointed to Mr. Wellington's room down the hall. He rolled his eyes but grinned all the same. "Okay, okay."

"Thank you."

Though letting things stay the way they were was what Brooke deserved, today I felt gracious. And deep down, I didn't want this situation to ruin her grade point average.

I needed to score points with the universe because you know what they say about karma. Yeah, I typically wasn't superstitious but I needed all the help I could get.

28

FIN

May 30— 11:47 a.m.

After I had sweet-talked Mr. Wellington to give our group project a passing grade, I left the campus and pressed the pedal to the metal on Ash's car. But no matter how hard I hit the gas, the thing wouldn't pass fifty-six, making me wish for my Jeep all the more.

The drive to Reno took a half an hour longer than expected, and I finally pulled up to the customer service building. The entrance brimmed with people of all walks of life, drifting in and out, most of them not looking up from their cell phone screens. I followed a girl in her twenties, completely oblivious to me, and slipped in behind her without needing a keycard.

"Who can tell me the source of a blocked cell phone?" I sang to her.

Her head lifted upward. "We don't have that information."

"Someone must."

She turned, eyes unfocused. "Try the IT department."

A placard on the wall listed that the Information Technology unit was on the fifth floor. Jackpot.

I ran up the stairwell and bounded out of the doors. A blonde at the reception desk startled at my entrance. She studied me through her large black-rimmed glasses. "Can I help you?"

"Yes," I sang. "I need to figure out who sent someone a text."

Her eyes drifted off to a spot off to my right. "I can't do that."

"Someone must. Do you know who could?"

"Who could what?" I guy in a suit approached, eyeing the secretary's behavior questionably. He didn't look like the typical nerdy IT type, more like management material, but I didn't care. He was breathing.

"I need to know the source of a text," I sang.

His eyes zoned out like normal, and my gut twisted. This was so not me.

"Do you have a warrant?" he asked.

"Yes, but you don't need to see it."

"Let him in," Suit Guy told her.

The blonde buzzed me in, and I followed Suit Guy to the nearest cube. He shooed aside the occupant sitting in the chair. "Let me drive."

"Yes, sir." The cube dweller turned and frowned at me.

"What's the phone number?" Suit Guy asked.

I told him Ash's number and the date and time of the text. He typed in something, and her record popped up. Then he scrolled through a list of numbers.

"Hmmm," he said.

"What does that mean?" I asked. "Did you find it?"

"Yeah, I have a number, but there's no information tied to it. Must be a burner phone."

"A burner?"

He turned and sneered at me. "One of those pay and dump phones you buy at drug stores. There's no contract, so I can't help you."

He stood to leave.

"But don't you know where the text was sent from? Like a GPS location?"

"Not at the time of the text, no."

I scrubbed my hand through my hair. This was going nowhere.

"Are you sure?" I sang.

He pressed his hands to his forehead. "I can see where the phone is now, that's about it."

"Now?" My throat tightened. "Then show me."

Suit Guy returned to the Cube Dweller's seat and pulled up another screen with a map of green dots. A red dot stood out in the middle of them.

"These green dots are cell towers. The phone is somewhere in this vicinity."

Suit Guy zoomed on the buildings surrounding the red dot. My heart nearly dropped to my shoes. The red dot hovered over the top of Ash's high school. I'd left her thinking she was safe. And he was there the whole time. Watching.

Hands shaking, I pulled out my phone and dialed Ash. The phone started to ring, then rolled over to voicemail.

"Is that all you needed?" Suit Guy asked, annoyed.

"No. I…" I had to warn Ash somehow. "Can you look up a cell phone even when it's off?"

He sighed, then nodded.

"Then look up this number." I gave him Ash's number again.

"Kenny, go ahead and do it," Suit Guy said to the Cube Dweller. "I have a meeting."

"Sure." Kenny took a seat and typed in the phone number. An additional red dot lined up with the first one. "They're in the same area."

I gripped onto the edge of the cubical.

"You okay?" he asked.

I couldn't think beyond the fear. What if he had her already?

"He's… he's stalking my wife."

Kenny yanked his head backward. "Do you think she's in danger?"

My eyes zeroed in on the pair of red dots. If the cops got involved, things would just get more complicated. In all actuality, I knew my mistake. I should have never left her alone. What we needed was an experienced mer there—my dad.

"No…" I pinched my eyes shut to center myself. "I need the cell records of that first number. Who the person texted, what was said, the recipient's info."

"I can't give you—" he started to say.

"Give it to me!" I sang.

"All I have is the numbers with dates and times."

"Fine, whatever." I dialed Dad while I was waiting for him to pull up the info. Of course, it rang four times, then rolled over to voicemail, too. "Dad, call me. It's an emergency."

Within minutes, sheets of numbers and data poured out of Kenny's printer sitting next to the monitor. I continued to redial Ash's number, continuing to get voicemail.

Once the printer stopped, I snagged the stack and ran for the stairs.

"I was never here," I sang.

Within moments, I was in Ash's car and pulling out of my parking spot. Once I made it to the main thoroughfare, traffic ground to a halt. I laid on the horn, my hands shaking.

"Get out of my way!"

Imagining the worst, I swerved around traffic while my foot hit the gas, breaking every law in the DMV manual. I'd screwed up again. Who was this guy and what did he want?

My phone rang. Dad's name highlighted the screen.

"What's going on, Son?" he asked when I picked up.

"The guy is at Ash's school! You need to go over there now and make sure she's alright!"

"Wait. Where are you?"

I honked my horn and tried to edge around the vehicle stalled on the road. "I went to Reno."

"Reno?"

"Ash's final was going to take two hours, so I decided to check on the cell records."

"In Reno?"

"That's where the main office is," I said, exasperated. "Please. We're running out of time!"

"I'm on it!" Dad moved the phone away from his mouth and yelled, "Badger!"

"Just don't scare her, okay? Just… don't let her know he's there."

Dad blew out a breath. "Next time, you need to let me know what you're up to. You should have never left her there alone. I said I'd take care of the phone records."

Yeah, when? I wanted to ask. Seriously? He was going to lecture me? I ground my teeth together. He was the one procrastinating, not me.

"Badger!" Dad yelled. "Get Jax and Jacob. We need to get to the school."

I blew out a frantic breath. "Just get there."

"We've got it taken care of." He hung up, but my heart wouldn't stop pounding. The phone chimed with a text.

ASH: I'm finished early. Everything okay? I saw the missed call.

I picked up the phone and dialed, working hard not to sound panicked.

"Hey, you. I'm starving." The smile in her voice made me a million times thankful, but the urge to vomit was still there.

"Hey, I won't be there for a bit. Where are you?" Birds sang in the background, and I gripped the phone tighter. "Are you outside?"

"I figured I'd see if you were in the parking lot. Are you hiding?"

"Ash," I said sternly. "Listen to me. Turn around and go inside."

"What?"

"Turn around quickly, and go back inside."

"Fin, you're scaring me. What did you find out?"

I pinched my eyes shut. I couldn't tell her, not in her condition. "Nothing. I'd just feel safer if you were indoors until I get there."

"Okay?" Her voice was questioning, but the soft crunch of gravel, and then the soft slaps of her shoes against pavement told me she was at least walking toward the building.

"Where's Georgia?"

"She's taking her exam." There was a pause. "Is the guy here?"

"He might be."

Her footfalls stopped, the silence deafening. "You just said it was nothing. This isn't nothing."

"It's okay," I said. "My dad is on the way."

She pushed air through her nose. "He is? Where are you?"

"I'm just leaving Reno."

"Just leaving?" She sucked in a gasp. "Can't I have my mom come get me?"

"No. It's better if my dad picks you up." I didn't want to terrorize her by explaining. "Just get inside."

The sound of doors opening and closing came through the phone's speaker. "I'm in the lobby now, but I don't see the white van."

"Good." I gripped the phone so tight my arm ached. "How was your final?"

"I passed. Easy peasy."

I pictured her there, sitting in the lobby, waiting, alone and defenseless. My foot hit the gas and pressed harder.

She abruptly screamed, then the phone made a crunching noise, and the call ended.

"Ash?" I looked at the phone's screen in disbelief, then tried to redial. It rolled over to voicemail. My skin burned, morphing with scales. I let out a grunt and punched the dash, denting it.

I dialed my Dad again while I raced down side streets. "He's got her, Dad! He's got her!"

"What?" The loud rumble of the truck came through the line, the noise growing louder with increased acceleration. "I'm almost there. Where is she?"

"She was just in the main lobby! Hurry!"

At the sound of a police siren, I hung up and set the phone down.

"Pull over," the voice boomed from the loudspeaker.

I screeched to a halt and jumped out, arms up. The cop spoke into his radio, then pulled his gun. "Stay where you are, young man."

"It's an emergency," I sang. "I need you to escort me."

He lowered his gun. "Emergency?"

"My fiancé has just been kidnapped."

"What's her name?"

I stepped forward. "It's Ashlyn Lanski. I was just talking to her on the phone, and she screamed. Then the phone died."

"Okay." He wrote it on a pad of paper. "Where is she?"

"At South Lake Tahoe High School."

He spoke into the radio attached to his collar. "Calling in a missing persons." He leaned toward me. "Age?"

"Eighteen."

"Eighteen-year-old Ashlyn Lanski."

"Red hair… slight build," I added.

Something crackled on the line. "*Ashlyn Lanski? Are you sure?*"

"Yes," I said, almost jumping out of my skin. "We're running out of time."

"*That missing case was solved already,*" the voice continued.

"Poseidon," I groaned. "She's been abducted for real this time."

The cop's eyes narrowed. "Wasn't she that Olympic hopeful? Wait. You look familiar, too."

"Forget all that, and escort me," I sang.

His eyes glazed over and he stuffed the pad of paper into his pocket. "Follow me." He returned to his car, and the siren blared as he sped off.

I jumped into Ash's car and turned the key. The tiny motor chugged to life then died.

"What?" I turned the key again, listening to the engine sputter, but not catch. "You've got to be freakin' kidding me!"

The cop car disappeared out of sight while I turned the key and pumped the gas. Then I noticed the gas gauge pointed to empty. My fist pressed against the horn, blaring loud and long. It didn't matter. The cop didn't look like he would return. I lifted my hand, but the incessant noise didn't stop.

"What?" I bashed my fist against the steering wheel to make it stop.

My phone lit up next to me. There was a missed call, but from a number I didn't recognize. Why wasn't Ash calling me back?

Posideon, I'll kill him if he so much as touches her.

I yanked the lever to open the hood. The phone buzzed against the console. Dad's name appeared on the screen. I answered.

"What's going on?"

"Fin?" Dad asked. "What's that noise?"

I got out and walked away from the car, stuffing my finger into my other ear so I could hear. "Just tell me Ash is okay."

"She is. Nothing's wrong."

"Then what happened?"

"Her friend snuck up and startled her. She dropped her phone and it broke. She's been trying to get in touch with you ever since."

I turned and glared at the car. I'd overreacted once again, and now some poor persuaded cop was on his way to rescue a girl who's first abduction ended up being a hoax. Great.

"Good," I said, just wanting to get off the phone. "I'll meet you at home soon," *after I get gas.*

I hit END when a text illuminated on my screen.

UNKNOWN: It's a big sea to leave your guppy all alone in.

Three pictures came in one after the next, all of them of Ash. Alone. Standing in the parking lot. Talking on the phone.

He'd been there.

Watching her.

My skin heated. That son of a bass was going to pay.

29

ASH

June 1— 1:24 p.m.

The car sputtered and Fin cursed under his breath as he drove me home from school. Ever since yesterday, he'd been quiet—deathly quiet.

"You okay?" I asked.

"Fine."

I bit my lip and decided to drop it. I figured he blamed me for what happened with the fiasco yesterday, and he'd been tightlipped about what he found out in Reno.

I marked an X over another day in my planner. Only one more and I'd be finished. Officially an adult. Oddly, I thought I'd be happier about it.

"So, I heard about your secret bachelor party."

He turned to me, baby blues hidden under sunglasses. "What bachelor party?"

I turned up the side of my lip. "The one Jax and Jacob are not so subtly planning."

Georgia had already gotten wind of it and wanted to crash it, that was until she couldn't find Natatoria in a Google search. She then redirected her energies into planning a bachelorette party for me. Any other time, I'd be all for it. But with our little one coming, the idea of putting on a slinky dress and high heels made me tired. Besides, without persuasion, no clubs would be open in the middle of the afternoon.

"They want to go out one night this week. Blow off steam." He side glanced at me. "But I said no."

I dipped my head. Not leave my side was more like it. "Is this a plot to get permission?"

"What?" He wrinkled up his brow. "No, never."

I gave him the stink eye. "Because there's a stripper?"

"What?" He pulled a face. "No. Never!"

I could think of a few mermaids in Natatoria who'd love to entertain them with a wag of their tail and a dash of pheromones, but I was just relieved we were talking again.

"Then what are you going to do?"

He leaned back in his seat. "Badge thought we'd chase dolphins, or do some deep sea fishing. You know. Mer against mer competition stuff." He pulled up to the house and parked. "I don't have to go."

"You're the groom. Why wouldn't you go?" I smiled.

"Are you really saying yes? Or just saying yes to make me happy? Because there is the matter of..."

He let the words hang there, like a disease. Mr. White Van was in the middle of everything now—every move, every conversation, every decision. I hated him.

"Look... now that we have our new pool, I can stay there." I perched a brow.

He gave me a sultry look. "How can I trust that you won't snoop?"

"With the same trust I'm giving you that you won't be entertained by a tail wagging stripper."

He clenched his jaw, his face growing serious. "I'm not saying this because I don't trust you. I'd just feel better if you stayed in the palace in Natatoria with everything."

Angered, I turned to look out the side window. First I hated going through the passage between Tahoe and Natatoria, reminded once again of the horrible things Alaster did to me. But being in Natatoria without Fin after everything Tatiana told me about what happened to her, especially now that I was expecting, terrified me. But I wasn't surprised he'd insisted on me staying there, especially after yesterday's events, and I didn't want to argue.

"Okay," I said reluctantly.

"Are you sure?"

I gave him a smile. "Yeah. It'll be fine. You have fun."

His whole body relaxed as he blew out a breath and stepped out of the car. He walked around to open my door with a refreshed countenance. "Where are all the girls?"

I scanned the dock, then remembered. Today was my dress fitting. Biting my lip, I tugged my shirt over my protruding abdomen. Whether I liked it or not, our little merling was starting to make an appearance, and I was worried the dress wouldn't fit.

"I'm trying on my dress today. They must all be inside."

"Oh?" Fin pulled me into his arms and squeezed, lingering extra long. "And I'm not invited."

"Of course you aren't." I spanked him on the butt. "You can't see me in the dress before the wedding."

He kissed me, then deepened the kiss. "I can't wait until you're officially Mrs. Finley Helton."

I relaxed in his arms. "Me neither."

We kissed again, but uneasiness prickled down my spine. Once he let me go, I scanned the area for Mr. White Van, seeing no one. Ever since the abduction, I couldn't shake the feeling I was being watched.

"You okay?" Fin asked.

"I'm more than okay. I'm perfect," I said to hide my worry. "You go now. I'm sure there's a lot to do, considering you've had to babysit me all morning."

He smirked as he handed me the keys, then kissed me one last time before jogging across the lawn and down the path, disappearing somewhere between the trees. Within seconds, I saw him cross the parking lot and walk up to his parents' house.

He turned and waved to me. I waved back, but the uneasiness grew stronger in his absence, and I quickly walked to the house. The typical hustle and bustle between the houseboat and my parents' was absent. Were they all inside for my dress viewing? Talk about ruining the surprise.

Once I stepped onto the porch, I heard "Shhh," from inside. I turned the knob and someone yelled, "Surprise!"

A crowd of thirty ladies gathered in my parents' living room: Tatiana, Georgia, Girra, Galadriel, my mom, Gran, Fin's mom and Desirée, along with a handful of the other mermaids who'd been helping out. In the center of the room was a mountain of presents.

"What's this?" I asked dumbfounded, dropping my backpack to the floor. They hugged me one by one.

"A shower, dear." Mom hugged me last and ushered me to sit on the couch.

My eye caught the spread of food on the kitchen table just beyond: sandwiches, sliced fruit, and a huge cake, all making my mouth water.

Tatiana sat next to me, handing me the first present. "You were surprised, weren't you?"

"I... yeah?"

"Be honest. You didn't have a clue?" She waggled her eyebrows.

"Not a clue."

The first gift, from my mermaid sisters, was a book filled with pictures of bedroom furniture from Crate and Barrel.

"This is an amazing dream book," I started.

"Dream book? *Pfffft*," Girra said. "That'll all be delivered next week. Oh how I love that mall place."

I swallowed, trying to keep from looking so surprised.

Mom leaned over, eyeing the book. "Oh, my."

"Thank you, that's very generous," I finally managed to say.

Tatiana put a gift bag on my lap. "This is from me and Jacob."

I felt something silky hiding in the tissue and pulled out a black nightie, if you could call it that. My cheeks burned at the lack of fabric. Someone whistled as I stuffed it back in the bag.

"Tatchi," I said brusquely under my breath.

She laughed and nudged my arm. "Tell Fin, you're welcome."

I gave her a sideways glare and reached for the next present.

After several minutes, the coffee table was overflowing with linens, dishes, towels, cutlery and appliances, yet I still wasn't done. My stomach growled audibly.

"The bride needs food. Stat," Tatchi snapped.

One of the mermaids jumped up and snagged me a plate of food, which I quickly devoured.

Lucy walked in the front door with a scowl on her face. "Why didn't you pick me up?"

"Oh, Lucy," Mom said solemnly. "I totally forgot with Ash's surprise shower today." She jumped up to hug her, but Lucy shrugged her away, walking off toward the kitchen.

With my supersonic hearing, I heard her mumble, "Yeah, because she's more important," under her breath.

"This is from Pearl." Girra handed me another bag filled with tissue, and I snapped to attention.

I looked around the room. "Where is Pearl?"

"She's watching Nicole." Tatiana propped her lips up in a grin. "Hopefully they're getting along."

I lifted my brows, knowing just how much of a sacrifice that would be, considering Nicole's attachment to Tatiana. "Tell her thanks from me, and that I missed her."

I felt inside the bag, feeling something satiny again. She wasn't gifting me lingerie, too, was she? Deciding to be a good sport, I took the item out.

"I wonder what this is." I smirked.

The garment unfolded into what looked like a white gown, but not something that would fit me. Something just the right size for a baby. Once I realized what it was, I shoved the garment inside.

"What is it?" Girra asked. "I didn't see."

"It's... private." I turned to Tatchi and mouthed, "baby outfit." Her eyes rounded. She knew just as well as I did that Mom, Gran and Lucy didn't know about the baby yet.

"Is it another nightgown?" Galadriel leaned forward. "Let me see."

I hid the bag behind my back. "What's next?"

"It's for the merling," one of the mermaids announced loudly from the back. "A birthing gown."

"Sterling, as in silver?" Gran asked while touching her ear. "That didn't look like jewelry to me. What is it Ashlyn?"

"Birthing gown? Let me see it," Mom prodded.

"Shhh, Rose. We're not supposed to talk about it," someone chastised.

Then things sunk in, and Mom's head whipped around to me. "Are you pregnant?"

Oh, crap.

"No, Mom," I lied. My glance darted to Desirée, terrified she'd see how horrible I was at keeping the mer secret with humans. "It's just not my size."

"Oh, fish poo." Galadriel jumped to her feet. "I'll be right back."

While Tatiana leaned forward to grab another package, I heard Galadriel yell for Jacob from my parents' porch.

"We have to keep cool," I mumbled to Tatiana.

Mom walked over, hand on her hip. "What's in there you don't want us to see?"

I looked up terrified our bubble of bliss had popped, recognizing the hardened expression I knew well—the one determined to get her way.

"It's nothing, Mom."

Something crinkled from behind my back. I turned just as Lucy pulled out the gown. The room quieted. "This explains the prego test I found in the trash."

My stomach dropped.

"Ash," Mom whispered.

I swallowed down my tears. Where was Jacob or Fin, already? Tatiana looked at me with a panic stricken face. We had to cover this up. We couldn't look like idiots in front of Desirée.

"It's well wishes for a future child. A custom we have." Desirée walked forward. "Where we come from."

Mom turned to her. "Where you come from? You're not American?"

"No. We're Nat—"

"Scandinavian," Tatiana interrupted, then laughed. "Yah, didn't ya know?"

I hit her arm and laughed. "Great accent."

"Then what's the positive test I saw in the garbage?" Lucy asked.

I wanted to jump up and wring her neck.

"I don't know. It's not mine." I rebuked myself for not hiding the test in Fin's garbage can instead of ours. "Can you hand me the next present?"

"In here," Galadriel said behind me. "Just sing away the last twenty minutes."

"No, it's okay," I started to say, but I was too late.

Jacob sang to the crowd. Gran, Lucy, Georgia and Mom's faces lost all composure.

Desirée's appraising eyes made my stomach turn. This was a

disaster.

"What... what were you saying?" Mom asked me.

I blew out a breath and fell backward into the cushions of the couch. "I'm starved. Let's eat."

The mer in the room didn't move for a moment, tension still thick in the air. I jumped up anyway and headed to the table. After I had finished eating, I opened more gifts than I knew what to do with, and I leaned back exhausted, wanting everyone to leave so I could take a nap.

"This is for you." Desirée handed me another sack of coins and gems.

I looked up at her in surprise, then stood and hugged her neck. "Thank you, Mother. For earlier, too."

"Of course, my sweet." She rubbed my back.

"Wow." Mom's eyes widened as she sifted through the gifts. "Everyone has been so generous."

I nodded in agreement, feeling extremely blessed.

Girra walked over. "Well, aren't we going to see the gown?"

I coughed, thinking she'd meant the birthing gown, then I remembered. My wedding gown.

"Oh, you don't want to see it, do you?" I looked at everyone, embarrassed. They all started chiming in at once.

"We want to see it."

"Yes."

"Put it on."

"It's upstairs." Mom's eyes twinkled. "But Wynie can have the honors."

"I'll help ya, love." Wynie's sweet smile comforted me as she took my arm.

We moved through the crowd toward the stairs. And like Mom said, hanging from the curtain rod was the most elegant dress I'd ever seen, trimmed with lace and tiny iridescent gems. My mouth dropped open.

"Oh my starfish, it's gorgeous," I told her, then gave her a huge hug. "You've outdone yourself."

"Just wait until it's on, Love." Wynie removed it from the hanger.

After I had changed out of my clothes, she held it up and I dove my hands through the middle. She tugged the dress over my hips, then zipped up the back. I barely had to suck in my gut.

"It's perfect. How did you—?" I turned, knocked speechless after spying my reflection in the mirror.

"Years of practice, sweetie." She watched me with so much love. "Where's your veil?"

The veil. I couldn't go down with Mom's veil on, and certainly not Desirée's headdress.

"I, uh…"

Wynie opened my closet, pulling out two hangers. "Looks like there are two in here."

"I haven't made up my mind yet." I placed my hand on the door to close it. "I don't need it yet."

"You should let the girls vote."

"No," I said a little too firmly. "I mean, I want to decide. They both have sentimental value, and I shouldn't show them everything today, you know? Save something."

"I see." She bowed her head. "Do you want me to help you down the stairs."

"I… I think I can do it. Just give me a second."

"Of course, dear." She left and closed the door.

I stared at the veil and the crown, at how they represented my dual life. Yes, being married to Fin and living in our house would alleviate all this tension, but what was I advocating for on behalf of the rest of the mers? Was this fair to let them believe it could be done? That pretending to be human was easy?

"Ash?" Mom cracked open the door. "Are you—?"

She let out a gasp. I turned to her and sniffled. "What do you think, Mom?"

She walked closer and pulled out my hands. "You've never looked lovelier."

"Do you think?"

"Do I think?" Tears trailed her cheeks. "It's all I've ever wished for you. Better. I can't believe Wynie made this by hand."

"I know." I swallowed, savoring the moment.

With our ups and downs, I'd never expected her to approve, to be proud of me like this.

"All it needs is my veil." She turned to fetch it from the closet. I stayed her hand.

"Mom. I… I want to save it for my wedding day. Okay?"

She blinked at me for a moment. I braced myself for her backlash. Then she just smiled. "Okay."

My hands jutted out, pulling her into a hug.

She resisted. "I don't want to smoosh you."

"You're not," I said with more sniffles.

"Okay… we need to stop this. I don't want to get tears on your gown."

"I know." The tears wouldn't stop.

I just wanted to hug her tighter, to wrap myself up forever in her love. We'd finally had a breakthrough. I could trust she'd finally just let all her nitpicking go, and just was my mom. No judgment. No suggestions.

"Thank you," I whispered.

"What for?"

"Just giving me the day of my dreams."

"Of course, honey. I love you."

"I love you, too."

Maybe what I needed all along was the love of two mothers, because for the first time I finally felt whole.

30

FIN

June 2 – 1:30 p.m.

When the bell rang, I stuffed the highlighted cell phone list in my pocket and slid out of the car to greet Ash, thankful I didn't have to spend one more minute in this dreaded parking lot.

Students poured out of the double doors, laughing and high-fiving one another. I'd expected Ash to come out all smiles. We'd pulled it off.

Brooke walked past, ignoring me.

"Hey, let me see your phone," I sang.

She stopped, her eyes suddenly vacant and reached into her jeans pocket to hand me her phone. I scrolled through her texts. Whatever the stalker had sent her wasn't on the phone anymore.

"Do you know this number?" I pointed to the stalker's phone number on the list.

She glanced over. "No."

"He texted you. What did it say?"

She blinked. "That I was supposed to tell him where Ash was."

My brow furrowed. "Why?"

"I don't know. He said not to say anything to anyone."

"And you listened to him?"

"I don't know. I just had to." She blinked, her eyes clearing.

Had to? "Thanks, and sorry for the partner mix up."

She scowled at me, eyeing me up and down. "I passed without your help thank you very much."

I let out a huff. What was it with girls being so mean?

"Be nice," I sang.

She shook her head and touched her forehead. "Yeah," she said slowly. "You, too."

I watched for Ash to exit, suddenly becoming worried. Finally, she walked out with Georgia by her side. They hugged, then separated. When she didn't see me, I jogged to meet up with her. She marched over to the garbage cans and dropped her backpack inside.

"What are you doing?" I asked.

She startled at my voice, then dusted off her hands and proceeded to walk past me toward the car. "Nothing."

I caught up with her. "Why'd you toss your backpack? Did you flunk or something?"

She stopped, frowning. "No. I passed. I'm done. I've graduated and now, it's over. I don't need that crap anymore."

I lifted my hand and backed up. "Okay."

She scowled, then stormed over to the passenger side of the car and tried the handle. The door was locked.

"Are you sure you want to throw away everything?" I asked.

"Yes!"

I scratched my head, not sure where this stemmed from.

"This is what you wanted Ash, to graduate. Why are you upset?"

"I'm not upset. Can you just unlock the door? I want to go home."

I moved closer to her. "You *are* upset. I get it if you don't want to talk about it, but if we're going to give this marriage a chance, you have to be honest."

She looked up at me, piercing me with her green eyes, and her lip quivered.

She rushed me with a hug. "I'm sorry."

A pang hit my gut as I held onto her. I wanted to fix it. Fix all of it. "Just tell me."

"No. It's stupid. I just... need to get over it."

"Over what?"

"The end… it just… got rushed."

"The end?"

She lifted her hand and gestured to the school. "I'll never know what could have been."

I tried to wrap her up in my arms again, but she fought me. "No. It's so stupid. I'm happy with you, and happy for our baby. I just… want to turn my selfish brain off!"

The tears poured down her cheeks, making me frustrated. "You're not selfish."

She pulled out a paper from her pocket and waved it at me. "This is from the most sought after swim coach in the world. He wanted me. Me! It was my dream to swim in the Olympics. I worked so hard and your uncle stole that from me. For what? Position in the kingdom." She started to rip up the letter. "Now I'll never know what I could have been."

"No, Ash. What are you doing?"

The pieces fluttered to the ground like snow, and she stared at them, her hands shaking. I grabbed her and hugged her hard. She sobbed on my shoulder, her body quaking.

"I'm sorry, Ash. I should have never left you alone and gone to Florida."

She sniffled. "It's not all your fault. I thought I could handle it on my own. I had no idea the depths of his ugliness."

I took her cheeks between my palms. "I promise I won't ever leave you again. I'll always be there to protect you, and our child, from now until eternity."

She sucked in a sob, then kissed me. I tasted her tears on my lips and regretted I could never avenge this injustice.

At 5:30 p.m., I knocked on the door to Ash's parents' home, and waited, my stomach tied in knots. The stiff collar itched my neck and the khakis made me sweat, and I wished I could have just sang a nice outfit in their minds instead of actually wearing one. It wouldn't be for long considering the plan, and I'd change back into my T-shirt and board shorts after my surprise for Ash.

Ash's mother opened the door. "Oh, Fin. Come in. Don't you look nice? Ash is almost ready."

"Mrs. Lanski, these are for you." I held out the bouquet of flowers toward her before crossing the threshold.

Her forehead wrinkled. "For me?"

"Yes. I figured..." *since I'm going to have to mind-mojo you in a little bit.* "You needed them."

"How thoughtful." Tears welled in her eyes, and she wiped one away.

All of this had to be hard, to watch your oldest child graduate, then get married in such a short period of time. The temptation to sing away her sadness rocked me, but I knew how dangerously close I was to turning her into a robot, which wasn't what Ash wanted.

"And you don't have to be so formal. Karen is fine, or even... Mom."

I swallowed, taken aback for a second. "Okay, Mom."

She swept me up into a hug and squeezed. Could this be working? Could we actually be mastering this blended family idea?

She opened the door wider and gestured I come inside. Tulle and bows hung everywhere like the wedding fairy had come and barfed all over the place.

Lucy sat on the couch in the middle of it with a scowl. "I don't get why I have to go," she whined.

"It's your sister's high school graduation," Mr. Lanski said from the kitchen.

"So."

"Aw, dear." Her grandmother sat down next to her and put her arm around her. "Your day is coming."

"I want to have a sleepover at Laura Jane's."

"You can tomorrow night," Mrs. Lanski said.

Lucy crossed her arms over her chest, and I wanted to sing the sass away. But I knew if I did that, Ash would definitely suspect something. Luckily, Ash had perceived Karen had a change of heart with the news. Good thing I had made her nicer. People acted the worst at funerals and weddings.

"So? What do you think?" Ash stopped halfway down the stairs, wearing her black gown and cap. Her red hair trailed down in loose curls, falling softly around her shoulders.

Her eyes met mine and my pulse quickened. She could be wearing a burlap sack and still be the most beautiful thing I'd ever laid eyes on.

Ash's mom put her hand to her lips. "You're… "

"Beautiful, pumpkin," Mr. Lanski finished.

He lifted his hand and helped her walk the rest of the way down the stairs. Once she stepped onto the floor, I could see the sadness creep into her eyes.

Mrs. Lanski wiped her tears off her cheeks and fumbled in her pocket to find her phone. "Okay, so let's get some pictures by the fireplace. Lucy? Stand by your sister."

Lucy didn't move.

"Lucy, come on," her mom prodded. "We don't want to be late."

"I'm not going," she said.

"Stop this. Of course you are."

"I'll go first," I said to rescue the both of them.

Lucy huffed, then moved to stand by her sister. Ash put her arm around her sister's shoulders, but Lucy remained stiff and refused to do the same. Reluctantly, Lucy smiled, but once Mrs. Lanski shot the pictures, her frown returned.

"Are we done yet?" Lucy asked.

"Just a few more family shots," Mrs. Lanski said. "Let's have a good attitude."

Lucy groaned. We most definitely were going to have a one-on-one chat after this, or I wouldn't be responsible for my actions.

Karen snapped a few shots with each family member, and then me. I set down the gift I'd gotten for her, and joined her in front of the fireplace.

"Hey gorgeous," I whispered in Ash's ear.

Ash rolled her eyes. "I can't believe we're doing this."

Mrs. Lanski had me take a few of the family, and we tried to set up a shot with the timer, but the camera kept moving and chopping off our heads.

"When are your parents and Tatchi going to be here?" Mrs. Lanski looked at her watch. "Maybe they can take a few of us at the school."

"Soon," I lied.

"Oh, look at the time." Mrs. Lanski grabbed her purse and sweater. "We need to get going. Lucy?"

I looked to Ash and her gaze fell to the floor.

"Mr. and Mrs. Lanski, Lucy and Gran, please come sit down," I sang.

Ash sniffled, then ran upstairs.

My chest constricted, but I proceeded to sing the family a memory of the evening anyway. Of driving in the car and having a tough time finding a parking place, of filing into the multipurpose room and watching the graduation ceremony amongst the anxious group of parents and kids. I'd never been to a graduation before, so I filled in the details Ash had told me earlier. Then I proceeded to tell them that the battery on Karen's camera had died, and she was unable to take any pictures at the event.

After I'd run out of any additional details, I'd told them that once they woke up, they'd assume Ash was at her all-night grad party.

"And knock off the attitude, Lucy," I added. "Be happy for once."

"Okay," she mumbled.

I sucked in a measured breath. "I mean, just be happy during your sister's wedding. Don't give her any more grief."

She nodded, and I thought of robots again. What was I doing? How could this be good for them, or Ash?

Snagging the gift I'd brought, I took the stairs by twos and knocked on her bedroom door.

"Don't come in," she said in a sniffled frantic huff. "All my wedding stuff is in here."

I backed up and waited in the hall. She stepped out, eyes rimmed in red, no longer wearing her gown. "Did you do it?"

"Yeah. We're clear… but where's your gown?"

She shrugged. "I took it off."

"Why?"

She deadpanned. "I'm not going to my graduation. That's why."

"Oh, yes you are."

Her eyes crinkled at the corners. "What?"

"Just get your gown on and come downstairs."

She frowned at me in disbelief.

I held out a gift bag to her. "Open this first, though."

Her eyes softened as she looked at the bag. "What is it?"

"You'll see."

She froze; her cheeks flushed red. "Is this—?"

"What?" I scrunched my brow.

"Never mind." She shook her head, then pulled out the stuffed kangaroo I'd bought her earlier. Her eyes lifted to mine.

"I thought… she's got a little joey in her pouch," I said. "See?"

Her lips pulled into a smile, then she wrapped her arms around me. "I love it. Thank you."

I blew out a relieved breath. "Good, but we need to hurry. The daylight is a wasting."

"You seriously want me to wear my gown."

"Yes," I demanded. "Go put it on."

"Okay. I'm going."

After she had put on the gown, I took her by the hand and led her outside. My family and a few of our closest friends sat in chairs along the beach. Between them was a path lined with tiki torches.

She turned to me in awe. "What's this?"

"Welcome to our graduation."

"Our graduation?"

I half-smiled. "I told you I had connections, remember?"

She nudged me in the side. "You didn't even take one final."

Tatiana, wearing a black robe of her own, cued the music. "Pomp and Circumstance" began to play over the loudspeakers, and the audience stood.

Tears welled in Ash's eyes, and she turned to me. "I know this is totally ridiculous, but can you sing to my family so they'll come?"

"Sure."

I returned to the house.

"Mr. and Mrs. Lanski, Gran and Lucy, we're having a graduation celebration for my sister and me. Ash has been invited to participate. It would be a great honor if you'd be in attendance, just…" I thought for a moment. "Remember this as happening Wednesday. Okay?"

The four blinked as if snapping out of their trance, and followed me outside.

"Go ahead and sit there." I gestured to the row behind Desirée and her daughters and their mates, including my idiot cousin, Colin.

"Wow. Isn't this special," Mrs. Lanski said.

I took Ash's arm and led her to the back of the aisle next to Tatiana. The girls embraced before Tatiana helped me shrug on my robe and hat. Once we were ready, Oberon, the officiant of Natatoria, who stood in front, nodded to me.

"What do we do?" Ash whispered.

"Follow my lead," Tatiana said before walking down the aisle.

"Your turn," I whispered, nudging her to follow.

She gave me a look of fear and thankfulness.

"It's practice for next Saturday," I added.

A smile sprung from her lips, and she walked down the aisle behind my sister. The girls stood to the left of Oberon, and I joined alongside them.

"You may all be seated." Oberon lifted his hands. "We are gathered here today to celebrate and uphold the graduation of studies for these fine individuals. The students you see before you have successfully passed this phase of their lives and will be ushered henceforth into the world as adults, to represent mer—" Jack coughed loudly, interrupting his mistake. "The, uh… graduated folk. May they grow in wisdom and grace and live long upon the land. May they find happiness and favor in the career of their choosing. May we all support them as they begin this new journey."

The crowd murmured in agreement.

"Ashlyn Francis Lanski," he called out.

Ash startled, then stepped forward and took his hand.

"Congratulations." He then handed her a piece of paper rolled up and tied with a red ribbon.

She smiled, then walked to the other side of the stage.

"Tatiana Renee Helton Vanamar."

Tatiana proceeded forward and received her diploma.

"Finley Samuel Helton," he finally said to me.

I took the parchment, knowing it was a fake, but felt pride swell in me anyway. My parents had given me lessons, yes, and with our mer, I had a photographic memory, but this felt different. Like I'd been given permission to feel like an adult and was expected to act as such. That I'd become one with my mermen brothers.

Oberon held out his hand to us. "I give to you the graduated students."

Ash grabbed onto the tassel of her hat, and then she moved it so it dangled on the other side. She signaled we do the same. I had no idea what that meant, so I just grabbed my hat and threw it into the air like I'd seen others do on TV.

Dad's eyes radiated with pride as he stood, clapping. Badger let out a wallop, startling Desirée and the princesses. Ash's family clapped with everyone else, eyes vivid once more.

Ash rushed me with a hug, squeezing hard. I spun her in a circle.

"Thank you," she said. "A thousand times thank you!"

"Anything for my Ginger Girl," I said.

Our future families embraced one another in celebration, then the hungry mob then headed for the buffet tables positioned on the grassy knoll between our houses. Tables and chairs were situated along the outskirts, and far too fancy for my liking. My sister and mother had had a field day planning and setting up for yet another party. Merriment and dancing followed, but I knew we didn't have long until the sun set.

Ash made her rounds, hanging with her family and enjoying a large slice of cake. I noted Desirée watching on, eyeing Ash with something I couldn't read. Jealousy perhaps. I moved to tell Ash to be sure to include her birth mother when Tatiana grabbed her hand and dragged her to the dance floor. Galadriel, Girra, and several other mermaids joined in. Garnet, though, stood pouty faced, next to her mother, and I was reminded once again of Lucy. Luckily crabby girls came few and far between, and thankfully my sister was not one of them. Where was Colin? After scanning the crowd, I couldn't find him or Lucy. Walking the perimeter, I headed over toward Badger's post.

"Hey, where's Colin?"

"Aye," he said, scratching his beard. I smirked, admiring his vest and

Scottish kilt he wore. "Haven't seen 'em. Did you try the main house? Yer ma is giving tours now. She can't wait for it to be finished after that big gift givin' party Ash had."

I knew that already. Mom had been bugging Dad every day, begging to get started on the décor for the interior.

"Yeah, right." I glanced over that way.

Movement from Ash's parents' driveway caught my attention. Then Lucy and Colin cleared the side yard fence and walked my way.

I stalked over to intercept them. "Hey."

"Hey yourself," Colin said.

Lucy gave me a smirk, then darted over to the buffet table.

"What were you two doing?"

Colin crossed his arms over his chest. "Nothing."

"You were just… talking?"

"Something like that."

My eyes tightened. "You of all people shouldn't be taking human girls anywhere unchaperoned."

Colin laughed. "And why's that?"

"You know why."

He shook his head. "I'm betrothed to Garnet."

"Another reason not to be improper."

"Lucy had something to show me, and there's nothing to worry about. She is after all… *family*."

The way he said "family," made my skin crawl. "Show you what?"

"If I tell you, it'll ruin the surprise."

I furrowed my brow. "At this point, I don't need any more surprises."

"It's a gift. For you and Ash." He grinned widely.

I was confused. Lucy hated my guts. Why would she give us a gift? Had my persuasion changed her heart entirely?

Desirée lifted her hand and motioned to us.

Colin nodded to her. "If you're done interrogating me, my soon-to-be mother-in-law wants to speak with me."

I shook my head at his insinuation that I was interrogating him and looked to find Lucy. She stood off to the side, trying her hardest to gain the attention of one of Badger's guards, but looked none the less harmed.

"Yeah. Whatever," I said.

He sauntered off, but I still had my suspicions that the fruit hadn't fallen too far from the tree.

31

ASH

June 6 – 10:10 a.m.

A motorboat zoomed overhead, and I woke up, encapsulated in Fin's arms, our tails twisted around one another's. I shook my head to clear the fog.

The sun flickered down from up above and brushed its warmth against my skin. My body jolted. I'd be late for school!

Then it hit me—no more teachers, no more books. All I had to worry about was the wedding. My heart zoomed again, this time in fear and anticipation. Four days and a wake up.

"Good morning, sleepy head." I wiggled my hips to free myself from Fin. "Time to get up."

"What time is it?" He yawned and stretched, then reached to pull me close.

I allowed him to but then looked down at my watch. "Holy carp. It's after 10."

"10?" Fin's eyes opened wide.

We kicked our tails simultaneously to propel us to the surface. The bright morning sunlight temporarily blinded me for a moment. Where were we? A tugboat horn sounded to our left while another boat chugged in our direction. We'd somehow drifted over to the harbor during the night.

"Ash, come on." He grabbed my hand and we plunged down, just avoiding the spinning propellers.

"I don't get why we can't sleep in our pool," I said after we neared our side of the lake.

"Only five more nights."

I pushed out my lip. "That's too long."

"Well, you have to have something to look forward to. I promise it'll be worth it." His lips pulled into a grin.

We swam through the tunnel to the porthole and phased in his parents' basement. As I walked over to my cubby on the wall, the nightgown I wore dripped puddles around my feet. I started tugging off my nightgown when I caught Fin's gaze.

He sat on the rim of the porthole, fastening the Velcro of his board shorts all wrong while his hungry leer undressed me. I let the gown fall back into place, snagged my stuff and walked behind the changing curtain.

"Where are you going?" Fin jumped up and tried to follow.

I held out my hand. "Uh-uh. You have to have something to look forward to, and I promise it'll be worth it."

"What?" His jaw dropped. "Technically we're married."

"No, we're promised. Five more nights and this is all yours." I flared out my hands to gesture the sides of my body.

His eyes tightened. "You don't play fair."

"Technically this was your idea," I reminded him before I shooed him away.

Once I changed into street clothes, we walked up the basement steps into the kitchen. Dust and tools lined the wood floors. The cabinets were in, but no countertops.

"There you are!" Tatchi ran in with Nicole in her arms. The babe was hanging upside down, fighting to get free, her tail flipping in her face.

"Uh… do you need help?"

"No, I'm ok—"

"Love you, Ash." Fin gave me a quick kiss before he left. "I need to finish the cottage. Make sure you check in with your parents."

"Oh, right." I watched him disappear outside, longing for more time with him.

"Okay, so… Ouch!"

I turned to see Tatchi hold her hand over her eye, just as Nicole smacked her in the face again. Her grip on the merling slipped. I lunged forward to catch the babe before she hit the floor. My fingers snagged on her tulle skirt, and we tumbled into a heap onto the floor. The girl threw up her arms and giggled, then blew raspberries at me.

Tatchi watched us, mouth pulled in a grin. I tried to hand her back, but Nicole's little hands gripped hard on my wrists.

"Mama," Nicole said.

"Oh. My. Starfish." Tatiana gasped.

I blinked, unsure what had just happened, but didn't want Tatchi's feelings hurt either. "I'm not your mama, sweetie. Here's your mama." I tried to hand her back.

"Mama," she said again, then blew another raspberry. Spittle fell on my face.

"She said her first word. She said it! Me! I won the bet!" Tatiana ran to the doorway. "Jacob! Jacob! Come quick!"

Slightly disgusted, I wiped off the spit.

Nicole shifted into legs and sat next to me, staring at me with eyes framed by long dark lashes. My countenance softened.

"You're kind of cute. You know that?"

She cooed. "Mama."

Then something thumped in my stomach. Hard. I leaned over. "Ouch."

Nicole rolled to her feet, reached over and touched my hand.

"Yeah. My little joey is in there, your cousin," I said. "You'll have someone to play with soon enough."

With a huge grin, she rolled to her feet, then tugged my hand. I stood and let her lead me outside.

Tatiana followed behind us, mouth agape. "Wow. She likes you."

Jacob walked up, chest bare and jeans slung low on his hips, and it wasn't hard to see what Tatiana saw in him, though I knew he had a good heart, too.

"Hey, babe," he said, kissing her.

"Watch this." She leaned over and smiled at Nicole. "Say Mama."

Nicole reached up and tweaked Tatchi' nose and laughed.

"Apparently my effect on kids is short-lived." I shrugged when my merling punched against my lungs this time.

I leaned over gasping. Nicole looked up at me, her head twisted to the side. I tried to talk when the punch happened again.

"You okay?" Tatchi put her hand on my back.

"I'm okay. I think this baby wants to get out of here."

"Not before you walk down the aisle." Tatiana led me to a bench. "Have a seat." She turned to Jacob. "Take care of Nicole, please."

Jacob ran off after Nicole while I sat and caught my breath. My protruding belly edged out onto my lap, and I tried to imagine becoming as big as a watermelon. "True."

Though I was finally showing, Pearl let me know that I'd grow overnight the last two weeks and that I'd need lots of food and rest.

And that's all I wanted. Glancing over at the sheets blowing in the wind, anxiety for this hoopla to be over with sounded wonderful. I so badly wanted to get the baby's room done.

Only five more days.

Tatchi took out a sketchbook and flipped to a page out of my view. "So... blue or green?"

"Huh?"

She eyed me over the book. "For your master bathroom."

"My master bedroom? What is that?" I tried to pull the book forward.

She yanked back. "Don't ruin your surprise."

"What surprise?"

"Just tell me the color," she insisted.

"Uh… blue?"

"Perfect." She marked something in the book and slammed it shut. "And about today."

"What about today?" I asked.

Tatchi rolled her eyes. "It's your bachelorette party, silly!"

"Oh, no, no, no." I waved my hands and stood. "I'm going to have Fin sing this away right now—"

Tatiana grabbed my hand and tugged. "Sit down, silly. It's not Georgia's doing. It's Girra's."

"What?" I exclaimed. "How the heck does Girra know anything about bachelorette parties?"

"Well… Georgia told her."

I huffed. The three G's, as I'd started calling them, were a menace. I was soon distracted watching Jacob crawl around on his hands and knees with Nicole on his back. He gently bucked and she slid off, just to jump up and beg to go again.

"Cute, aren't they?" Tatiana mused.

"Yeah." I sighed and rubbed my belly. This would be Fin in a few short months. Would we have a boy, like I'd been calling him, or a girl?

Tatiana took my hand and squeezed. "Have you thought of names yet?"

"Names?" Other than Joey, I hadn't given it much thought.

A tear trickled down my cheek as I watched Jacob and Nicole play. How could I not want this for us? Was there anything more precious?

Jacob sat crisscross while Nicole put flowers in his hair, and more tears fell. "I don't know. Maybe something after my parents… my adoptive parents."

"They *are* your parents, Ash," Tatiana said quickly. "Just like we're Nicole's parents. It's who raises you that matters—who loves and chooses you."

"Desirée loves me," I said in her defense.

"Yes," Tatiana nodded, "but she also traded you because you weren't a boy. That has to hurt."

I smashed my lips together to withhold my tears. I'd cried enough over this, but it still hurt worse than I'd led on, and the rawness told me that I hadn't gotten over it.

"I'm fine," I croaked out.

"Don't stuff it down," she said softly, rubbing my back. "It's okay to feel it."

"I can't fault her. It was either that or die. She didn't have a choice, and we've changed those laws now."

Tatiana nodded. "True."

Then it hit me. It wasn't necessarily Desirée I was hurt over, it was Phaleon—a father I'd never meet, a father that craved a son, and ended up creating a monster like Azor.

"Owww!" Jacob yelled.

I looked over to see his arm gushing blood out of two half-moon crescents.

Tatiana gasped and ran over and scooped up the child. "No, Nicole! No biting."

"It's okay," Jacob said. "I'm fine."

The child, completely uninjured, wailed loud and long, shifting into her tail and smacking Tatiana on the hip.

Tatiana tried to fuss over Jacob and get Nicole to quiet down at the same time, but he just laughed. "Like mother, like daughter, right?"

I creased my brow in confusion until I remembered that Tatchi had once told me that's what happened when he tried to drag her from the palace against her will.

"That's not funny." Tatchi frowned.

"A love bite. It'll heal." He kissed her, then motioned to the water. "Take her in the lake and let her swim around. She'll calm down there."

Tatchi gave me a forlorn expression over her shoulder. "Sorry. I need to go. I'll see you later at the party, okay?"

"Yeah." I waved my hand. "Go. Go."

She ran down to the dock, wrestling with Nicole the entire way, and after a soft splash, the crying ceased.

Jacob walked by me, bowing. "M'lady."

"Stop that. Just call me Ash."

He just smiled and continued on toward the cottage. I lifted my hands. Old habits did die hard.

Sucking in a breath, I glanced at the droplets of blood marring the concrete. For just being bitten, he sure handled it well. I didn't know what I would have done if the same happened to me? Maybe I wasn't ready for this parenthood thing after all.

32

FIN

June 6 – 10:48 a.m.

Jacob ran in just as I finished painting one of the last sections of the trim in the main room, my shoulder aching something fierce.

Dried blood covered his arm.

I stood. "What happened?"

"Nothing. Uh… just a little accident."

He ran his forearm under the water. Two little pink bite marks were next to an even larger crescent—the one my sister had given him the day of her fake promising to Azor.

"It's fine." He dried off his arm and hands. "So you finished with the trim?"

"Yeah, just about." Whatever had happened, he wasn't going to tell me. "Good thing, too. The girls are going to storm the castle, so to speak, if we don't finish up and get out of here. They're eager to play house."

Jacob shrugged. "Poseidon love 'em for it."

There was a knock at the door.

"Uh, hello?" A guy stood with a clipboard. His eyes skimmed over the tools and materials spread across the floor.

I dusted off my hands. "Can I help you?"

"I have a delivery for F. Helton."

"Delivery?" I asked.

"Yeah. Sign here, please." He handed me a pen, pointing for me to sign the bottom of a receiving order that listed row upon row of furniture items.

"But this stuff is supposed to come next Monday."

The guy shrugged. "It is Monday."

"What?" I smacked my forehead with my hand, then looked around at the chaos. We needed a day to clean up the mess, at least.

"If you don't accept it, I don't know when I'll be able to redeliver. Possibly another week or two. And you'll be charged again."

"Over my dead body." Galadriel stormed past. She stopped and gasped at the mess. "What in Poseidon's name is this?" She huffed. "Sing and tell him to wait."

"Galadriel," I grated through my teeth.

She put her hand on her hip. "I'll make a scene. You know I will!"

"Can you hang for a bit?" I asked the driver. He looked at his watch. "I've got another delivery to do after this."

Galadriel spun and stepped forward. She leaned in and dragged her finger across his jawline. "We just need a pretty minute to get this *junk* out of here."

The guy's eyes closed, then opened half-lidded. "Whatever you want." He walked backward, tripping down the stairs as he went back to his truck.

"That's how it's done." Galadriel gave us a satisfied smile.

Jacob and I looked at one another, then just shrugged.

"Girls!" Galadriel yelled outside while she clapped her hands twice. "If it's not nailed down, it goes in the yard! Get to work!"

The gaggle of mermaids poured inside. Girra sauntered in last and plucked the paintbrush from my fingers. "I'll take that."

"Oh, no you won't." I took the brush back.

She stamped her foot and looked up at me. "You can paint later."

Jacob snagged the brush from me. "Just give us ten minutes, Princess, and then we'll get out of your hair."

She let out a huff, but clearly she'd allowed his charm to change her mind. "Ten minutes. And that's it."

"Come on, Fin," he said with a laugh. "Before they kick us out."

"I think you're right." I grabbed another paintbrush and followed him.

We quickly painted the trim in the main room, then rinsed out the brushes before Galadriel had a hissy fit. Jax joined us as we stood outside, far away from the mayhem surrounding sweating movers. Poor guys were forced to follow their every command.

"Dude, do you think we should help?" Jax asked.

"And be steamrollered? No, thanks, brother." Jacob folded his arms. "We're paying 'em. Let them do it."

Jax pointed to his brother's arm. "What happened to you?"

He let his arms fall. "Nothing."

"Is that a bite?" Jax leaned over for a closer look. "You and Tatch doing—"

"No! Geez!" He stepped away from him.

"Maybe we should sing," I suggested, still watching the movers.

"Sing what? The funeral song?" Jax laughed. "They'll be done soon."

I shook my head. Each time I thought they'd unloaded the last piece; they took another out and unwrapped the plastic off of it. At this rate, it would take all day—a day I didn't have to waste.

Jax nudged me in the side. "So, your bachelor party."

I glared at him. I'd completely forgotten about that.

"It's tonight, you know," he added.

I let out a measured breath. "What? No. I—no. We can't go now."

Jax lifted his hands. "Dude! Can't go? Why not?"

I gestured to the movers. "How can you suggest we go party in the Pacific when we're behind schedule?"

Not to mention, I still needed to follow up on Ash's stalker, which kept getting bumped for one reason or another.

Jacob put his hand on my shoulder. "It's just cosmetic stuff. Your furniture is in, so you're pretty much there. You need this break."

"I want it done. We're having a kid."

Jax laughed. "It's never done. She'll want to change stuff. Add stuff. Move stuff. Just embrace it. We all need to let loose after the schedule Jack's had us under. You're wound up tight! Look at you."

"No, I'm not." I rolled my shoulders to prove I wasn't wound up tight, feeling the ache. "We'll go… next week."

"No doing," Jax said. "Gladdy has my social calendar booked."

"And with the baby. This is the only night Tatchi is letting me out of her sight," Jacob added.

I sighed. Going to the Pacific meant leaving at 4 p.m. at the latest to drive there. "Then let's cancel it."

"Whatcha be doin'?" Badge walked up, put his burly hands on my shoulders and shook. "Watchin' the women folk work?"

"More like staying out of trouble," Jax said with a snort.

Badger laughed. "Never."

Jacob jerked his chin to me. "Fin wants to flake on tonight."

"What?" Badger squeezed his hands, hurting me. "You ain't doin' no such thing."

"Owww." I wiggled free and turned to him. "There's a lot to do and not a lot of time. It's fine. We don't need to—"

"We are leavin'!" he barked. "And not another word!"

"Let me handle this." Jax cupped his hands over his mouth. "Gladdy!"

She marched over mad as a hornet fish. "Can't you see I'm busy?"

I frowned at the both of them. Galadriel, of all the mer, didn't have any say over anything I did or didn't do.

Jax leaned over and whispered something in her ear. All of the anger melted off her face, a half grin took its place. She tugged out her necklace from between her cleavage. The vial of black liquid attached sent a shiver through me. I took a few steps backward.

"I'll go!" I held up my hands. There was enough octopus ink inside to knock out every merman in Natatoria. "No need to use that."

"Darn right ya will." Badger hit me on the back and howled with laughter. "We got some stuff planned that'll put hair on yer chest!"

Afraid to ask what that meant, I was going whether I liked it or not. Poseidon, have mercy.

Then again, maybe the furniture delivery came at a good time. I could drive to Reno, find out where Ash's stalker was right now, then grind his face into the dirt… I mean, mind-wipe him.

"Hey, Jacob, you busy?"

He glanced over. "No."

My lip curled. "Wanna go hunting?"

He returned my smile. "You betcha."

"Just…" I said, eyeing his attire, or lack thereof. "Put on a shirt. Will ya?"

A scream came from somewhere inside the cottage. Jax, Jacob, Badger and I bolted to the front door just as a dark-haired mover tried to run out.

I latched onto his arm, smashing him into the side of the wall. "Where do you think you're going?"

"It's him!" Girra yelled out of breath. "The guy! The one who tried to take Ash!"

"Get your hands off me," he yelled.

I grabbed his collar and pressed him up against the siding, spotting the stitches just under his hairline.

"Explain yourself before I introduce you to the bottom of Lake Tahoe," I seethed.

The guy swallowed, sweat beading on his forehead. "I didn't. She lies—"

"Hey!" another mover yelled as he marched toward us. "What's going on here?"

"Shut yer gob and get back to work!" Badger sang, finger pointed at the truck.

The guy's expression relaxed into that of a zombie, and he turned and went back to the truck.

"It was him. I'd know that face anywhere," Girra raged.

"Talk!" I pressed my forearm harder against the guy's throat. "I swear to Poseidon if you don't tell me—"

"I don't know what you're talking about," he choked out.

"Does calling my wife a guppy ring any bells?" I reached for his phone attached to his belt with my free hand.

"Hey! What are you doing?" He tried to swing a punch at me.

I jumped back and sang, "Don't move."

He froze in place, arm outstretched in a weird angle. The tendons on his neck pulled taut as I retrieved the phone from his belt and touched the screen of his cell phone.

"What's the password?" I sang.

Powerless against my commands, he spouted out, "Superman."

I chuckled. "Figures."

Flipping through the texts, I found the ones to Ash and her friends. I turned the phone to his face, sticking it an inch away from his nose.

"Explain yourself, asshole!" I raged.

"You could do this easier with—" Jax started.

"Don't!" I warned.

I was done with persuading people. He'd tell me of his own accord or lose a testicle and remember every last detail of it.

His eyes widened. "I... I... I was just doing what I was told."

"And what was that?"

"To watch her... and..." He clamped his mouth shut.

I lifted my hand, then slowly balled my fingers while singing for him to stop breathing. His eyes started to dart around as his face reddened. Then he opened his mouth like a fish out of water, his jaw flapping.

"Uncomfortable, isn't it." I kept my glare trained on him while the others shuffled nervously around me.

Still stiff as a statue, the guy started to go limp, his lips turning blue, then purple.

"Fin," I heard Jacob say.

"You can breathe," I said, voice hard.

The guy pushed out a strangled breath. "What are you?"

"I'm your worst nightmare. Now tell me."

"Yes," he whimpered. "I was hired to do surveillance, and then try to kidnap Ash. I'm sorry. I'm *so* sorry."

My hackles rose, but I kept my cool. "By whom?"

"A company with the initials ARC. That's all I know." He grunted, still fighting the grip I'd sung on him.

ARC?

"And what have you told them?"

"That Ash is engaged to you. That you live here with your parents and sister, and Ash and her family are your neighbors. And you're planning to marry her this Saturday, here on the beach, which is ..." He stopped talking, and the curious crowd grew around us.

I leaned in. "Continue."

"No one in your family is on social media, but Ash, her sister, Lucy, and mother. And that Ash climbs out of her bedroom window every night and doesn't return until morning, and that your family and friends have come here daily for weeks now, without cars or any form of transportation. The house is big, but it's not finished, so you all can't be staying there, especially when after sunset, there's no noise, lights, or anything. Then I saw Jack on the beach with a big fish tail. I was able to get a picture of him. I sent it to all of Ash's friends to see their reaction. Most of them didn't believe it."

The crowd shifted around us, whispering their worries that our secret had gotten out, but I didn't care at this point. It would end here.

"How does ARC know about us?"

"Ash's blood test from her school."

"Her blood?" someone said softly.

My shoulders slunk. Her coach had said the test had gotten lost, and I'd been a fool to believe her. But I didn't think there would be anything odd in her blood, considering I'd healed her so long ago. "Is there anyone else working on this case?"

"Not that I know of."

I pressed him up against the wall again. "Take me to them."

"Aye," Badger said. "We'll teach 'em cute *hoors* a lesson."

The guy shuddered, face becoming pale. "I don't know where they are, man. Honest. They just drove up in a black sedan with tinted windows. Gave me a package with money, and keys to the van." He continued to shake. "Like I said, they offered me a deal I didn't think I could refuse."

I stepped forward, the song bursting off my tongue, "Go back and tell them that they are nothing but a bunch of—"

"Fin!" Dad yelled.

Badger put his hand on my shoulder. "I know you want to give 'em a kick in the bollocks, but ya need to think this through."

Dad pushed through the group of mer. "What's going on?"

I swiveled around and exploded. "This son of a bass is Ash's kidnapper! She's wanted for her blood!"

Dad's eyes widened. He turned to the crowd. "Okay… enough of this gawking. Everyone get back to work!" Once the crowd disbursed, he pulled me aside. "What do you think you're doing?"

"What you've been too busy to do." I jutted out my jaw.

Dad's face hardened. "You need to check yourself, Son."

"No, you do," I fumed. "You seem to think we're protected in this bubble you've created, but we're not. We're being watched and this is my wife we're talking about."

"And what did this spineless urchin get away with?" Dad asked exasperated. "Who did he hurt?"

"No one, because I'm handling it." I didn't want to mention Girra recognized him.

Dad gave me a glare, apparently warring with what to say next. "Can I suggest you do it away from prying eyes?"

My nostrils flared. Could he give me a freaking break? "I'm handling it."

The guy grunted, still frozen solid. "What are you going to do to me?"

"Aye, can I suggest ya tell this bloke to be leadin' his faceless cowards away from Ash," Badger said steadily. "That'll stop this."

Dad shook my head. "I think it's bigger than that."

"Let me handle it. It's my problem."

Dad lifted his hands. "Are you sure?"

"Yes!" I spat.

"Then be my guest."

I faced the abductor, tempted to tell him to go play on the freeway, but I knew they'd just send someone else in his place. I needed to find his boss and mind-wipe everyone at ARC. "Just forget everything that's happened here with the mer and don't ever come back again."

His eyes glazed over. "Okay."

"And if they contact you again, you get a name, and then come back and tell me. You got it?"

"I will," he said robotically.

"Now get out of here."

Once the song released him, he crumpled onto the porch. Then he bounded up and ran off, not looking back.

"Well, that's just great," Galadriel said from the doorway.

"Don't worry. We'll find this company," I said to her.

"No." She put her hand on her hip. "Now I'm down a mover."

Badger laughed, loosening the tension. "Aye. We've got ya covered, don't we boys? Let's show these movers what we're made of."

But I couldn't calm my mind down. This company knew all about my family, where we lived, about Ash's blood and our wedding. Would what I'd just sang to him be good enough? Or would they just send someone else. Ash could never be out of our sight.

"Wait," I barked, turning around. "No one breathes a word to Ash about this or Desirée, understood? No one! I'm not going to ruin her day."

Galadriel and the rest of the mermaids all nodded, eyes wide.

"You don't need to worry, Son." Badger clapped me on the back. "Nothin's getting by us."

"Okay," I said, hoping to get out of my bachelor party.

"But yer comin' tonight whether you like it or not."

I closed my eyes and sighed. "As long as Ash goes to Natatoria for the night."

"Yeah, sure." Galadriel popped her gum like what had just happened was nothing. "Now can we get back to work? I've got a lot to do."

I screwed up my face. "Yeah."

"Get to work!" she yelled.

The group snapped to and disbursed, under the command of her shrill voice. But I couldn't help but watch where the guy ran off to. He might not be back, but someone else would be. And when they did, we'd need to be ready.

33

ASH

June 6 – 4:32 p.m.

I tried to sit once more, as Tatchi grabbed my hand to lead me to the dance floor. "Oh, no you don't!"

I fought against her tight grip, watching the three G's laugh and spin in circles under the pulsing lights. Girra had Fin mer-mojo the club owner to let us in early, and we were the only ones here.

"I can't. I'm so tired," I begged.

Though it was the middle of the afternoon, all I wanted to do was sleep. I took off the plastic crown with pink feathers and leaned against the back of the booth. Little Joey chose to swim to the beat inside my tummy.

I rubbed my belly. The fact I'd be a mother very shortly felt so surreal. My eyes slid shut, and my mind wandered to little socks and baby powder.

Someone shook my arm moments later. "Wake up, Ash."

The house lights were on and the music had stopped. I yawned and straightened, confused what was happening. "Sorry."

"It's okay. We have to go." Georgia tugged my arm.

"Ice cream?" Girra asked, clearly not wanting this party to end.

My head bobbed automatically. I was always up for ice cream.

After getting giant cones at a shop just a short walk away from the club, we sat by a fountain on the patio and people-watched.

"Do you think they're in love, for like real?" Girra pointed to a couple holding hands.

Georgia turned to her, brow pinched. "Is there any other kind?"

"Well, the pro—" she started.

Galadriel coughed. "I think they're totally in love. Just look at them."

I nibbled on my Rocky Road, too tired to care that Girra had slipped. Another couple walked by and congratulated me. "Can't I take this crown and sash off yet?"

"No!" Girra pouted out her lip. "This is still part of the party."

Tatiana pulled out the layout of the wedding on a hand-drawn map. "Okay, so I need you to see this."

Tiny chairs were spread out like a fan, filling most of the beach. On the parking lot that would be covered in grass, were tables and chairs. Too many guests. How could we not think this would be a disaster?

"No wedding stuff," Girra demanded. "You promised."

"This is important. We need to get the ceremony down," Tatiana said to her.

My eyes, though, couldn't stop staring at the little black dots posted around the edges.

"What are those?"

Tatiana moistened her lips, her gaze flicking to Galadriel. "Overseers."

"Overseers?" I asked. "Why?"

"I think she means guards, and it's overkill if you ask me." Georgia smirked. "Those three are freaked we're going to have wedding crashers."

Girra, Galadriel, and Tatiana gave me fake smiles, but I knew why. They could have just said it was to keep Mr. White Van away from me. I straightened, so as not to show my concern as the near abduction replayed in my mind.

"Oh, that reminds me." Galadriel bent forward, taking off her necklace. "Here. I've been meaning to give you this."

On the end was a vial filled with black liquid. "What is it?"

She clasped it around my neck, then whispered. "It's octopus ink. It'll knock out a whole room of mermen. I always have it on me."

"Why?" I asked.

She put her hand on my shoulder. "You're still a princess. You can never be too careful."

A shiver wove its way through my stomach, jolting little Joey awake. Was this because we were going to Natatoria for the night? The horrific things Tatchi had told me she endured in Natatoria while promised to Azor tensed my shoulders. Was something happening that no one wanted to tell us about? If that was the case, I didn't want to stay there. Not without Fin.

"Thank you," I said, unsure what to say.

"What is that?" Georgia asked.

"A good luck charm." Galadriel winked. "So... enough wedding stuff. Let's talk about your gift to Fin."

I blew out a low breath. Between school, swimming, the merling, and the wedding, I'd completely forgotten.

"Well, I'm glad I brought this up," she finished.

"Is Fin getting me something?" I asked, unsure if I wanted to know the answer, terrified of the pressure to come up with something just as good.

Galadriel laughed. "Uh, yeah... the cottage, silly."

"Oh, that." I massaged my temples.

"But don't worry. I have something I know he wants," she said, eyes bright.

"You do?" I asked.

Guilt that my practically identical sister knew Fin better than I did hit me. She bit her lip, almost as if she was thinking of something kinky. I wanted to slug her considering my body was nowhere near sexy anymore and had started to resemble a growing blimp.

"His Jeep," she said in a hushed whisper.

My mouth fell open. I totally didn't expect her to say that with her look, but she was right. He'd been talking about missing his Jeep every time he drove my ratty car.

"But how would I get it here from Florida?" I asked.

"I made a call to Hans and Sissy, today. They're arranging transport. It's coming Friday night."

I blinked at her.

"Consider it an apology. For everything I put you guys through." A tear welled in her eye.

Without another thought, I stood and hugged my sister.

"Apology accepted." A tear slithered down my cheek.

"What happened? Why are they crying?" Georgia whispered to Girra.

Girra jumped up and hugged the two of us, then Tatiana. Georgia just sat dumbfounded. I grabbed her by the wrist, pulling her into the hug.

"I love you girls so much," I said. "Thank you for the wedding… the house… everything."

We all cried and hugged. In spite of everything, I had the best friends and family ever.

Returning to the house alone, I took off the sash and stuffed it in my purse. Once Lucy found out that she, the maid-of-honor, hadn't been invited to my bachelorette party, there'd be hell to pay. But I was glad she wasn't there. After having such a touching moment with my biological sisters over ice cream, I couldn't imagine what would've happened with her there spoiling it.

Glancing at the dock, I watched Tatiana, Girra, and Galadriel slip into the lake to return to Natatoria for the night. Though Fin had insisted I stay in the palace while he was gone, after Galadriel's little gift, I'd made the excuse that I was too tired to swim the distance. Considering I'd slept through most of the bachelorette party, they agreed to let me stay. What they didn't know was that I'd planned to spend the night alone in our pool.

But I had to go to my room first, then sneak out of my window. Thank Poseidon my stomach wasn't any bigger, or I'd have to lob myself out like a whale.

Mouthwatering smells of garlic, oregano, and basil hit me as I entered the house.

"There's the bride." Mom's fork clattered to her plate as she stood from the dinner table. "Let me warm up your plate."

I put down my purse on the sofa, careful to check and make sure the sash was well hidden before I sat down.

"Hello, dear," Gran said extra loud. "Have fun?"

Lucy looked up at me, and I braced myself for whatever vitriol she'd spew while Mom was out of hearing distance.

"What's with the crown?"

"Oh!" I pulled the crown off my head and set it on the floor. "Just something Georgia gave me. Spaghetti and meatballs, huh? I'm starved."

Lucy continued eating but watched me warily. The microwave dinged, signaling my food was heated.

"So, how'd the party go?" Mom handed me my plate before sitting down.

Ix-nay on the arty-pay, I wanted to say. Why couldn't mermaids have the power of mind-erasing song, too?

I stuffed a meatball in my mouth and lifted my pointer finger to signal I was chewing. Though I kept my eyes low, I could feel Lucy's eyes on me.

"What party?" she finally asked.

"The bachelorette," Mom said.

"In the middle of the afternoon?"

I wanted to sink into my seat.

"In my day, we only had wedding showers. None of the bachelorette business," Gran started.

My gaze went to Gran as I shoveled food into my mouth and listened to her story. My peripheral vision was tuned into Lucy.

"Where'd you go?" Mom asked.

"Uh… Déjà Vu." I put my fork down and braced myself for her tantrum. "Sorry, Lucy, it's an eighteen and older club, otherwise we would have invited you."

She crunched on her garlic bread and lifted her left shoulder. "No big."

I prepared my retort, until her response sideswiped me. No big? Gran continued to talk about clubs in her day, and how she'd been a singer in one once before she was twenty-one.

"You haven't told me this story," Mom said.

"I haven't? I'm sure I have."

I continued to eat, trying to listen, but was confused why Lucy wasn't making a bigger fuss. Maybe she didn't want to be involved just as much as I didn't want her there.

"And the girls' dresses are done. Wynie and Maggie finished them today. They're so gorgeous," Mom said proudly. "Lucy, would you mind trying yours on for Ash?"

"I'll take care of these," Gran snagged her plate and mine, taking them to the sink.

Lucy looked at me, and I expected her to make a face. Instead, she grinned, then stood and walked out of the room.

I splayed my hands on the table.

"Do you need help?" Mom asked her.

"I've got it." Lucy then disappeared upstairs.

Mom's eyes panned to me, then she shrugged. Yeah, I was just as shocked at Lucy's behavior, too, but didn't want to say anything to jinx it. What had gotten into her?

"Uh, Mom?" Lucy called down the stairs. "I do need help with the zipper."

Mom ran upstairs as I walked in the living room and within moments, Lucy walked down in a strapless, emerald ball gown, flowing and long, adorned with beads and sequins sewn along the top. The fabric along the bodice was folded and curved, resembling that of a rose bud.

I gasped, bringing my hand to my mouth. "Oh, my gosh. You're gorgeous."

Lucy turned around, smiling. "I think so, too."

My jaw dropped open. She actually liked the dress?

"The other girls' are a shade lighter, just to set off the maid of honor, and all," Mom said.

Lucy curtsied.

"Lovely, my dear. Just lovely," Gran said.

"I can't wait to wear it," Lucy finished. "But I should probably take it off so it doesn't get ruined."

"I'll help you."

Once Lucy and Mom left the room, I pressed a couch cushion to my mouth to exuberantly squeal. What had happened to change Lucy's attitude?

"It's going to be such a beautiful day," Gran said, startling me before she returned to the kitchen.

I jumped up and spun in a small circle, marveling at everything that had happened. This would be the wedding of my dreams. We'd done it. We'd integrated.

"I'm going to my room for the night," I said to Gran. "Goodnight."

"That's a good idea, dear." She walked over and kissed me on the forehead. "You need your beauty sleep."

I took the stairs by twos and rounded the corner to my room.

"Going to bed already?" Lucy came into the hall, back in her street clothes.

"Yeah. I'm kind of tired." I started to rub my stomach, then dropped my hands to my sides.

"You're not going to watch that zombie show with me?"

I opened my mouth, then closed it. She never asked to watch TV with me. "Maybe tomorrow."

"Okay."

I stared at her in shock as she walked into the bathroom and shut the door. Mom walked past, smiling and headed downstairs. So surreal. I returned to my room. Once closing my bedroom door, my phone started to ring.

"Hey, my Ginger Girl," he said. "We made it okay. How was your bachelorette party?"

"Fine." I could hear the guys making noise in the background along with waves.

"You going to be okay for the night?"

"Yeah." The bathroom door opened and Lucy started singing.

"The girls waiting for you?" he asked.

"Uh… yeah," I lied.

"Well, get outside. I'm not hanging up until you get to the water and go with the girls."

"Okay." I didn't want to tell him I'd changed my mind. "I have to change first."

"Put me on speaker and tell me everything you're doing." His voice grew husky.

My cheeks burned. "Fin! Stop it!"

He laughed. "No one is listening."

I heard Jax laugh in the background. Had they been drinking or something? "You like to do that to me, don't you?"

"It's adorable when you blush. But hurry. Badger is about to steal my phone and chuck it in the Pacific."

I quickly changed into a dark blue nightgown and opened my window. The evening breeze blew inside, pushing against the curtains. Scanning the parking lot and the street connecting our houses, I didn't spot Mr. White Van, thank Poseidon. I pocketed the phone and climbed onto the roof, then down the trellis.

I ducked as I passed the windows, hearing the TV show Lucy was watching, and headed to the dock. I probably could have watched it with her, considering we'd had at least an hour before sunset, but I didn't want to chance a fish-out.

"Okay. I'm here," I whispered. "Have fun."

"I love you, Ashlyn. Always remember that."

I swallowed my nerves of staying alone and lying to him. "I love you, too."

Then, he was gone.

I slid into the lake and headed toward the portal tunnel into our enclosed patio. Once inside, I locked the hatch behind me. White wicker chairs with cushions decorated the edges. I shifted into legs, then walked up to the sliding glass window to peek inside. A sheet hung across the doorway, blocking my view.

"You and your darn sheets," I mumbled.

I tried to slide the door open, finding it locked. Curiosity bloomed inside me anyway as I pressed my nose against the glass. Saturday just seemed like forever away.

I blew out a breath and flopped into the pool. Within a minute, I was restless and bored. We needed a TV in this room at least, or bar taps like his parents had and a refrigerator. Guilt that I didn't return to the palace instead with the others washed through me.

I lay on my back, counting the stars beyond the windows when I heard glass breaking. I popped my head up and held my breath.

The sheet shifted as if something hard had blown against it.

"Jack? Maggie?" I asked softly. "Is that you?"

A dark shadow drifted past the sheet, shooting panic into my limbs. I ducked down and pulled in a gulp of water. Someone was in the house.

My heart pounded in terror as I swam to the other side of the pool toward the hatch. My trembling fingers couldn't unlock it. I pressed my palms on the deck to lift myself out to get a better angle when a black gloved hand pulled back the sheet and clicked the lock open.

I slipped down into the water, and darted to the bottom of the pool, covering myself with the underwater blanket.

My hands shook, and I grabbed onto the vile of ink just in case. The silhouette of someone crossed over top—someone that resembled Mr. White Van.

A siren yelp escaped my lips, and I gripped my hand over my mouth to stop the noise. Bubbles wove their way to the surface instead. Whoever was up there, stopped and stared. Were they watching me?

My teeth started to chatter with fright, then my stomach clenched, sending horrible pain through me.

Whoever was there didn't do anything, just stood on the side of the pool, watching. I knew I'd be okay as long as I stayed down here, but their ever watchful presence creeped me out all the same. They could never get to me, let alone pull me to the surface. I'd drown them first.

Then some sort of liquid splashed into the pool.

"Here fishy fishy," a man's voice said.

Mr. White Van. My heart pounded harder as I waited. Then I smelled it. Chlorine.

The gel covers over my eyes started to burn at first, not bad, but just enough that it felt better to close them, and I wondered why this was the first time I'd had a reaction to chlorine. Was it because my gel eye lenses and gills hadn't made an appearance in the pool? Even still, I grabbed the blanket, and wove it around my neck, hoping to stop the chemicals from spilling into my lungs.

I sat, unmoving, for what seemed like forever, watching upward as the moon slowly crossed in the sky above. When I couldn't stand the pain anymore, I closed my eyes and waited, listening for what he had in store next. His footsteps could be heard shuffling about, echoing in the room above me. Did I dare try to make a swim for the hatch? How much chlorine did he bring?

After a few minutes, my gills began to burn. I glared at the shadow up above as visions of me leaping out, digging my claws into my assailant's neck, and pulling him underwater gripped me.

I'd risk my life for our child. I'd do anything.

34

FIN

June 7 – 8:02 a.m.

I drove Dad's Yukon up and over the ridge, completely exhausted. The guys crawled out and took the ice chests filled with tuna to the houseboat, spoils for tonight's feast.

"I'm starved," Jax said.

"Me, too," Jacob added.

Though I could use some food, too, I wanted to check in with Ash. She hadn't yet called this morning, meaning she most likely had taken her time to get back from Natatoria. Then I wanted to take a quick nap before finishing Galadriel's to-do list for the cottage.

"Hey, Dad." I waved. "Are the girls here yet?"

He stood on a ladder, painting the trim of the house. "I think they just left to go shopping."

"With Ash?"

He shrugged. "I don't know."

My gaze swung to the cottage. She better not have spoiled her surprise, or else. I ran over, unlocked the door and walked inside to make sure. New furniture and draperies greeted me, making me excited to share it with her. Home. Our home.

Walking across the tiled kitchen floor, I stopped at the sheet and noticed it was stuck in the door jam. Placing a call to Ash on her cell once again, I unlocked the slider. The sound of a phone ringing came from the patio.

I pulled the slider open the entire way. "Ash? Are you in here?"

Walking to the pool, I peered down into the water. A redhead was curled up on the floor in the corner in a fetal position. I dove in and my legs snapped together, the bones crunching into place, and swam down to her. Knowing her body was busy making our baby, I didn't want to wake her if she was just taking a nap. But she wasn't sleeping. Her hands were clenched firmly around her fin tightly, her body shaking.

"Ash?" I swam next to her, concerned at first, then alarmed. "Ash! What's wrong?"

She lifted her hand and flashed the vial of octopus ink.

"Stay back!" she hissed.

I sculled backward. "It's me, Ash. It's Fin!"

She blinked as if to clear her eyes, then dashed for me and latched her arms around my neck, holding on tight. "Don't leave me."

"What's wrong?" I wove my arms around her and rubbed her back. Her body shook from her accelerated heartbeat.

"He… he-e-e," she stuttered.

I caressed her cheek, lifting her head so I could see her eyes. "He what?"

"Wa-a-a-a-s here-e-e-e," she finished, her voice almost sirening.

"Who?"

"Mr. White Van!"

I pulled my head backward, unbelieving what she was saying. "Who?"

"Th-h-h-h-e guy who-o-o tried to-o-o-o take me."

The water next to my scales bubbled from the heat radiating off of me. How could that be? I'd mind-wiped his sorry ass just yesterday.

"He was pouring chlorine into the water," she spluttered out. "Burning me."

"Chlorine?"

"Up above." She stabbed a shaky forefinger upward.

I sniffed the salty water. "Ash, there's no chlorine."

Had she been hallucinating?

She detached herself from me, eyes wild. "Are you calling me a liar?"

"No." I reached for her. "Let's get you out of here."

"He's there... up there. Watching."

I looked upward, only seeing the sun filtering down through the evergreens. "He's not in the house now. I just checked."

Her breaths pulled through her gills in rapid succession, somewhat disjointed. She latched onto me again and buried her face in my neck. With a pump of my tail, I surfaced.

"No one is here but us. I promise you."

With a little coaxing, she finally looked, her frantic gaze darting around the patio room. "He was here. He broke a window when he came inside. He unlocked the slider, and then found me."

The slider door had the sheet tucked inside, but I didn't notice any broken glass. Maybe I didn't look hard enough. I smoothed her wet hair. "Okay. Let's just get you out of the water."

Lifting her to sit on the side of the pool, she remained clamped onto my arm.

"Listen to me, Ash," I said firmly. "I think you just had a bad dream."

Her eyes grew wide. "What?"

"I didn't tell you, but I ran into him yesterday, and wiped his memories. He couldn't have possibly been here yesterday," *or so help him.*

She shivered none the less. "You did?"

"Yeah."

She blinked at me, tears streaming down her face. "I imagined it?"

"I think so. Probably all the stress." I ran my hands down her arms, heating her skin with mine. Why didn't she stay in Natatoria like planned? The girls had some explaining to do. "But I'll double check the house if that'll make you feel better."

She grabbed onto my wrists. "No. Don't leave me."

"Okay." I pulled her into my arms and rocked her until she stopped shaking. "I promise you. I'm not going to leave you, Ash. Never again."

"Okay," she said, whimpering.

"No one is going to hurt you."

She snuggled her head into my neck, and within moments she was asleep. I pulled her underwater with me and sunk to the bottom, prepared to push everything off our to-do lists and just rest.

35

ASH

June 10 – 1:02 p.m.

The next few days flew by, and before I knew it, Friday had arrived. Tatiana and the girls had outdone themselves. The entire area for the wedding and reception had been encircled with a rod iron fence, decorated with green ribbons, white flowers strewn on wire, and tulle. At the junctions were tall stanchions with hooks on the top for the lanterns.

White chairs lined the beach, facing an arch covered in white and pink flowers and garlands mixed with deep green ferns. Strands of beads, decorated with shells and starfish lined the chairs next to the aisle. The tables for the reception held large glass vases filled with flowers, ferns and willowy branches that dangled starfish ornaments. Even the walkway leading from my parents' house to the back of the aisle had arches covered in flowers and tulle.

My heart pounded in anticipation of tomorrow, of everyone sitting in those seats watching us commit our lives to one another. In twenty-four hours, I'd be Mrs. Finley Helton.

"What do you think?" Dad asked, eyes shining.

"It's everything I've ever dreamed it would be."

He squeezed my arm tight. "Good, pumpkin."

"Cue the music!" Tatiana commanded while clapping. "Let's get this thing started!"

Nicole toddled around her feet, wearing a deep green tulle skirt. She'd already dumped over her basket of flower petals twice before even having a chance to walk the aisle.

"Cannon in D" by Pachelbel started, but through the wall of flowers, I could barely see anything. Fin was supposed to be seating his mother while Jax seated mine. Tatiana paced behind the wall that blocked my view of the audience, then turned and motioned to us. "Now you come!"

Dad looked at me. "You ready for this?"

I could barely contain the butterflies in my stomach from flying free. "As ready as I'll ever be."

He batted a tear off his cheek, then squeezed my arm tight with his. "Let's go, pumpkin."

We walked together down the tiny walkway, hidden behind a wall of flowers and fabric, spanning between my parents' porch to the back of the aisle. If the little cobblestones under my feet could talk, they'd tell a story of my life. Of memories of me learning to walk, of learning to run, of bare feet and booted feet. Of snow and rain, of lost and found treasures. Of being a vast world for my dolls to live. Of holding secret hidden spots for hide and seek. Of providing a path to a beach where I got lost in another world with my book in hand. Of fast friendships and secret crushes. Of a place where I discovered the mer for the first time. And when I thought those days were over, today symbolized dreams had become anew, that this would be where our child would play, too.

"Once the ceremony is over, we'll take that down." Tatiana pointed to the fabric billowing in the wind, snapping me from my thoughts.

"Girra. Go."

One by one, the bridesmaids followed behind Girra. Lucy looked back at me, her eyes twinkling. I couldn't believe after everything, we were getting along. Tatiana walked down with Nicole, and I peeked around the corner to see. Nicole reached for a hanging starfish on the garland.

"Come on, baby," Tatiana prodded, pulling her from her treasure.

Nicole let out a wail, threw down her basket, and plopped on her butt in the middle of the aisle, kicking and screaming. Then she shifted into a mermaid. Jacob dashed over, scooped up the merling, and darted toward the houseboat.

I bit my lip, hoping Tatiana would just concede and let Pearl keep her during the ceremony instead of forcing a child too young to participate. Lucy reached out and squeezed my hand. "It'll be okay tomorrow. Just you wait."

Then she let go and walked down the aisle, a little quicker than she should, but happy nonetheless. She stood next to Oberon and smiled. I couldn't help the tears from falling. Everything had come into place.

Then a piano rendition of the "Bridal March" began. My heart leaped into my throat just as Dad took charge and started ahead. We cleared the wall and the few sitting in the audience stood.

Fin's eyes met mine, an azure blue glistening in the sun, and then he smiled, that smile I adored when he drove his Jeep over the ridge. My dreams had come true. And we'd done it. We were finally getting married on land under the evergreens.

Dad continued to walk me down the aisle, and I couldn't stop my happiness from flowing down my cheeks. Once we arrived at the front, Dad stopped and Mom took up my other side.

"Who gives this woman to this man?" Oberon asked.

"Her mother and I."

Mom sniffled and squeezed my hand before she took her seat next to my father. I glanced back and spotted Desirée sitting on the groom's side, close to the wall of white fabric. A pang of regret stabbed my stomach as she smiled at me. I hadn't expected her to be here, but then again, she was family and her daughters, my sisters, were in the wedding, why wouldn't she?

Then I thought of the veil I'd wear tomorrow. I needed to mojo mom and Lucy so I could wear Desirée's crown instead. Maybe that would be enough.

Oberon placed my hand in Fin's. "This is the part where I greet the audience," he said with a kind smile. "And then we'll have a song by the boys' choir."

Ten boys filed in, all dressed in kilts. We turned and listened to them sing the Natatorian anthem. At the end, Badger belted the song along with them, until Sandy, his wife, gave him a glare from the audience. He cleared his throat. "My apologies."

Oberon explained what he'd say, and then he gestured to Fin. "And this is the part where I tell you to kiss your maid… er, I mean, wife."

Fin gave me a wicked look, then dipped me backward before he kissed me. My cheeks burned red hot, but I accepted the sweetness of his lips anyway.

The "Hallelujah Chorus" started to play, and I gave Tatiana a fiendish look. This wasn't the song we'd chosen. She shrugged with a coy smile. After everything, though, it seemed apropos.

"By the power bestowed upon me by Chancellor Merric—"

"He's dead!" someone yelled from the water.

The music stopped abruptly.

"What son?" Oberon asked.

"The Chancellor is dead! Regent, come quickly!"

Desirée stood, marched down the aisle, and waded into the water.

"Dead?" I gripped tightly onto Fin. "How?"

My Dad's face paled. "Why was that boy swimming? And where did Desirée go? It's freezing in the lake."

"You didn't see that," Fin sang to Lucy, Georgia and my parents. My dad sat down and joined my bewildered Mom.

Jack crossed over to us. "I'll see what's going on. Badger, take care of things here."

"Aye, Captain," Badger said. "Let's be finishing this up. Oberon?" He gestured to the officiant.

"Yes." Oberon cleared his throat. "By the power bestowed upon me by Chancellor Merr—uh, Regent Desirée, I now pronounce to you, Mr. and Mrs. Finley Samuel Helton."

My parents stood and clapped exuberantly while the rest of the audience sat somewhat still. Fin and I strolled down the aisle, but I no longer felt like celebrating. Would the mers even come tomorrow? Merric, though technically not the king any longer because of the new laws, was just as loved and adored.

"Who's Merric?" Lucy asked.

"He's a friend of the family," Girra said behind me.

"Yeah."

"Oh. I'm sorry," Lucy said.

I eyed her suspiciously. This was not the Lucy that I knew at all. Then it clicked what had changed. My glare landed on Fin. He'd done what I asked him not to do, and he was going to get it.

36

FIN

June 10 – 1:42 p.m.

Ash grabbed me by the arm and pulled me off to the side.

Her nostrils flared. "Did you sing to her?"

My heart galloped. "What?"

"Lucy. She's been *nice*, ever since… graduation." She leaned in, her fists balled at her sides. "Did you sing to her or not? Answer me."

I ran my hand through my hair, caught. "I just told her to knock off the attitude, either that or…" *I was going to slap her across the face.* "I mean… she's your sister, and this is a special day for you."

"Not by blood, she's not." Ash hardened her jaw. Then her eyes flashed with horror. She stepped back, almost knocking over the fabric wall. "You sang to my mother, didn't you?" Her voice raised an octave. "Didn't you?"

"Ash." I took her arm gently, but she yanked it away.

"Answer me!"

"I might have…" I grunted, fumbling for what to say. This was horrible and she was going to hate me. "Let's go talk somewhere *private*."

Her body shook with anger. "No. You will tell me now!"

"I asked her to be… cordial."

"Cordial?" Her eyes widened, filling with tears. "You mean this whole time, she's been persuaded?"

I opened his mouth, but nothing came out.

"I'm marrying a liar!" she yelled.

"Ash. Come on." I moved forward to touch her, wishing I could sing this away instead.

"No!" She put up her hands, and when I fought to touch her, she batted me away. "I don't want anything to do with this. With you! Leave me alone!"

Horror flooded through me. Was she calling things off? "Ash, please."

She turned to run and slipped on the path. I moved to catch her but missed her arm. She collapsed to the ground, landing on her hip. She rolled onto her butt, then grabbed her stomach, moaning. I tried to pick her up.

"Stop it!" She slugged me in the arm, then curled up on the walkway, sobbing. "Go away."

"Ash." I knelt down to help her up, wanting her to stand because she was exposing her underwear. "I wasn't trying to lie to you... I just wanted to help. I'm sorry."

I'm so *so* sorry.

She just sat there crying and shaking her head, mumbling something I couldn't decipher. I wanted to fix it, but I didn't know how.

"What's going on here?" Tatiana came around the wall. "Oh, my starfish! Ash! Are you hurt?"

"No." She dusted off her bloody knee that had started to heal. "I'm fine. I just want to be alone."

Tatiana leaned over and pulled Ash to her feet.

"Ash." My voice sounded breathless like I'd been punched in the gut. "I'm sorry."

"What did you do now?" Tatiana seethed through her teeth.

"It's not his fault." Ash lifted her chin, her gaze not looking at me. "I just need a minute."

"Ash, honey?" her mother asked as she made her way up the path.

"I heard you yell. Are you—Oh, my heavens. You're bleeding!"

"I'm fine." She pressed past all of us and marched down to our designated table sitting on the lawn, her mother following behind.

I watched them stride off, then glanced at Tatiana.

"Don't look at me," she snapped. "If you screwed this up, so help me, I'll knock your barnacles into next week. I swear it!"

"I… just…"

With a snide tone, she said, "You will go down there, and you will make her happy! Got it, limpet breath? I didn't do all of this for you to screw it up!"

I startled. She hadn't called me that since we were kids, but I knew she was right. "I will."

She stormed off toward the party, but I couldn't shake the pit filling my gut. I pulled in a breath and joined Ash at our table.

She sat rigid, hands folded in front of her. Smells of freshly baked tuna that we'd caught made my stomach rumble. And though I needed to eat, if Ash hadn't planned to, neither would I.

"Here," Tatiana brought a plate of food and set it before Ash. "You should eat."

"I'm not hungry," she said sharply.

Tatiana's face grew wary. "Okay, well…" Her glare cut to me. If we were underwater, she would have chewed me out via mind-talking. "Tell me if you need anything, okay?"

"I'm fine," Ash said, short.

The smells of her food made my mouth water. My nerves earlier had taken my appetite, and now I was starved. I leaned back and tried not to think about my stomach aching.

Our family milled about us, eating and drinking, but as witnesses to our fight, they steered clear of us. News of Merric's death didn't help matters either. With the somber mood, I didn't see anyone sticking around long. Even still, I just wanted this fight over with already.

I reached over to take her hand. She jerked away and deadpanned.

"What?" I asked.

She turned to stare straight ahead again, her expression emotionless.

"Are you going to ignore me all evening?"

She sighed, but remained quiet, technically answering my question.

"I'm sorry," I mumbled. "What do I have to do to fix this?"

Her glare landed on me and she threw her napkin on the table, then got up and stormed off.

Everyone's gaze followed her stiff jaunt across the lawn, then panned to me. Unable to hide, I rubbed the back of my neck, then just took Ash's plate and dug in.

"Fin?" Mom approached. "What's going on here?"

"Isn't it obvious? They're fighting." Galadriel walked by, stuffing a piece of cake in her mouth. "Aren't we going to dance? Where's the DJ?"

"Merric died! Don't you have any respect?" I snapped.

"*Pssht!* Your barnacles are in a bunch."

"Galadriel, could you give us a moment?" Mom asked far sweeter than she deserved.

"By all means." She gave a curt smile and headed to the DJ station.

Mom took Ash's seat next to me and the music started. "Trouble in paradise?"

I shrugged, unsure how to respond.

"What is going on?"

"I don't know anymore. Ash wanted this wedding. She wanted everyone to be here, but yet, she didn't want me to sing to anyone." I let out huff. "That's nearly impossible."

"I'm confused… you mean the messenger that just showed?"

"No." I turned to her, speaking a little louder than I should. "Her mother."

Mom's eyes widened. "Oh."

"On any given day she can be a royal pain in the anal fin," I whisper-yelled, trying not to cuss.

Mom gave me a harsh look to keep my voice down and leaned in whispering. "Who Desirée?"

"No, Karen," I said through my teeth. "You didn't know her before."

"And what did you tell her?"

"Just to be cordial. That's all."

Mom stared at me pensively for a moment. Then she put her arm around my shoulder. "Listen, Fin. The song manipulates people, yes, but unless you've been singing every decision Karen has made regarding Ash, you haven't been manipulating her. Yes, asking someone to be cordial can definitely change someone's attitude, but it won't stick around unless that's already inside a person. Women have a lot of… hormonal issues, especially ones that are Ash's mother's age."

"You're blaming this on hormones?"

Mom chuckled. "No. I'm just saying that Karen most likely wanted to be happy for her daughter, but couldn't for whatever reason—responsibility, stress, the fact you two are very young. That all plays into it."

"So you're saying she is acting like who she wants to be, but couldn't before," I said.

"Yes."

I paused, letting her words sink in. "So I didn't manipulate her?"

"I think what you did was set her free," Mom suggested.

My gaze panned to Ash's parents dancing in the middle of the floor, happy and in love. Then I found Ash sitting alone on our bench by her parents' dock, her back to me. "I think she wants to be alone."

"No girl wants to be alone. I think she wants to know her mother loves her and all of this has been real. But maybe right now, this isn't something to fix. Just listen."

Telling a guy not to fix something was like asking him not to breathe. But at this point, I would try anything. "Okay."

"Good." Mom smiled. "'Cause this is the 'for better or for worse' part of a relationship."

"I know."

"And I'm going to tell you what my mother told me. Never go to bed angry."

My eyes slid shut. Getting Ash to not be angry at me seemed impossible, but I was willing to try. "Okay."

"And remember she's dealing with a lot of hormones herself. I had terrible nightmares when I was pregnant with you two."

My head swung around to meet her gaze. "Nightmares?"

"Vivid ones where people were hunting me down, trying to take me," she said. "I couldn't tell what was real sometimes. I almost drove your father nuts."

That confirmed what I thought happened to her earlier this week. "Thanks for the advice."

Mom's face brightened. "Good. Now go talk to your girl. You've got a big day tomorrow!"

I jumped up and jogged across the lawn. Slowing my pace as I approached. With caution, I stood beside her. "This seat taken?"

She looked up at me, and shrugged, cheeks stained with tears. This was going to be one tough unfixable clam.

I sat next to her. "I understand if you're mad at me."

"I'm not mad." She crossed her arms.

Okay.

"Do you want to talk about it?" I asked specifically from my mother's advice.

"No," she said, clipped, and crossed her legs.

Fighting the urge to get up and leave, I just sat there, waiting. Mom said not to fix it, so I wouldn't.

Her wrap-around skirt parted ever so slightly, revealing the faint scar on her leg from when she'd fallen off the boat.

Not thinking, I reached over and traced the line. "I fixed that. Right here. Remember?"

Her skin broke out in goosebumps. "Yeah."

"Feels like a lifetime ago, doesn't it?"

"Yeah."

The silence ticked on, slowly passing. When I didn't think I could take another moment, she leaned against my shoulder.

"I don't know why this bothers me so much," she confessed. Though tempted to tell her that she should brush it off, I kept my mouth shut. "It's just so disgusting you had to persuade my own mother to get her to be civil. Desirée should have the place of honor tomorrow, not her. I think you should sing her out of the wedding."

My jaw dropped at how much this hurt her. "Ash, I just told her to be kind. Everything else she did after that point was her choice."

"Yeah, right."

"No." I hooked my finger under her jaw and lifted so she'd look at me. "Singing changes memories, yes, but if I sang to this whole world to be kind, it would last for their next decision, then they'd relapse into whoever they were."

"But Lucy is being kind, too, and we both know she has a black heart."

I shrugged. "Maybe that's not who she wants to be."

She moved her chin from my fingertip. "Yeah, maybe. I don't get why it bothers me so much. Why I feel like I need to earn their love."

"They both love you," I said.

"Do they? It feels forced."

"Well, I can persuade your mother and sister to be mean, if you want."

"No… don't do that." She sniffled. "I like them like this. Maybe I just feel guilty."

I put my arm around her shoulder and squeezed gently, tempted to tell her I'd sing whatever she wanted me to. But didn't. Her body grew limp like she was giving up the battle.

"Maybe she'll surprise you," I said.

She let out a long sigh. "Maybe."

"Are you still going to walk down the aisle to me?"

Her face puckered in that cute little way I adored. "Of course I am."

"Good, 'cause I was worried there for a minute. Besides, I didn't want to live in our house all alone."

"Oh, Fin." She wrapped her arms around my torso and squeezed. "I'm sorry I've been so emotional."

I smoothed her hair. "Don't worry about it. This was my fault. I should have told you sooner."

"Actually." She looked up at me and pulled her bottom lip between her teeth. For a second I wanted to ravage those lips. "I have something to show you."

I straightened, worried for a second.

"No, it's a good thing." She jumped up and pulled my hand, leading me toward her parents' garage, and I wondered what she wanted to show me.

37

ASH

June 11 – 12:45 p.m.

I sat at my makeup table in my bedroom, staring at my kangaroo, knowing this room would no longer be mine. That my single life was no more. That from now on I'd be known as Fin's wife, partner, soulmate.

"Alright. Let me have your ring." Tatiana stood behind me, looking at my reflection in the mirror. She wore her blonde hair pinned in endless curls with beads and pearls woven throughout. Her green gown accentuated her lithe frame.

I pulled off the diamond ring and handed it to her. "Great. And a ring for Fin?"

"Yeah, it's right here." I opened my jewelry box and the ballerina started to twirl to "Für Elise". Something about the song made me think my life was ending somehow. I snapped it shut and handed her Grandpa Frank's ring.

"I need to go and get everything started. Are you going to be okay?"

I bit my lip, the tears welling in my eyes. "Yeah."

"Don't do that," she said sharply with a fierce point. "Or I'll start crying, too."

"I'm not crying." I pinched my lips together, swiping a finger under my eyes. We looked at one another, then embraced. "Thank you, Tatchi. For everything."

"Of course." She pulled away and put out her pinkie. "Best friends forever, right?"

I hooked my pinkie around hers and squeezed. "Forever."

"Okay. You have about twenty minutes. And then I need you and your Dad on that porch. You hear me?"

"Loud and clear." I saluted since she'd repeated this drill several times now.

Her eyes tightened on me, but I knew she was playing. "He's waiting for you downstairs."

"Okay, okay." I shooed her out the door anxious for a minute alone. "Go already."

She gave me one last up and down glance to make sure everything was in place. "Veil!"

"I got it… I got it."

She gave me a thumbs up. "Alright. Let's do this!"

I smiled, then heard the door click shut. My gaze drifted to my reflection, and I smoothed my hands over my bump. It had become so much more pronounced the past few days, but Seamstress Wynie had done an excellent job making the skirt appear fuller all the way around to hide it.

The merling kicked, and my heart thumped harder. "You ready, Joey?" I asked my stomach. "Let's go see Daddy."

For the last hour, a steady stream of mers had continued to flow out of the Helton's front door. Most of them had taken their seats—a sea of multicolored fabrics undulated in the wind. I was surprised that even in the wake of Merric's death, they showed. My eyes zeroed in on Fin in his tux, standing on his parents' dock, watching, waiting. My heart squeezed, knowing I was cheating in this moment. How I loved him.

His Jeep, now decorated with crepe paper, and a "just married" sign was parked in front of our cottage. His excitement yesterday, after I'd revealed its hiding place in my parents' garage, made me able to forgive him and smile again. It had been the perfect wedding gift.

A giant red ribbon encircled the cottage beyond with a bow on the front door. After the reception, Fin planned to carry me over the threshold, and I couldn't wait.

"You ready?" Lucy popped her head in my room.

"Oh, yes."

"Mom thought you might need this."

She handed me a glass of what looked like orange juice. My mouth watered as I took it from her. "Really? Thank you!"

"She said it would give you that extra oomph of blood sugar so you don't pass out during the ceremony."

I smiled. Mom knew me so well. Maybe Fin was right, that his request just brought out the good inside her. I took a sip, tasting something creamy and sweet mixed inside. "Ooh, it's good. Want a taste?"

Lucy lifted her hands. "No. I already had some. I guess it's her secret recipe."

"It's yummy. I'll have to ask her for it." I handed her the empty glass. "Could you help me?"

I walked over and pulled Desirée's crown from the closet, then handed it to her. "Put this on me?"

Her eyebrows pulled together momentarily.

"What?" I asked, panicked. Had Fin already unmind-mojoed her?

"Nothing. It's gorgeous."

She fastened the crown on my head and positioned the strings of gems in the back.

I took her hand. "Thank you," I said, squeezing. "This has been the best week of my life. I'm so glad we've bonded."

"Me, too." She smiled, but it didn't seem as warm as it had the past week. Maybe Fin did unmojo her.

"After you." She held her hand out. Her eyes twinkled with excitement, and I couldn't believe the day had finally come.

I walked to the stairs, heart pounding, and felt a dizzy spell hit. Grabbing onto the banister, I waited for it to pass before continuing down. My ankles, wobbly in my heels, didn't help matters, but all I wanted was for this moment, this grand entrance with my father, the one we'd talked about ever since I was a little girl.

I cleared the middle of the stairs and looked around the empty living area, but it was empty.

"Dad?" I asked.

A man with a white beard walked around the corner and my heart nearly stopped. "Well, aren't you lovely," Alaster said, eyeing me up and down.

A shriek escaped my lips as I gripped onto the banister, then turned and tried to run back upstairs. Lucy stood in my way.

I pressed into her. "Lucy, it's a trap. You have to run. Hurry," I whisper-yelled.

She put her hands on her hips and let out a long sigh.

"Come on! move it! I'm not kidding."

"Neither am I." She smirked. "I've had to be nice to you this entire time. So disgusting."

"Nice to me?"

"You and all your mer friends." She reached out and grabbed ahold of my arm, pinching. "Get downstairs."

"What?" I pulled my arm away from her and reached for the chain at my neck that held the octopus ink, remembering I'd put it in my jewelry box. It didn't matter anyway, since she was human and not a male. What I needed was the pepper spray tucked away in my purse.

I elbowed Lucy in the side and edged my way past her. She let out a groan behind me as I stepped into the hallway. If I could get to my window and scream for help, maybe. Then suddenly, I was yanked backward by the skirt of my dress. I fell onto the floor as something ripped at my waistline. My fingers broke open with talons, and I clawed my way across the carpet.

A guy grunted behind me, as someone held onto my dress. Then hands latched onto my ankle, and I kicked.

Pulling harder, I tried not to think about all the hard work Seamstress Wynie had done, as my skirt tore free from my bodice. I crawled forward, finally making it to my room when hands cinched around my waist.

"Oh no you don't, Princess."

I screamed, flailing my arms, but they suddenly felt like strings. His rough hands flipped me over onto my back. Mr. White Van leered down at me with a sick and twisted smile, then his face blurred and weaved around in my vision.

"Just hold still, Princess," he said with excitement. "It'll all be over soon."

I fought to keep my eyes open, but no matter what I did, I couldn't. Then, I felt myself being lifted, and I floated off into nothingness.

38

FIN

June 11 – 12:55 p.m.

My heart pounded in anticipation as I waited on the dock for things to start. Mer after mer had poured in from my parents' house, bright-eyed and smiling, like our wedding was the perfect distraction after Merric's death.

"You look great, Son." Mom kissed each cheek.

Dad stood alongside her. "We're so happy to add Ash to our family today. I'm proud of all your hard work with the cottage and handling the situation."

"Thanks, Dad." I grinned, but I hadn't exactly handled everything with ARC, though we'd been on the lookout.

I couldn't stop my nerves, though. How was Ash handling all of this? Badger had taken my phone when I tried to call her earlier, and threatened to throw it in the lake.

"That's cheatin'," he'd told me.

I thought of last night, and how she'd surprised me with the Jeep. We, of course, had planned to wait until tonight to celebrate, but with the fight and the stolen moment alone, we didn't have much self-control.

After that, Ash, Tatiana, Girra, and Galadriel stayed in the basement pool of my parents' house as a final hurrah. I stayed in the lake—my last night having to sleep alone. I couldn't wait until the moment I carried Ash over the threshold of our new home. So much love would be shared there, especially after our child was born.

Tatiana bustled over in her green dress, her hair a mess of jewelry and pearls. "You ready?"

"Ready as I'll ever be."

"Good." She glanced up at Ash's house, but with a floral barrier, neither of us could see the porch.

"I'm going to have them start the music. You seat the parents, then do as we practiced yesterday, okay?"

I nodded and followed her around the back of the audience. Once the music started, my nerves went into full gear. If only my Ginger Girl were here, then I knew they would fade. I just had to see her green eyes shining at me.

I proffered my arm, and Mom took it, clasping her hands around mine. "You'll do fine."

"I know."

My feet felt like they barely touched the sand as I walked my mother down the aisle. All eyes were on me—hundreds of pairs, not only anxiously awaiting the ceremony, but curious to see what life was like interacting in the human world. Today marked a momentous feat—that we'd done so, and may others could join in and enjoy the same privileges.

Once Jax seated Ash's mother and we took center stage, the audience turned. Girra started first, followed by Galadriel, then Georgia. After the fiasco with Nicole yesterday, Tatiana decided against her attending, and she walked down alone—eyes trained on Jacob. Lucy appeared at the back of the audience, a catlike smile on her face. Once she made it to the front with the rest of us, the music changed and my heart began to pound.

I held my breath and waited, watching to capture this moment in my mind forever. But Ash didn't appear. After ten long seconds passed, she still didn't appear.

"Where is she?" I heard Tatiana say between her teeth.

"She was right behind me," Lucy said softly, lips unmoving. "I don't know."

After thirty seconds, Tatiana left her spot and rushed down the aisle. The audience broke out in a hush of whispers, then I heard my sister gasp. The top of her blonde head bobbed along the walkway, headed toward the house. She threw open the front door, calling Ash's name.

The DJ stopped the music, and the audience's voices grew louder. Some stood to try and see over the fabric wall.

"Stay seated," Oberon said calmly. "We'll start the ceremony in a few moments." He leaned in and whispered to me. "Go find your bride."

I walked firmly down the aisle, terrified she'd gotten cold feet or was mad at me again, and then marched up the walkway to the Lanski's house.

"Fin," Dad called behind me. "What's going on?"

I quickly glanced over my shoulder before heading inside. "I don't know."

Tatiana came down the stairs toward me. "She's not here!"

"Where is she?" I looked around the living room and spotted the sliding glass door open. Behind the kitchen table, Bill was lying passed out on the floor.

I quickly checked that he had a pulse, then ran onto the back porch, and scanned the side yard, not seeing anything. "Ash?"

"What happened?" Bill groaned.

"We were hoping you'd be able to tell us," Dad said.

The entire wedding party flooded into the tiny living space, everyone but Lucy.

"What's going on, Fin?" Galadriel asked.

"Ash isn't here." I pushed past everyone to find the person who saw her last.

Audience members were now standing, and milling about the beach and walkway, asking questions. Ash's sister stood off to the side, watching with a smirk on her face.

"Where is she?" I sang to her.

Lucy blinked at me, but her eyes didn't lose its normal clarity like it should have with the song. "I don't know."

"You were with her last."

"Maybe she didn't want to marry you."

My hand formed into a fist. Who had mer-mojoed her back into her snarky self? Then the horror hit, and I grabbed her hand to confirm she didn't have the promising tattoo, not finding anything.

She yanked her hand away. "I beg your pardon."

Then her eyes lifted, finding someone in the audience.

I turned to see where her gaze landed, spotting Colin. He cocked his head to the side, his lips holding a knowing sneer. I charged him and pummeled my fist into his jaw. We collapsed into a group of guests. Garnet shrieked, screaming for her mother, as Lucy screeched behind me to stop.

Blood spewed from Colin's split lip. The women nearby started to squawk, backing away. Colin picked himself up and prepared himself to hit me when I grabbed his collar. "Where is she?"

"How the heck am I supposed to know?"

"Out of my way!" Desirée barked. The sea of mers parted. "What is going on here?"

"Ash is missing," I said, dropping Colin and straightening my jacket. "And he did something to Lucy to cover it up."

"I did not!"

Desirée lifted her chin. "Or maybe she's changed her mind."

I curled my fingers into a fist, not caring that she was the Chancellor pro-tem until the people had a chance to vote, or not. "She didn't."

"Silence!" Desirée barked, and the mers around us stopped talking. "I can't hear myself think. Now, Finley, why do you suspect Colin has something to do with this?"

I clenched my jaw. Blaming Colin was far easier than telling Desirée Ash's life had been threatened by the ARC, especially after we'd sworn over and over that we had control of our secret on land.

"Because Colin took Lucy aside and sang Poseidon knows what at the graduation party."

"Son." Dad came up behind me and put his arm on my shoulder. "Let's talk."

"What is the meaning of this?" Desirée asked him.

"Fin!" Tatiana ran up to me crying. In her hand was a bunch of white fabric. "It's the skirt from Ash's dress. I found it in the closet. It's been completely ripped off! She's been kidnapped!"

"Jacob! Jax!" I called, pulling out my keys. "Let's go!"

We tore through the audience, as Desirée commanded me to stop, but I ran up the hill toward the Jeep anyway. After yanking off the sign on the back, I jumped into the driver's seat. Jax and Jacob climbed into the back.

"Fin!" Dad called, running up the hill. "Wait. We need to regroup. Figure out—"

I tore out of my spot. "They took her, Dad! And I can't just wait around and hope she comes home. I have to find her! I'll call you—"

I patted my pocket for my phone when I remembered Badger had it. "Shit!"

My mind raced, trying to think of what to do. My only lead, after my search for ARC online was a bust, was to interrogate Ash's former stalker. But in order to do that, I had to return to the cellphone headquarters in Reno and see if I could track down his cell phone like I'd done before.

Dad stood in the way of me backing up the Jeep, hands lifted out.

"Just wait. We can interview the guards. Find out if they saw anything first."

A scream came from Ash's front yard. I craned my neck around, then turned off the engine. The three of us jumped out and followed Dad as he ran over to the lawn behind Ash's house. A mer woman wearing a fine dress sobbed over the lifeless body of a guard. His blood had pooled in the street.

Hysteria broke out. Women screamed and men yelled, as mer trampled one another and rushed for the lake, diving in en masse. Desirée ran to the podium and snatched the microphone.

"Everyone, calm down," she said. "I need the Council members, the wedding party, and the king's guard to meet me inside Jack and Maggie's house. The rest of you need to return to Natatoria peaceably through the hatch. Oberon, you're in charge."

The mass of mers slowed, but they continued to head for the lake all the same, completely ignoring the fact they were instructed not to be so obvious.

Desirée sighed and motioned to Colin. He took the microphone.

"If you're human, it's time for you to go home as well," he sang. "The wedding has been canceled, and that's the only detail you'll remember."

His satisfied smirk found me as he returned the microphone to its stand. I clenched my fists. If he had anything to do with this, there'd be Hades to pay.

The few family members and friends Ash had invited gathered up their things, and returned to their cars, but we were running out of time.

"Dad, I'm going!"

He grabbed my arm. "No, Son. You can't."

"Why not?"

"This is a security breach. The Council has to come up with a plan first."

"The plan is I go to Reno and find this son of a bass."

"Yes, I agree with you, but you must abide by Natatorian law!"

My hackles rose. How in his right mind did he think Natatorian law had any say over whether I tracked down this guy or not? "This is my promised mate's life we're talking about!" I blew out an angered breath. "So help me if something happens to her—"

"I know. A few extra minutes to come together and hatch a plan could save hours in the long run."

"Fine." I threw up my hands and headed to my parents' house completely unwilling.

39

ASH

June 11 –2:11 p.m.

Noise from the room assaulted my senses, and I pulled in a breath, my throat parched. The pungent smell of antiseptic and cleaner flooded my nose. Looking through half-lidded eyes, I tried to see who was there, but my vision was blurry. I lifted my hands, only to find them tethered to the bed. My heart started to pound, making a machine close by beep faster. I checked my legs, instead flipping my tail.

My tail!

"It's okay, honey. Just relax." A dark-haired woman dressed in a white coat placed a gloved hand on my arm.

I pulled in a deep breath and squinted in the dim light. IV's were attached to my arm. One had clear liquid while the other had red. Blood maybe? The tube ran somewhere I couldn't see.

"Where am I?" I croaked out.

"Just relax," she said.

The beeping didn't slow, then something warm flooded into my arm. My eyes slipped shut. "I'll die out of the water."

"I'm almost finished."

Finished? With what? And why wasn't she freaking out over the fact I had a tail?

My mind felt warm and soft once more. I opened my eyes again when the thirst was too great. The red IV was gone. Only the white remained.

Alaster stood at the foot of my bed. I tried to scream, but nothing but air came out of my throat.

"Catfish got your tongue?" he asked with a slippery smile.

Around his neck was a silver ring that shot orange light onto his face, casting horrific shadows.

"Alaster," I croaked.

"Good to see you've remembered my name."

I looked at the drying scales on my fin. If it was night already, why wasn't he a fish, too?

"You're alive?"

"Of course I am." He chuckled, darkly. "Don't sound so surprised."

"Why am I here?"

"Oh, I think you know."

My fingers throbbed at the memory of what he'd done to me in the cave—the forced promise and then how he'd cut off my fingers to pawn me off as Galadriel. This couldn't be for power, could it? There wasn't royalty in Natatoria any longer. Was this all for revenge?

My stomach tightened with a cramp, but I was too weak and restricted to clutch my stomach. "I'm going to die."

"No, you're not." Alaster took out something from his pocket and flipped a switch. Light turned on from a similar device that circled my neck. My fin shifted into legs. I tried to tuck them under me, but they wouldn't move. Luckily, what remained of my wedding gown covered the tops of my legs, but my chest constricted in fear. Fin was waiting for me to walk down the aisle. He'd be hysterical with worry to find me missing.

"Imagine my thrill when investigators showed up at your door looking for the girl with magical blood," he said. "An opportunity waiting for my exploitation."

I licked my chapped lips. "What?"

"Yes. After you left us with my Dradux friends, I returned here to

Lake Tahoe to clean up your mess. And I've found a better partnership than what Natatoria could give. One more lucrative and responsive to my tastes."

He snapped his fingers and three girls ran in, a redhead, a blonde, and a brunette, all in heels and tight dresses showing way too much cleavage. They fought over who would get to stand next to him.

"Meet Candy, Brandy, and Sue," he said.

They scowled at me.

"He's mine tonight," the blonde said.

"You had him last night," the brunette whined. "Don't you remember?"

"If you would have remembered to check the schedule, girls, you'd see he's mine," the third said as she rubbed her hand over his chest. "Aren't you, Al?"

Alaster's smile broadened as he brushed the redhead's hair off her forehead. "There's enough of me to go around, ladies."

A sick feeling washed over me, watching him toy with these women, and I turned my head. Then the light clicked off, and my legs phased into a fin.

"Wow!" the blonde said with a giggle. "Do that again."

He let her click the button, and my legs returned.

"I want one of those." The redhead pointed to my fin.

"All in good time, my pet." He leaned over and gave her a sloppy kiss. She leaned against him, moaning. The other girls watched on longingly.

I tried my hardest not to cry, but the tears formed on my lids anyway, then another cramp gripped my stomach. I withheld a groan.

He broke from the redhead's lips, and stepped forward, tracing his finger along my ankle and up my leg. "But I might have a change in plans. It is, after all, Ash's wedding night, and I'd hate for her to have to sleep alone."

I slid my leg away from him. "Don't touch me, you son of a bass."

He lashed out and grabbed onto my leg, hard. "I'll do what I want!" I yelped out in pain. The tears falling freely down my cheeks now.

"Oh, Al. Stop teasing. You can't rearrange the schedule, you promised," the redhead whined. "I'll be your bride."

"Me, too," the blonde said.

"Me, four," the brunette followed.

But even with three willing participants, Alaster's eyes raked over my body lasciviously. My skin crawled.

"I guess you're right," he said to them. "I'll have to put Ash on the schedule like the rest of them."

"Nooo." The redhead clicked her tongue. "Then that means less time with you, and you already have a redhead. Me."

"That's right, I do." He kissed her again, and the ghastly memory of his lips on mine made me gag. "We'll work it out, now that I've added another." Alaster's eyes gleamed with treachery.

The redhead pouted. "You said if we added anyone else, it would be a girl with black hair."

"You're right, Candy." He ran his finger down her arm. "And I wonder who that could be."

I felt my stomach clench, deeper and harder this time and prayed he wasn't talking about my little sister, Lucy. I hated how she tricked me yes, but if she'd been kissed, she'd be loyal to my worst enemy. Tied to him until death.

A memory of Alaster swearing he'd go after Lucy if I didn't cooperate packed a punch to my stomach, making it knot in pain. Is that what he meant by revenge? My body started to tremble as the four left the room. I rolled over and clutched my stomach with the closest hand, praying Fin would find me, praying it wasn't too late.

40

FIN

June 11 – 2:16 p.m.

"You lied to me!" Desirée bellowed at my father while standing at the head of the table. Six Council members, including my father, sat three on each side.

"We didn't lie," Dad defended.

"You didn't tell me that Ash had been stalked by some assailant that tried to take her," Desirée clarified.

A few of the men mumbled their disdain.

Girra folded her arms and glared at her mother as she sat on the couch in the corner of my parents' great room where the rest of the mer sat. "We mojoed him," she mumbled.

"Silence!" Desirée slammed her fist on the table. "We have a problem, Jack. This has been mismanaged and is now completely out of control."

"We can fix it," he said.

"Fix it?" She turned her back on us and stared out of the bay windows. "We have one guard dead and now my daughter is missing."

"Yes, and we know an employee who works for the company. Fin just needs—" Jack started.

"Company?" She swiveled around, her eyes narrowed.

"Companies are places that hire people and make stuff," Girra explained.

"I know what a company is." Desirée's chin lifted. "Are you telling me this man was *hired* to steal my daughter?"

Dad took a deep breath. "We mind-wiped the employee. Unfortunately, he wasn't privy to where the company was located, and we've been looking for it ever since."

Desirée's eyes hardened. "Then if you didn't find the source, the wedding should have been canceled and Ash returned to Natatoria."

Yes, that probably would have been the best idea, but that was hindsight now. I clenched my jaw to keep from speaking and looked to the ceiling. We were wasting time casting blame.

"We didn't think it required such drastic measures," Dad stated. "And it was, after all, Ash's choice."

"You left it up to a headstrong, pregnant girl who has no idea of the consequences of our secret being discovered?" Desirée chuckled. "This is preposterous, Jack. Even for you. What makes you think you're above the law?"

"We aren't above the law." I stood, my muscles strung tight. "But while we're pointing fingers, your daughter is in trouble. I need to go to Reno now."

Desirée turned to me as if it shocked her that I spoke. "Where is this Reno?"

"It's an hour away."

Her expression turned reflective, almost like she appeared to be mulling it over. "What do you need?"

"Nothing other than Jax, Jacob, and my dad. Once we find the employee, we'll question him." I flipped my keys in my hand and motioned we leave.

"You can have Jax, Jacob, and... Colin." Her eyes tightened. "Jack, you're under arrest!"

"No!" Maggie jumped up and tried to prevent a guard from grabbing him.

"This is insane," one of the Council members said. "We need to vote on this."

"As Chancellor Pro-tem, I must take charge," Desirée stated. "In two short months of doing things your way and changing the laws, our secret has been exposed. You may not have agreed with how things were run in the past, but they were there for a reason, and just look what Jack's foolish ideas of mer living with humans have given us. We cannot afford any more mistakes and at this moment I am stopping this foolishness. The Council will no longer have governing rights until Ash has been returned to us. Fin. Go to Reno and report back to me. Only me!"

I stared at Dad, torn to defend him or leave for Reno.

"Go, Son," Dad said curtly. "I'll be fine."

My mother's expression was filled with worry, but I ran out anyway, keys in hand, and rushed to the Jeep.

Badger followed behind us. "Aye, Son!"

I turned and he tossed something in the air to which I caught. My cell phone.

"But I thought—" I started, looking at it.

"I wouldn't be tossing your technology into the drink. Now go and get our girl back."

Jax and Jacob hopped in the back while Colin took the front.

"Oh, no," I said. "You'll wait here."

"The Queen said for me to go."

"She's not the Queen," I seethed.

Colin didn't move out of the seat.

"Fine, but you'll stay in the truck." I threw the Jeep into reverse and spun out of my spot. We'd get there in an hour since I finally had some power underneath me.

41

ASH

June 11 – 2:58 p.m.

I rolled over onto my side and clutched my stomach with one hand. The cramps had been squeezing my abdomen every so often, growing with intensity each time.

The next one hit and all I could think about was the pain. Then hot water gushed between my thighs. Holy heck. Was I going into labor? I couldn't be. It was too early. I panted for air. I needed help. I couldn't do this alone.

"Ohhhh!" I groaned as the ring of fire between my legs only grew hotter and more intense, shooting pain up my back.

Then the contraction hit again, but a new urge hit me. One to push. I sucked in a breath, fighting it, but the fire spread and burned down my thighs instead and I couldn't stop myself.

No, Joey. Stay inside. It's too early.

Another wave hit, and I grunted through it, finally giving in. Grabbing onto my knee, I bore down. Pushing felt so good, freeing, and I had no choice but to let my body take over. Another contraction hit, and I pushed again. Then another.

After several pushes, something slipped out of me and plopped onto the white fabric between my legs. I sucked in a tortured gasp and looked down at a tuft of fiery red hair. A tiny silver tail flipped upward, then smacked the liquid.

"Oh." I tried to reach for the child, but couldn't with my wrists tethered.

I could feel the child wiggle against my thighs, but it made no sound. Was it a girl? A boy?

"Help!" I called out, but no one came. "I need help!"

I grunted again, trying to break free of the straps on my arms. Eventually, I just scooted my butt upward so I could see. A tiny body, small and pink, lay in the goo between my legs. A boy, my son.

"Oh, Joey." I scissored my legs closer so they pressed softly against him to cradle him. "Mommy is here."

But I knew something was wrong. He wasn't moving. I tried to nudge him, but he didn't respond.

"No. NO!" I cried out. "Please, someone help me!"

"What's going on in here?" The dark-haired woman who'd been in my room earlier stood in the doorway, hands on her hips.

I looked over at her, desperate. "My child needs help. Please."

"Child?" She walked over, then her eyes grew as she looked at the baby lying between my thighs. "Oh my stars!"

"Untie me!"

She ignored me as I continued to beg, and instead fumbled in the drawers of the metal cart against the wall. She pulled out a blanket, and then bundled up the child into her arms—a tiny bundle no bigger than a shoe. "Edna! Come quick!"

I tried to reach for him as another blonde woman arrived. The dark-haired nurse passed off the bundle to her, and they looked at one another. I watched Edna's lips move and say, "dead."

Panic overwhelmed me. I yanked my arms, jolting the bed.

"No, he's not! I want my baby! He's mine!"

Edna looked over at me with sadness in her eyes, but the nurse shooed her out. "Just… deal with it."

"No! Give him to me."

"Shhh… Now, now." The nurse smoothed the hair off my forehead. "This will make you feel better."

"I want my child! I want my Joey!" Something warm filled my veins, and I fought to keep alert, keep my eyes open. I wouldn't sleep. Couldn't sleep, not when my son was being taken away by strangers. "Give him to me, please. I'll do anything." My voice slurred, foreign to my ears.

But no matter how hard I fought, sleep overtook me anyway.

42

FIN

June 11 – 3:21 p.m.

After just having broken every traffic law known to man, we squealed into the parking lot at the customer service building fifteen minutes earlier than expected.

"Stay here!" I jumped out and nodded at my passengers, who were still white knuckling the roll bar for dear life. Wussies.

"Sure, man. Whatever," Jax said.

I couldn't worry about it. Unlike the last time I'd come here, the place was a ghost town. When no one exited, I waited for several minutes, then decided to bang on the doors.

An older gentleman in a blue uniform approached, hands on his hips.

"Open up," I sang.

He held his hand to his ear and mouthed, "Can't hear ya. We're closed to the public."

"I need to get inside," I sang louder.

He merely shrugged, then walked back to the reception desk. Some security guard. I fisted my hands and marched back to the Jeep. The guys stood around uneasy, watching me cautiously.

"What's going on?" Jax asked. "Isn't this the place?"

"Yeah, but…" I trailed off. How would I get inside now? And once I did, was anyone going to be there to help me?

"Why isn't he letting you in?" Jacob shifted his stance, sizing up the door like he was ready to strong-arm it, or something.

"We should go," Colin advised.

I stared at the shredded decorations hanging off the back of the Jeep, clenching my jaw when the idea hit. Running over, I slipped into the driver's seat and turned the key. Then I threw the stick into reverse. I revved the engine.

The guys' eyes widened.

"You better get out of my way," I warned.

Jax and Jacob gave each other a look, then hopped aside, giving me a wide berth.

Without another thought, I sped backward, smashing the back of the Jeep into the plate glass window, shattering it.

"For the love of the Kraken, are you nuts?" Colin bellowed.

But I was out of the Jeep and running across broken glass to the stairwell before anyone could stop me.

Taking the stairs by twos, I bolted upward and busted into the Information Technology office. Without flinching, I hopped the counter.

"Ignore me," I sang as I ran past the purple-haired girl and headed toward Kenny's cubical. But it was empty

"Where's Kenny?" I yelled to the receptionist. When she didn't answer, I ran to her desk. "Hey!"

Her legs swiveled the chair around, her glare framed against a pierced eyebrow and heavy makeup. I startled for a moment as visions of mermaids danced in my head.

She gave me a once over, then pulled one earbud out of her ear. "What's with the tux?"

"Uh…" I glanced at her name placard, which also had a mermaidish tone to it. "Is Kenny here, Delphina?"

"He's off today. You late for your wedding or something?"

"Where's his boss?" I asked, impatiently.

"Where do you think they are? It's Saturday." She snapped her gum and everything inside me wanted to strangle her with her earbud cord as she popped in the bud and returned to her computer monitor.

I stepped closer. "I need someone who can track down a cell phone signal," I sang.

No response.

I pushed the monitor aside and put my face into her line of sight.

"What do you think you're doing?" she said extra loud.

I made a motion she needed to remove her earbud, either that or I'd do it for her, and trust me, they wouldn't work after I was finished.

"I need a cell phone traced," I sang.

The sass melted from her face as she picked up her phone and dialed. I could hear ringing coming from somewhere behind us in the sea of cubicles. "Hey, Barney? I have someone…"

I sprinted to where I'd heard the sound coming and stopped before an overweight man with a month's worth of soda cups and food containers occupying every open space of his desk. He swiveled around in his chair, phone receiver in hand.

"Barney?"

He gawked at me. "Yeah?"

"I need you to pull up the location of a cell phone," I sang.

His eyes clouded over and he turned to his keyboard, first minimizing a window of what looked like a horror movie he'd been watching. He then pulled up another window and signed in.

"Hurry," I said.

"Going as fast as I can. What's the number?"

I gave him the number, and he punched it in. We waited for the site to pull up the coordinates. Then a red circle appeared on a map and hovered over a building in Carson City.

"Where is that?"

"It's…" He zoomed in. "It's 24333 North Carson Street."

I wrote it down on a slip of paper, then prepared to leave.

"Hey, do you have a business card?" I asked him.

He squinted. "No. Why?"

"What's your number?"

He told it to me, and I wrote it down. "When I call," I sang, "you do whatever I want. No questions asked. Got it?"

He nodded, eyes glazed over. "Yeah."

"Great. I was never here."

I took off running again, jumped the counter, and headed for the stairs. Jax and Jacob were standing in the lobby. The old guy, who sat frozen with a phone receiver in his hand, watched me with wide eyes.

"Let's go!" I yelled. "I've got the address."

"You're free to go," Jax said to the man, "But we were never here."

Within moments, we were on the road back to Carson City.

"I think there's glass in my ass," Jax snipped.

Jacob laughed.

"Where are we headed to anyway?" Colin asked, unamused.

"Some place in Carson City. We passed it on the way," I said. "Hold on!"

The tires skidded as I turned onto the highway. Bits of glass skittered off the back of the Jeep like falling stars. All I could think about was Ash. She needed me. I just knew it.

43

ASH

June 11 – 3:45 p.m.

I opened my eyes again, shaking uncontrollably, hoping that the events that just happened had all been a terrible dream. Finding the spot between my legs incredibly sore and still wet confirmed I'd given birth. I strained to listen, but there was no baby's cry. Tears slid down my cheeks. I didn't think I could take any more abuse, especially not from Alaster.

He had everything, including my son's life.

I just had to get out of there.

"Fin," I whispered between chapped lips. "Please. Find me. Save our son."

44

FIN

June 11 – 4:16 p.m.

Colin shifted uneasily as I pulled up to the building and parked.

"Is this it?" Jacob glanced warily at the darkened interior.

"Doesn't look open." Colin glared at me. "And I don't think you should bust into this building, too."

"Maybe the reason it showed him here was because he left his phone at his desk," Jacob suggested.

Though the guy didn't seem like a white-collar cube mongrel to me, I wasn't going to leave without at least checking the building first.

"Dude, why don't we just call the number and find out?" Jax stretched his hand out for my phone.

I'd thought of that earlier, but I didn't want to tip him off. At this point, I'd try anything. "Yeah, sure."

He dialed the number, then put the phone on speaker. It rang several times.

"See? He's not here." Colin lunged for the phone. "Let's go back."

Jax pulled his hand away. "Hold up."

Someone picked up on the last ring.

"Yeah?" the guy asked.

"Yo, where you at?" Jax asked, deepening his voice.

"Who is this?"

"I'm here with dat pizza you ordered." Jax waggled his eyebrows.

"Pizza?" There was a pause. "I didn't order a pizza."

"Well, it's paid for and I'm standin' outside yo building on…"

"24333 North Carson Street," I whispered."

"24333 North Carson and no one's answerin' the door," Jax finished without skipping a beat. "It's gettin' cold."

The phone muffled. "Anyone here order a pizza and put my name and number on it?" A couple people answered "no," in the background. "I think you've got the wrong guy."

"Well, it's paid for, so," Jax added. "I guess I'll eat it. See ya."

"No, I'll come out," the guy said quickly.

"Great." Jax hung up the phone and shot us a big goofy grin. "Now that's how it's done boys."

"Good job." I jumped out of the Jeep along with Jax and Jacob.

Colin remained in his seat and blew out an annoyed breath. "This is stupid. What's he going to know? Ash isn't here."

"Stay in the Jeep then." I pressed him with a sideways glare before jogging over to the doors. We leaned against the wall and waited. Within a few minutes the doors opened, and the same guy with dark hair stepped out.

Jax grabbed him and put him in a chokehold.

"Where's Ash," he sang before I had a chance to.

His eyes glazed over instantaneously. "In the building."

My legs weakened as Jax yanked the guy inside and forced him forward. I grabbed the guy's collar and lifted. "Where?"

He shakily pointed to the hall. "Down there."

The creak of the passenger door sounded behind me, meaning Colin had finally gotten out of the Jeep.

About time.

My mind raced as we marched across the linoleum floor of what looked like a hospital. Stark white walls with abstract pastel designs hung in cheap frames. Chairs covered in vinyl lined the small waiting area wall. What was Ash doing here?

"Did you take her?" I sang.

"Yeah," he said apathetically.

My hands balled into fists. After I mojoed him and everything, he still took her. I should have killed him. "When?"

"Before the wedding."

My heart pounded and it took everything inside me not to grab him and break his puny neck on the spot. "Take me to her," I sang.

We rounded the corner and stopped before a set of locked double doors marked, AUTHORIZED PERSONNEL BEYOND THIS POINT. The guy swiped his card against the reader and the doors opened magically.

A woman walked out into the hall, wearing a mask and a white coat, quickly glanced at us, then yelped in surprise.

"What are you doing in here?"

"Don't move," I sang to her, then smashed the kidnapper into the wall. "Where is she?"

He whimpered. "I don't know."

I turned to the woman in white. "Where's Ash?"

She shrugged, too.

"A redhead with green eyes!"

She tilted her head. "Do you mean Candy?"

"No! Son of a—!" I grunted in frustration, then turned to Jax and Jacob. "Split up. Sing to anyone you see and don't let them leave." Colin leaned against the double doors as if he was terrified to be there. Figures. "Colin, just stay here and keep an eye on these two. I'll be right back."

He nodded.

I bolted forward, scanning the opened doorways as I moved as quickly as I could. I continued singing, freezing whomever I met, asking if they had seen a redheaded girl. Their answers were conflicting and they kept mentioning Candy. After about five minutes, I'd checked every room without success.

"Fin! Over here!" Jax called.

I tore around the corner and entered a room at the end of the hall. Ash lay strapped to a table still wearing her wedding gown, torn and shredded around her waist. Blood covered the sheets and her dress.

"Ash!" I ran to her and touched her face.

"She's breathing, but unconscious." Jax unbuckled the wrist restraints.

I glared at the IV's attached to her, and then at the necklace radiating orange light. "What is all of this?"

Jax shrugged. "I have no clue."

A dark-haired woman entered, then shrieked and ran out.

"Stop!" I sang, and she froze. "Get this stuff off of her!"

She robotically walked over and started unhooking the wires and tubes. The machines next to us beeped with alarms, but she didn't silence them.

"Why isn't she awake?" I asked.

"I gave her something to sleep," the woman said.

"Why?"

"Because," she turned to me, eyes sad, "she lost her baby."

The world swayed, and I had to grab onto the gurney. Our child had died? How? When? My hands then lashed out and grabbed on to the woman's shoulders, squeezing tight. "How did this happen?"

She flinched, her face pained. "We didn't know she was pregnant. She didn't look pregnant."

"Why is she here?" I grunted.

"Her blood. It has a special protein. We were to collect it. It didn't hurt her. Just... the stress must have thrown her into labor."

"Must have?" I raised my hand to hit her.

She turned her head downward, flinching.

"No," Jax restrained my hand. "She's not to blame, and you have to focus on getting Ash out of here. She needs a healer."

"Not to blame?" I yelled. "What kind of place is this?"

"We're a research facility for cancer," the woman said, voice quivering.

"And you just take people and steal their blood?"

"She'd volunteered. She just…" the woman stopped talking.

"Restraints aren't needed when one volunteers," I grated.

"I don't know…" She swallowed, then shook her head as if to clear away the song. "I just did what I was told."

"When will she wake up?" Jax asked as he wrapped Ash in a blanket.

"Soon." Her eyes panned across Ash's frail body, sorrowful. "I'm sorry. I don't know why I went along with this."

"Money, I'm sure," I seethed.

Her eyes flashed to mine. "I didn't know she was pregnant. Honest."

I carefully lifted Ash's unconscious body into my arms. If I didn't get her out of there, I'd commit bloodshed on this pathetic existence of a person.

"You'll forget we were here," I sang to her. "You'll destroy any samples of her blood. Any tests. Any records. Any evidence she was here. And if you can't do so, you will call me," I sang her my number. "And then you'll quit, you miserable excuse for a human!"

The woman's head lowered, but I couldn't watch her grovel now. Ash needed to get home.

Jax followed me into the hallway. "Dude, I'll stay and clean up."

"No, you can't. Just sing to the crowd, and tell them to get out of here. Once I get Ash home, we're coming back and torching this place."

"This mess is too big to leave," he insisted as we approached the people. "And if we burn it down, we'll destroy any leads to where

Ash's blood or research went."

I sucked in a measured breath. "How will you get back? We're too far from the lake."

"I'll persuade someone to drive us, but don't worry. Just take Ash home."

"We need to stay together," I said.

"I'll be fine." Jax put his hand on my shoulder and squeezed. "Let us handle this."

Jacob called out from down the hall. "I found more of them."

We ran to him. Three girls in high heels and dresses that barely covered their bodies stood off to the side with their hands on their hips.

"You can't keep us here," the redhead said.

"I don't know what's up with these three. They don't have promising tattoos, yet they won't answer me," Jacob said.

"Answer you?" I asked, not having enough brainpower to unravel the mystery.

"Yeah." Jacob scowled. "Could you be too dumb to be persuaded?"

"I heard that," the redhead said.

"I don't know. I gotta go." The guilt of failing Ash, of losing my son because I let the basswipe go, started to unravel me. "You two handle it."

"Where's Colin?" Jax asked.

My gaze swung to the doors.

Jacob shrugged. "He was there a minute ago."

I gritted my teeth. "Find him, fix this, and get back before sunset. I'll meet you at the house."

Jax saluted me before I walked out of the research lab with Ash in my arms. I'd failed her. I'd failed everyone.

45

ASH

June 11 – 4:59 p.m.

At the sounds of a horn honking, my eyes pulled open. Wind beat against my face as the bright sunlight pelted down on my skin. I gripped onto the armrest and shrieked.

"Ash, It's okay. It's me. Fin." He reached over and held onto my knee. "You're safe."

I tensed at his touch and yanked away.

He withdrew, confused. "It's okay. We're going home."

"Home?" Beyond the words "congrats" scrawled in paint on the windshield, the green of the pines covering the mountains, and the white shale sand on either side of the road blurred past. I couldn't process what had happened. He'd found me? How?

"Where are we?" I croaked out, trying to clear my head of the lingering grogginess.

"We're on Highway 50."

After everything, I didn't trust my eyes. Glancing down at the blanket, I saw the blood, then remembered what had happened, of what I'd lost. Tears started to fall again. How would I ever tell Fin? How did this get so out of control?

Once we knew we were expecting and even when I was taken the first time, I should have never let my selfish wedding fantasies get in the way of our family's safety. For what? To pretend to a mother and sister that I'm human when they despised me? To matter to a father and to a grandmother who weren't my blood relatives?

My head drifted to rest against the cold windowpane, my legs curled up underneath me, my insides numb. I had naïvely thought that once I was freed of that hellhole, it would be over. But I knew differently now. I'd been branded forever and wherever I went, it would follow, eating me alive. If I told Fin that Alaster was alive and behind it all, he'd go crazy and never let it go.

Within twenty-five minutes, we pulled down our street and up to the cottage. A moving van stood parked on the dying grass of the lot, where movers loaded in tables and chairs. Leftover wedding decorations blew in the wind like funeral pyres, and I turned my head from it, all of it raw and a reminder of my stupidity.

Fin parked and walked around to my side, opening my door.

"Come on, my Ginger Girl." He slid his arm around my waist. "Let's get you inside."

His warm touch felt wrong, and I recoiled.

"Congratulations!" one of the movers called while waving.

Fin turned, and waved back, embarrassed. "Thanks."

I used the opportunity to pivot my hips and slide out of the Jeep. The sharp rocks met the soles of my feet upon impact.

"I've got you." He tried to grab onto me again.

"Stop!" I yanked up the blanket. "I'm fine!"

He lifted his hands and stumbled backward.

Hugging the blanket tightly to myself, I walked on weakened legs toward the cottage complete with a picket fence, the white-trimmed windows and the red heart at the peak of the roof—the epitome of cuteness. I hated it.

"I want to carry you—"

I pushed him away. "No."

"Ash."

"Just let me deal with this, Fin!"

He clenched his jaw and stood stiffly. "I know you want to. You're not alone in your pain."

I turned to him, eyes hard. "How could you say that? It wasn't you that was taken. It wasn't you that…" *watched our child die.* A sob lodged in my throat. Maybe sleeping through the pain was the answer.

"The nurse told me."

I swallowed down the lump threatening to choke me. "Told you what?"

"About our son."

My nails bit into my arms, piercing the skin, while I poised my legs to run. I'd hoped the pain would distract the ache inside my heart. It didn't work. My body only grew tired from the strain of standing.

Fin steadied me. "Come on inside."

This time, I didn't fight him as he led me over the threshold and into a house that rivaled magazines, but I wanted nothing of it. It all reminded me of Joey, and I'd give it all back just to have our son in my arms.

Fin quickly took down WELCOME HOME signs and helped me down the hall. The closest door was cracked open. Fin reached over to pull it shut, but not before I spotted a crib.

"The bathroom is down here." He led me inside and started the water. My eyed drifted to my reflection. Stringing hair matted with pearls and gems hung haphazard around sunken eyes and gaunt skin, illuminated by the necklace Alaster had put on me. Death warmed over.

Fin worked to undo the buttons on the back of my gown, one by dreaded one. I'd dreamed of a moment when his fingers would help remove this dress before he made love to me, not like this, not when I wanted to burn it.

"What's this?" he asked as he tried to remove the necklace.

I reached up and grabbed a hold of the metal. "Leave it."

He didn't fight me, only lifted the remains of the dress over my head. Then he helped me into the shower to the stone seat.

The hot water pelted my skin as the blood swirled down the drain. He lovingly removed the pins from my hair, then lathered it with shampoo, then conditioner. I didn't have the strength to fight him.

Though I would have loved to have just stayed in there, crying, until the water ran cold, he turned it off, wrapped me in a towel, and led me to our bed.

"Are you hungry?" he asked as he tugged a T-shirt over my head.

Fin's scent enveloped me, and I wanted it off. I didn't deserve his love, or attention. In fact, I never wanted to move, let alone eat again. "No."

"I'll be back. Just rest." He kissed my cheek, and I heard the door softly shut along with the door to my heart.

I slid to the floor, then curled up in the corner, rocking my body back and forth. I'd never allow anyone in again—this hurt way too much.

46

FIN

June 11 –5:46 p.m.

I picked up what remained of Ash's wedding dress off the bathroom floor, and marched outside to the garbage. Cussing, I threw it away. And then I kicked the garbage can, before smashing my fist into the side, making a dent in the plastic.

"Son of a—!" I'd let it happen. All of it. We'd lost our son because of my stupidity.

Glancing at our bedroom window, then at my parents' house, I was thankful no one came out to greet us. Though I knew I should find out what had happened, I wouldn't leave her alone again like I'd promised her I wouldn't.

"Fin!" Tatiana ran off the porch, still wearing her bridesmaid dress, carrying Nicole in her hands. "Did you find her?"

"Yes," I said unenthusiastically.

"Is she okay?" Tatiana's face wrinkled in confusion. "What happened?"

"No, she's not okay," I said brusquely. "She lost the baby."

"What?" Tatiana shrieked, and just stood there, mouth ajar. Then she pushed past me to get inside. "I need to see her."

"No." I grabbed onto her arm. "She doesn't want to see anyone, and don't take this the wrong way, but especially not you and Nicole!"

Tatiana's eyes welled with tears. "Why not?"

"She's been traumatized, and…" I gestured to the merling, who sat in her arms, sucking her thumb.

"Oh, right." Her shoulders fell. "This is horrible. Does she need her mom?"

I wrinkled my brow, not sure if she meant Desirée or Karen. "She has me, and that's good enough." I paused. "Wait. What do her parents think happened?"

"That the wedding went off without a hitch and you two went on your honeymoon."

"Really?" My eyebrows rose. "And what about Lucy?"

Tatiana shrugged. "She's fine, too, I guess…"

I pressed my palm to my forehead. "I don't get how they got in and out with no one seeing them. It was like they timed it perfectly when no mers were around."

"We were all distracted." Tatiana's gaze drifted off toward the movers. A tear trickled down her cheek. "I should have listened to Ash and kept things small, especially with the baby coming."

"It's not your fault…" *it's mine.*

Tatiana put her arm around my shoulder. "What happened?"

I blew out a breath and quickly explained what the research company was doing, and how Jacob, Jax, and Colin were cleaning up the mess.

Tatiana's eyes grew. "Are they going to be okay?

"Yeah. They'll be fine."

Tatiana wiped away her tears. "I'm so sorry, Fin. What can I do to help?"

"Where are Mom and Dad?"

"They took Dad to Natatoria to be put in irons in the square. Mom followed." She pressed her eyes shut for a moment. "I didn't go back so I could be here when you and Jacob returned. I had to know what happened to Ash."

I pulled out my phone, then pocketed it, remembering that none of the guys had one. "They'll be back soon, but I gotta go."

"I don't know what to do."

"You think I know what to do?" I barked.

Something crashed inside, and I looked at the cottage, then I took off running.

"Fin, where are you going?"

I bolted inside and ran to the bedroom. Glass from the mirror lay in broken fragments all over the floor. Ash was in the bathroom, arms shaking, blood dripping from her fingers as she held a shard of broken glass.

"What are you doing?"

She looked up at me, eyes glazed over. "Don't stop me. I want to be human."

Her hand tightened and the blood poured onto the floor.

"What? No!" I lunged for her, fighting over the shard of glass. Eventually, I was able to wrangle it from her hands. It toppled to the floor and shattered.

"Stop it!" Ash fought me weakly, trying to reach for another.

I grabbed onto her and shook her. "What are you doing?"

She sucked in a tortured breath, her eyes terrified. I blinked at her, then hugged her tight. "I'm sorry."

"Ash?" my sister called from down the hall. "What's going on?"

"I've got things handled." Footsteps came closer, raising the hackles on my neck. "Go home, Tatiana!"

"What's going on?" she asked.

At Nicole's wail, I screamed at my sister. "Get out of my house!"

"Mother of Pearl, I'm going!" Within seconds, the door slammed.

Ash pushed me away and turned her cheek. "I'm hideous. Don't look at me."

"Ash, please. Listen to me."

Her fierce glare zeroed in on me. "No, you listen! I'm done! I can't live this life! Always looking over my shoulder! Never knowing who's my friend or enemy! Not having the power to defend myself! Not even being able to trust the man I love!"

I pulled back, wounded. She was right. I'd betrayed her to the point of ultimately failing her, time and time again.

"You mind-mojoed my mother, and that's who I was doing all of this for!"

I didn't know what to say, paralyzed with guilt and regret. The desire to apologize pulled at my lips, but how do you say sorry for this? Our son was gone and it was my fault. I couldn't do anything right.

Her sunken eyes narrowed on me. "You may have stopped me, but I'll do it later. I can't live with this pain. I need this to go away!"

I leaned against the wall, defeated. "You think you're the only one hurting?"

Her chin lifted. "I don't deserve you."

"You're wrong. I don't deserve you. And none of this was your fault, you hear me? And I get it—"

"Get what?" Her voice shook. "You didn't see him slide out of you, see his red hair… see him die!"

The knife dug into my soul, and I no longer wanted to live either, to know every day that I'd failed her and our son, to see the condemnation in her eyes. I'd ruined everything.

A tear trickled down my cheek.

Her mouth turned in an ugly hard line. "I want the pain to be gone, the memories gone! If I'm human again, I'll forget it all. Swim for the Olympics. Go to college. Have the life Alaster stole from me."

My eyes lost focus. Maybe this is what I deserved? A life without Ash, without love.

"Fine." I took a shard of glass off the ground and held it out to her. "Do it."

Her eyes rounded. "What?"

"You're right. This is too much." My hand shook, holding the glass shard as it cut into me, the blood dripping onto the floor between us. "I'll revive you, then I'll no longer be in your life."

Her lip quivered.

"If you get to end things, then I will too," I continued.

She furrowed her brow. "But you don't have anyone to revive you."

I lifted my shoulder. "Why does it matter? You won't remember me anyway."

I knew it was cruel, but it was honest.

She batted the tears falling off of her cheeks with the back of her hand, smearing blood on her face. "No, Fin."

My tears fell free, unrestrained. "It's fine. Just do it."

She knocked the shard out of my hand and lunged for me. Her arms squeezed around my neck as the silent sobs wracked her body.

Then she pulled away. "I can't live without you."

Her lip quivered, and she let out a strangled whimper, then she put her palms on my jaw. Her trembling lips covered mine, soft at first, then more passionate. Our tears mixed on our lips as our kiss ripped open the rawness hiding inside, at the sadness pouring from the gaping hole. We pressed ourselves against one another, heart to heart, holding and hurting, groaning and pressing. Our bodies hungered for the other to take away the pain, and put the broken pieces together, at just a chance to make things right.

"I'm just so sorry," I begged. "Please… I'm just so sorry."

"I am, too," she whispered.

Then I felt something in my soul settle, a peace I hadn't felt before, and Ash's body relaxed into mine. A hope that we could survive this. That we just had to get through the worst of it together.

I crushed her to me, rocking her gently, as we grieved the loss of our son.

47

ASH

June 12 – 8:34 a.m.

Staring off toward the lake, I sat on the lounge in the enclosed patio where I'd stayed the entire night, watching the sunlight dance on the water. I'd faked I was sleeping so Fin would give me a moments peace.

My fingers traced the lighted necklace. I'd put it back on after I couldn't sleep so I could shift into my legs. Though I hated that it reminded me of Alaster, with it I could avoid the thing I started to loathe most—my tail.

After we had realized we couldn't live without one another, we curled up together in our pool. I'd had every intention of staying in his arms the entire time, but every time I closed my eyes, the nightmares began. I had to escape the suffocating guilt that I'd kept my abductor a secret, terrified how Fin would react. I needed time. I needed to think.

It didn't help that my breasts ached with the need of a child to the point I had to express them or suffer a soaked T-shirt. I wondered how long it would take before they dried up.

Fin had begged me to see Pearl, but I refused. There was nothing physically wrong with me, and I didn't need any more pity. Being subjected to his was enough.

I took out my sketchbook and began to absently draw, red hair and a pink button nose, the child I'd never know. I missed him with a pain so great it took away my very breath, of dreams hatched that would never be fulfilled, of a joy robbed from the depths of my soul. I didn't know how I'd ever recover.

The light on my neck suddenly flickered and went out. I yanked it off and tapped it. Nothing. Inspecting the edges, I noticed a screw. Maybe it just needed more batteries.

Conversation in the house drew my attention away, and I padded across the patio tiles to listen.

"Colin returned and told Desirée that the humans know mers exist and their blood cures disease, and that we can never go on land again, which unfortunately Jax said is the truth." Galadriel frowned. "She's freaking out and wants all mers to return home, meaning you two."

My hackles rose. That dirty jackfish's father was the one exposing the mer, not us. Was that their plan all along? To create a catastrophe so big and pin it on us that the mer would be frightened into submission? That by schmoozing up to my mother and charming Garnet was nothing but a power grab. Did they even know Alaster was alive?

"I'm not going anywhere, especially with the state Ash is in," Fin said.

You bet I'm not leaving.

"Well, then, you should hide, or go somewhere, because there are two guards waiting on the dock to come get you if I'm unsuccessful," Galadriel warned.

"Let 'em come," Fin said, voice clipped. "I'd love to send them home with a message to my mother-in-law."

"Fin," Galadriel whined. "This isn't a joke. Mother has kicked out the Council members who'd approved of the wedding. They've clamped down on everyone and everything, demanding we return to our old ways, and things don't look good for your dad."

Fin cussed. "Do you think I don't know that? What am I going to do? Defend him? I'm just as much to blame. Desirée most likely is looking the other way because I'm her daughter's mate, but Ash can't be expected to leave."

"Well, I don't think you have a choice. And with Colin and Garnet expecting, whispers of coronation are stirring."

I covered my lips with my fingers.

"No." Fin sounded shocked. "When did they get promised?"

"They *have* been this entire time, hiding their marks with flesh toned bands." She let out a sigh. "It's a disaster."

My stomach rolled over. Colin? King? I gritted my teeth. *Over my dead body.* If anyone, Fin should be King, considering… but I didn't want to be Queen. Sadness rolled over me, and I gripped the wall to keep from smashing it with my fist. It was like I kept forgetting the loss of my son, then remembering over and over again, and now I'd lose my freedom, too.

"I'm concerned what Ash would do if we forced her to come home—" Fin started.

I burst into the living area. "I can make decisions for myself."

"Ash." Fin turned toward me, face ashen. "You're awake."

Galadriel rushed me with a hug. "Oh, my dear darling. I'm so glad to see you. I'm so sorry."

I let out a measured breath, forcing myself to accept her condolences as kindness and not pity. "Thank you, but what's this about having to return to Natatoria? I'll die first before I bow to that son of a bass."

Galadriel chuckled nervously. "Well, considering how everything is lining up, you might have to die, or run…" she looked over her shoulder at the dock through the windows, "like now."

Fin gripped my hand. "We're not going anywhere."

My eyes lost focus. I was in no mood to leave in my weakened condition. Of course having the lighted necklace would make things easier. But if we ran, they'd just hunt us down. We'd never be free.

Did my mother even care? If she'd heard of my return, not to mention my miscarriage, why didn't she come herself? What was I supposed to think when she sent her minions to drag me out of my home if I didn't come willingly?

To Hades with her. It was time she was taught a lesson of her own.

"What if we did die?" I asked.

Galadriel's eyes widened. "Are you serious?"

"I mean faked our deaths," I explained. "Because as far as I'm concerned, I'm an American citizen and I'm not leaving. She can't suddenly force me to abide by Natatorian law just because I pose some imaginary threat, especially when she abandoned me, and not the other way around. If converting is not an option, then I'd rather be dead to my mother. Can you make us look dead?"

Fin gaped at me, speechless.

"Uh." She rubbed her hands together. "Yeah. I guess."

I knew in my gut it was now or never, and I wasn't going to return to Natatoria and hear all the apologies for our disastrous wedding and miscarriage, just to watch Colin be crowned.

"Aren't they going to check on us soon?" Fin asked.

Galadriel laughed. "They're so terrified, especially after that poor guard was stabbed. They think all humans are evil and lurking around every corner to steal their blood."

"But they can sing," Fin said.

Galadriel shrugged. "I think they've forgotten that, but it's to our advantage, right?"

"Well, then let's get started." I sanded my hands together. "What do you need?"

"Makeup for starters," Galadriel suggested, then her eyes brightened. "There's some in your bathroom."

"In my bathroom?"

Galadriel laughed. "You think I would decorate your home and not stock it, too? I'll go get it."

I reached out and snatched her hand, remembering we hadn't cleaned up the blood and glass yet. "Let me get it."

She tilted her head. "Are you sure?"

"Yeah." I waved my hand dismissively. "Get everything else set up in the kitchen."

I brought her the makeup sets, and while Galadriel quickly painted Fin's skin gray and applied a gel mask that looked like peeling skin, I worked on my own face and thought of how we'd make this look believable to the point they wouldn't cart off our supposedly rotting bodies to Natatoria.

"So what does Natatoria do with their dead?" I asked.

"We take them to Bone Island," Fin said, "or have a funeral pyre."

I bit my lip. "Then we have to make this be our Bone Island, right?"

"I guess so." He eyed me in terror like he had no idea what I'd suggest next.

I moistened my lips, tasting the powdery makeup. "What if when the guard arrives, we're carted off by humans instead, like… to the morgue."

Galadriel glanced toward the window again. "They might freak about that, because, you know… cutting you up and stuff."

"True," I said. "But do they know about autopsies?"

Galadriel pushed out her lips. "No, I don't think so."

"So, what if they see us dead, then the ambulance comes."

Galadriel's dragged her teeth over her lips. "They'd be terrified."

"Too terrified to sing?"

Her fingers slowed while she thought. "Just leave it to me."

After we were sufficiently covered in makeup, Galadriel grabbed the ketchup and started squirting it on us as we lay on the floor in the kitchen.

I wrinkled my nose. "This stuff smells too much like tomatoes. I don't think it's going to work."

"Oh. There's a can of tuna in the pantry." Galadriel leaped over us to get it.

"You bought us food, too?" I asked.

"Of course I did!"

She opened the can, then spilled the juice on the floor.

"Thank you for doing this." I kissed her cheek before lying back down. "You know the drill?"

"Yes, yes. Just get into your places." She flapped her hands and glanced out the window again.

Fin draped his body over me while Galadriel laid the suicide letters next to us. I'd penned a story that mirrored the pain oozing from the cracks in my heart, and Fin's said he couldn't live without me—the irony too biting to think about.

"This is actually very romantic." Her voice was soft as she positioned us. "Like Romeo and Juliet."

A book nerd after my own heart.

"Except we aren't really dying," Fin said, annoyed.

"True… just, stop moving." She sighed, contented. "Perfect. Okay, I'm calling 9-1-1 now." I heard her footfalls retreat to the foyer, then her hysterical voice telling the dispatcher the address of the house.

I squeezed Fin's hand. How or why he'd chosen to support me on the eve of his father's court battle showed how much he loved me. How much he cared.

"All done," she yelled to us. "Here goes."

A blood-curdling scream sounded from her lips, then trailed away as she ran outside. It took a little bit, but within the minute, footfalls crunched on the gravel path.

"What's wrong, Princess? Is that—?" one goon started, speaking in thick Natatorian.

"Blood?" the other finished.

"Yes." Galadriel panted, out of breath. "I tried to save them! I yelled for help! But... you didn't hear me, and I couldn't save them! What are we going to do?"

Her muffled sobs sounded like she'd pressed her mouth against her hand, or to one of their chests.

"Don't cry," the lower voiced one said.

"Poseidon," a man squeaked from what sounded like the doorway. "What do we do now?"

"Well, I don't know!" Galadriel shrieked.

"Are you sure they're dead?" Squeaky asked.

"Of course they are. Look at them." She sniffled.

"We should get a healer," Deep Voice suggested.

"It's too late for that! First the wedding disaster, now this?" Galadriel began sobbing. "I can't take anymore."

Bare feet slapped the wooden floor of the house. "How do you know they're dead?" Deep Voice asked.

"I felt for a pulse, and there was nothing. You check!" Galadriel pressed.

"No," Squeaky said abruptly. "I trust you. You're family and all."

Galadriel continued to wail. "They killed themselves because they couldn't... handle... the pa-a-ain." Above her hysteria, there was the sound of paper flapping in the wind. Our letters?

"I can't read it... it's English... whoa," Squeaky grunted. "Catch her."

There was a thump on the floor.

"Poseidon!"

"I told you to catch her," Squeaky exclaimed.

"I know, but you were closer, you jackfish! What's that smell?" Deep voice asked. "It's like dead fish."

Galadriel sucked in a breath. "What happened?"

"You fainted, Princess," Squeaky explained.

"I need my mate. Get me Jax!"

A siren from a fire truck wailed far off in the distance, coming closer.

"Poseidon! What's that?" Deep Voice asked in a panic.

"I don't know." Galadriel's voice scaled an octive. "It's… an ambulance. Oh shoot! They're coming! They know! We gotta hide."

"They know? How?" Squeaky said.

"Coming. Who's coming?" Deep Voice said, panicked.

"The authorities! We have to hide!" There was a rustle of feet. "Not here! Outside!"

After a few grunts, the room grew quiet. Then the rumble of a diesel reverberated outside. I peeked to see red lights flashing through the window. At the knock on the door, I held my breath.

Boots pounded against the hardwood floor and entered the room.

"George," one of the guys said tensely. "Is that Bill's kid?"

"Oh, shit," the other said. "I think you're right."

Warm fingers touched my neck.

"Pronounce us dead," Fin sang.

"Uh… you got a pulse?"

"No," the other said. "They're already cold. What are we going to do?" the first guy asked.

"I can't believe this." The other stood with a grunt, taking off his rubber gloves. "We gotta call the coroner."

"Don't tell Bill," Fin sang. "Turn us in as Jane and John Doe."

Peace settled over me. This way they wouldn't find out we'd died.

My body was lifted and slid into a body bag. The zipper slowly made its way upward, sealing me inside the claustrophobic space. Then there was silence. I strained to listen.

"The other one is ready," one of the guys said.

"George, what's going on?" I heard my mother ask out of breath, hysterical.

"Oh, crap," I mumbled. "Fin?"

There was silence. Did they take him already?

"Fin," I whispered-yelled, then my heart stopped. Had he suffocated in the bag? "Fin!"

"Oh my—" Mom choked back a sob, still outside. Was she viewing Fin's body? Where was he?

"Ma'am," the guy pressed. "This is a crime scene. You need to step back."

"No!" Her voice shook. "Show me the girl!"

The boots returned, pounding the ground. Hands tugged on the bag, and fresh air flooded the suffocating space. I held my breath. A strangled shriek of my mother cut the silence. I willed Fin to sing something, to do something, but I didn't know where he was, and I had to play dead.

The zipper once again sealed me inside, and I worked to keep my breathing level as not to create movement. Mom left crying, and I strained to listen. Sweat beaded on my brow as the stench of ketchup and tuna fish wafted around me. Then my back began to ache. How long would I have to stay here?

Unable to wait another minute longer, I shredded my hands into the plastic by my face and freed myself. There wasn't another body bag next to me. Looking out the windows, I didn't see the truck. As far as I could tell, I was alone.

I wiped off my hands, caked with ketchup and makeup. Why did they leave me behind? Where was Fin?

The keys to the Jeep on the counter caught my eye. I'd have to go to the hospital or the coroner. Of course, after a shower.

48

FIN

June 12 – 9:44 a.m.

My body was lifted and carried on a gurney across the gravel walkway outside.

"George, what's going on?" I heard Ash's mother say, hysterically.

Oh, crap.

The heavy doors squeaked and my body was shoved inside. Then something clicked, encasing me in silence. Heartbeats passed. Was Ash's mom outside still? What was happening?

I tried to maneuver my hands to tug on the zipper, but whoever bagged me, cinched a strap around my middle. But if I did get out and sing to Karen, Galadriel, and the guards would see, ruining everything. I'd couldn't do anything until I returned, the poor thing.

The blood pounded in my ears as the moisture filled air of the tiny space left my gills confused if they should appear or not, especially now that I was encased in darkness. Then the engine of the vehicle rumbled to life. The bag jostled, signaling we were on our way to the coroner. Sucking in deep breaths, I wished for fresh air, for freedom.

Then the doors opened again and then slammed shut. Someone outside banged twice against the back of the van. The vehicle began to move.

I sang, "Open the body bag."

The zipper pulled down, and my eyes focused on blue eyes. Then my blood froze.

"Uncle?"

"Faking your death? How original," he said with a sickly smile.

You would know. My hands gripped onto the edges of the body bag to free myself, but I couldn't move my arms. "You're alive," I said more as a statement than a question.

"Of course I am."

"Where are you taking me?"

He pressed his finger to his lips. "I think you know where."

I know where… what?

"When I get out—"

His laughter interrupted me, a sick and evil sound. "That's not happening."

"What are you going to do with me?"

He rubbed his hands together. "So many plans. So little time."

The joy in his voice made me sick to my stomach. My heart continued to pound. Did he have Ash, too? I gritted my teeth. I had to keep him as far away from her as possible. "It doesn't matter what you do to me. Ash is dead."

His lip picked up at the side. "Oh, you're little plan didn't fool me."

I deadpanned. Did he have her?

"And just so you know, I so enjoyed our quality time together, though short-lived."

Enjoyed their quality time? Just now? What was he talking about?

Alaster jerked his chin upward, then his brows pulled together. "She didn't tell you? How poetic."

Tell me? Tell me what? I shook my head and laughed it off like I knew what he was talking about. "What's your deal? Did Grandpa and Grandma not give you enough attention as a kid?"

His fist punched into my chest, knocking the wind out of me before he put his face inches from mine. "Shut your mouth! I own you!"

I coughed, adrenaline surging through me, and I pushed my arms against the restraints to get free. "You're a coward. You can't get the respects of mers on your own merit, so you have to manipulate them. Guess what? It might work, but it doesn't last long! Your true colors will show, and though your little lap dog Colin is snuggling up to the most despicable of all princesses, you still won't win."

"Won't I?" He smirked. "With you and Ash officially dead, and your father arrested for exposing the mer, they all think humans are gun wielding murders ready to drain them of their blood like vampires. Once Garnet and Colin give birth to a son, the mer will be salivating for a King to stop this madness. Not before your father is executed, of course. Then I'll come to the rescue, having wiped away our secret from the minds of men, and guide my son as he rules his kingdom."

I ground my teeth. He'd used this entire fiasco to swoop in and claim his prize. My blood drained from my face.

And now that he'd taken me, I was at his mercy. "Where's Ash?"

Alaster smirked. "Dead, isn't that right?"

I struggled to get free, but I knew it was futile. Alaster had thought of everything. There would be no rescue for me this time.

49

ASH

June 14 – 9:08 a.m.

I paced the living room, my insides crawling with worry. Fin had been gone for two days, and I hadn't slept a wink. The coroner, the hospital, even the guys at Dad's work, knew nothing. He'd simply vanished. I tried not to think of the worst—that Alaster had him—but there was no other explanation. Most likely, once I was freed, Alaster had been waiting for the perfect opportunity to strike.

Always there.

Always watching.

Tears drizzled down my cheeks. First my son, and now Fin. I didn't know how much more I could bear. I pinched my eyes shut and screamed. Alaster needed to die!

Gentle knocking pulled me from my grief. I stopped and listened, then walked onto the patio toward the locked hatch door. The rapping started again.

"Ash, it's me! Tatiana! Open up."

I unscrewed the wheel and the door popped open with a soft whoosh.

Fingers gripped onto the rim and a blonde head emerged from the porthole.

"Tatiana?" I asked breathlessly, not trusting my eyes.

"Galadriel told me the truth." She leaped up from the hatch, phasing midair, and crashed into me with a strangling wet hug. I broke into sobs on impact. "If I ever lost you."

I buried my head into her shoulder and clung onto her tight, my body convulsing. She was all I had left.

"I'm so sorry," she kept saying. "I should have never insisted on a big wedding. This is all my fault."

"No. It's not." I wiped away my tears. "It's Alaster. He's back."

Tatchi's eyes widened in horror. "What? I thought he was dead."

"No." The bile crawled up my throat once again. "And I'm pretty sure he has Fin. He's the one who's been behind the guy in the white van; all of this."

"What?" Her mouth gaped open. "You have to tell your mother. She has to know. She has to let Jax and Jacob free so they can find him!"

I pressed my palm to my forehead. I couldn't go, not with the chance she'd force me to stay. Not to mention all the questions and sympathetic looks.

"I need to stay here and find Fin."

Tatiana's tiny frame went slack. "Okay. Where have you looked?"

"The coroner, the hospital…" I whimpered. "He's probably at Alaster's research facility."

"Research facility?"

"Yeah… don't ask. But I don't know where that is, and I don't know where else to look."

Her expression turned hopeful. "Jacob does. He was there when Fin found you. He knows the building."

I grabbed onto her hand. "You have to get him here then."

She gripped me tighter, her face pained. "I don't know how, but okay."

Goosebumps pebbled my skin. "I'll wait here for you in case he does come home."

"Of course." She kissed my cheek, then rushed to the open porthole.

Bubbles popped along the surface of the water. Then a head full of dark hair from a guard immerged.

Though I didn't recognize him, he startled to see me. "You're alive?"

"Run!" Tatiana yelled.

I turned to run and slipped. My body skated along the wet tiles, my legs smashing into the glass door. I rolled over to get up. Strong arms clamped onto mine and yanked upward.

"Let go of me!" I shrieked, kicking and biting.

"Cooperate, Princess."

Why did they insist on these stupid titles? I continued to fight as he dragged me to the hatch, but not before he secured my mouth with a strip of cloth so I wouldn't siren once underwater.

He dropped me down the hatch and pushed my head underwater. I heard Tatiana's muffled cries from somewhere in the distance, but I couldn't see her.

The wish I'd kept the ink necklace Galadriel had given me slipped through my mind along with her warning. Royalty was never safe. I was going home whether I wanted to or not, and I had a lot of explaining to do.

50

FIN

7:26 p.m.

I awoke in a room similar to the one I'd rescued Ash from, throat parched, unsure how long I'd been asleep. Light came from a contraption around my neck, the same as Ash had worn when I found her. My gut squeezed when it hit me. Alaster and the ARC were one in the same. He'd been behind it all: the stalker, the murder of the guard, Bill being knocked out and Ash's abduction. Colin had been his front-runner, mind-mojoing Lucy, and feeding his dad details so they could set it all up. It was an inside job.

My head swayed. Why hadn't Ash told me Alaster was the one who took her? The regret we didn't torch this place when we left ripped through me. But then again, Jax and Jacob wouldn't know where to look for me, and might have only set him back a few days.

Two tubes, a clear one and one with red fluid were attached to my arm, doing something to my veins. I fought against the restraints tying me to the gurney, rocking the bed. Maybe if I could get it to tip over, I might be able to break free and sing my way out of this shit hole.

"I wouldn't do that." The same girl I'd seen before entered the room, the redhead they'd called Candy.

"Let me go," I sang.

She laughed. "That won't work on me, darlin'."

I swallowed and studied her hand, not seeing a promising tattoo. Then it clicked and my head sunk back into the pillows. Why hadn't I figured out earlier that she'd been promised via polygamy? Candy wouldn't have a tattoo if Alaster was promised to someone else, but she'd be loyal to him and unaffected by the song.

"What am I doing here?"

"Curing cancer." Her eyes crinkled with her huge grin. "But you need to be cooperative, or else I'll do this." She pulled out something from her pocket and pressed her thumb against it. The light around my neck turned off. Instantly, my fin spread from my hips, silver and sleek, and busted through the sheet tucked under the mattress. The second it happened, I began to crave the water.

An evil grin spread over her lips. "Uncomfortable, isn't it?"

"Not at all," I sneered at her, then swiped my tail upward, aiming for the restraints. The barb sliced through the binds on my left wrist, then the right. Her eyes widened in fright.

With a wicked laugh, I launched myself off the bed, yanking and ripping out the cords tethered to me. I landed in front of her, grasping for her ankle. She screamed, tripping on her overly high-heels, and fell on her butt in the hall. I slapped my hands to propel me forward. My scales squeaked as they rubbed against the linoleum floor, competing with her incessant shrieks. I had this one chance to get free, but I had to get my hands on that remote.

She skittered away from me like a crab, but as the adrenaline evaporated, exhaustion set in. I stopped, wheezing for air. Once Candy realized I'd never catch her, she popped to her feet. Then her eyes lifted to something behind me.

I flipped over, tail barb out.

"Are you done fighting?" Alaster asked from further down the hall.

Whipping my tail around, I poised myself to sting him in the leg. Then the light turned on. My tail split into two legs before contact. But that didn't matter; I jumped to my feet to charge him anyway. Then the light flickered out. I fell onto the floor with a loud thwack, fished out again. Groaning, I worked to catch my breath when the light came back on. My legs returned, but I wasn't going to go through that again. Placing my palms on the floor, I remained on all fours.

"I like you cowering before me like a dog," he bit.

The opened seam of board shorts, exposing my junk, made this all the more humiliating, but I wouldn't let him see that it bothered me. He'd make a mistake and when he did, I'd strike him dead.

"You finished?" I asked, "because I can do this all night."

"Can you?" He pressed the button again, making me shift. "Actually, without water, things might get a little... difficult."

I rolled over and began scooting away from him on my backside.

Alaster's eyes tightened. "Looks like I'm going to have to teach you to behave."

"I'd like to see you try."

The pinch in my shoulder made me reach back. Something fuzzy stuck out of my skin. I tugged it out, finding a dart with a red tip. My vision started growing fuzzy, my limbs weak. The dart fell out of my fingertips onto the floor. A girl's laughter echoed in my head. I tried to stay upright, but my body slumped over. Eventually, I collapsed to the floor.

"Hurry, help me," I heard Alaster say as someone grabbed me and yanked.

I willed myself to fight against them, but my body didn't obey. They lugged me back to the same room and dumped me on the floor. I lay on my side, not sure if I were a man or a fish.

"You *will* learn some manners," my uncle grated through his teeth somewhere behind me.

I lay there, panting. *No. You're the one who needs a lesson, dear Uncle.*

Somehow, someway, he'd make a mistake and I'd be ready once he did.

51

ASH

June 14 – 9:09 p.m.

"I'm confused." Desirée sat perched on her velvet chaise inside the palace library, staring at me bewildered with piercing blue eyes.

I pushed out a measured breath, trying to keep my fidgety hands steady on my lap. I'd hoped after everything, she'd at least understand this whole thing was a setup.

"Like I said, Alaster came into the house right before I was supposed to walk down the aisle, knocked out my dad, and persuaded my sister to slip me something in my drink, then he kidnapped me. He'd also been behind this stalker, and made it look like some company was interested in my blood for a cure to cancer."

"How is that possible? There were mer everywhere, and guards, too. They're not persuadable."

"Well, one of them died… I bet he was at the wrong place at the wrong time," *and Colin had to have been helping.*

She crossed her arms. "I'm sorry to say this, but I think you hallucinated it, with the stress and pregnancy…"

I swallowed down my tears. Hallucinated? "Someone took me. You can't deny that."

"Well, even if Alaster were alive, I'd have a hard time believing he'd ever do that. He was always so kind."

"Kind?" I chuckled bitingly and thrust my scared finger in front of her face. "He cut off my fingers so I'd look like Galadriel. Force promised me to control me, not to mention stabbing Colin in the stomach and trying to burn us alive in the basement. I know what I saw."

"We all make mistakes, my sweet."

My mouth hung open. Mistakes? At least the mistakes I'd made didn't purposefully hurt people. "Well, he hasn't changed," I seethed. "And now he has Fin."

"But you didn't see him take Fin."

I sighed, refraining from rolling my eyes. "No."

Desirée stood, and then abruptly pulled me to my feet and into a hug, squeezing tight. "My sweet, you've been through a very traumatic loss—"

I pushed her away. "Fin is out there and he's in trouble. I know it!"

Her lips pursed. "Okay. I'll send my men to find him. Where is this building?"

"It has to be Jax or Jacob. They know where the building is."

"Or Colin," she said resolutely. "I would think he'd want to go, but I think we should keep your… incident…. to ourselves. That would be so painful to get Colin's hopes up."

I tried not to let the fact that the news bowled me over show on my face, but Colin was there, too? Dang. How was Fin ever able to escape with me and live to talk about it?

I clenched my teeth. "I don't think it's a good idea for Colin to go, considering."

Desirée dipped her head appraisingly. "Colin is Fin's cousin—"

"Alaster is Fin's Uncle!"

She looked at the floor, her chest heaving. What had happened to the woman I thought was my mother? Why didn't she believe me?

"Well, for now, you need to stay here. Because whoever took you, is still out there, and it isn't safe on land."

"Stay here? And do what?"

"Wait." She took my hand and patted it patronizingly. "It's what mermaids do."

I swallowed down what I wanted to tell her to do with that suggestion, along with the curse words I'd use to embellish it. When it came to her loved ones, she didn't wait. Apparently Fin wasn't important enough, or me for that matter. She, just as I, would move heaven and hell for them, the only difference was I wouldn't switch my child no matter what the cost.

"But for now," she continued. "It's best you wear this."

Quick as a flash, she pulled a gold circle from her pocket and clasped it snuggly on my wrist before I could stop her. The heavy metal shushed with what sounded like trapped liquid inside. The Natatorian symbol was engraved in the metal.

"What is this?" I tugged on it, trying to take it off.

"It's a bracelet that will inject sleeping serum in you if you try to leave Natatoria. It's for you own good."

"What?" I screeched.

She lifted her hands. "Now, Ash. Please… calm down."

"I am not staying here!"

"Yes. You need to. For your safety."

I stood. "You are not in charge of me. I'm an American citizen. I have rights."

"Guards," Desirée called. "Take her to the infirmary!"

"What?" I backed away when two burly men entered, one of them my earlier abductor from my house. "No! Please!"

They grabbed onto me and carted me down the hall, kicking and screaming.

52

FIN

June 15 – 8:35 a.m.

For hours, Alaster had switched me from mer to human and back again countless times. The exhaustion hit a point of hallucination. I even had a conversation with a talking donut.

I blinked, and slowly focused on a figure sitting at the other end of the dimly lit room. The orange glow coming from his neck cast sickly shadows on his ugly face that would terrorize children everywhere. He was too ghastly to be a figment of my imagination.

Though I might have been able to get up, I didn't want to. He'd broken me and there was no fight left inside.

"Just let me die," I begged.

Ash would be better for it anyway. She'd be free to convert and forget all about our insane way of life.

"I'm disappointed," my uncle said. "Where's all your sass?"

I merely grunted in disapproval. He stood and walked closer to me. I closed my eyes and cringed. When he didn't do anything, I looked up at him and grimaced.

"Why?"

"Why what? All of this?"

I couldn't even nod. "You could persuade anything you wanted."

He laughed. "Yes, but… that got boring after a while."

My eyes slid shut and he pressed the button, forcing me to shape into a fish. I grunted, wheezing for air but really wanting water.

"Stay awake!" he bellowed.

Playthings. That's what he needed. Something to torture to make him feel powerful, alive.

"I'm trying," I whispered.

He leaned over. "Do you know what it's like to watch a man who's conquered the world, amassed wealth beyond his wildest dreams, and has the respect of his peers, cower before you because you hold the key to his life?"

My eyes slid shut again unable to stay open, and he pressed the button.

"Answer me!"

"No," I grunted, shifting into human form.

"I have. They pony up every time. Any amount I ask. They even make me amazing inventions, like this." He tugged on his lighted collar. "It's hilarious, really."

"So you... manipulate people for real?"

"Why yes. It's far more entertaining." He straightened and returned to his chair. "But cancer is quite a hungry beast and I only have so much blood to give. And with so many people sick, I don't have enough of a supply."

"Is that why you want me?"

He put his hands behind his head. "Partly, yes. Partly no."

But I knew that neither money or the accolades of humans wasn't what he really wanted. His entire life, he'd been contending for position. A seat on the Council, Captain of the Guard, promised to a royal. And every time he was passed up, mostly by my dad. Alaster's ultimate desire had always been for the top, for the mer to bow and revere him. My family stood in the way of that. That's why he hated us.

He shot to his feet. "But I'm finally going to get what I really want." His fingers snapped. "Get up. We're going."

Get up? I couldn't even sit, let alone stand.

"Where?" I asked, frustrated it took all my energy just to talk.

His lips perked up in a big grin. "Home."

53

ASH

June 15 – 9:47 a.m.

I sat in my room in the infirmary, furling and unfurling my fist around the fork I'd stolen. The fact I'd been imprisoned by my own flesh and blood not only made me enraged, but it also made me question everything. Why didn't she believe me? To top it off, my inflamed breasts ached with milk. And although I'd bound them with a strip of fabric I'd torn from a sheet, nothing relieved the pressure.

No one had come to see me, except the same lame guard who'd brought me a meal every so many hours. But the last time, I'd kept the fork and he hadn't noticed.

The lock clicked as the knob turned, and I startled, my muscles pulling taut. He'd be sorry he'd locked me up. The metal felt hot against my fingertips as I waited until they'd cleared the door. Then I charged.

"Whoa!" The woman darted out the way just as I stabbed the empty air. She turned and lifted her hands. "I come in peace."

"Galadriel?" I stumbled backward, speechless. "What are you doing here?"

She pulled off her hooded robe and slid it over my shoulders, tying the cord at my neck. "I'm here to save you."

"Save me?"

"Yes. Jax and Jacob are at the Tahoe Gate ready to take you home to find Fin."

My mouth opened in excitement, and then I remembered. I jutted out my wrist to show her the bracelet. "They need to go without me because I can't now."

She flapped her hand forward. "I was afraid of that, but don't worry."

Her oversized beaded bag dropped to the floor with a clunk. She pulled out a flat piece of metal, which she slid between my skin and the bracelet. Then, she took out a bolt cutter.

"Ready?" she asked.

I eyed the bolt cutter but nodded all the same.

The metal crunched under the sharp jaws, then made a loud pop. The metal ring hit the floor, splattering green gunk everywhere. Sharp barbs that hadn't been there before stuck out on the underside of the bracelet.

Galadriel jumped back, pulling me with her. "It's cassava poison. Don't touch it, or it'll kill you."

"Kill me?" I backed up, massaging my wrist. "Mother said it would make me go to sleep."

"What?" Her mouth hinged open. "I'm beginning to think she's lost it. No, Ash. This would have killed you, which…" she trailed off, looking horrified.

"You have to be wrong. It couldn't have killed me." I laughed nervously as she gawked at me. "Why are you looking at me like I'm a ghost?"

"Because Mother hasn't told anyone you're alive. If it weren't for Tatiana, I wouldn't have known you were even here."

I blinked at her. "Where's Tatiana?"

"Mother locked her up in her room for escaping."

I pushed out a breath, my eyes losing focus "This is insane. I have to get her free."

"No." She took ahold of my shoulders. "You have to get out of here. It isn't safe. They're having Jack's trial in the square today. His punishment is being served."

"What?" I asked, breathless.

"I know, but it's the best time to sneak you out of here because everyone will be there."

"What are they going to do to Jack?"

A grimace marred her beautiful face. "I don't know. Charge him with something. I'm hoping not—"

"Bone Island?" I said slowly.

"Well, if you guys are on the outside, then you could go check on him, just to be sure. But Mother has never supported banishing people, so…"

I blew out a relieved breath. "Okay. What about you?"

"I have to stay here, you know… keep things in line. You never know what might happen." She quirked a grin.

"Are you sure?" I looked into her sad eyes.

She nodded. "Do you have that ink I gave you?"

I licked my lips and shook my head. "I took it off on my wedding day."

She removed her necklace and put it on me. I caught a glimpse of her missing fingers, of what our father had done to her when she'd disobeyed. Thank Posideon she was such a rebel."Here. Take mine."

"Are you sure?" I asked.

She forced a smile. "I have more. You just do whatever you can to find Fin, okay?"

I bit the inside of my cheek. "Okay."

We quickly hugged, then peeked out of the door. She pointed I go to the left.

"Be safe," she whispered.

We embraced one last time before we ran in opposite directions.

54

FIN

June 15 – 9:48 a.m.

When I awoke again, I was in the back of a vehicle, bouncing around, rolling from side to side. The white van? Apparently whoever was driving hadn't studied the DMV manual. I tried to brace myself with my hands, finding them bound. Then the vehicle lurched to a stop.

The back doors flew open. Sunlight poured in, blinding me. I blinked, trying to focus on my surroundings. Alaster grabbed onto my wrists and tugged me forward.

"Get out!"

My bare feet crunched on dead grass—the parking lot. Just beyond was our beach and the lake. No one was around.

I glanced over my shoulder at our house. Was Ash inside?

"Don't worry, pretty boy. She's in Natatoria waiting for you." Alaster pushed me forward.

"Natatoria?" I mumbled.

Then I glanced to my right at Ash's parents' house. Lucy came bounding down the walkway.

"Mr. Helton! Mr. Helton!" She waved her hand, confirming my suspicions she'd been working with him. She then stopped and stared at me, mouth agape.

I looked down. My T-shirt, stained with ketchup and stinking of fish must have looked fabulous with my board shorts dangling around my waist, Velcro unfastened.

"What are you wearing?" she asked.

I closed my eyes slowly, wanting to sing, but not having the strength. This was another problem that would need fixing later.

"He's fine," Alaster said, voice clipped.

"Where's Colin?" she asked, touching her lips.

Fury rose inside me. Had Colin done more than just persuade her? If so, Lucy was only fourteen and way too young to be promised. But then again, like father like son. I wanted to strangle both of them all the more.

"Go inside," I tried to sing, but my voice merely cracked.

Her brow furrowed. "When is he coming back? He promised me he'd be back. It's been four days."

"Yes, he's been busy, but I plan to see him today," Alaster explained.

I'll say.

Her shoulders relaxed, then she eyed me malevolently. "Where's Ash?"

Didn't she think we were dead? I could have sworn I'd heard her mother's voice when Alaster took my supposed dead body away. Alaster must have sung it all away.

"I'll tell Colin you're looking for him," Alaster interrupted, sugary sweet. "Now go home and wait like a good little girl."

"Are you sure?" She pouted.

"Very sure."

She squinted her eyes at me and then turned toward the house.

Was she polygamy promised, or not?

"She's only fourteen," I said, exasperated.

"Only?" Alaster laughed. "All that matters is if she can bear a shoal or not."

Or a new addition to your vampire lab, I almost said. "You're sick." I spat.

"Save your judgment." He shoved into my back to get me to move toward the dock.

Once we reached the end, I fell in and tried to shift. My gills appeared, but my exhausted muscles refused to work, and I began to sink downward.

"Come on little guppy." He grabbed onto my wrists and dragged me toward the gate, legs and all.

Guppy. Ash's text came to mind and the water around my skin boiled. I should have known Alaster was behind all of this.

Once we hit total darkness, my reluctant body finally phased.

"You need to take better care of yourself," Alaster joked.

Before we entered the Tahoe Gate, he slipped some contraption that looked like a gas mask over his face and neck.

"What's that?" I asked.

"Another little trinket from a grateful patient." He grinned, but I didn't trust why he'd need it.

Once we entered the tunnel and swam through to the exit into Natatoria, I heard Jax and Jacob's voice.

"Hey!" I yelled.

Alaster slammed his fist into my back, shoving the water from my lungs.

"I wouldn't do that," he warned as he dumped something black into the water.

Then I realized what the mask was for. I flipped my tail and jetted toward the Lake Tahoe side, but not before the octopus ink took hold and pulled me into her watery depths.

"That's right, pretty boy," I heard echo in my mind. "Just sleep."

55

ASH

June 15 – 10:17 a.m.

I slipped into the current through the Northern exit in the palace and pulled the robe tight to conceal my face. Discontented murmurings of the large mass gathered floated over from the square. Curiosity to see what was happening made me pump my tail and swim closer just for a quick look.

Desirée hovered before five thrones, all empty except the one occupied by Girra. Below them, Jack was chained by his neck to a pillar in the middle of the square, surrounded by guards. Several hundred mers gathered just beyond, watching her.

I scanned the crowd for Galadriel. Did she get out of the infirmary okay? Maggie whimpered, hovering not too far away from Jack, held back by the guard. Tatiana, probably still locked up in her room, wasn't with her.

"What do you have to say for yourself?" Desirée bellowed.

Jack held his head low and said nothing. Was he not going to defend himself? I knew, after my chat with my mother, whatever he could have said wouldn't matter. Desirée had already made up her mind. We'd have to rescue him from Bone Island with Sissy and Hans' help, and then run as a family, which meant I needed to get out of here before she caught me.

"Eirion, Poseidon rest his soul, is dead as a result of your malfeasance and so is my daughter and your son!" Desirée continued.

My tail flared to make me stop. I swiveled around. Why would Desirée blatantly lie to him? Jack's shoulders convulsed anyway. Had no one told him our deaths were faked?

I swam closer, hoping to get his attention, hoping he was acting. Galadriel should have told him our plan and not left him in such a tortured state. He might do something drastic like take his life, something I'd contemplated myself.

"We must not let this happen again," she commanded. "We were the safest when we had a king on the throne."

The mer murmured, some agreeing and some disagreeing. A chant broke out.

"King! King! King!"

The hair prickled on my neck. If it weren't for Alaster ruining my wedding, they'd be chanting something totally different today. He'd set this up, knowing how the mer would react, and put his son in the right place to claim the throne when the opportunity presented itself.

A merling's sudden wail made my milk let down. I put my arm over my breasts to stop the ache. My heart twisted painfully as I scanned the crowd for the source. Who would bring a child to a trial?

Then I saw them. Garnet and Colin arrived and sat behind Desirée. A dark-haired merling wiggled in her arms, and although her face was red with embarrassment while trying to console the crying boy, jealousy settled in anyway. Why was it that they'd get their happily ever after? What had I done to deserve such heartache? My tears bled into the water. My life had been torn from me, and I hated everything the mer stood for. They were a cruel and crooked race I no longer wished to be a part of. I'd rescue Fin, get Jack from Bone Island, then we'd leave and never return, damn their stupid laws. Damn my birth mother.

The baby's wail made me kick harder. Even the merlings hated it here. I had to leave before I completely lost it.

"He's not dead!" I heard a familiar voice say.

I flared my fin to stop and turned. Had someone finally gotten the guts to say something?

All the blood drained from my face when Alaster floated above the square, tugging Fin's lifeless body upward by his shirt collar.

"I've found your traitor, selling his blood for money! They both deserve Bone Island!"

"NO!" I screamed and pumped my tail to get closer.

"She's alive!" the mer began to say. "Ashlyn is alive!"

Desirée turned, blue eyes flashing. She put her hand to her mouth in concern.

"See?" I yelled, flipping the hood off my head. "Alaster *is* alive. He was behind selling our blood and kidnapping me, and I can prove it!"

Desirée puffed out her chest. "That cannot be true."

The mers murmured more. The merling's continued shrieks added to the tension.

"It is!" I yelled, but beyond my word, I really had no proof.

"She lies, your majesty," Alaster said while bowing. "I found them, trying to pass themselves off as dead. I was able to get Fin and fix the situation, but Ash got away."

Your majesty? What?

Desirée dipped her head. "Though it pains me to say it, guards, arrest my daughter. For faking her death and exposing our secret to humans."

"What?" I backpedaled.

How could she still defend this known criminal over her own flesh and blood? But at this point, even if no one believed me, I had to stand up for Fin's family, for myself.

"Please! Natatorians, listen to me! Alaster was the one who killed Eirion so he could abduct me from my wedding to make it look like the humans knew our secret. He set Jack and Fin up to take the fall,

all to scare you into thinking you need a king! Do you think it's a coincidence his son is in line to take the throne? That his secret promising to Garnet and the timely birth of their son are merely a fluke?"

The crowd began to stir, uneasy. Several guards left their post next to Jack and surrounded me. Maggie, free to swim to Jack, put her arms around him and tried to undo the chains that bound him.

I swam above the crowd to keep my distance from the guards. The merling's wails heightened and pierced the water, so loud people were putting their hands over their ears.

Then Garnet yelped, and the child stopped. "Ouch! He cut me!"

Before I knew it, the merling had escaped and was making a beeline for me. Black ink trailed behind his head, fading in the current, revealing bright red hair.

"Get that child!" Desirée demanded.

I sucked in a gasp as he came closer, my body breaking out in goosebumps. He stopped before me, eyeing me with blue eyes framed with dark lashes—Fin's eyes.

I couldn't breathe. "Joey?" I asked.

He let out a happy cry, darted forward and clung to my neck. My arms wrapped around him, pressing him to my bosom, the tears flowing free, my heart unfurling. Joey let out a soft coo of relief. He was alive!

Then my vitriol began to boil. Alaster had stolen my child and let me believe that he'd died. And after everything, my mother was trying to trick the mer again—all for the throne!

Pointing to Desirée, my eyes filled with hate. "You stole my son!"

"What?" She puffed out her chest. "That is Garnet and Colin's merling! Give him back."

"Are you kidding me? Only a merling torn from his mother's breast would behave this way and you know it!" my voice bellowed.

"You're the one who should be arrested."

"Ash is the rightful heir," one of the mers cried out.

I swallowed hard. Heir? To the throne? That was the last thing I wanted. Freedom on land was what I craved, unencumbered and away from this madness. But the guards, confused what to do, bumped into each other, some heading for me and others changing direction and returning to Desirée.

"This is not true!" she shrieked. "That's Garnet's child! She is the rightful heir to the throne." She backpedaled in the current. "Get your son, Garnet!"

"Let her have the brat!" Garnet snipped and swam off from the square toward the palace.

"Wait, Garnet?" Desirée cried, reaching for her though she was too far away to catch.

The crowd began to mumble louder, waving their fists in the air for answers.

"Desirée's heir has produced a son!" one cried.

"Who does the merling belong to?" another yelled.

"Ashlyn and Fin can take the throne!"

"We need a king!" a group chanted.

Though it was clear to the mer Desirée had committed treason, I didn't want the throne.

"Stand up to her," a nearby girl said to me.

My chin jerked upward, and I held onto my son, my body trembling. Why wasn't Fin waking up? "Desirée, you've committed treason. Not once but twice."

Desirée laughed. "I have not. I watched Garnet give birth to that child and he belongs to her. If anyone has committed treason, it is you and Fin, for exposing our secrets!"

"No, Mother. You have overstepped your authority as Chancellor Pro-Tem, and as a voting citizen of Natatoria, I motion that you be stripped of your title."

"Aye," Badger said.

"Aye," the crowd said in unison, their voices growing louder.

"Royalty has no say here," I continued. "The Council is in charge, the ones the mers elected. By their voice, you've been stripped of your title as Chancellor Pro-tem, and you will be tried in court for kidnapping my son, along with…" I pointed to where Alaster had been hovering, finding he'd disappeared. Panic spread through me. We couldn't lose him again. "Where is he?"

"Aye, get yer mangy arse back over here." Badger pressed a trident to Alaster's back. A wall of mers with weapons stood behind him. "Whatcha wanting me to do with him, My Queen," he said to me.

My eyes widened at the moniker. Did he not just hear what I'd just said?

Alaster raised his hands. "I didn't do anything. The Heltons are the ones at fault!"

"You took me, then stole my newborn and made me believe he was dead!" I seethed.

"I did not!" he defended, incredulously. "This is all lies! And that is *my* grandson you're holding! Give him back!"

The mer murmured, still wavering in who to believe.

56

FIN

June 15 – 10:34 a.m.

I shook my head, trying to focus on my surroundings. The tails of mers flipped above me as I lay prostrate on the stones lining the square, the water charged with anger and fear. My father was chained to a block a few feet ahead of me.

Alaster swam directly above me, the son of a bass, and Badger had a trident pressed into his back.

I swam upward. "What's going on?" I asked Badger.

"Fin!" Ash cried out.

My glance swung wide to find her, my vision finally clearing. I swam forward, fighting the searing pain in my head from the ink. Then I saw him, a redheaded merling clinging to her chest. I blinked again. This couldn't be. Our son had died.

"He's alive?"

Ash smiled hugely, biting her lip and nodding as she swam forward.

Yes? What in Hades had happened? I swam toward her when Desirée charged forward. "It doesn't matter! When Merric died, while you were planning your wedding, the people voted me Chancellor and requested I revive the laws that have always protected us. I'm here to announce that I will assume the throne as Queen because I have taken a mate!" she shouted. "As decreed by the fact, my daughters are mated!"

The crowd burst into a cacophony of questions.

"Can she do that?" the mer asked. "I thought it had to be her son?"

"Yes, she can!" another shouted. "Any heir will do!"

"Who's her mate?" they asked collectively.

"Alaster is my mate!" She pointed to him. "Unhand him! Unhand the King!"

Alaster? What the hell? The blood drained from my face as the guard shifted positions, surrounding Badger and the mers next to him, freeing Alaster.

He gave me a smug smile. "I always win."

"Aye, stand down men," Badger said when his men started to struggle.

"No!" I yelled. "We must fight!"

I charged the closest guard, just to be punched in the gut and pulled into a chokehold.

"Desirée, this is ludicrous!" Jack barked. "This isn't how we do things!"

"Silence him!" Desirée commanded, pointing to Jack.

I glanced over at Ash, giving her a pleading look. Helpless, I couldn't do anything to stop them. She was the one who needed to stand up to her mother and take her birthright.

Instead, she glared at Desirée and her decisions leading to this point all made sense. She and Alaster had used any means possible to regain power, even by betraying our family. And we'd given her the perfect setup by the fact we were distracted with the wedding. Did she have something to do with Merric's death, too? The betrayal was evident on Ash's face, stabbing me in the heart.

"Arrest them and bring me the child," she seethed.

My hackles rose. Why did she want our child?

Ash held tight onto our son. "I am the rightful Queen! Arrest Desirée and Alaster for treason against Natatoria!"

The guards didn't listen to her, instead grabbing her hands and putting them behind her back. She opened her mouth when one slapped his palm over her face. The guard holding me swam me forward.

Ash glanced over at me, but I could barely stay lucid. Fear we wouldn't survive this roiled through me. Weakened beyond words, I still fought to get free.

Desirée glared at my son as he clung to my wife, his tiny body pressed tightly against her.

"He is not your son," Desirée said, voice hard.

"Like hell he isn't," I mumbled

Her lip sneared upward and she leaned in. "You should have remained dead."

Ash's shoulders slunk down, and her countenance fell. This was the only thing she'd craved—a mother's love.

My heart seized for her.

You don't need it. Rise above this. You have love. You don't need her approval, I tried to say, but couldn't.

Desirée charged, grabbing ahold of my son. The merling screamed, thrashing his tail around, nicking her arm with the sharp edge. Ash fought back, smacking her tail against Desirée and the wall of guards behind her.

"Hold her still!" Desirée barked.

The guards stiffened and pressed forward.

"Ash," I groaned, completely helpless. "Help her."

Would no one stop this madness? Where were the rebels? Could the mer not see this power grab for what is was and do something to stop it? Or were they so paralyzed by the law, they couldn't act of their own accord for what was right. So desperate for a leader.

In a last ditch effort to stay connected to Ash, Joey grabbed onto her necklace and yanked. Black ink flooded into the current, making the babe's eyelids heavy.

Octopus ink.

Then the guards started dropping around me like flies, and I quickly joined them.

57

ASH

June 15 – 11:00 a.m.

Desirée's eyes widened once she saw the ink. "Where did you get that?"

Instead of answering, I punched her in the gut with my tail, then snatched a weapon from an unconscious guard floating next to me and slipped behind her, pressing the blade against her throat.

She tensed and let out a gurgled choking noise. "What are you doing, my sweet?"

"I am not your sweet!" I pressed the blade harder. Blood spilled in the current. "Tell them!"

She sputtered and coughed like she was trying to get air, but I knew better and I didn't care at this point. "Tell them what?"

"The truth! Now!"

The females watched us with rapt attention.

"I'd rather die," she said softly.

"So be it!" I moved my hand to slit her throat when Galadriel stayed my hand.

"Don't go there." She took ahold of the weapon and handed me my sleeping son. "It's tempting, yes, but it's what's ruined her."

My hold loosened, and Desirée swam away, free. Her hands touched the cut as it closed up.

"You think you know me." She narrowed her eyes at the both of us. "But you don't! Life is about making the tough choices."

Maggie and Sandy swam up behind Desirée, grabbing her wrists and shackling them with irons.

Desirée startled, then shrieked, tugging against them. "What are you doing?"

"We'll handle her, My Queen." Maggie bowed. Sandy, though, yanked the crown from off her head and swam toward me.

She placed it on my head, then bowed. "Your majesty."

"No," I started to say.

"What?" Desirée screamed. "No! That's mine!"

Sandy winked, then the two swam Desirée, flapping and sirening, toward the palace.

"We have to arrest Alaster, too," I shrieked, turning to find him not sleeping amongst the men. "Where is he?"

"Uh…" Galadriel scanned the bodies. "He was right there."

A dark figure swam toward us, trident in hand, and wearing what looked like a gas mask.

I backpedaled in the current, clutching Joey to me tightly.

"You will not take the throne," the man said through the contraption.

"Alaster?" My eyes tightened, but with all the mermen passed out, I was at his mercy.

Galadriel swam in front of me just as he thrust the weapon forward. He punctured into her gut and she groaned. Blood filled the water.

"NO!" I sirened. "You son of a bass!"

He yanked the trident from her stomach, clearly unfazed by my song, and pointed it at me.

"Next time I won't miss," he seethed.

Galadriel's body slowly sunk downward, her stomach filleted open, but I couldn't save her. My gaze was glued to the end of the trident, gleaming in the sunlit waters.

"Save the Queen!" a mermaid shrieked.

"She's mine!" Alaster laughed as he reared back his hand, ready to stab, but the water around us rippled and writhed as a swirling cyclone of hissing mermaids rose up and surrounded his body in a constricting vortex.

I swam backward as the circle grew tighter, undulating outward with each swipe of his trident.

"Get back, wenches! All of you!" Alaster yelled, but I couldn't see his body.

I tucked Joey's face into my neck as their sirens grew louder and louder, then I heard Alaster scream in terror, and the water grew bloodied. Schools of fish swam in, gobbling up the bits of flesh.

Then the group of mermaids slowed and disbanded, bowing to me before they swam back to take their places amongst the crowd. I cowered in disbelief. Had they shredded him to pieces with their talons?

Galadriel's moan stole through me, and I rushed to my sister's side. She held onto her stomach, looking up at me, her face gray.

"I'll be fine," she rasped. "Just get me Pearl."

"Pearl!" I yelled as I placed my hands on top of hers. "Please get me Pearl!"

She forced a smile. "You were very brave today. You'll make a great Queen, much better than I'd be." She reached up and touched my son's hair. "I knew something was fishy about his hair color, but they knew better than to ask for my help."

"Don't tell me I have a box of color in my house?"

She laughed. "Maybe. But it's not black."

I gripped tighter onto her hand and once Pearl showed, I gave her some space to work.

"She'll be fine," Pearl promised me.

"Your audience awaits," Galadriel nudged her chin forward. "Look."

The mermaids still hovered behind me, watching wide-eyed, for what, I wasn't sure. I turned toward them, terrified of the power they held. So instead of commanding their allegiance, I did the smartest thing I could do. I bowed to them.

Angry murmurs crossed the crowd.

"Wait!" I lifted my hand. "If what you want is for me to be Queen, then I'd rather serve you as your humble servant instead."

Heartbeats passed as eyes tightened on me. What did they want from me? To be another dictator like Desirée?

"No. Hear me out!" *because I don't really want this job.* "I'm not going to lead you with an iron fist. What we need to do is govern ourselves, and live peaceably. And I don't want to keep you here if you don't want to stay."

The women looked at one another, confused.

"I don't want to be bowed to, and held higher than you. I want to be your equal. Are you with me?" I raised my fist.

They turned to one another, speaking in hushed voices, then one by one, they raised their fists, copying me. Their voices began to agree in a resounding yes.

My chest heaved in relief just as the men started to wake up. The women disbursed, finding their mates. I scanned the audience for Fin, unable to find him.

58

FIN

June 15 – 11:00 a.m.

At the horrific noise of a multitude of mermaids sirening, I opened my eyes. A vortex of water pulled at my fin, tugging me out from under the pile of mermen pinning me. I fought to be sucked into the vortex when I heard Alaster scream.

Bloodied bits spit out of the top of the funnel of water. Fish swam in and gobbled them down.

What the hell?

When I opened my eyes again, mermen and maid were hugging one another in the same space. Was I dreaming?

"Fin?" I heard Ash cry frantically.

I pumped my fin and swam forward, reaching out for her and my son. Enveloping them in my arms, I held them close and kissed their heads, never wanting to let go. We were finally together and whole.

"What happened?" I asked. "Where's your mother?"

"Arrested."

"And Alaster?"

She just shook her head, speechless, when it hit me. It hadn't been a dream at all. I glanced to my left, then my right as mermaids watched me with narrowed eyes. A shiver trailed my fin. Had they always had this power but never used it?

Ash looked up at me, her green eyes sparkling. "We never have to worry about him again."

"Good riddance," I muttered, somewhat terrified. "You're wearing your mother's crown?"

"I..." She turned her lips up in a grin. "I'm Queen."

"And I'm King?" I grimaced.

"I guess."

I blinked at her. "Well, this changes things."

She laughed, and I leaned in and kissed her, trapping the delectable sound inside me. Then I closed my eyes and held onto my family, relieved.

"Where's Alaster?" I heard Colin yell. "Where's my dad?"

Letting go, I turned toward him. "You're under arrest."

His eyes widened, then he darted off, almost running smack into Badger's trident. "Aye, you scum sucking sea sack, yer arse ain't goin' nowhere."

Colin shrieked, holding up his hands. "I didn't do anything. It was my dad!"

"I don't think so," I said. "He committed promise polygamy. Lock him up."

Garnet turned to him appalled, then slapped his face. "That's it! It's over!" She swam off in a huff.

Ash sucked in a gasp. "He did? With who?"

I shook my head. "I'm pretty sure he kissed Lucy."

She rubbed her hand over her forehead. "That's how they did everything."

"Yeah... well." The only way to break the bond would be for him to die, or strip him of his fins. Both were just as appealing to me.

But I hovered in the current, feeling somewhat useless. Ash and her mermaids disposed of Alaster and locked up Desirée. I'd done nothing but passed out.

She looked up at me, a smile in her eyes like I was her hero, squeezing me tight. All the hurt and pain was gone. My Ginger Girl was back.

"Can we deal with it tomorrow?" she asked. "I just... I want to go home."

I grinned. Finally, something I could do. "You're wish is my command."

Her laugh cleansed me as we held hands and swam for the Tahoe Gate.

Epilogue

ASH

"So, I was thinking..." Tatiana tentatively leaned forward as Nicole and Joey played at our feet at the cottage.

I threw a couch pillow at her. "Don't even start—"

"What?" She quirked a smile. "Oh, come on. I have to plan something."

"I'm just trying to get motherhood down, and this Queen thing keeps getting in the way of everything. So no baby showers, or whatever you've got going on in that head of yours."

"I was thinking honeymoon."

"What?" My voice pitched an octave. Joey looked over, his bottom lip quivering. I scooped him up and hugged him. "Oh, baby, I'm fine. Don't cry."

He whimpered, then recovered. He quickly squirmed to be let down.

"You're handling motherhood fine." Tatchi gestured to Joey. "See?"

I glared at her. Did she not see the bags under my eyes?

"And once he's weaned," she continued, "you could use a vacation. That's what grandparents are for."

I wasn't leaving my son, not now, not ever, but before I could argue, someone cleared his throat from the kitchen doorway, startling me. "Ladies. Can I get anyone a refill?"

I looked over at the source. "Of course you can, Colin."

He bowed then walked over with a jug of iced tea and topped off both of our glasses. "Dinner will be ready in an hour."

"Thank you."

He bowed once more before leaving, and I smashed my lips together as to not smile.

Tatchi busted up into giggles once he left. "Well, I think his punishment is working out swell."

"Stop it, will you?" I shook my head. "I agree with the converting part, but mind-wiping him to be our maid?"

Tatchi kept giggling. "Well, at least he's not wearing the French maid uniform anymore.

I rolled my eyes. "You and Fin. I swear."

"So how is… everything?"

A sigh escaped my lips. "Okay, I guess. Alaster's business consisted of one customer who owned the building and it's suspect if he ever had cancer to begin with. Destroying our samples was easy enough. Candy and company, after having their promises' broken, went back to their regular lives. But we felt bad about the employees, and gave severances, along with glowing recommendations."

"That's nice of you," she said.

"And after we converted Colin, Lucy's promise broke but that didn't stop her from still having a crush on him."

"Oh, sweet urchins. Is she hanging around here all the time?"

I nodded. "Yeah, something like that."

Nicole shrieked, playing tug of war with a rattle Joey had first.

"No, no." Tatchi took the toy from Nicole and returned it to Joey. "We need to share."

Hissing, Nicole lunged for the toy. Tatchi scooped her up and held her tiny fists tight. "No."

Angered, Nicole spit in her face. My eyes widened, and I wondered if Tatchi would let her get away with that.

"I said no," she said firmly.

Nicole's face turned bright red and she arched her back, letting out a wail.

There was a knock at the door. I jumped up to answer it.

"Ash?" Mom's eyes darted to Tatchi and the shrieking merling. "Did I come at a bad time?"

"Not at all." I led her inside.

She bent down and picked up Joey, who was watching Nicole curiously. "How's my little man?"

Nicole shifted into her tail, shredding her diaper.

Mom gasped, holding Joey away from her. "Oh, my."

I leaned in. "She's a fish, too, Mom. Remember?"

She blinked at me, then nodded. "I remember."

With a little song, we were able to finally reveal Fin's fishy side of the family. Well, and mine too, because, at this point, there was no way we could keep the grandbaby a secret from my parents if we were to be neighbors.

"I brought you a little present." She handed Joey a stuffed bear.

Nicole saw the bear and screamed louder.

"I think I should go," Tatchi said apologetically.

I side hugged her. "Okay. I'll see you later?"

"Sure." She smirked, then disappeared out the door. I closed it, thankful for the silence.

Mom's eyes crinkled at the corners. "Terrible twos?"

"Something like that."

Fin walked in from the patio area, hair still wet from the lake.

"Hey!" he said. "There's my buddy!"

Joey squealed and reached for his dad. Mom handed him off reluctantly.

Fin threw Joey into the air, sending him into a chorus of giggles. His contagious laughter had all of us going after a few seconds, bringing such happiness. In awe, I watched them: father and son. I still couldn't believe this was my life.

Mom gave me a sweet smile and squeezed my hand. "I'm so happy for you," she said softly. "I'll see you later, okay?"

I returned her smile.

She nodded and opened the door.

A messenger from Natatoria, shirtless and wearing a manskirt, stood on the steps dripping wet.

"Your Majesties. There's an urgent matter at the palace."

"Your Majesties?" Mom asked.

I looked at Fin. Would we ever catch a break?

"It's nothing," Fin sang to her. "It was nice to see you, Mom."

The messenger's eyes widened at his mistake as Mom walked down the path.

Once out of her earshot, Fin asked. "What's the emergency?"

"You just need to come."

I looked at Fin. "It never ends, does it?"

He shrugged. "Guess not."

THE END... maybe?

If you want more of Ash and Fin, let me know in a review of EVERMORE. I listen to my fans!

GLOSSARY

Alaster Helton: Brother to Jack Helton, Uncle to Fin and Tatiana, father to Colin, pure-born.

Ashlyn (Ash) Lanski: biological daughter to Phaleon and Desirée, raised by Bill and Karen, sister to Lucy, promised to Finley Helton, a pure-born but was switched and changed into a human at birth.

Azor, Prince: (deceased) Bill and Karen's biological son, switched at birth and converted to human, raised by Desirée and Phaleon, betamer.

Barlemede (Badger): friend of Jack, betamer, rescued from the sea by Sandy when human and later became her mate

Beta-mer: when a human is converted to mer by drinking essence.

Bone Island: the island were mers are taken to be dried to death when banished from Natatoria, or where the bodies of deceased mers are left.

Brooke: Callahan's ex-girlfriend from Ash's high school who blames Ash for their breakup.

Callahan O'Reily: Ash's date to the Senior Prom.

Colin Helton: Son of Alaster, cousin to Fin and Tatiana, pure-born.

Desirée, Queen/Regent: Ash's biological mother, mother to Girraween, Garnet, Galadriel, pure-born. Promised mate to King Phaleon.

Dradux: Azor's crooked guard who were murdered after Merric and the Lost Ones restored order in Natatoria.

Essence: a blue sparkling liquid that gives a youth like appearance, or if ingested, makes one turn into a mer.

Finley (Fin) Helton: Son of Jack and Maggie, brother to Tatiana, promised to Ashlyn Lanski, pure-born.

Frank Delatore: (deceased) Human grandfather of Ash, married to Iris.

Galadriel (Gladdy/Lia), Princess: Eldest daughter of Phaleon and Desirée, sister to Ash, lost her ring and pinky fingers after Phaleon chopped them off when she secretly promised to Jax, pure-born.

Garnet, Princess: Daughter of Phaleon and Desirée, sister to Ash, pure-born.

Georgia: friend of Ash from high school.

Girraween (Girra), Princess: Daughter of Phaleon and Desirée, sister to Ash, pure-born.

Hans: Sissy's mate, resides in and runs the Florida safe house for runaway mers later known as the Lost Ones, pure-born.

Iris (Gran) Delatore: Human grandmother of Ash, Mother to Karen.

Jack Helton: Father to twins Finley and Tatiana, mated to Maggie, pure-born.

Jacob Vanamar: former royal guard, Tatiana's promised mate, father of Nicole, pure-born

Jaxtonian (Jax): Mated to Galadriel.

Karen Lanski: Mother of Lucy and Azor, raised Ash from birth, married to Bill.

Lost Ones: those who escaped Bone Island and survived.

Magdalene (Maggie) Helton: Mother of twins Finley and Tatiana, mated to Jack, betamer.

Meredith Hamusek: Rival swimmer to Ash from another high school.

Merling: a baby mer

Merric, King/Chancellor: Phaleon's father, presumed dead after Phaleon murdered him to become King, pure-born.

Natatoria: the mer kingdom under the mantle of the earth, home of where the pool of essence resides.

Nicole: Azor and Xirene's orphaned child who was passed off as Tatiana's child when Azor and Tatiana were King and Queen. Named after the servant Nicole who risked her life to save Tatiana's during an attack at Azor's compound, pure-born.

Pearleza (Pearl): former servant, healer, assistant to the former Queen Desirée, pure-born.

Phaleon (Leon), King: (deceased) Ash's biological father, mated to Desirée, pure-born.

Promise polygamy: When a mer kisses more than one person, making them bonded to the kisser.

Promise tattoo: The mark that shows on the ring finger of a promised person: colorful for women, black for men.

Promise: the bond created when a mer kisses another (human or mer), the intertwining of two souls.

Pure-born: Born of two mer parents.

Sandy: Badger's mate, pure-born.

Sissy: Hans' mate, resides in and runs the Florida safe house for runaway mers later known as the Lost Ones, pure-born.

Tatiana (Tatchi/Tatch) Helton-Vanamar: Daughter of Jack and Maggie, sister to Fin, best friend to Ash, mated to Jacob, mother of Nicole, pure-born.

William (Bill) Lanski: Human father of Ash, married to Karen.

Wynie, Mistress: former servant, royal dress maid.

Xirene: (deceased) servant that was secretly promised to Azor, died during childbirth of Nicole.

GET FREE CONTENT

Building my readership has been one of the most rewarding parts of being an author. Occasionally, I send out newsletters alerting readers of sales, contests, and new releases. By signing up at www.brendapandos.com, you'll also receive a free copy of Glitch (a $3.99 value) along with a Talisman short.

ENJOY THIS BOOK?
YOU CAN MAKE A BIG DIFFERENCE!

Reviews are the most valuable tools I have when it comes to getting attention for my books. As much as I'd like to have the marketing budget of a big publisher, or take out a full page ad, it's just little ole me.

But I do have something publishers would love to get their hands on.

You! My loyal and committed readers!

Honest reviews give my stories wings.

If you enjoyed this book, I'd very much appreciate if you'd take five-minutes to leave a review (a short one is totally fine!) when prompted at the end of this book.

And if you do write one, please send me an email at brendapandos@gmail.com so I can thank you personally. Or visit me at www.brendapandos.com to find out how you can get some signed swag by me!

Acknowledgements

To my husband, for not rolling your eyes when I say, "I have to work now," and my kids, when I say "Mommy is almost finished, then we'll do something fun!" You're all so very patient with me through this process and NOW we can do something FUN!

To my incredible PA: Julie "Jewels" Bromley, and beta team Nicole Hanson, Debbie Poole, Janille Dutton, and Stacey Nixon, thank you! To my DYNAMIS sisters: Jamie Magee, Kristie Cook (my BAFF!!!), Morgan Wylie, Lila Felix, Delphina Henley, Kallie Morgan, S.T. Bende (Yay for my amazing synopsis!), Rebecca Ethington, and Julia Crane, for sprinting with me and supporting me. I would have never hit my writing goal without you! A special thanks to my #1 fan, Rhonda Helton, for all of the gorgeous swag you make from my stories and your friendship. And the rest of my fans on Facebook, Instagram, and twitter, you encourage me daily to keep going and there when I need you most. I'd be nowhere without your support of my stories. A million hugs and thank yous for the best job eva!

To Karen of Crain Editing, thank you for working on a tight deadline and always having room for me. You're the best! To Kelsey Keeton, and Laura Deal for that AH-MAZING photo on the cover!

And last, but not least, to my Heavenly Father. For being my hope and strength. As always, you continue to grow and shape me in this journey. Thank you for expanding my dream.

ABOUT THE AUTHOR

Brenda Pandos is the author of several fast paced paranormal, sci-fi, urban fantasy and contemporary romance books. She lives in California with her husband and two boys, eight two (sniff) chickens and a grumpy cat, and loves to be contacted by readers.

Connect with me online:
facebook.com/brendapandos | brendapandos.com